FOREVER YOUR GIRL

A Katie Parker Production: Act 6

JENNY B. JONES

Sweet Pea Productions

Sweet Pea Productions

Cover Design: Llewellen Designs

FREE BOOK OFFER

CHAPTER ONE

Something is in the air. And I don't just mean the popcorn.

I sit beside my sweetie Charlie Benson at Bubba's Big Picture Cinema and wonder at this anxious knot in my belly. After moving to Chicago to be with Charlie, the two of us have hardly made it back to our hometown of In Between these past two years. Tonight, we're parked beneath the stars at this national treasure of a drive-in. We share a diet soda, a tub of popcorn almost as big as our rental car, and the occasional kiss.

But this evening, Charlie's kiss is different. And it has me on high alert, my lady intuition tingling.

Charlie taps an erratic beat on the armrest with his hand. The boy is not the nervous, fidgety sort. "Are you okay?" His question interrupts my attempt to decipher the tune he's hammering. I was torn between "Amazing Grace" and "Fat Bottomed Girls."

"Yes," I say. "I was about to ask you the same thing."

"That's the fifth time you've checked your phone in the last minute." More tapping as he nods towards the large screen in the distance. "I thought *Overboard* was one of your favorite movies."

It's true. I'm a sucker for a good amnesia love story.

With no small amount of regret and hesitation, I stick my phone back into a purse that's spilled into the floorboard. "It's fine. Everything is fine." Though my boyfriend's apparently developed a tick. Oh, and there's the fact that I'm awaiting the fate of my last audition. Only a huge new play that could determine the fate of the rest of my life. No big deal. "Yeah, nothing wrong with me."

My last role at the Winnifred Theater in Chicago was a school-girl in *Wicked.* While it was an honor to have a part in my all-time favorite show, the line "Oh, my!" didn't exactly propel me to stardom. I've been on a hundred auditions in the last year, and let's just say I've kissed a lot of frogs. The only thing substantial that's turned up is rejection. So much so, I've quit telling Charlie about my auditions.

But last week, I read for an incredible part. And I have this feeling.

Could be reflux.

Could also be God finally throwing open the doors to my future as a Broadway actress.

"This place was one of our first dates," Charlie says. "Remember?"

I smile and reach my hand into the popcorn bucket between us. "Bubba's does hold a lot of great memories." When Charlie and I were in high school, we saved this place when it was about to be demolished. "It's still the best spot to watch 80s movies." And sometimes, like tonight, the popcorn tastes like it's just as vintage.

I return my attention to the screen as Goldie Hawn's butler gets philosophical. "Most of us go through life with blinders on. Knowing only that little station to which we were born..."

Suddenly the butler freezes. Then the screen flicks twice before going dark.

I hear groans from outside and realize I've never seen the drive-in so packed. It seems the whole town of In Between has shown up for tonight's double feature.

"At some point, Buford's going to have to update his equipment." I reach for the drink and take a deep sip.

"That would ruin part of the charm," Charlie says.

We watch as the screen snaps, crackles, and pops. Bubba's Big Picture is as fickle as the weather, but Buford always gets the show back on. "I wonder what's happening."

"Probably some new kid operating the reel." Charlie leans forward in his seat, and his dark hair falls across his forehead. “Look at that full moon. Let’s get out and sit on the hood until they get the movie fixed.”

Opening my car door, I breathe in the evening air, taking in the scent that is solely the drive-in—a mix of peanut oil, car exhaust, and stale cotton candy. Charlie throws an old quilt on the hood of the rental sedan, then with a hand, helps me up.

The speaker box coughs and sputters as if blowing out the cobwebs. A voice comes through loud and clear over the sound waves as an image begins to take shape on the screen.

I’m instantly on alert because what I’m looking at is not Goldie Hawn and Kurt Russell.

“We apologize for the interruption, folks,” says a voice through the speaker that sounds suspiciously like my grandmother Maxine. “There seems to be a glitch in this classic love story.”

I look at my boyfriend as he takes my hand. “What’s happening?”

"Just watch.” With a laugh, he wraps his arm around me and pulls me to the warmth of his side. “I think we’re about to get to my favorite part."

Soon there’s a new movie playing for the large crowd. I choke on a breath of humid air as I see a video of Charlie and me on the screen. “That’s us.”

Maxine’s recorded voice begins to narrate. “Once upon a time, a sixteen- year old girl fell from a tree, landing with a splash into a pool. And one very lucky boy helped fish the girl out. Little did he know, the girl didn’t just crash into the water. She crashed into his life.”

I hold a hand over my parted lips while familiar songs from our high school years play. A progression of images and videos come to life, as Charlie now tells the story of our relationship. I see the pictures of us during my first year at In Between High School, both wearing Fighting Chihuahua T-shirts. There we are in our church youth group. I laugh as a photo scrolls by of Charlie sitting in a church row beside a pretty blonde, while I scowl in the seat behind them, fuming at the sight of my future boyfriend. Video plays of my first theater role as Juliet, and Charlie passing the football at the state championship his senior year.

“Our first dance,” I whisper as a new photo appears. “I’d been grounded, and you showed up on my back porch with a bouquet." I'm pretty sure I fell for him that night. Who could've resisted a boy on your porch in a suit and tie, bringing music and a slow dance?

As Charlie's voice narrates the starts and stops of our long journey, newer memories flash on the screen. The two of us skydiving in Chicago. Our vacation in New York last summer for one of my many auditions. Photos of our families. The two of us kissing beneath the mistletoe last Christmas.

"Katie Parker and Charlie Benson are a love story for the ages," his recorded voice says. "And now it's time for their happily ever after."

My heart stutters as Charlie slips off the hood and tugs me with him. His smiling eyes on mine, Charlie drops to one knee and pulls a velvet box from his pocket. "Katie..."

Tears fill my eyes, and I hate that I already look like a blubbery cliché. "Yes?"

Voices around us pull my attention, and I startle to see the entire town of In Between has gotten out of their cars and now circles the two of us like nosy neighbors.

Or people who love us.

Frances waves over to my left. My grandmother, grandfather, and parents wave to our right.

This is happening. Charlie is about to propose marriage.

That knot in my stomach does a little flip. And tightens.

Charlie clutches my fingers as the evening air breezes through his hair. "Over the years, we've built a friendship. Together we've saved a drive-in theater, we've saved a town, and we've saved your Valiant. But you...you saved me." He pauses as his gray eyes glisten. "You've become my best friend in adulthood, my confidante as we navigate our life away from In Between. We've taken the long way to get here."

"Like *forever*, kiddies!" Maxine calls. "For-ever."

"We had a few rough patches, taking breaks, and doing life separately. But it was always you, Katie Parker Scott. My heart always led me back to you. I know our futures aren't certain. I don't know where my job will ultimately take me. You don't know where your next play might lead you. But here's what I can say for certain—I would follow you to every stage, every theater, every play. Anywhere. I want to be the guy waiting for you at the backstage door, roses in hand, for the rest of your life. I love you, and I am your biggest fan." He fumbles with the box, finally releasing the lid.

The crowd gives a collective, "Awww."

A stunning diamond solitaire set in rose gold glitters in the moonlight. "Katie Parker Scott, will you marry me?"

"I..."

A retrospective of memories flashes through my mind. Life with my biological mother. The fights, the hurts, the drama. The day the caseworker left me with my foster parents, James and Millie. I'd cried into my pillow that night, praying one day I'd get my own fairy tale ending. The night Charlie kissed me on the stage of the Valiant theater, and my heart had forever set its tempo to beat in time with his. The time before my mom's funeral, years later, when I'd kissed *him*, wishing and hoping that one day we'd be together.

Now here we are. Standing in the circle of family and friends who are suspended in a joyously expectant tableau, waiting for my certain response.

"Yes." I nod and smile as my future husband rises and reaches for my hands. "I'll marry you, Charlie Benson." The crowd erupts into whoops and cheers. Millie and James embrace, while Maxine whistles through her fingers, then high fives her husband and everyone around her.

Charlie slips the engagement ring over my finger. I'm vaguely aware of the thought that I'm glad my nails don't look terrible, and I'm having a good hair night. The ring wobbles in its final resting place and will need to be sized. "It has room to grow. Kind of like us." He smiles then draws me to him. "I love you, Parker."

"Love you, Charlie."

Then against a background of celebratory cheers, a canopy of stars twinkling overhead, and Maxine breaking into the first verse of "Going to the Chapel," Charlie kisses me.

My first kiss as an engaged woman.

Charlie smells like shampoo, safety, and sunlight when his lips capture mine. I can feel his smile, and I lean into it, wanting to burn this moment into my memory. His arms hold me tightly as my hands curve around his back. The ring on my left hand provides a new weight, a new anchor to this boy who's become a man. *My* man.

Charlie's lips are soft on mine, feather strokes of promises I know he'll keep. The crowd finally falls away in my head. It's just Charlie and me.

Anxiety tries to push every button I have, but I take a deep breath and hold on tighter to my new fiancé. There will time enough later to worry about all the details: a wedding, the cost, the statistical probability of staying married past six weeks with my dysfunctional DNA.

Charlie's eyes meet my gaze as he reluctantly pulls apart, placing one final kiss on my forehead. "Ready to celebrate?"

Grinning, I tuck my head into his shoulder and nod.

"She said yes!" Charlie yells, igniting more whoops of glee. "Nachos, popcorn, and pizza on the house." If I thought the enthusiasm was loud for our engagement, it doesn't come close to the crowd's response to an open snack bar. "I was going to have it catered, but this seemed more you."

"Low-quality snacks? Very me."

The large movie screen flickers, then *Overboard* flares back to life. People mill about, with just as many heading toward us as beelining for the snack bar. I think how much easier greeting everyone would be with a bowl of nachos, but I suppose I can press through and soldier on.

Because I'm engaged!

"Katie, sweetheart." Millie is the first family member to congratulate me, hugging me close against her cotton dress. "I'm so happy for you." Tears glaze her eyes, and she tries in vain to blink the waterworks away. "We're going to have so much fun planning." She hugs Charlie. "How much time do we have?"

"Six months," Charlie says, just as I blurt out, "A year."

Charlie and I exchange a look, but I keep my smile in place. "It's going to be a while."

"Welcome to the family." James shakes Charlie's hand. "It's about time."

CHAPTER TWO

Two Years Later

Change was in the air. I could feel it in my bones and taste it on my lips. My role in my latest play had come to an end, by choice, and Charlie and I would be bound for New York next month. I had another job lined up, and Charlie easily transferred within his company to the Manhattan office. That wasn't the change coming.

It was something else. The winds had shifted in my spirit, and I felt unsettled.

Maybe I just needed to return to my favorite place and reset.

Last night we'd stayed out till two a.m. celebrating the end of my run as precocious Alice Roosevelt in *The Widow*, a play about her father Teddy, and I was exhausted. I was ready for a bedtime before midnight and a town that didn't move so fast.

"Katie? *Katie.*" Charlie waves his hand in front of my face, pulling me back to the moment. "You okay?" he asks, and I realize the car has stopped moving, and we're once again sitting in my parents' driveway, home on this Saturday night for the Fourth of July weekend.

"Yes, of course." My lips curve into what I hope is a believable smile. With our suitcases stowed in the backseat, we're each staying at our respective parents' houses for the next two weeks until our New York apartment is ready.

Charlie leans over and kisses me, though his eyes regard me with caution. "We're settled on the wedding date, right? We can tell our families?"

I wrap my hand around my convenience store fountain drink, my palm damp from the cool condensation. "Yes. Sure. Unless you think we should wait until I hear back from my last audition." Mary, my agent, had said we'd hear before the weekend was out.

"No." The rental car door opens with a loud, creaky protest. "I don't."

"Katie!" Millie rushes out of the front door, a sight for sore eyes. I haven't seen her and James in six months, and I've missed them more than I care to admit. "Give me a hug."

"Hi, James." Charlie sets down two worn carry-on bags and shakes my dad's hand before James claps him on the back and yanks him into a hug of his own.

"We've missed you both," James says. "But what a six months you've had, eh?"

It's true. The last two years have been a whirlwind. *The Widow* began as a small play in Chicago, but word-of-mouth launched it into the stratosphere of theater success. It's set to open in New York in the winter, and Charlie and I are moving with it. I'll be returning as teenage Alice. Unless something else better comes along. Like a lead role.

"There's my girl." My grandmother Maxine sashays into the yard, her golden highlights a thing of perfection, her skin smooth and flawless, and her nails a glossy fuchsia. I look like I've been traveling all day by way of camel, while she always looks as if she's just stepped from the spa. "Kisses all around!" Her husband, Sam, trails behind her.

I laugh as I kiss her silky cheek, inhaling the light air of her floral perfume. "Hello, Granny."

She swats my hand at that, then her frozen eyebrows attempt a frown. "What's wrong?" she whispers.

I love Charlie, but no one gets me like my Mad Maxine. "Nothing. Just excited to be the grand marshal of the Fourth of July parade."

"I hear that sarcasm," Maxine snips. "But you're our local celebrity."

"I'm hardly famous."

"Did you or did you not get invited to the Tony Awards and present with Daveed Diggs?"

"She did." Charlie grins. "She'll be hosting it in no time."

"We have a bit of news," Charlie says as we stand next to Millie's rose bushes like yard gnomes. "We've updated the wedding date. Again."

Everyone turns to me, and I put on my best smile. "Yep. We mean it this time." Or I do. We've had two dates rescheduled, and each time the fault has been mine. The theater is a demanding mistress.

"Don't keep us in suspense," Maxine says. "When are you two finally going to make it legal?"

Charlie reels me into his side and kisses the top of my head. "The last Saturday in January. Assuming the In Between Community Church is available."

"We'll make sure it is," James says.

"That's not much time to plan." Millie guides us inside, past the living room and into the kitchen, and we follow her like little ducks.

"Not much time to plan what?" Amy Scott stands at the stove as a kettle cries.

Amy's story is as complicated as my wedding date finalization. She's the Scotts' only biological child, and after high school, she bought a first-class ticket to crazy town where the in-flight snacks were opioids, and the beverage cart served nothing but Coke and Crown. She flew those not-so-friendly skies for over a decade before checking into a treatment center in the wilds of Montana. Two years later she left, a new person, and is now on staff at James's church helping families in the throes of addiction.

"Katie and Charlie have set a new date." Millie opens the fridge and pulls out a pitcher of lemonade that I know is freshly squeezed for our arrival. "Isn't that wonderful?"

Amy pours hot water into a chipped In Between High School mug, and the steam curls around her brown head. "Perhaps third time's the charm?"

My smile wobbles as I accept a glass from Millie. "Something like that." Did I mention that Amy and I had a less than auspicious meet-cute when I first became a foster kid in the Scotts' home? Neither one of us has forgotten it, and though we avoid the issue, we've also never hugged it out and became besties. She currently lives in the small apartment in the back yard the Scotts built for her a handful of years ago. I probably won't be making too many visits back there to see her.

"It's hard to plan when success comes at you nonstop." Maxine gives me a comforting wink. "Something I know all about. Have I mentioned I'm running for mayor of In Between ?"

The lemonade tastes tart on my tongue. "What?"

"Don't get her started on her platform," Sam says. "You'll never get her to quit yapping."

Maxine ignores her husband. "Yeah, the previous gal was a total crook and got forced out, and now we have an interim mayor. The town decides the first week of September in an emergency election, and I don't want to brag."

I return to my drink. "Sure, you do."

"The informal polls show me in a huge lead."

James slips on his apron, a sure sign he's about to get serious with the food. "Yeah, informal as in Maxine asks everyone at the Burger Barn who they're voting for."

"Don't forget my sweetie Sam polls the senior center." Maxine gestures toward the door where the sun begins its descent. "Now, James, fire up that grill for the steaks. We've got a wedding to finally plan."

Hours later, as the crescent moon levitates above the back deck and the stars blink and twinkle, I stand outside, ignoring the mosquitos and every violent bite they take.

"Okay, sweet pea, spill it." Turning, I find Maxine standing behind me. She holds two steaming mugs of coffee and hands me the one that's been diluted with cream, just like I prefer.

"Spill what?"

"Tell me whatever's going on in that red head of yours."

"Nothing." Holding the mug with both hands, I let the warmth seep into my skin. "What else could be on my mind but wedding plans and giddy happiness?"

Maxine takes a slurp of her coffee, then narrows her eyes, zeroing in on me like an eagle ready to swoop in on its prey. "Either you talk or I'm going in there and telling James and Millie about the time you got a tattoo in college."

"That tattoo is long gone."

She toasts me with her drink that I know contains more sugar than the candy bar she's probably hiding somewhere on her person. "As is the boyfriend whose name was temporarily on your shoulder. But wouldn't they still love to know all about it?"

I huff out a breath, then collapse into a blue Adirondack chair. "You wouldn't understand."

"I've been married twice. Try me."

"Charlie is so...Charlie."

"Was there someone else you wanted him to be? Because you know my sister Sylvie in Arkansas is ex-CIA. If you want him turned into someone else, she could make this happen. For a price."

"No."

Maxine's still pondering the possibilities. "Maybe a Chris Hemsworth face? Though I'm not sure Charlie has the jawline to pull it off."

"I meant, he's so normal, so grounded and solid."

"And you'll have to live with that?" She rests her hand against her brow like a geriatric Scarlett O'Hara. "What a burden you'll bear."

"I mean, we're so very different. I'm an actress. I work insane hours that are barely conducive to a life."

She leans toward me with a conspiratorial whisper. "I'm pretty sure Charlie's aware of this."

"But he's on the fast-track in the corporate world. He sees himself running a Disney or Google one day. I'm not cut out to be an executive's wife. I don't schmooze. I don't like cocktail parties. I loathe small talk and have nothing in common with the wives and girlfriends of his co-workers."

"So, then hang out with the menfolk. It's one of my favorite hobbies."

"That whole world isn't for me." But here's the real issue. "What if one day Charlie realizes I'm not what he needs?"

Maxine settles herself in the chair beside me and leans into me. She could not be more in my space if she used my left nostril to draw air. "Is that what you've been waiting for?"

"I don't know how to be a wife. How do I know if I'm ready?"

"Hon, no one's ready. It's like senior citizen mud wrestling. You don't wait until you're ready. You just tighten your bikini top and jump in."

Ugh. "When have you ever—"

"Stay on topic. We're talking about you and your insecurities. Sweet pea, do you love Charlie?"

"Yes. Very much."

"And he adores you. What else do you need to know?"

"I—"

"You don't have to have everything figured out. You're an engaged woman. And you're going to marry a boy you've probably loved since tenth grade. If that isn't a fairy tale romance, I don't know what is. Sweetie, if I had even an inkling that Charlie wasn't the right hot dude for you, I'd happily be plotting a way to break you kids up. But I'm not. Because I believe in you two. And minus my ordering sushi at Gus's Getcher Gas last night, my instincts are pretty spot on."

I want to believe her. I want to hope I don't marry Charlie, and five years later he wakes up and realizes he got it all wrong. "This is scary stuff. I didn't expect that."

"Is that why you've postponed the wedding twice?"

I don't want to think about that right now. "Work got in the way."

"Hmph." She ponders her black coffee. "Big life changes often are scary. But babe, they're sure worth it."

I know Maxine's right. I'm not sure why my head and heart can't get in alignment. "There is one thing I'm absolutely certain of."

"What's that, toots?"

"I want you to be my matron of honor."

Maxine covers her gasp with a well-manicured hand. "Me?" Her eyes pool with tears. "Are you sure?"

"You're my best friend. There's no one else I'd want by my side."

"Or to clothesline you when you attempt to escape down the aisle?"

"That too."

She pats her arm. "My biceps and I stand ready."

One wedding detail finalized. "I think this is finally happening."

"And that's a good thing." Her bracelets clank as she tweaks my chin. "For the bachelorette party, do you want the guy jumping from the cake to be naked or on fire?"

"Neither."

"This isn't Bachelorette Party: Amish Edition."

I smile, but a dark thought squeezes my conscience and begs to be shared. "I've been praying for God to give me confirmation that marrying Charlie is truly the right thing to do."

She blinks at the topic change. "Asking for signs?"

"Yes."

"Here's you a sign," Maxine says. "Your darling grandmother says it's the right thing to do."

"Did God tell you that?"

"Jesus and I are like this." She holds up two crossed fingers.

Just as I'm about to tell her about my missing engagement ring, my phone buzzes from its place on the picnic table. Walking to it, I read the screen. "It's my agent. I should take this."

"Okie dokie." Maxine shoots me some sassy pistol fingers. "I'll be inside calling guys for your bachelorette party. Do you mind seventy-year olds? Leroy Sykes is very fit."

I wave her away and answer my phone. "Hi, Mary."

"Katie, have I got news for you."

I glance down at my hand, where an engagement ring should be. "I guess I have a little news myself."

CHAPTER THREE

"HOLD YOUR NEWS." My agent smacks her ever-present nicotine gum in my ear. "I guarantee mine's better. Are you sitting down?"

I settle back into my chair, watching Millie's potted herbs dance in the breeze. "Yes."

"Well, get to your feet because... you got a part!"

"That's great."

"Great?"

I review the handful of plays I'd auditioned for in the last month, many of them lead and supporting roles. "Let me guess, Rizzo in that revival of *Grease*?"

"Not even close, babe. Are you ready for this?"

My heart returns to that frantic gallop, and despite the humidity, my skin pebbles with a chill. "Tell me."

"Katie, you got *the* part."

"No."

"I'm talking to the next Amelia Earhart, star of the next Broadway smash *Amelia Takes Off*. Girl, this thing is going to be huge."

"Mary, that's impossible."

"You're the star! Do you have any idea who you beat out for the role?" She lists off a handful of familiar names, a few of whom I now call friends.

"Are you sure?" I'd auditioned on a whim—a lark. The role was too big, too famous. It was meant for some Hollywood A-lister or a recognized Broadway star.

"The director loved you. She said you had an *it* quality she hasn't seen in years. Says she adored you in *The Widow*."

Shock sings through my blood. "Thank you. This is amazing."

"Block out your schedule for the next two years."

"Two years?"

"Didn't I tell you? She's already got this thing majorly financed. That's how big of a sure bet this production is. Rumor is, Elton John is one of the backers."

Two years of consistency, of steady work. "So, a little update for you—my fiancé and I set a wedding date tonight."

"Is that so?" My agent cackles in my ear. "Better get married fast. In two months, you report for duty. You won't have more than a day off for ages."

"But—"

"Either get married now or do it in a couple of years."

I repeat her words in horror. "Get married *now*?"

"I don't care which, but starting September 4, you're nobody's lady but the theater's."

"Katie's getting married now!" I hear from inside the house.

I spin around, only to find Maxine lurking behind the screen door, her face stretched in a wild grin. She jumps up and down, clapping her hands in jubilant glee. "My Katie's getting married now."

Numb, I end the call with my agent and step back into the house.

Charlie stands by the kitchen sink, holding a plate and wearing a ridiculous grin. "I don't think folks in the next town heard, Maxine. Care to repeat it?"

"Katie was on the phone with her agent." Maxine addresses the room as if unwinding a grand story. "Not that I was eavesdropping, but I heard Katie say she got a part."

"I was outside," I remind my favorite snoop. "With the door shut."

"Privacy is overrated." Maxine returns to her update. "Then I heard her very loud agent say Katie got her dream role."

At that, I can't help but smile. "I got the lead in a new play. On Broadway."

"Katie, that's wonderful." Millie sets down a steaming pan of peach cobbler, then wraps me in a hug. What follows next is a huge squeal fest. Everyone piles on me, and together we jump up and down, shouting and laughing. "My girl's going big time!"

Soon I've been squeezed and congratulated by everyone. Everyone except my fiancé. "Charlie?"

Charlie grabs my faces and kisses me like we're the only two in the room. "I'm so proud of you, Katie. When does it start?"

My heart makes a slow sink toward the floor. "In two months."

His hands fall away and tuck behind his back. "What?"

"I start in two months."

Maxine pops her head between us. "That agent said Katie would be working nonstop for the next year few years. So, you know what that means, don't you?"

I can hardly breathe. "That you back up, so I'm not staring at your chin hairs?"

She takes a step in reverse. "It means you guys gotta get married right away."

Is the air thinning in this room? There seems to be a distinct lack of oxygen available. "That's not what that means."

"That's exactly what your agent said—you need to do it pronto, or you won't have a chance for ages." Maxine skips to the stove and dishes out a serving of cobbler for herself. It's large enough to feed the entire family. "Sounds like you kids need to speed up these nuptials."

My pulse escalates at the very idea. Is this what cardiac arrest feels like? A coronary? "I don't think—"

"When will your next break be?" Charlie asks. I can tell from the way his head's angled and his brows slant that he's really giving this serious thought.

"I...I don't get one. I mean, sure, I could ask off for a few days later in the season, but that's not what the new kid with the lead role needs to do."

James retrieves some spoons from a drawer. “I know a preacher who’s available.”

“What about a destination wedding?” Maxine pulls her phone from her pocket, clicks and swipes, then produces a scenic photo. “Helen Chang’s granddaughter got married in Scotland this past February. It’s very windy there.” She pulls up another picture and chuckles. “Helen had a total skirt alert. Caught a swift gale off the loch, and everyone saw her bloomers.”

“Are you talking about Emily Chang?” Millie pulls the lid on a carton of vanilla ice cream. “Sweet first-grade teacher, who goes to our church?”

“That’s the one.” Maxine shows us a photo of Emily in her wedding dress, a halo of flowers around her head.

“She’s already filed for divorce.”

My stomach sinks at this definite lack of happily ever after. “How about we discuss this later? Charlie and I have only had minutes to absorb my news.”

“I think a destination wedding sounds great,” Charlie says. “How about next month?”

What? No, too soon! Too soon, people. “Or we could wait until the show’s run a while—maybe a year?” I smile reassuringly. “People in the military do things like this all the time—lengthy waits due to work. Same with astronauts. Can’t get married when you’re on Mars for a year, eh?” I hear the irrational edge to my voice and try to take it down a notch. “What’s our rush?”

“Because we’ve already rescheduled a few times. And because we want to be married.” Charlie reaches for my hand. “I’m ready. Aren’t you?”

“Sure she is,” Maxine shouts. “She’s been ready to be Mrs. Benson for longer than I’ve been president of the In Between Justin Timberlake fan club.”

Sam leans toward Amy. “That would be a ridiculously long time.”

Maxine takes a giant bite of cobbler, and her cheeks fill like a squirrel’s. “I know a divine travel agent.”

“A destination wedding would be a cheaper option.” James catches his wife's glare. "Not that you need to worry about that. But the church is booked through the fall."

"I'll pay for your wedding party to attend," Maxine offers. "And a big celebration when you return. It'll be my gift."

"Kind of hard to turn that down, isn't it?" Charlie leans down and kisses my cheek, his gray eyes intense on mine. "What do you say? Want to get married next month?"

My eyes take in the room, and I nearly melt at all the expectant gazes trained right on me.

Then I look at Charlie, a boy I loved before I even knew what love was.

And despite the slight nausea and the chorus in my head telling me to slow down, I nod my red head. "Okay. Let's get married."

CHAPTER FOUR

My Sunday starts off with a bang, from the moment Maxine wakes me with a serenade beneath my bedroom window and goes a hundred miles per hour from that point on.

"Eliza Biggles is *the* best travel agent in In Between." Maxine holds open the door for Charlie, me, and our small entourage of family.

I step inside and swear I smell mothballs. "She's the only travel agent in In Between."

"We're lucky we got her to come in on the Lord's Day," Maxine says. "Usually, she heads to the casino and closes the place down."

"Katie, dear, I'm so excited." Charlie's mother, Donna, has accompanied us this morning, and she vibrates with excitement. "I think a destination wedding is brilliant."

"Of course, it's a brilliant idea," Maxine says. "It came from me. Donna, have I talked to you about your mayoral preference for our September election?"

I didn't sleep a wink last night. I even woke up at four a.m. and took something to help me nod off, but my brain was like, "No, thank you! We have more thinking to do!"

Instead of counting sheep, I counted all the ways I was completely overwhelmed. I've just gotten the part of a lifetime, something I don't know that I'm prepared to successfully pull off. What if I'm a terrible Amelia? If I screw this up, I'll be forever relegated to supporting roles or bit parts.

Another insomniac item was the fact that I've gone from being an engaged woman with no looming wedding date to someone who is now a month away from getting married. It's a lot to take in. What do I know about being a wife? Or successfully navigating a marriage that doesn't implode? Nothing. I come from a long line of women who never had a successful marriage. My mom never married my dad. Her only marriage had lasted months. My mom said my grandma had married many times but died clutching the divorce papers that ended her marriage to step grandpa number five. We were a bloodline of cursed women. What if I'm bringing inevitable bad juju to my holy union with Charlie? Did a good man deserve that? What if when I said, "I do," I magically transformed and got a hankering for Jim Beam and dirt road honkey-tonk?

"Dear, Eliza." Maxine rushes toward a peacock of a woman wearing an Auntie Mame kaftan and kisses her cheek. "How are you, you fashionable thing, you?"

My grandmother is a style maven. If there was a runway for senior citizens, she'd be walking it. This fawning over Eliza Biggins' rainbow-colored tent dress is Grade A Maxine Dayberry Suck-Up.

"I'm just swamped, darling." Eliza's fur-trimmed high heels looked like she's stepped out of a 1980 soap opera. "But when I got your call, I knew I had to fit your granddaughter in. Please, sit." She points a long red nail to a seating area circling her desk. "Who do we have here?"

"I'm Charlie Benson." He sticks out his hand for Eliza to shake. "And this is my fiancée, Katie."

"Aren't you adorable?" Eliza hugs me like we're old friends, and I'm smothered in a cloud of old lady perfume.

Charlie introduces our mothers as Eliza opens a drawer in her desk and pulls out a one-subject notebook. "Let me boot up my computer here." She snorts as she laughs. "My son buys me a new computer every year, but I'm old school. These young whippersnappers think I'm the fuddy-duddy, but when the world implodes, and we're all living without electricity and modern amenities, who will be laughing then, huh?" She licks a finger and flips through ink-stained pages. "They can keep their technology. Everything I need is right here in my spiral notebook."

"And what a cute *Paw Patrol* design it is." I shoot my grandmother a look. *What have you gotten us into?*

Maxine ignores me. "Eliza, I know you said it was impossible to book a destination wedding with our timeline, but I was hoping you could work your magic."

"And work my magic, I have." She flips a few more pages, her eyes glowing with victory. "I searched high and low for something wonderful, and I've found just the thing." From the top drawer, she extracts a brochure and pushes it toward Charlie and me. "Behold the wonder."

I pick it up. "A clown cruise to the Caribbean?"

"Oops. Wrong pamphlet. Let's try this one." She whips out another. "Read it and weep with joy."

Charlie frowns. "A singles getaway to a haunted castle in Transylvania?"

"Oops again!" She swipes it from his grip. "But that one does come with a certified matchmaker and vampire hypnotist, if things go belly-up for you two."

"I'll keep that in mind." Charlie's lips quirk, and he gives my foot a light nudge with his shoe.

"Okie dokie, my blissfully-in-love artichokies, here is the wedding destination of your dreams."

I expect to see yet another ridiculous getaway, maybe a bus tour of chicken farms or an all-inclusive trip to the wax museum in Branson, Missouri. But what I'm looking at is actually pretty impressive. Photos of crystal blue ocean water, regal palm trees, a luxury hotel suite with a gorgeous lanai.

"Now I have your attention." Sitting in her desk chair, Eliza wheels herself closer, the ropes of beads around her neck pooling on top of her prized notebook. "This is Santisto Resort. It's a five-star resort in Santisto, Mexico, and a hop, skip, and a jump from Cancun. Food and drinks are covered, as are daily spa treatments. As you can see from the brochure, there's a lazy river, three giant pools, and you get your own cabana to lounge in on the beach. Your rooms would have an ocean view and are within walking distance to all the other restaurants on the resort."

"It looks beautiful," Millie says from her spot beside me. "What do you guys think?"

"It's okay," I manage. "Not bad."

"Not bad?" Eliza slaps her knee and guffaws. "This kind of deal rarely comes along. Kiddies, this resort is where A-listers stay, and they just happen to have a cancellation that I grabbed. If I don't sell it to you, I've got a waiting list of other interested parties." She reaches for her avocado green corded phone. "Customers who are waiting for my call."

"No!" Maxine grabs the receiver from Eliza's claw of a hand. "Don't be so hasty. My granddaughter here is still a little overwhelmed and starstruck. She just landed a mega role on Broadway, tomorrow she's the grand marshal in our Fourth of July parade, and now she has to endure the sudden shock of having to speed this wedding along...well, it's been a lot to take in. Right, Katie?" Her eyes are a silent plea to cooperate.

"Sure." I manage a smile. "But I think we'd like to hear more."

Charlie's hand reaches for mine, and he presses a kiss to my fingers before resting my hand in the safe crook of his arm.

A total swoony move.

Or maybe he's just afraid I'm about to bolt out of here like a summer Olympian doing the fifty-yard dash.

"So, we could get married on this Santisto Resort?" Charlie asks.

"It's their specialty, they tell me." Eliza peers at us over her bifocals. "Their wedding package is separate from your inclusive stay, but it includes a professional photographer, a seaside ceremony, a two-tier cake, an ordained minister, and a small reception afterward." She taps on a glossy photo. "This is a wedding they've done. And you didn't hear this from me, but this place is so nice that Beyonce and Jay-Z renew their vows here yearly." She makes a criss-cross over her heart. "Look at me, blabbing. I swore I wouldn't tell anyone that, so now it's your secret to keep as well, right?" She slaps her hands on her desk and proceeds to laugh at herself yet again. This woman seems to think she's an endless supply of punchlines. "What do y'all say?"

Donna scans the brochure. "I think it's lovely. And what a blessing that a trip like this is available on such short notice."

"I agree," Millie says. "If you're sure you don't want to wait, then this sounds ideal."

"What do you think?" Charlie asks me.

I stare at the smiling couple staring back at me from the brochure. "It's something to consider. Maybe we can talk about it for a few days."

"Days? That's not gonna work." Eliza shakes her **orange** head. "This deal will be gone within the hour. I'm only offering it to you because I owe your grandma a favor."

Maxine inspects her flawless manicure. "We won't rehash old wounds, but it did involve a cheating husband, a prenuptial agreement Eliza should never have signed, and forty-eight hours of surveillance embedded with a grunge band in Austin."

"Thank you for your time, Ms. Biggins." Charlie rises and shakes her hand again. "We'll definitely give this trip some thought."

"Best of luck to you, kids." Eliza Biggins closes her notebook with a snap. "It's going to be near impossible to find a destination that can handle your wedding with such a quick turnaround." She doesn't break eye contact as her phone rings. She presses the antique receiver to her ear. "Eliza's Exciting Expeditions, Eliza speaking. Yeah. Uh-huh. Okay." The notebook is opened once again. "Funny you called. The Santisto Resort has a last-minute cancellation of rooms that will absolutely meet your needs. With this package, you'll get an all-inclusive stay at the resort, plus a five-star destination wedding that includes a two-tier cake, an ordained—"

"We'll take it."

I stare in something akin to horror at Charlie's words. "What? Charlie, I don't think—"

"We'll take it." Resolutely, he pivots in his seat to face me. "I know it's rushing things, but we can keep things simple." Eyes gray as a summer storm hold mine captive. "At the end of the day, I just want to marry you. I don't care where or how. I don't want to wait more than a year, especially not for some vague, indefinite date we won't know until the distant future. Let's do this, Katie. You, me, our family, and a few friends. It'll be an adventure—together." He holds out his open palm. "Are you with me?"

I stare at that hand and know there's only one right answer here.

But why is it sticking to the roof of my mouth, afraid to trickle off my tongue?

"Katie?" Charlie's brows rise, and everyone around us leans in.

Finally, I place my hand in his. "I'm with you."

The room expands with the collective sigh of relief, and Eliza hangs up on her customer.

The travel agent then turns to her dusty computer and fires it up. "Let me see if I remember how to work this thing so we can make some reservations." She gives it a love pat, and it whirs to life. "Congratulations, kids. You leave in twelve days."

Stars dance before my eyes, and a dustbowl settles in my lungs. "Excuse me?" I manage to croak out. "Twelve days?"

After shoving her bifocals onto her nose, a squinty-eyed Eliza click-clacks on her keyboard. "Yep, you head out on a Friday, then marry that next Monday. Better get to shopping."

For the next half hour, decisions are made, credit cards are swiped, and I sit in my uncomfortable chair and nod my head while I sweat right through my shirt.

My wedding is in fifteen days.

"So nice doing business with you." Eliza later escorts us to the front doors. "I'll be in touch. Bye-bye now."

I step onto the sidewalk, and the blast of sunshine brings an immediate headache.

Or maybe it's the impulsive trip we just booked.

Millie falls into step beside me. "How are you feeling?"

I sniff the aroma wafting from the coffee shop two doors down and know I'll be detouring for a triple shot espresso. "I feel like I got run over by a semi-truck bound for Mexico."

Her motherly face softens. "Eliza's right—we don't have much time. We have a lot to buy and better get started."

"I don't even know where to start."

"That's an easy one." Maxine hoofs it down the sidewalk and inserts herself between us. "Let's go find you a wedding dress."

CHAPTER FIVE

"WELL, HERE WE ARE." On Monday afternoon, I give Charlie a kiss, grab my phone, and exit the rental car. Though the parade won't start for another half hour, the town square is already buzzing with activity. "See you at the end of the route. I'll try not to bean you with a lollipop."

"Katie, wait."

With sweat already dotting my brow, I turn to my fiancé. "Yes?"

His frown could scare the small children already lining up along the sidewalks. "Are you okay?"

"Yes. Sure. Perfectly Fine. Gotta go now."

His hand reaches for mine, halting my escape. "You didn't tell me how dress shopping went this morning."

"No luck in Houston. We're going to try the new shop in town tomorrow." Though we found a flower girl dress for Charlie's sister, Sadie, who's ten going on sixteen. It's the perfect mix of not too mature, but not too young. And cheap.

"You've barely said two words to me since we decided to move up the wedding date."

Oh. That. "Just feeling overwhelmed...with love."

Charlie ignores a passerby who waves in our direction. "I think I just witnessed your worst acting performance ever. Don't you want to get married?"

Is this really the time for this conversation? We have a country to celebrate and heat strokes **to endure**. "Of course I do."

"Then what's going on?"

"Charlie, I—"

"Hey, sweet peas." Maxine blares an airhorn twice, causing a nearby flock of geese to squawk and scurry away. She inserts herself between the two of us. "Charlie, you have the rest of your life to monopolize my girl. Right now, I need her for parade duties." She gets a look at my outfit as I exit the vehicle. "I thought I told you to show cleavage."

"I don't have any."

"You're an actress—you could've improvised. I have a lot riding on today. You could be my ticket to earning the millennial vote."

My eyes drop to my chest. "Guess you'll have to lure them in with something else."

"But with what? Free televisions and coupons for queso at Nellie's House of Nachos?"

"I was thinking with sound ideas and forward-thinking policies."

She rolls her eyes. "You don't know politics at all."

I squeeze Charlie's hand and give him a quick kiss. "See you later."

"This conversation isn't over," he says quietly.

And that's exactly what I'm afraid of. How do I communicate my hesitance to marry the boy when I can't even understand it myself? I love Charlie with every cell and molecule in my body, but yet...the delays on our way to the chapel have not disappointed me the way they have him.

"Kissy time later." Maxine pulls me along and escorts me down the sidewalk where cars and floats line up like they're posing for a new Norman Rockwell painting. "Sam's waiting for us with the Cadillac."

The good people of In Between mill about, and the clouds above us breathe out humidity and filter happy sunshine. The air buzzes with an energy that seeps into my skin and momentarily pushes away all my dark, tangled thoughts. I wave at Frances, who stands on her NASA float like an avenging ship captain. I spot two former high school teachers and call out a hello.

"Miss Katie?" I glance down at a short, curly-headed blonde girl who holds a notebook and a smile. "Can I get your autograph?"

I grin at the child who can't be more than ten. "Sure." I give her an enthusiastic version of my name, the loops and swoops taking up the entire page. It's only been this year that the autograph request phenomenon has hit, and while it's no longer the out-of-body shock it initially was, I'm still not used to it. "Here you go. Have fun at the parade."

"Wow." She clutches the notebook and looks at it like I've given her a thousand dollar check instead. "This is the coolest."

"You bet it is." Maxine hands the girl a 'Maxine for Mayor' koozie. "My granddaughter here is about to be the reigning princess of Broadway. That signature will be worth big bucks this time next Fourth of July. Now move along, little darlin.' We've got a parade to start."

"Thank you!" the girl squeals, then breaks through the crowd. "Mom, look. I got Idina Menzel's autograph!"

"Adorable little brat." Maxine cracks her knuckles. "Do you want me to go straighten her out?"

"You can do it later."

"Right. Way to stay focused. Onward to the Caddie."

We walk another block, intercepting well-wishers and calling out hellos. Sweat gathers on my upper back as we swim upstream in search of Sam. While I owe much to the town of In Between, participating in a parade in July in Texas means my debt is now more than paid.

"Here we go. Sam! Yoo-hoo!" Maxine throws her hand up in the air and waves at her adorable husband. "Isn't he a hunk? Girl, check out the backside of that dreamboat."

"Not really the visual I want of my grandfather," I say as we reach the car.

"I meant the Cadillac." Maxine pats the dusty pink car that nearly takes up more than its share of parking spaces. "Get a load of these curves, would ya? And check out that leather interior. Cars today are tiny Hot Wheels compared to this beaut."

Sam sits in the back and pats a fin. "This here's a Cadillac Eldorado. Rumored to have been used in a movie starring Marilyn Monroe."

"Got it from one of Sam's friends," Maxine says. "See Katie, this car's got good juju."

"It also has 'Vote for Maxine' signs plastered all over it." I walk around Maxine's dreamboat. "Is my name on here anywhere?"

"No, but it can be." She digs into her purse and extracts a pen. "Do you spell Indina with two N's or one?"

"Dagnabbit, Maxine." Sam hops out of the vehicle and inspects her banners. "Where did these banners come from?"

"Straight from my heart."

He rips one down, and beneath it is a sign emblazoned with my name and my title of grand marshal. "There. Now take the other signs down while I rev up the Eldorado."

"But this is the perfect opportunity for my campaign," Maxine protests. "Me, riding with *the* famous Katie Parker Scott. Who wouldn't vote for that?"

Sam slips off his sunglasses. "Me, that's who. And if you think I didn't notice the T-shirt gun, you are mistaken. With your luck, you'll take out someone's eye."

Maxine sighs. "No, this one has a scope and sights. So easy to operate even Katie here could do it." She pats my shoulder. "And she will. In between throwing out quality candy and Maxine Dayberry bumper stickers."

"Let's go!" A burly man yells as he walks down the road, clutching a clipboard and inspecting each car. "In Between Fourth of July Parade kicks off in three...two...one."

Patriotic music begins, and I see cars begin to slowly crawl forward.

"No time to unload any of our supplies," Maxine says. "Let's hop in before they take off without us."

I join her in the back seat, my vintage gingham skirt swishing around my legs. "Ow. That's hot."

"Yeah, that's the price you pay for luxurious, vintage leather." Maxine flops a towel in her seat beside me. "Old things can't all be perfect."

Sam shoots his wife a look in the rearview. "Don't I know it."

"Just drive, you geriatric stud muffin."

Five minutes later, after everyone else has gently rolled on, Sam puts the elongated car into drive, and we ramble on.

I toss candy and wave, feeling every bit like a Meghan Markle or Kate Middleton. Minus their inherent grace. And model good looks. And with the addition of a bug in my mouth.

"It's a new day with Maxine Dayberry!" my grandmother shouts, tossing candy to waiting kids.

"That's some quality chocolate you've got there." I notice she's sharing an expensive brand from a local chocolatier.

"I can't afford cheap stuff when so much is on the line. My opponent, Gus McGillicuddy, cannot win this election. He has the personality of a lint roller." And with that, she digs into a canvas bag, grabs a wad of something, and lobs it like a hand grenade. "T-shirts for my sweeties!" She throws more, with an aim any pro baseball team would envy. "That's a nice poly-cotton blend. Preshrunk. Won't change—like me. I see you, Mr. Dinkus. Here's an XXL just for you. Oops, sorry about your nose!"

As I smile and wave my arm like a beauty queen, I study the faces of the people lined up and down the street. People I know, people I grew up with. There's Angie Frazier, who manages the night shift at Tucker's Grocery. I see her twin sister Stephanie Goines who runs the post office and knows everyone in town by name. Mr. Fisher, my junior English teacher. The pastor of the Methodist church who lives a street away from my parents and sings when he waters his lawn. Mark Jacobson, a boy I graduated with who now runs a tax prep service downtown. They wave at me as if I'm queen for the day, and though it's a bit discomforting, it feels good to be so accepted and loved.

We pass by my old drama teacher Ms. Hall who cups her hand over mouth and yells, "You're In Between's pride and joy!"

Maxine waves back. "Thank you, dear!"

I laugh and throw Ms. Hall the truffles Maxine thinks she's hidden in the seat.

My grandmother's arm comes within an inch of my nose as she chunks another T-shirt. It nearly takes out a toddler. "You wanna tell me what's going on with you?"

"Tammy Nelson's baby almost got himself a knee replacement? Also, I swallowed another bug, and I'm sweating through my dress."

Maxine digs in her bag and hands me a water bottle. "I mean with this wedding business."

Why does she keep asking me that? It's certainly not helping the nerves. "I'm fine."

She lobs a candy bar and beans the interim mayor right between the eyes. "Sweetcheeks, if I was about to marry Charlie Benson, I'd be grinning from ear to perfectly aligned ear and bragging to anyone who'd listen."

"Excuse me for being humble and subdued."

Maxine cackles and slaps my leg. "We're not talking about your bust line. We're talking about your pre-wedding demeanor."

"It's a lot to take in."

"I told you I was kidding about staying the whole week with you and Charlie on the island. I swear I'll leave with the rest of the family."

I was too tired and stressed to tell my grandma I saw her fingers crossed behind her back. The travel agent had made arrangements for Charlie and me to stay seven days on Santisto, while everyone else left on day four. Nothing like spending part of your honeymoon with family.

"You've had two years to mentally prepare," Maxine says. "What's the problem?"

"I just..." Can hardly explain it. "Something feels off."

"Like your brain?"

"Katie! Katie!"

"Wow, you really do have adoring fans." Maxine gestures to a woman running toward our car. "Maybe she wants a T-shirt." She readies her pitching arm.

"Wait." I hold a hand to stop her, the noise of the crowd fading away as the woman draws closer. "Oh, no."

"Is that a rabid fan? I'm not afraid to be your bodyguard," Maxine says as the woman nears. "Need me to body-slam her?"

"Katie Parker Scott?" The lady's long, raven hair blows around her face, and the angles of her flushed cheeks, as well as her green eyes, look hauntingly familiar.

She rushes the car, and it's not until she's jogging beside the vehicle that I see she's not alone.

"Yes?" I manage to say.

"Do you know who I am?" she yells.

Words escape me, so I slowly nod and watch the wide-eyed child with her.

"You have to help me."

"I..." My hair loosens from my ponytail as I shake my head. "What are you doing?"

She lifts up her child, depositing the girl into the warm seat beside me. "I need you to take care of my daughter."

"We have a looney!" Maxine yells, searching the crowd for help. "Call 9-1-1."

But the police are already here.

Two cops dressed in crisp navy rush the woman, each taking an arm.

"Save my daughter," she yells as they haul her away. "Please save my daughter!"

"Good heavens." Sam pushes the brakes on the car, and the leather scrunches as he turns. "What kind of crazy fan would ask you to take her child?"

I stare at the little girl, pulling her to me as she cries. "One who knows she's my sister."

CHAPTER SIX

WHEN PEOPLE ASK me about my family tree, I usually tell them it got wiped out in the In Between tornado when I was in tenth grade. That tree was broken, split, and probably hauled off to the paper mill.

So, to be sitting here now, in the In Between Police Department, with one officer, one grandmother, and one fiancé expecting me to explain this family is not my idea of a pleasant time.

"I've heard this happens to Reese Witherspoon all the time." Maxine takes a sip of police station coffee, grimaces, then tosses it in the nearby trashcan.

"Well, someone asking me to take her kid is a first for me." I cross my legs and bounce a nervous tempo with my leg.

Charlie rubs the back of his neck like there's a pain there with my name on it. "You have a sister, and you've never told me about her?"

"It's fairly new information for me as well." I try to keep my voice as calm and pleasant as possible for the sake of all the listening ears in the office.

"How long have you known about her?" Maxine asks, clearly hurt I've kept a secret.

I shrug. "Not long. Can we get back to Officer Kramer's questions?"

The police officer types into her keyboard, shaking her head. "You celebrities are so weird."

"I'm definitely not a celebrity."

She raises a red eyebrow. "Only celebrities get to be grand marshal of the Fourth of July Parade."

"That's true." Maxine nods. "Last year, Curly Monroe brought up the rear, and Lord knows he's a big deal."

Officer Kramer gives her a hearty amen. "Huge."

"Who's Curly Monroe?" Charlie asks.

Maxine snorts. "Only the most famous potbelly pig this side of the Mason Dixon."

I bite my lip and go to bouncing my other leg. "I can only hope to aspire to that level of fame."

"Curly Monroe can skateboard on two hooves," Officer Kramer states. "It is a very high bar."

"Sorry, I'm late."

We all turn at the voice of the new arrival, and when I see the woman walking into the office, I nearly drop the water bottle in my hand.

"Mrs. Smartley?" As I live and barely breathe, there stands my old caseworker. "What are you doing here? I thought you'd retired." And lived in another county hours away. Grateful for an excuse to get up and move, I get to my feet to meet her.

"Katie Parker, as I live and breathe." She hugs me, something that would've been a complete violation of the Teenage Katie Parker Code of Physical Boundary Protocol.

Mrs. Smartley and I stayed in touch for years after my adoption in high school, still writing old fashioned letters like we'd done when I was in care. But I'd gotten busy and somehow ran out of time to chit chat with the woman responsible for bringing me to James and Millie Scott.

"Look at you." She holds me at arm's length, her eyes taking in the sweaty sight before her. "My gosh, I love a success story. Reviewing those used to help me sleep at night."

"What are you doing here?"

"Moved to In Between when my daughter had a baby, and then I retired. I'm filling in while the department deals with some turnover." She greets Officer Kramer. "Just got through talking to Haven Mitchell. I hear her daughter is here somewhere."

"She's in the break room getting a snack with Chief Higgins."

Iola pulls up a chair from a nearby desk. "Give me all the sordid details."

"Mom is Haven Mitchell, age 24." The policewoman reads from a report with a tone reserved for grocery lists and appliance manuals. "At approximately four a.m., we conducted a raid on a property at 939 South Arnica Drive. Inside were Mitchell, her five-year-old daughter, and the owner of the house, Benny Caprizio."

"The drug dealer, Benny Caprizio?" Mrs. Smartley inquires.

"That's the one. In the home, we found a whole arsenal of guns, as well as twenty-thousand in cash."

"Any drugs?" Maxine's leaned so far on her chair, one small tap would empty her into the floor. "I watch a lot of BBC mysteries, so I might be of help."

Officer Kramer locks eyes with Mrs. Smartley, and a silent message is conveyed. "We found a lot of interesting items. Drugs and a significant amount of cash were found in Haven Mitchell's purse."

Mrs. Smartley types notes into her phone. "I missed the part where you lost Haven and her daughter."

Officer Kramer clears her throat as a patchwork of pink splotches appears on her neck. "We used flash-bang to gain entry into the house, predictably catching Delgado by surprise, as per our intent. We did not know the home contained other occupants." Iola does not look impressed with this portion of the story, but the cop continues. "Haven Mitchell and her daughter were apparently in the other end of the house and managed to take off on foot. They sort of eluded us. For a while."

Iola looks up from her phone, her wiry gray hair still a bonnet of chaos on her head. "Until Haven approached Katie at the parade."

"Something like that."

Iola gives one of her classic eye rolls before turning her attention to me. "I hear you have a niece."

"News to me as well." Charlie's jaw is as taut as fishing pole line.

Iola pushes up her oversized glasses. "We'll be taking Haven's daughter into care." She gives me a warm look meant to comfort. "Her name is Daisy."

Charlie shifts in his seat. "Katie probably knew that."

Officer Kramer stacks some papers on her desk a little too aggressively. "Ms. Scott, I'd like to hear how you're connected to Haven Mitchell."

"Haven and I had the same biological father. He left my mom when I was two, and remarried multiple times, has numerous kids all over the country I'd imagine. I've never had contact with my bio-dad, but apparently, he raised Haven until his death some years ago. She contacted me by way of my Instagram last fall when the play I was in took off, and I got a little press."

Maxine raps her hand on Officer Kramer's desk to gain her attention. "My granddaughter, Katie, is a theater star in Chicago. She's about to headline a major show on Broadway."

The cop lifts one dark brow by way of response.

"So, you started communicating with this Haven?" Charlie asks. "You didn't tell any of us?"

"We swapped some infrequent emails, traded bio information. Honestly, she never bothered to tell me she had a daughter." Though she had asked some strange questions about my life and personal beliefs.

"Did you know you're the child's godmother?" Iola asks.

Lowering the water bottle pressed to my lips, I can only gape in confusion. "Says who?"

"Haven."

"I don't think that's how that works." Give me some credit here.

Mrs. Smartley wears the unfazed expression of a woman who has seen it all. "We're going to make some calls and investigate, but Haven says you're the only family."

"I think she has a mother somewhere."

"To hear Haven tell it, her mom didn't raise her very well," Mrs. Smartley says. "But, aside from you, she's kin." Iola levels those caseworker eyes on me. Eyes used to persuade, as well as comfort. "Look, Katie, Haven's probably going to be in jail for a while until this goes to court. She swears she didn't sell or use drugs, but for the last six months, she's lived with a known dealer and endangered the welfare of her child."

"Chip off the family block," I mumble.

"Daisy's going into foster care tonight."

My heart aches at the thought. "That's terrible."

"Haven is begging you to take her daughter."

"My Katie can't be babysitting right now," Maxine sputters. "She's got a quickie wedding to plan and a booming career."

"We could take her with us." Charlie's words are clipped, and though he sits beside me, he feels miles away.

"No, that's impossible." Panic pulses through my tired muscles. "We don't live here, and I'm not trained. Licensed. Ordained. Whatever you call it."

"We have workarounds for family." Iola's steady gaze meets mine, and she communicates pages of information in one glance. We both know how this shakes out. We both know the system. The question is, what am I going to do about it? "Haven says her sister's a big star."

My cheeks flame. "Not a big star. More like a medium-sized one in a small constellation. I'm a total Little Dipper." I swear Iola bites her bottom lip on a grin. "I work six days a week, with strange, late hours. And Charlie and I are moving to New York in weeks. We both start new jobs. I can't keep Daisy."

Mrs. Smartley has never been one to tolerate excuses. "You sure?"

"Definitely." Guilt and urgency are twin heat-seeking missiles soaring around me, about to land in one big explosion. "Plus, I'm getting married. Did I mention that?"

"I think you might've."

"Yep. Getting married. Getting hitched. Becoming the ole ball and chain. Making it legal. Making an honest woman of myself. Saying I do to—"

"Where do we go from here?" Charlie asks, eyeing me curiously as if he'd like to check my forehead for a fever.

"Daisy goes with me," Mrs. Iola says. "I'll work all day and evening, calling around until I find an open home who will foster her. If I don't, the two of us will probably spend the night in the DHS office. She'll sleep on the couch, and I'll catch some Z's in a chair. Then if we can't find a placement, Daisy will be sent to a girl's home a few hours away."

My stomach lurches with a familiar pang I haven't felt in years. "The one I lived in before the Scotts?"

"That's the one. But it's improved somewhat." Iola extracts her car keys from her purse. "They painted it, so probably just like new, right?"

I will never forget that place. It's where I met Trina the Knife Wielder, the girl who slept with weapons beneath her pillow. I was never so glad to leave. "Daisy can't go there."

"Maybe we should talk about this in private," Charlie says. "Assuming my opinion matters here."

"Of course, it matters." On top of everything coming at me, Charlie's furious. Can't say I blame him. "Charlie, we can't care for Daisy. Who would watch her when we work? And then, there are visits and court dates to consider. We definitely can't bring her back to Texas for that."

"We could handle all that remotely." Mrs. Smartley looks quite proud of this answer.

That fixes nothing, really. A few court dates are the least of our problems. "We can't bring her back to New York."

"I think we should give it a try." Charlie acts like this is one of his work negotiations. "You're Daisy's family."

Maxine pipes up. "I like this idea. I could visit and play the doting grandma. I could even nanny for you in New York."

I have to make Charlie see reason. "You can't be serious about fostering a child."

"I'm serious about considering it."

"My career's just taking off, and we'll be adjusting to life as husband and wife. Mrs. Smartley will find Daisy a good home. She's a pro at that—the best. And I know nothing about taking care of little girls. My mom fed me Pop-Tarts and Hot Pockets. We're not ready to be parents for years yet, and there's simply no way I can commit to—"

Any remaining words fade away, drifting into the precinct ether as my world shifts like God turned the page of my script and rewrote all the lines.

Because a burly cop walks from a room, his arms wrapped around a wiggling five-year-old. She wails and screams, pleading for the one thing she wants in this world. “Gimme my mama. Please let me see my mommy!”

Those heat-missiles of guilt and urgency land their target.

I feel the jagged edges of shrapnel and fire sear my heart.

“Okay,” I hear myself say as the cries grow louder. “We’ll take her home.”

CHAPTER SEVEN

"SO...A SISTER." Charlie sits with me hours later in the office at the Department of Human Services while Iola prints off some paperwork. Maxine tries her best to entertain a hollow-eyed Daisy on the other side of the room.

I pick at unraveled threads on a worn couch that probably predates Iola. "Technically, yes."

"You didn't think the fact that you had a sister was worth mentioning to me at any point in our relationship?"

He asks this in the same tone one might ask, "Did you know there was a dead body in your trunk?"

Though I've gone through this a few times now, Charlie still needs to hear the answer. Like the next time I say it, it will finally make sense. "Andy, our bio dad was never my dad, ever. Do I share his DNA? Unfortunately, yes. Was he ever a parent to me? Thankfully, no. He never paid child support, never sent so much as a birthday card, and did not even get his name added to my birth certificate. Haven's dad is as much a stranger to me as the next person who drives past this building. I've had enough trouble in my life being associated with my bio-mom, so the last thing I wanted to do was take on any of Andy's dysfunctional brood."

"But, Haven had been contacting you."

"A few times. She didn't seem too crazy, so I responded. I thought that was the end of it." But, of course, in my dysfunctional world, it was just the beginning.

Charlie runs a hand through his hair. "This is serious. What are we going to do?"

Not what am *I* gonna do, but what are *we* going to do. My nervously beating heart expands in my chest. "I don't know. You had a normal upbringing. Maybe you can take the lead on this parenting thing."

"I think you should consider bringing Daisy back to New York with us."

"Nuh-uh. No way. I've agreed to a few weeks, but once we step on the plane to Santisto Island, our responsibility is over."

"We could make it work."

"No, Charlie, we can't. You're gone for months at a time, and my schedule is insane."

"I could ask for family leave. Maybe request a different position that doesn't require so much travel."

He was driving Indy car speeds with this idea, ready to crash through all roadblocks and alter our lives. "You just got a promotion. You can't give it back."

"I'm only saying if we need to—"

"We don't. We won't." My breath hitches, and I force myself to pull air into my lungs. "I'm certain."

Charlie watches the little girl bite into a cookie as she shrugs a shoulder to whatever Maxine's telling her. "I think we don't make any final decisions tonight. Let's take a few days to pray about it, give it some thought."

"Charlie, I—"

"She doesn't have anyone, Katie. Besides her mother, who you never mentioned, we're her only family."

"We're not Daisy's family." I feel the need to remind him. "Because Haven's not my sister."

Charlie rubs his hand over my cheek and presses a kiss to my forehead. "Life with you is never boring, Katie Parker."

I blink back the sting of tears and lean into him. "I'm not ready to be a parent, Charlie."

"I know," he says. "But I guess she wasn't ready to be a foster kid."

~

An hour later, as Charlie and Maxine walk Daisy to the car, I hand a stack of signed paperwork back to Iola Smartley. If I were on the Titanic, the ship would've just hit the twin icebergs of Regret and Panic. I'd be sinking so fast, Leonardo wouldn't even have time to find me a floating door.

What have I done? Did I seriously agree to fostering? How is this my life? I'm about to get married to the best man God ever created and start the job any actress would kill for, and *this* happens? Haven Mitchell couldn't wait to date a drug dealer and get busted *next* year?

God, where are you? Is this how it works—something wonderful happens like my Broadway production, and bam! Here comes a disaster to temper it?

"Don't forget," Iola warns. "You'll have a probable cause hearing this Wednesday. The judge likes the foster parents to be there."

Court? Oh, gosh. I still have nightmares about sitting through court when my mom had to appear. "I don't suppose they've improved on the experience with halftime entertainment and snacks?"

Iola stuff papers in a blue folder and hands it to me. "Afraid not, but if you're terribly bored, it's a chance to get frisked by security."

"Iola, I don't know how to take care of a young child." I've lost count, but I'm pretty sure this is the twelfth time I've made this claim.

She flops a veined hand, completely unaffected. "I suppose you'll figure it out."

"This is a very bad decision, Mrs. Smartley. I could totally mess up this kid, which could ruin your career forever."

"I'd love to return to retirement, and I dare them to fire me daily, so give it your best shot."

"One time, I had a pet goldfish, and I frequently forgot to feed it."

"Good to know. Next time I get a case and need a home for a guppy, I won't call you. Look, you've got all Daisy needs right now—a safe home and a good heart. If you think I'm worried about leaving a foster kid in your care, you are mistaken."

"Fine. Let me run a few parenting questions by you."

Iola leans on a faux wooden desk and crosses her arms over her faded sweatshirt. "Shoot."

Sheer terror has me trying one more time for a reprieve. "For her milk formula, do you think Similac or Parent's Choice?"

Iola's lips twitch. "You can skip that and hand her a cup."

"Do you think Daisy would prefer her Mountain Dew in a 44-ounce tumbler or just give her the two-liter?"

"I can bring her one of those backpacks with the straw." Her drawl is as Texas as a bluebonnet. "That way, she can mainline it by the minute."

"And how do you think Daisy takes her morning coffee?"

"Three shots of espresso with a Red Bull chaser." Sandpaper couldn't be dryer than Iola's voice. "Nice try, kid, but I'm not buying what you're selling. You'll be fine, and so will Daisy May."

Daisy *May*? "Mrs. Smartley..." That's it. That's all I have to say. The rest goes unspoken and surely is written all over my dazed face. Her name is a plea, a prayer...a reluctant surrender.

My old caseworker smiles and puts her hand on my shoulder. "Let me tell you something, Katie Parker."

Oh, gosh. I know that tone, that softened expression. What's about to follow will pair well with an inspirational soundtrack. This is the same way Iola's pep talk began as sixteen-year-old me sat in her van before meeting two strangers called James and Millie.

"If I didn't believe you could handle this, I wouldn't leave this dear child in your care. You think I only know who you were when you were in the system, but you're wrong. Believe it or not, I've got a pretty good idea of who you are now. I've kept up with your progress since day one."

"You have?" I want to write out her words on pretty paper with fancy calligraphy and press it into a memory book.

"I have. I've taken care of thousands of kids, and there are a handful that will always be extra special to me, children who had so much potential, who were either gonna be accomplished criminal masterminds—or presidential candidates."

"I don't really have an interest in politics so—"

"You've made it, Katie. You've come out on the other side, and you're a stunning success, just as I knew you would be. But more important than any personal achievements, you're a fine human being."

My sniffle sounds loud in this dim room. "I do recycle and always return my shopping cart."

"You could've had a hardened heart, a penchant for anger, a soured spirit. You'd be justified if you did. But look at you." She tilts her head, her eyes now sparkling with tears behind her outdated glasses. "You're a social worker's dream story, and a parent's wish come true." She reaches into her pocket, then hands me a much-needed tissue. "Who better for this little girl to spend a bit of time with during the most traumatizing moment of her life? What a gift to her that you're not only her aunt, but you know exactly what she's going through."

"I'm not her aunt."

"Fine. You're a distantly connected...friend."

My voice comes out squeaky and hoarse. "I'm so afraid of doing the wrong thing and not having any instinct for taking care of her."

"Nobody's asking you to teach Daisy algebra and Latin. Keep her safe, keep her fed, and let her be the hurting child she needs to be. Like the Scotts did for you."

"Okay." I sniff and blot my leaky nose with the Kleenex. "I guess I can try that. But you promise it's temporary?"

"I'll take whatever you can give me. We'll start work on finding a long-term home for Daisy. Can you give us a few weeks?"

"I leave for my wedding in eleven days."

"I'll get you respite care for Daisy while you're gone, then find another family after that as the long-term placement."

I feel like an insensitive ogre. But let the record show I don't know this child or her family. And the timing is terrible—for Daisy and for me. My life doesn't even allow a dog, let alone a child. "I can do this for a few weeks."

"Sure, you can." Iola pats my arm then holds walks me to the exit.

Pushing open the door, I hesitate as the night air swoops in. “Mrs. Smartley?”

“Yes?”

“Do you give every reluctant foster parent such a personalized sales pitch?”

“When necessary.” She flicks off an overhead light and grabs the same messenger bag she used to carry a decade ago. “I’d hate for anyone to miss out on the blessing I know is coming her way.”

CHAPTER EIGHT

THE TRIP BACK TO MY PARENTS' house yawns by, every mile fueled by the silent, pervasive angst within the car.

Daisy sits in the back, saying very little. She clutches her hands in her lap as if the death grip keeps her tethered to the seat. I was that kid once, though ten years older than Daisy's five. I recall the fear snaking through every vein and limb, my hands cold, my heart racing like I'd sprinted through a deadly obstacle course—zero idea where I'd end up. While home was unsafe, even at a young age, you recognize it could be worse.

When Iola Smartley picked me up from the scary girls' home and drove me to the unknown of the Scotts, I'd briefly considered a movie-esque leap out the car door, jumping to freedom. Fortunately, logic and my dislike for vertebrae fractures had prevailed, and things turned out better than okay for me. But not every foster kid gets that happy ending. The unknown can be a much larger monster than any terror you might've come from. It's a powerless form of torture.

"Daisy, what kind of music do you like?" I turn in my seat, hoping to coax her into an answer while Charlie drives. She says nothing but continues to look out the window, the evening lights creating shadows across her pale face. "I like it all," I say. "Show tunes, rap, country, pop, bluegrass. What about you, Charlie?"

He turns onto Smith Street as his voice turns jovial and silly. "Oh, man, I love 'Old MacDonald.' And Katie won't admit this, but she sings that a lot when she thinks no one's looking."

My hand flies to my chest. "You know about that?"

He cuts me a look. "I know it all, babe."

I'd be a fool to miss his sarcasm. Yet, I ignore it anyway. "Please *do not* tell her how 'Baby Shark' is my second favorite, because that would totally embarrass me."

"The way you combine quality dance moves with convincing fin motions is a thing of beauty." He flicks the blinker and adjusts his brights as a car passes. "Do you like any of those songs, Daisy?" Charlie sings an off-key verse of the obnoxious oceanic masterpiece.

Daisy doesn't look ready to commit to our conversation, but I see her eyes flit toward me, and I count it a victory.

Our car eases into the driveway, and I notice every light in the house is on. No doubt Millie's running around like mad trying to prepare for this unexpected guest.

"Here we are." Charlie shifts the car into park and regards us both with a smile. "I'll get Daisy's stuff while you help her inside." He allows his gaze to rest on me for a moment, his hand on the door handle. "Later, we'll talk, okay?"

His words are light, but I hear the strain, the disappointment. "Right. Okay, Daisy, here we go." Then I lead Daisy into the house, the two of us connected by DNA and a common membership in a club no child ever wants access to.

"There's my girl." James greets us at the front door, and as soon as I walk in, I smell cookies. Whenever Millie wants to comfort, she breaks out the baked goods. James kisses my cheek, gives Charlie a solid pat on the shoulder, then grins at young Daisy. "Hey, sweetie." His voice is soft as spun cotton. "My name is James. I'm Katie's dad."

Tears arrive unannounced, and I blink the moisture away. How is it those words can still completely undo me? He's my father. James Scott is my dad. How did I ever get so blessed? Meanwhile, Daisy here gets the father figure of a drug dealer. *Great going, Haven.*

"Who wants snickerdoodles?" Millie breezes into the living room, her silvery blonde curls dancing around her flushed face. I'm sure she moved at warp speed to fluff her two-story nest.

"Daisy." I shift closer to the girl. "This is my mom." While the moment is welcome, it's no surprise when my niece gives a small smile at the sight of Millie. Millie radiates tranquility and safety, and everything about her is a giant hug.

Millie searches the coffee table for the remote, then turns the TV on to a cartoon. "Katie, why don't you and Charlie take Daisy's stuff up to the guest room, while Daisy helps me in the kitchen with dinner. Are you hungry, sweetie?"

Daisy shrugs a dainty shoulder, her big eyes on Millie.

"You can think about it," Millie says as she leads Daisy toward the kitchen. "But tell me, how do you feel about dessert first?"

Charlie and I ascend the stairs, the Walmart bags in his hands crunching with every step.

"Dessert first, huh?" Charlie turns left at the landing, where a collage of family photos happily hang. "You know things have gone Defcon 3 when Millie pulls from the bottom of the food pyramid."

"Something life with me taught her." I slip into the room across from my old one and flick on the light, illuminating the place where Daisy will spend her first evening as a ward of the state. A full-sized bed sits in the middle of the room, normally covered in a vintage white quilt. But tonight, somehow, it's decked out in a pink spread and held down by a trio of teddy bears. I have no idea where those stuffed animals came from, but if anyone is capable of conjuring comforting toys from thin air, it's Millie.

I inhale the faint scent of Charlie's woodsy cologne as he walks by and sets the white plastic bags on the floor.

He peers inside one then pulls out a small T-shirt bearing the face of a familiar cartoon character. "Are these two bags all she has?"

"I guess." Some kids arrive with nothing, and the caseworkers have to quickly shop before drop-off. "We can ask about stuff from her house."

He lays a nightgown on the bed, the tag dangling from the sleeve.

"Is this how you came to the Scotts? With only a few meager articles of clothing?"

Memories of that day crash to the forefront, and I take a moment to reorganize the pieces. "I carried a trash bag of stuff to the group home, but when Iola picked me up to come here, she gave me a small suitcase." It was new and shiny purple. Everything I'd owned had fit in that case I'd been so proud of. "The department had to buy me a few things. My shoes weren't fit for anything but the trash, and I was in dire need of new underthings." I also remember Millie taking me on a shopping spree fit for a princess. I still have a few of those items, just mementos I can't part with and keep in a box at the top of my closet.

Charlie stares at the bags. "It kills me to think of you living through that."

Sentiments like these always unsettle me. "One time in college, a cute boy told me it made me who I am today."

"I was pretty adorable." Charlie sits on the bed, and the mattress dips as he braces his hands on his knees. "Is there anything else I don't know about you that you need to share?"

I sit down beside him and drop my head to his shoulder. "I sponsor three dogs at the shelter down the road from my apartment, and when you order fries, I think of them as ours."

"At least one of those is not a revelation." He turns to face me head-on, his eyes full of hurt and confusion. "I still can't get over the fact that you have siblings out there. Since when did you stop telling me important stuff?"

"When Haven first reached out, you were in London." I trace the tension across his forehead. "You've had so much going on at work, and it's not like I see you a lot."

"The distance means we stop talking? That you shut me out of your life?"

"No. I'm sorry. I don't know why I kept it to myself. I guess old habits and the old shame reared its head."

"Your sister is not your shame, no matter who she is.

"I know that." In my mind, I do. But in my heart, it's like *here we go again*. Another woman in my family line who can't keep it together and can't parent a child.

He sighs and gives a slight smile. "So, you're an aunt."

"Biologically, yes." It's odd to think I have blood family out there. Growing up with my mom, we had almost zero contact with relatives, and those we did see did not make me want to seek out anymore. "When we get married, I guess you'll be an uncle."

"We are still getting married, right?"

"We definitely are." I frown so hard, I'm sure I'm laying fertile groundwork for wrinkles. "Why would you ask that?"

"We got engaged two years ago. I don't want any more delays."

"Okay." Though a child dropped in our laps seems like a solid one. "We won't let this stop us."

But how do you stop a natural disaster?

Because I feel certain one is coming—or already here.

CHAPTER NINE

LEAVING Charlie upstairs to take a call from his family, I descend the stairs with trepidation and dread. What am I supposed to do with a stranger's child?

Walking into the living room, I find Daisy propped on the couch next to Millie, eating from a plate piled high with baked goods while *Daniel Tiger* sings a song on the TV about being upset. Pretty sure the fuzzy little guy knows nothing about the kind of trauma Daisy does.

"Hi, Daisy." I sit on the chair next to her, hoping my face appears as kind as Millie's and not pulled into an unintentional "psycho stressed twenty-something who has no idea what to do with you."

"We were just watching a little TV and talking." Millie hands the girl a napkin. Maxine sits on the floor near Daisy's feet and conducts a running commentary on the fashion choices of the animated characters.

"What do you think about those cookies?" I'm struggling here for any quality conversation topics. "Are they the best or what?"

Daisy says nothing, and my guess is *the best* would be a one-way ticket back to her mother.

"So...I'm a friend of your mom's."

Daisy's quirked eyebrow is so blonde it's almost white. "Mommy says, you're my aunt."

Technicalities. "We do have some family in common." I push out the next sentence like I'm about to explode with joy. "You're going to stay with me for a little while. Isn't that fun?"

"No." She shakes her head, and tears spill down her cheeks. "I want my mommy." Sobs shake her shoulders, and she folds inward, a wounded bird forced to shelter herself against the wind.

Going to my knees, I get eye-level with the girl. "Hey, do you know what?" I pause but still get no reaction out of her. Daisy's not here for chit-chat. "One time, my mama got in trouble and went away for a little bit. I was a foster kid, too, and had to stay with some people I didn't know. It's scary, isn't it?"

Head lowered, and her gaze hidden behind a curtain of hair, she nods.

"Those people I stayed with turned out to be very nice." I hold out a word that would've been gold to foster-kid me. "They were safe. *I* was safe." I hold off telling her they're now my parents. I don't want to scare her with the thought she might not be reunited with her mom. "Daisy, would it be okay if I held your hand?"

She sniffs, her bottom lip pooched with a powerful sorrow that nearly sends me all the way to the floor.

Slowly, I reach for her small hand, wrapping my fingers around hers. "I know what it's like to be away from home and away from your mom. It's very yucky, isn't it?"

Her hazel eyes pool. "Yes."

"You can trust me, all right? I won't let anything or anyone hurt you. I've been through a lot of the things you're going through, and I'd love to be your friend as we handle it together." For as long as I'm in town, anyway. "I'm a little scared too."

She wipes her nose with the entire length of her arm. "You are?"

"I've never been a parent before."

"You don't have any kids?"

"Nope." I muster up a smile. "But we can figure all this out together." She gives me another faint nod as if verbal responses are a privilege

I haven't yet earned. "Do you want to talk about what happened today?"

"No."

Fair enough.

Daisy's eyes hold scorn. "I heard you say to the gray-headed lady that you didn't want to bring me home with you."

Oh. I look to Millie for help, but she merely picks up the TV remote and turns down the volume.

"I'm sorry you overheard that," I say. "What I meant was that it wasn't a good time. I've got a lot going on."

She grabs another cookie. "Same."

"Yeah, I guess you have a lot to deal with as well. I'm unexpectedly getting married in less than a couple of weeks, then I'm moving to a new city to start a big job." Daisy looks like I've told her I need to file my nails and rearrange my sock drawer. "The thing is, I don't know anything about taking care of children." I barely had a childhood myself. "But it can't be too hard, right?"

Maxine stifles a chuckle before stealing a cookie.

"Nothing can hurt you here, okay?"

"I want to go home."

"I know."

"I want my mommy!" She throws a cookie on the floor and launches herself at Millie.

I try again, though this feels like I've accidentally put a tedious song on repeat. "Your mommy wants you to stay with me for a little while. And as soon as I know anything more, I swear I'll let you know. No secrets from me."

"It's late." Millie puts the plate of cookies on the coffee table. "Time for bath and bed for Daisy." When she sees my look of mild panic, she holds out a hand to Daisy. "Come on. Let's all go upstairs and talk some more while we get you ready for bed. I have a new Barbie toothbrush I think you're gonna like."

Daisy reluctantly places her hand in Millie's, then we all follow our sainted leader upstairs.

My feet fall heavy on the steps as we ascend. "I guess I need to cancel my appointments for tomorrow's dress boutiques."

Millie regards me over her shoulder. "Not necessary. If Daisy doesn't have a daycare to return to, Amy's volunteered to babysit while we shop."

"Nice try getting out of that one," Maxine whispers as she passes me on the steps. "This wedding is going on whether you show up in a trash bag or a fancy Vera Wanger."

An hour and a half later, after more tears (on Daisy's part and mine), a stack of books, and goodnight prayers, I stand in the doorway of Daisy's bedroom and turn out the light. Her hair falls over her yellow pillowcase, and her arm clutches a whiskered teddy bear. Even in sleep, her forehead furrows, as if she's brought her troubles to dreamland.

"I used to watch you sleep." Millie's arm rests on my back as she runs her fingers through the length of my long, red hair. "I remember many days your sleeping hours were the only ones I didn't fear you running away."

"Nighttime was the worst part of my tenure as a foster kid." I don't bother explaining the one hundred and one reasons why.

"I'd come up to your room sometimes in the middle of the night," Millie says quietly. "I'd pray over you and hope you didn't wake up and see the crazy woman standing at your bed."

"I never knew this."

"It takes work to love a kid. Sometimes those prayer sessions were for me as much as they were for you."

"I'm sorry for every moment of grief I gave you."

She rests her cheek against mine. "Sweetie, I'd do it ten times over. The hard things are almost always worth it. Especially when they're a part of doing the right thing."

"You and James were in a different season of life."

"Very true. And if only a few days or weeks is what you give Daisy, then that's okay too. But know on the off chance you're considering taking Daisy back to New York, God's in the business of filling in the spaces where we lack, supplying energy and ability that we don't have. Sometimes all we have to do to receive it is just show up."

"Millie, I—"

"I love you." She hooks an arm around her mother. "Let's get some rest, so tomorrow we can find that perfect wedding dress." She turns back at the end of the hall and calls out. "Oh, and Katie?"

"Yes?"

"James put the rest of the chocolate chip cookies in your room. He thought you might need them."

I stand in the shadows of Daisy's room for a few minutes more.

Then I do what Millie did for me all those years ago.

I pray.

Give Daisy a hope and a future. Give her a childhood that doesn't look like mine.

Please, send her somebody to take care of her.

Because God...it can't be me.

CHAPTER TEN

"How did Daisy do last night?" Maxine asks as we walk the downtown sidewalk of In Between. We're on our third store in search of a wedding dress, and, so far, I've found nothing that says casual beach bride who also loves herself some sweeping romantic drama.

"She woke up four times." I slip my sunglasses from my purse and slide them onto my face. "That two-way talk feature on the monitor is a blessing and a curse. When Daisy figured it out about three a.m., she used it to order snacks and a slushie."

Millie laughs and steps over a crack in our path. "She sounds like someone else I know."

Maxine hands two passersby a vote-for-Maxine flier. "You can use this baby gizmo to order food and drinks? Where do I get one of these?"

"Pretty sure yours is called Sam." Millie swings open the glass door of Vivi's Bridal Boutique and steps inside.

Frances greets us, her black hair in an elegantly messy knot, her glasses slightly askew, and beaming at our arrival. "This place is just as great as ever, huh?"

Vivi's is a little diamond in the rough of our small town. Though it's only been in business less than a decade, an article in *Southern Living* and several shout-outs on TheKnot.com haven't hurt. People drive hundreds of miles, eschewing the fancy bridal boutiques in Dallas and Houston for the quaint, cozy shop. Once owned by Vivi Moreau, who made most of the dresses herself, Lovella Jackson bought it a few years ago upon Vivi's retirement and filled it with more brand name gowns than not.

"Hello, darlings." Lovella Jackson herself sashays toward us, wearing all black attire as if she's promoting funerals instead of weddings. Red rubies drip from all her fingers today, and her ears sparkle with matching stones big enough to stretch a lobe. She walks with an easy confidence that few have, and I will probably never know. I still trip over air on a regular basis. But Lovella glides with a smile on her lips and a swing to her ample hips. "Katie, when I heard you'd made an appointment at our little store, I nearly died from the thrill." She clasps my hand in hers, and I wonder if she has a conceal-and-carry license for those long, pointy red nails. "Too bad you're not getting married in a few months."

"I've said this very thing at least ten times today." But Millie told me to nip it and accept my abrupt wedding date.

"We're doing a trunk show next month, with designers from all over. Lots of discounted items."

"I'll be sure and attend," Maxine says. "I'm about ready to renew my vows with Sam. Gives me an excuse to throw a party and take a vay-kay." She rights her huge diamond ring that's turned sideways on her finger. "If he's lucky, I might even invite him this time."

Lovella returns her attention back to me. "Do you know I saw you last year in *The Widow*?"

"I didn't. I wished you'd have let me know. Charlie and I could've shown you the town."

"Oh, girl, I know Chicago like I know In Between. It's where two of my boyfriends live." She gives me a saucy wink. "But next time I'm there, I'll certainly look you up."

"Katie and Charlie are moving to New York," Millie says. "They've got an apartment picked out in Brooklyn and will move right after the wedding."

"New York, now that's my kind of place." Lovella grins at Maxine.

"Girl, are you ready for your debate with Gus McGillicuddy next Wednesday?"

"You betcha." Maxine roots around in her bag then produces a Vote for Maxine koozie. "Here you go, sweetie. I hope you'll be in the audience at the debate that Wednesday night so you can see me take down that newcomer with hardly an effort."

"Gus has some sound ideas." Lovella inspects her koozie. "What he doesn't have is personality. The guy's about as prickly as a porcupine."

"Did my Sam deliver one of my signs for your yard?"

"He did." Lovella's micro-bladed brows sag. "It's been right next to my tiger lilies for months, but yesterday when my lawn boy went to mow, it was gone. Strangest thing."

"Now that you mention it," Frances chimes in, "our neighbor said he needed another one. His disappeared too."

"This can't be a mere coincidence." Maxine taps a finger to her chin. "Something is afoot, and that Gus McGillicuddy is surely to blame."

Oh, boy. In terms of feeding Maxine's paranoia, these two just handed her a triple-dip with sprinkles. "Two signs walking away is hardly a reason to claim a conspiracy."

"Au contraire, little starlet." Maxine sniffs the air. "I smell treason."

"That's probably my new potpourri." Lovella jerks her thumb toward her front desk. "Smells like moldy roses. I told my assistant Fiona to throw that stuff out. Now, what are we looking for today, Katie? Princess? Fit and flare? Blinged out? Avant-garde with a little Manhattan punk?"

"She's getting married on the beach in Mexico," Maxine says. "Do you have anything in a palm tree print?"

"I do not."

"Maybe some ivory lace leis?"

"Just sold my last one to a Kardashian."

"Drat." My grandmother gives an exaggerated sigh as she spins 360 to take in all the elegant grandeur. "Well, I guess we'll try to make do."

"I'll help you push through." Lovella puts on her game face, ready to get down to business. "Now who'd like a mojito or coffee?"

Our hands shoot up.

"I'll take coffee." I think of my sleepless night and the bags beneath my eyes that seem to be growing in weight by the hour. "Black. Strong and black." For once, I'm foregoing the milk.

Lovella nods toward a younger employee straightening a shelf of shoes.

"Coffee with creamer for us," Millie says, including her mother.

"How about you, sweetie?" Lovella's Southern voice booms as loud as her personality. "Frances, girl, what can we get you?"

"Nothing for me, thanks."

"My coffee's a nice organic blend from a fair trade farm in Brazil," Lovella continues as Frances continues to shake her head. "It has notes of vanilla, chocolate, and—"

"Nope." Frances holds up a hand. Her bangs swish-swash across her forehead as she shakes her head. "I'm trying to quit the sauce."

"Since when?" I ask, trying not to ogle the display of pasties and bra inserts near her. Every bit of that looks like torture.

"Joey and I are eating clean. Don't tempt me. Get thee behind me, java." She adjusts her red glasses. "Let's get started, eh?"

"I love that enthusiasm." Lovella chuckles. "Ah, here's Fiona with your beverages."

Her assistant distributes drinks from a tray, with one remaining. "Who had the mimosa?"

"None of us," Millie says.

Fiona extends the glass. "Would anyone like—"

"Me." Maxine grabs the drink like it's drawn from the fountain of youth, then regards a stunned Millie. "To throw it out would be wasteful. I can't have that on my conscience. Sustainability is one of my core campaign principles."

Lovella's arm swoops in a half-circle. "Now, before you is a paradise of wedding gowns, from vintage classics to the cutting-edge latest. Katie, you tell me what you have in mind, and I'll select a few while you peruse the collections. Any questions?"

Maxine accepts her drink from the young staff member, then takes a sip of the beverage that is definitely not coffee. "Yes, quick Q." She taps the rim of her fluted glass. "Can I go ahead and order two more?"

~

"GARTERS AND GROOMSMEN, THAT'S A GORGEOUS DRESS." MAXINE whistles through her fingers as I do a slow twirl before the three-way mirror. "Those other nine do not compare."

Maxine, Millie, and Frances sit in plush velvet chairs and watch my fashion show with all the rapt attention given to a Paris runway. I've tried on Lovella's suggestions, my crew's suggestions, and a few I'd found myself. So far, everything is pretty, but I haven't made a love connection with any of them.

"How does the dress make you feel?" Lovella asks as she joins us again.

I study myself in one of the mirrors, taking in the simplistic lines of a very pretty dress that would look perfect for a beach wedding. "It makes me feel...comfortable?"

"Comfortable?" Lovella fans herself with a pair of silk gloves. "Tell me there's more to it than that."

I hold up the skirt and move around a little. "It would look great with a tropical flower in my hair."

Millie sighs dreamily. "And your hair all flowing in waves."

"Don't forget," Maxine adds, "if you don't find anything soon, you can always use the gown I wore when I married my sweet Sam." She nudges Frances with a pointy elbow. "Had a butt bow as big as Texas. You don't find those at most weddings these days."

Frances chokes on her cup of water. "There's a reason for that."

The dress is beautiful, and I do feel lovely in it. With a sweetheart neckline, the strapped gown manages to look elegant with the lace, yet still casual with the thigh-high slit. My waist looks deceptively thin thanks to a grosgrain-band on the bodice, and it wouldn't take much to make it fit. "It has pockets."

"Pockets?" Maxine brightens. "That sells me, right there. All brides should have pockets."

"What for?" Frances asks.

"For storing cake leftovers."

"How about we take a breather?" A sleeve of bracelets jangle like chimes as Lovella walks my way. "I know when a bride's brain is overly saturated. Fiona can bring y'all some of our famous strawberry muffins, and after you have a little boost of carbs, then you can stroll through the store one more time."

Back in the dressing room, I crawl out of the dress and jump into my jeans in record time. Let me at those muffins. Nothing like stress-eating before you have to squeeze into the most important clothing of your life.

When I reappear, I find the ladies already munching on their second round of muffins and tipping back water bottles emblazoned with Lovella's label.

"Katie, you're not picking dresses based on cost, are you?" Millie asks. "I told you we were happily covering it."

"It had crossed my mind." My parents had given me a generous budget, but I knew this wedding was a financial drain and didn't want to go too crazy.

"Forget about it." Millie hands me a muffin dotted with bright red strawberries. "It's our joy to do this. And shopping for a gown is so fun." She pops a bite between her lips. "Right?"

"I should call Amy and check on Daisy." I walk out of the store, hoping when I return I'll find a dress.

And feel like a bride.

CHAPTER ELEVEN

"I don't know, Joey. Your parents are divorced, and you've got to accept that." Frances all but hisses into her phone a half-hour later. She stands between two racks of ivory dresses, her top knot bobbing like a buoy on the lake, and her glasses angled on her pert nose.

Worried I'm about to interrupt an argument with her husband, I hesitate and pretend like the green bridesmaid dress is the most fascinating thing to ever grace a velvet hanger.

"Joey, your mom and dad will both be at the wedding, so suck it up. And if you run off to surf while I run interference, I promise you, you'll regret it. What do I mean? Oh, your sister's birthday party last month comes to mind. Yes, I am still upset about that. You left me to mediate a scream fest between *your* parents. Don't tell me to calm down. This is calm. I'm so tired of..."

Frances's voice trails off, and out of the corner of my eye, I see she's noticed me.

"I gotta go, Joey," she snaps. "And tonight, *you* pick up something for dinner. The Frances Benson kitchen is closed."

My, this blue organza dress is pretty. Would really complement Maxine's eyes. Though there is zero butt bow, and immature me would like to get revenge for what she made me wear to her wedding. Moving on to this yellow one, I care nothing about, but need to look as if it's the only thing that has my attention....

"That yellow dress is terrible." Frances appears at my side, fraught with anxious tension.

"I think I'm going to stick with pale pink, but it's good to check out other options."

She sighs raggedly. "I know you heard me on the phone."

There's no use denying it. Half the store probably heard it. "It's okay to tell me to mind my own business, but are you and Joey okay?"

Frances hesitates, then reorganizes a handful of dresses that are just fine the way they are. "All couples have their ups and downs. We've had a lot come at us in the short time we've been married—my Ph.D. program, moving back to In Between, Joey opening up his own business, my new job at the Space Center, his dad almost going to jail, and his parents' divorce. I'd hoped we'd get a breather soon, and things would settle down this summer."

"Has something else come up?"

She opens her mouth to answer but then closes it just as quickly.

Oh. I get it. "Then Charlie and I threw a wrench in things, and we're dragging you to Santisto Island, right? Frances, I'd understand if you don't want to go. What if you and Joey sit the wedding out, and we'll see you at the reception when we get back? I never thought about how selfish it was to expect you to drop everything and come with us."

"No, I want to be there. There's no way I'd ever miss your wedding."

"Are you sure?"

"Katie, I'm positive." She chews the inside of her cheek as she consults a price tag on a terrible orange gown. "I guess when you're an adult, something's always coming up, right? I need to learn to roll with that and chill out." Her face looks anything but chill. "But back to you. You're getting married. My best friend is finally tying the knot with Charlie Benson. And just think, we'll be sisters-in-law. Family! I mean, you've always been part of my family, but soon it will be a literal fact. Hey, did I mention we're throwing you a wedding shower at the church Sunday?"

"This Sunday?" As in five days away?

"Yeah. Quickie wedding, quickie shower, right? So that means we need you to register like yesterday. No problem, right?" Her phone buzzes from her back pocket, prompting her to check the screen, scowl, then return the device to its hiding spot. "Anyhoo! Let's get serious about this dress shopping. That last one was a fabulous pick. Love the bodice."

I follow Frances past tall racks of dresses in every nuanced shade of white and cream. Stopping at a section of cap-sleeved gowns, I study my friend. "Are you still happy you're married?"

Frances nearly drops a gown. "What?"

"If you had to do it over, would you still marry Joey?"

She returns the dress to the rack. "Today's not a great day to ask me this." Frances drops her gaze, reaching up to slide a dress to the left and consider its lacy merits. "Of course, I would still marry Joey. Getting married when we did—with moving, being away from our families, and all we had going on—was a challenge. And so was the fact that we didn't know each other that well." She wags a finger in my face. "Which you warned me about half a dozen times."

Yes, but then I saw the error of my ways. "But you're making it work, right? He still gives you butterflies and all that?"

"Butterflies? No. But he does bring me French fries on a regular basis, so that's better than flying insects, right?" Frances jokes, but the smile does not reach her brown eyes.

"So, it's been hard?"

"Yes." She sees my disappointment. "But I think it's supposed to be. We've also had a lot of good times, and he's still who I want to spend the rest of my life with. Though I do wish he'd pick up his dirty socks, not leave his greasy tools in the kitchen, and learn to tell me what he's feeling instead of making me guess. I'm sure he has a laundry list of ways I bother him as well."

Great. If marriage is trying for Frances, I can't imagine what it will be like for me. "I'm afraid when Charlie and I get married, our relationship will change."

"You should be afraid."

"What?"

"You wanted real talk, and I'm giving it to you."

I signal for Fiona. “Can I get another coffee, please?” The blonde girl nods and zips away, clearly taking note of my slightly panicked tone. “Frances, what changed for you and Joey?”

“Dating and hanging out is a completely different world than living together and being in each other’s way day in and day out. I loved it at first, but then I learned we both needed some space in our tiny Pennsylvania apartment. He’d go hang out at the auto part store, and I’d go to the laundromat, toss in some towels, and read a favorite dragon novel. That saved us the first year.”

“Dragon novels saved you?”

“No, realizing we needed little breaks from each other. Otherwise, you start to annoy one another, and it builds up so much it finally quakes like a volcano.” Her fingers splay wide as she mimes a cataclysmic explosion. “Maybe I’m not the person you should be talking to right now. Joey and I are in a bit of a rough patch if you want to know the truth. I love him...but I don’t currently like him.”

I think of the string of men my mom went through, never able to truly commit. What if that’s my destiny? Maybe Mom didn’t push through because it was so hard—universally hard, not just “Bobbie Ann Doesn’t Finish Well” hard. If Frances, who succeeds at everything she touches, isn’t handling marriage well, then how will I ever be able to sustain it? The last thing I want to do is make Charlie miserable.

“Hey, don’t mind me.” Frances flops a hand in dismissal and laughs. “I’m just in a sour mood and taking it out on everyone. You and Charlie have been in love since high school, so this next step is as right as it can be. It’s not like you’re me and blindly rushing into everything, right?” Her posture lifts as she takes a cleansing breath. “Right. Now let’s find those dresses fit for a destination wedding.”

“Frances—”

“Come along. I already spy a potential winner.”

~

“It really is beautiful, Katie,” Millie says ever-so-patiently, as I try on the grosgrain-banded bodice dress for the third time.

I can’t argue with her. Of all we’ve tried today, it’s my favorite.

"Don't forget, you're in a bit of a time crunch." Maxine scrolls through her phone checking her campaign Facebook page yet again.

"And alterations do take time," Lovella adds.

"Okay." Here comes a decision. Brace yourself, family. I've made up my mind. "Let's get it."

Everyone's ecstatic responses are interrupted when the bells chimes over Lovella's door.

"Lovella, darling. I bring goodies for you!" A short man with black eyebrows as thick as inchworms and hair bleached so white it's nearly yellow interrupts my moment as he enters the store. He wheels a rolling clothing cart toward Lovella, and I can smell his heady cologne long before he reaches us.

The shop owner claps her hands together like a child at Christmas. "Frederico, you get over here and let me at them."

"Ah-ah-ah." He swats the air near her. "No grabby hands. I show you my fabulous creations." He reaches into the rack and extracts an ivory strapless gown that sparkles beneath the store lights. "Look at these and tell me you have not died and gone to the heavens."

Lovella gasps, and I swear her eyes tear up. "Gorgeous as usual. The things you come up with, Frederico." She stares in rapt awe as the designer turns the dress so she can see the back. "Truly a work of art."

He goes through the same overly dramatic process for several more dresses, each one eliciting a response from Lovella worthy of a Tony.

Smiling at the theatrics, I turn my back on the duo, giving my appearance one last look in the three-way mirrors.

"You promised me you'd bring some discounted gowns," I hear Lovella say. "Gimme a quick peek at those, then I'll have Fiona take them to the storeroom."

"I had limited supply," Frederico tells her. "But, I pulled some of my stock from the Dallas boutiques and bring you what I have."

"I can sell them. Don't you worry." At her sharp gasp, I spin around.

And behold the dress of my fantasies.

The bottom half is a simple, A-line skirt, but the top. Oh, holy garter belts, the top half could have its own display in the Smithsonian.

"The bodice is hand-sewn lace," Frederico says.

Lovella runs her hands over the gown. **"I love how the paisley design blends seamlessly with the nearly invisible net, but the large embroidered scallops create the neckline and the sleeves. Frederico, you're an absolute genius."**

As if an invisible force tugs me toward the gown, my tired feet move of their own volition, and before I know it, I stand before the dress. A dreamy sigh escapes my lips. "That is...exquisite."

Frederico throws up his hands and mirthlessly laughs. "I thought so too, but three stores have carried it, and has she sold? No. Bella's Bridal in Houston even marked it down forty percent, but no takers."

Lovella shakes her head in disbelief. "Those brides must've been out of their minds. This dress looks like it belongs on a celebrity. Very reminiscent of classic Hollywood. I could see Grace Kelly in this beauty."

That's it exactly. It's elegant, with a vintage nod to a Hollywood knockout, like those black and white movies from the Fifties Maxine and I used to watch during summer breaks.

"It's a work of art!" Frederico cries. "It's not for everybody, but I just *knew* it would be for someone."

"It's me." Melodic wedding bells chime in my ears, and chills dance along my skin as I reach out and touch the texture of the embroidered shoulder. "I can totally see this with my hair in loose waves and pinned up loosely at my nape. A long veil that attaches to a crown, but for the reception, just delicate diamond clips that hold up the hair."

"Yes!" The designer flips open a trunk. He digs through it until he grabs a white bag. "Behold." A vintage veil floats into his hands, and he lifts it high. "Eez perfection, no?"

"Absolutely perfect." I shake my head and force myself out of this silken stupor. "What size is this dress?"

"A ten." Shrewd eyes assess my figure. "So we geeve it a leetle nip and tuck. It would fit you like a glove. But like a comfy glove. Comfy, elegant glove."

"Can I try it on?"

"Eees for de trunk show we have next month." Frederico tsks. "So sorry. Strict policy that Frederico does not sell from the selection early."

But...this could be my dress. "I'll pay double." Pretty sure my credit card just flatlined in my purse.

Lovella rests her cat woman claws on my shoulder. "Fred-o, sweetie, do you know who this young woman is?"

"Looks a lot like my brodder's ex-wife Luisa Espinoza." His bleach blond head tilts one way then the next. "Are you also a mafia princess who occasionally robs dee banks?"

"No."

He gives a doubtful curl of his lips. "That's what she would say too."

"Frederico," Lovella interrupts. "This girl is Katie Parker Scott. She's from In Between and now is a megastar on Broadway."

My face warms. "Not mega. I mean, maybe on a scale of one to ten, I'm coming in at a two. Okay, possible a four, but definitely not in the eight range or—"

"She's getting married soon and is looking for *the* dress." Holding up the gown, Lovella frowns. "But hers is a destination wedding."

Frederico crosses his arms over his slender chest. "What's your destination, theater chica? Paris? Roma?"

"Santisto Island. Near Cancun."

"Oh." His face falls slightly. "I am so sorry, but this dress will ruin if it's in water."

"I don't plan to actually be *in* the water."

Maxine sidles up beside me. "Though that would be cool. Kind of a mermaid type of thing where you spring up from the waves and land on a large rock? Do you have any lace-covered nose plugs?"

I ignore her and appeal to Frederico. "The dress won't get wet. We'll stay on the shore. I can make sure of that."

"That's what they all say. I am telling you, this dress will ruin if it gets wet. Instant water stains, and it goes see-through. I'm talking peep show for all the guests and natives."

Maxine considers this. "If you charged for the show, it might pay for the reception."

"Plus, the train is four feet long." Frederico lists another handful of reasons he thinks it's a bad idea. "Listen to me when I tell you that you do not want a long train dragging the sand."

"He's right about that," Lovella says. "This is a dress for something a bit grander. Fancy indoor wedding, lots of people, maybe a historical or quirky locale."

"Our locale offers underwater unity candle lighting," Maxine says. "Is that quirky enough?"

"I am sorry." Frederico washes his hands of the whole idea. "I do not feel right about selling to anyone before the trunk show, and my heart says this dress would not want to be at your particular destination."

But my heart completely disagrees. Yet, I see his point. It's way too formal and delicate for a quick, seaside vow exchange. "Okay."

"I'm sorry, babe," Lovella says. "Would you like to try one of your earlier picks again? Maybe with different accessories?"

"No." I turn back to the mirror and meet Millie's eyes there. "Let's get this one."

"Before you decide," Maxine whispers as the designer walks away. "If that retro thing's the one you want, I can make Freddy-poo change his mind. Just give me twenty-four hours. Plus a Ginsu knife, a 1998 Puff Daddy CD, and some duct tape. Problem solved. And probably with an unexpected discount."

"No. But...thanks anyway." I've got enough wedding worries without concerning myself in kidnapping crimes and musical misdemeanors. And questionable soundtracks. "It's okay. They're right. That's way too formal a gown for a beach resort ceremony."

Maxine's blonde head nods. "And it would balloon too much when the helicopter lowered you from the sky."

"Helicopter? What helicopter?"

"Oops." She hugs me tightly and guides me toward the fitting room. "I guess I just spilled the beans on my wedding gift surprise. Silly me."

CHAPTER TWELVE

"ARE you sure you like the dress you chose?" Millie asks as she navigates her Subaru into the driveway. "It was beautiful on you, but if it's not what you want, then we'll keep looking."

"It's a great dress. And we're out of time." I open the car door and step onto the sun-warmed concrete. My stomach rumbles because, as everyone else had double-stuffed burritos at Tito's House of Tacos, I decided to stick with grilled fajita chicken and guacamole. Visiting home is normally all about comfort food, but I don't want to be the bloated bride of Santisto Island. Currently, I'm worn out, carb-deprived, and barely containing my anxiety dressed up as crabbiness.

Then an unfamiliar giggle carries on the breeze and reaches my ears. Millie, Maxine, and I all share a look.

Millie's lips curve in a smile when the sound repeats. "It's coming from the backyard."

We walk around back, running into Amy, who carries a box toward her car.

"Hey, girls," she says. "We've had a great day of playing. Dad has taken over, and I'm headed to the apartment."

"Thank you for taking care of Daisy." Amy and I have had our differences over the years, but ever since she returned from Montana, I have to admit, she's different. I need to accept that maybe she's not going to revert to the tweaked-out junkie she used to be. I've never seen anyone survive recovery myself, but I understand plenty of folks do.

"Anytime, Katie." She gives me a small smile then heads to her car.

We open the wooden gate of the privacy fence, and the sight that greets me nearly unwraps all the old ivy still growing around the edges of my heart.

I see Daisy perched in a swing, while James stands behind her, hands on her back as he gives her a gentle push. Her musical laughter floats into the humid air, mingles with the butterflies, then flutters to me. Though I didn't know James until I was sixteen, I can completely envision what I missed—how loving and compassionate he would've been with a five-year-old Katie. How my life would've been different if I'd been raised in such attentive normalcy.

"Hi, there, sweetie." Millie kisses her husband's cheek and surveys the scene.

"How'd dress shopping go?" James swipes at beads of sweat on his brow.

I give Daisy a silly-faced wave. "Good."

"Good?" When James says the word, it sounds almost accusatory and strange. "I've seen you more enthusiastic for a plate of nachos."

Maxine extracts a bedazzled water bottle from her cavernous purse. "Katie found a dress, and it looks lovely on her."

"Do I need to refinance the house or sell Millie's car?"

"Nothing that extreme," I say. "But how attached are you to both kidneys?"

"I could part with one." He sends his mother-in-law a pointed look. "Does it have to belong to me?"

I pull out my phone and show him a series of photos of the dress. He ooohs and ahhhs appropriately.

"Where did the swing set come from?" Millie studies the small metal frame that holds a blue slide, a wobbly teeter-totter, and two swings.

"Amy tracked it down. A church friend needed to get rid of it."

James puts a little more muscle into his next push. "We like it, don't we, Daisy?"

Her response is to lean back in the swing as she laughs, her blonde hair flying behind her as she soars.

"It looks like you've had a good day," I say to her. "You're very good at the swing. Look how high you can get."

I remember being her age and watching the sky, seeing things in the clouds that became part of my escape fantasy—a fast horse, a flying carpet, a big bunny to follow to his happy den.

"We had fun," Daisy says in her reluctant, wisp of a voice as if she's still unsure if she's allowed to talk.

"Yep." James looks ten years younger today, and I imagine how wonderful he'll be as a grandfather *way* out in the future. "We played, went to the park, stopped by the Burger Barn for some ice cream, then watched some cartoon she likes about pygmy unicorns."

Maxine takes a chug of water, then wipes her mouth. "I once dated a pygmy unicorn."

"James gave me some cookies, too." The little girl grins at Millie. "Did you know he has a secret cookie spot in his office?"

Millie steps closer. "Where exactly is this cookie stash, sweetie?"

"Anyway!" James steps between them and resumes his post as swing conductor. "Let's talk of more important, less caloric things. Iola Smartley called and said to remind you about court tomorrow."

I couldn't forget it if I tried. "We'll be there."

"Then I saw your travel agent on our ice cream run downtown, and she said to let you know the island is having some stormy weather and to plan accordingly, but nothing to worry about."

Great. "Maybe Charlie and I should cancel it all and get married in your office at the church."

"Nonsense and horse feathers." Maxine stuffs her water into her bag. "We're going to Santisto Island if I have to hold umbrellas over the whole lot of you."

A clanging, rustling commotion has us all turning around, and there walking across the lawn is a modern-day Santa Claus.

"Charlie." I rush to him, taking some of the overstuffed shopping bags from his hands. "What is all this?"

He kisses me quickly, a brief peck from one perilously weighted down. "I was in town, so I picked up a few things for Daisy."

My nosiness overtakes me as I settle the bags on the ground near the swing and rummage through them. "I see two Barbies, some Legos, a jump rope, a basketball." I mentally catalog the cost of Charlie's time and money, melting with love for this man. "Some puzzles, a few coloring books, and sidewalk chalk." I hold up a teddy bear with fur soft as a baby's breath, then reach for a small hot pink bottle. "Nail polish? Is this for you or Daisy?"

Charlie waggles his fingers at Daisy. "I'm willing to get in touch with my feminine side for our girl."

I drop my hold on a bag, and a ball bounces out and rolls toward a tree. "Charlie." I stand in his space and speak for his ears only. "She's not *ours*. Daisy's temporary."

"I know that."

"Do you?"

"A girl needs some toys."

"First of all, we're waiting for Iola to bring toys from her house. And second, Millie and I were going to take her shopping tonight."

He rubs the sunburned back of his neck. "So, I overstepped?"

"A little." This churlish response gives me an instant knot in my stomach. I can't be mad at him. Not when he brings a whole toy store to a girl who just wants her mom. "No, you didn't. It was really sweet of you."

"Daisy, look at all those toys!" Maxine calls. "My, whoever brought you all this is a prince among men."

I wrap my arm around Charlie's waist and pat his chest. "That he is."

"You should marry him," Maxine suggests.

"I think I might."

Daisy's hesitation gets abandoned on the swing as she all but does a full-body dive into each bag. She holds up a flaxen-haired Barbie in one hand and a black-haired one in the other. They dance in her hands as Daisy squeals, her elated expression like an arrow straight to my conscience. What if she gets attached to us before she has to move onto her next home? What if that next home isn't a good one? Surely Iola will make sure it's a quality family. Her instinct for matching kids with foster parents is second to none. She'll find Daisy a safe, loving home perfect just for her.

The idea gives me some measure of peace.

But strangely, not enough.

"Did you find a wedding dress?" Charlie asks as Daisy and her playmate Maxine kick the soccer ball back and forth.

"I did."

Charlie looks down at me, and his eyes go serious. "We're really getting married this time, Katie."

"Indeed, we are."

"Starting to panic?"

"Nope. Not me. Why would I?"

"It's okay if you are." He pulls me closer, tucking me beneath the crook of his arm, then kisses my temple. "But promise you'll talk to me about it and not let it grow to giant proportions in your head."

"I'm not panicking." I inhale the sunshine on his skin and frown. "Did you know your brother and Frances are having problems?"

"Who says?" Charlie drops his arm, instantly on alert. "Did Frances tell you that?"

"I overheard a phone call. Then later, she told me they've hit a rough patch."

His gaze darkens as he scratches the stubble at his chin. "I'm not sure this family can handle more turbulence. My dad informed me he's bringing his girlfriend to the wedding."

"Does your mom know?"

"I told her today. She's not happy."

"That's even more stress for Joey and Frances." And us.

"I'm sure they're okay," Charlie says. "It's not like they're splitting up." A frown cuts across his forehead. "Right?"

"Right. I'm probably overreacting. It's all the carbs I've not been eating." My eyes shift toward Daisy as she skips around a seated Maxine, stopping every few steps to stick a yellow dandelion into my grandmother's hair. What if Joey and Frances get a divorce? I don't want to think about the word divorce—not for Frances and Joey, and definitely not for me. What if I can't hack it as a wife, and I'm the cause of another Benson divorce?

"Katie?" Charlie waves his hand in front of my face, and I realize he's been talking. "Did you hear a word I said?"

"Sorry." I point to Daisy, grateful for the adorable excuse that she is. "Got distracted."

"I said I talked to my brother just last week, and he didn't say a word about any trouble."

"She told me I should be afraid of marriage, and he no longer makes her feel butterflies."

He leans in and nuzzles my neck. "Do I still give you butterflies?"

"Definitely." Though at the moment, a double-stacked cheeseburger would as well. "She seems unhappy, Charlie. Something's up."

"The honeymoon can't last forever."

"I guess." Was two years how long the good days lasted? And then what? After two years and one day, would I look at Charlie and want to claw his eyes out over dirty socks on the bathroom floor? Would he look at me and see amplified flaws and regret his decision? "I don't want that to be us."

"It won't be." My fiancé hugs me to him, squeezing extra tight as if to smother my dark thoughts. "You and I won't let it."

CHAPTER THIRTEEN

When you're a foster kid, odds are you have a healthy fear of cops and courtrooms. Today I get to see both. And unfortunately, so does Daisy.

"Tell me what this is again." As he drives, Charlie adjusts his air conditioning vent so it points toward Daisy, who sits quietly in the back.

It's hard to find a volume that reaches over the air on maximum blast but is low enough that conversation doesn't reach small ears. "It's called a probable cause hearing. Basically, all parties are there with attorneys, and they review the case before the judge, letting her know what's going on and why they took a kid into care."

"Did you have to go to one of these?"

"Yeah. I went to court quite a few times." I remember cold tile floors beneath my feet, gray and white squares that showed years of grime and wear by parents and kids whose lives had been dismantled. I'd always been taken out of school to attend, the last time sitting by James and Millie. They'd flanked either side of me, like shields in a battle. I remembered thinking how I'd finally felt somewhat safe in that courtroom with them surrounding me like an impenetrable forcefield.

"Will I see my mommy?" Daisy pipes up from the back, her arms around a stuffed bear with a crooked ear. "I want to see my mommy."

If you can hear that and your heart doesn't break, you might as well cash it in as a human being and go home. "I don't know." I have to be honest with Daisy, even though I'd like to give her the answer she wants. "Mrs. Smartley said she hoped they'd let her come in person and not just attend by way of video." Because your mom's in jail. Like mine was.

"I bet she misses me." The little girl twirls a lock of corn silk hair around her slender finger. Today she wears a cute bow of hot pink and sparkles. It's the tenth hair accessory I've bought for her, and I could see this turning into a problem. Given my family history, I suppose there are worse addictions to have. Also, this particular bow sits on the top-center of her head like a satellite and is big enough to signal Martians. But she loves it.

"Maybe she even cries sometimes," Daisy says.

"I know she misses you." Charlie turns down the music, a playlist of kid's songs he downloaded for her. "I bet she's happy you're safe with your aunt and getting to spend some time playing with Katie."

Daisy's no dummy, and she looks less than convinced. "I miss my mommy."

I try to make my voice as soothing as Charlie's. "If we don't see her today, we'll make her a card, okay?" I close my eyes and attempt to breathe away the tension that pulls down my shoulders, then silently offer up a quick prayer.

Dear God, please let Haven be there. Every time Daisy has a sad moment, out of lack of anything helpful to say, I hand her a new toy. I'm all out of toys, and this girl is all out of patience. God, you tell me you care for the sparrows, so I know you care for Daisy and see her. And you see me. Right? You do still see me? *Well, I need some serious help here. If you haven't noticed, I do not know how to raise a child, let alone a traumatized one who does not understand why she isn't home with her mom.*

"I miss Petunia too."

I turn back to study Daisy, her bottom lip quivering as tears spill onto her cheeks. "Who's Petunia?" Another stuffed animal?

"My dog."

Charlie nearly sideswipes a car. "You have a dog?"

"Uh-huh."

"Where is it?" I ask, sharper than I intend.

"My house. It's a new puppy. We keep it in a crate sometimes."

"What if that puppy's still in that house?" I whisper to Charlie.

"If it is, we'll be fostering that too."

I never had a doubt. I just hope this dog's still among the living.

Charlie wheels the car into a tight space at the Belmont County Family Courthouse.

If this courthouse was a cookie, it would be a stale, off-brand vanilla wafer. The beige building sits on a hidden, easy-to-miss sideroad. It's unassuming and boring, with no adornment, no landscaping, as if it doesn't even want to have a personality.

The sun beats down on us with a vengeance on this July day as I take Daisy's right hand. I smile to myself when Charlie takes her left. We look like a three-person family.

But we're not.

This is not my child, and certainly not Charlie's. But if I squint my eyes, I can almost see a red-headed girl with Charlie's light eyes and his skin that doesn't revolt against a tan. Maybe she'd have my freckles and his contagious smile. She'd be tall like the two of us, perhaps with a love for his sports and an affection for show tunes.

"There you are, sweet peas." Maxine interrupts my futuristic thoughts, waving like a crazed circus clown as she waits for us at the door.

"Hi, Maxine." I give her a quick hug and let her make over Daisy. Until Maxine whips out her cell phone.

"This is mayoral shoo-in candidate Maxine Dayberry coming to you live from the Family Courthouse in Belmont County. Our family has a history of foster parenting, and today that tradition continues as my granddaughter and her incredibly handsome fiancé usher in their young charge."

"Maxine, what are you doing?"

She waves me away with one hand out of the shot. "I am honored to be a foster grandmother once again."

"Great-grandmother," I correct, knowing she'll edit it out later.

"So happy that I'm sitting in this courtroom today to support my dear sweet Katie, who's a Broadway legend, you know? Katie, real quick, tell the good people of In Between how many Tony Awards you have."

"None."

"She doesn't do well with numbers, but the girl is the world's best actress. I bid you adieu for now, In Between. But just know as your mayor, I will have a heart for the less privileged, the displaced, the orphaned, and the mathematically challenged. So remember...a vote for Maxine is super keen!"

"Ladies, I think we better get inside." Charlie opens the door, and a push of cold air escapes outside. Where I'd rather stay.

I kneel down and get eye level with Daisy. "We'll be right here with you every minute." And then I accidentally utter what could be the most traitorous words. "Everything's going to be okay."

Security check runs much like an airport. We surrender any jewelry and metal to a bowl, and pass through an archway that probably x-rays right to my galloping heart. Then we walk to a waiting police officer who runs a wand over me like he's attempting to knight me with electromagnetic waves.

A mass of people sit bunched together in the lobby, and the bits and pieces of random conversations I hear sound about the same as they did years ago.

"I don't know how the drug test was positive. I'm telling you I didn't do drugs last week."

"I'm gonna step outside and smoke."

"That vending machine doesn't have anything gluten-free. It would be nice if they'd get with the times."

"I don't even want to see him, Mom. How much longer are we gonna have to wait?"

After taking my seat and getting Daisy settled, I hand her a coloring book and a few crayons. "Why don't you color your mom a picture?"

"Okay. I'll make her a really pretty one. But she says I don't have to color inside the lines like Grandpa Andy says."

I adjust the bow on her head. "I think she's right. You color it however you want."

Maxine joins us, dropping into a seat and looking completely put out. "What does it take to get frisked around here? I swear I could tell them I'm packing heat in my girdle, and they'd wave me on through. Does this face just look too young and innocent?"

Daisy answers before I do. "Nope."

The minutes pass slow as a snail's crawl through sorghum, and when the bailiff calls the case name, five coloring pages, two snacks, and an hour has ticked by.

"Here we go." I lead Daisy inside with my parenthood posse behind us. She sticks close to my side, her eyes searching the intimidating courtroom for her mother.

"There's my mommy!"

Haven sits at a table beyond the seating area, having courtside seats to the main event. Sans makeup and her hair in a tight, no-frills ponytail, Haven still looks beautiful as she waves and smiles at her daughter. If Daisy's noticed her mom's in prison stripes and cuffs, she doesn't seem to mind.

Iola leaves her table on the opposite side, opens a waist-high wooden gate, and greets us. "Hi, Daisy, sweetie. How are you doing, hon?"

"You never called me sweetie and hon." I brush back Daisy's hair from her face and smile at my old caseworker.

"My daddy always told me not to pet wounded pit bulls." Iola turns her attention back to Daisy. "We're gonna have a little meeting here in a few minutes, and then when it's over, you can see your mama for a short visit. How does that sound?"

"Good." Daisy looks like she's been promised a whole store of Barbies and bears.

A few minutes later, Judge Mendoza breezes in, looking every bit as business as Judge Judy ever did. "We'll now hear the case of the state vs. Mitchell."

Half an hour later, Mrs. Smartley escorts us out of the courtroom and directs us toward a small room filled with a handful of chairs and some well-used toys, only to disappear again.

When Haven enters the visiting room, she's escorted by a young, scrawny police officer she could take without even trying.

"Hi, baby." She shuffles over toward Daisy, and I find myself tearing up when Daisy throws herself at her mother, her tiny arms wrapped powerfully tight around her mama's waist.

"Oh, my goodness, I've missed you." Haven is full-on crying, though I can tell she's trying to keep it together. "Are you having fun at Aunt Katie's house?"

Daisy gives a slight nod, an unenthusiastic gesture meant to convey things are not fun, but I've managed to keep her alive.

While Maxine mingles with some potential voters outside, Charlie and I sit in on the visit.

Though I try not to scrutinize, I take in every micro-move Haven makes. Her eyes follow Daisy as if she's afraid her daughter will disappear, and her face glows with what could *possibly* be motherly pride. Though cuffed, her hands are never far from Daisy, touching her hair, holding her little fingers, rubbing Daisy's arm. Straightening the tire-sized bow.

I'll have to consult my findings and reflect on them later for a more educated conclusion, but my initial observances tell me it's slightly possible...it's marginally a tiny consideration...that Haven isn't as bad as my mother, Bobbie Ann Parker.

And I don't know what to do with that. It's easier to think of her as someone like my mom—a woman who can't take care of her kid, shouldn't be a parent and is a menace to the future generations.

But if today is any indication, that's not what I see at all.

Granted, maybe convincing performances run in the family, but Haven looks at Daisy like she hasn't seen her in years instead of days. She peppers her child with a hundred questions, then listens intently as Daisy replies, responding with exaggerated enthusiasm, feigned shock, or focused concern, as the answer requires. Daisy shows zero fear or hesitation, climbing all over her mother and peppering her with kisses that are matched in duplicate.

"I made you a picture." Daisy presents her mother with a selection from her courthouse coloring time and waits for Haven's response, leaning into her like I never would have with Bobbie Ann.

"Oh, Daisy. Isn't that beautiful? I love what you did with the blue shading. And that violet contrast? Very artistic and clever. Don't you think, guys?"

Charlie and I both startle as we realize Haven's talking to us.

"A natural talent," Charlie says.

"Yeah." I lamely echo, my brain on overdrive at this thought overload, this incongruent meeting of expectation and reality.

"Mommy, I miss Petunia." Daisy plays with the hem of her gingham dress, twirling in a semi-circle. "When can I get her?"

"That would be up to Katie," her mother says.

"Is there a puppy still at your boyfriend's house?" My tone could be nicer, but hurting animals and kids tends to bring out the shrew in me.

"The dog's at my attorney's home for now." Haven gives a pointed look over Daisy's head, letting us know we need to translate her message. "He says if I don't find her a home in the next week, she'll have to stay somewhere else."

Like the shelter. "Have your attorney contact Iola with the address, and I'll see what we can do."

Charlie gives my shoulders a gentle squeeze as if trying to pass on some of his calm.

Iola Smartley steps back inside, her left arm clutching a small laptop and her frizzy gray hair showing no signs of improvement. "We'll start doing video visits twice a week," she tells Haven. "Katie, will you be able to handle that on your end?"

"Yes." I spare a quick glance for Haven, feeling her eyes heavy on me. It's so strange to see her face-to-face, this person I'd only communicated with a few times via social media. I'd known it was probably a mistake, but I'd felt emboldened and safe behind the security of my computer, knowing we'd never actually meet.

But this was my life, where my plot twists would probably make M. Night Shyamalan envious for their creativity and shock. I should sign up to teach a master class—Hallmark movie devotees need not apply.

Iola points to the far corner. "How about I take Daisy over there to that bucket of questionably sanitized Legos, and you two sisters can talk visitation details."

We're not sisters, I want to say. But instead, I watch Charlie follow Iola as they direct Daisy to this new, hopefully distracting task.

Haven clears her throat and keeps her voice low. "How's my daughter doing—really?"

"As good as can be expected." I can't keep avoiding eye contact, so I finally look at Haven. She looks nothing like me, minus the shadows of fatigue. Her height lacks a good four or five inches from mine, her eyes are as dark as mine are light, and her dyed black hair doesn't seem to have so much as a highlight of auburn. "Daisy's sad and quiet. But she also has moments where you wouldn't know what she's been through. She plays and watches TV and eats well. Charlie got her some toys, and the Barbies are her favorites."

"Don't be afraid to mention that Barbie is an independent woman and doesn't need Ken."

"Okay. Sure. Right after we do our feminist flashcards and sustainability dumpster dives."

"And that Barbie's waistline is not in any way representative of a real woman." She gives me a quick once over. "Like us."

"Haven, the girl is five. How about I just let her play and not worry about registering her to vote and penalizing toys for lack of platform."

Her gaze roams longingly back to Daisy. "I don't want her to end up like me—dependent on a guy and paying the price for it."

"How long does your attorney think you'll be in...um..."

"A correctional facility?" Her head hangs, and she takes a moment to collect herself. "I can't believe it either. Katie, look, you don't know me from any of those other strangers in the courtroom, but I'm telling you, I love my daughter. While I serve my time, DHS will make a list of items for me to complete before I get Daisy back. I'm gonna knock that list out faster than they've ever seen it accomplished—anything to be reunited with Daisy. I made a huge mistake. I admit that."

"Yeah, you did. And Daisy's paying for it." Not one family member fought for me when I was treated like crap by my mom, then finally in the system. Not one. "I won't let Daisy be mistreated anymore."

"I don't mistreat her." She sees my blatant disbelief. "Yes, living with Benny was wrong, and it hurt her. I thought he'd changed. He told me he had. I'd just lost my job and needed a place to stay. I had no idea he had a whole arsenal of weapons and drugs in that house."

"You do realize I was in that courtroom when the judge mentioned the cops found drugs and ten thousand dollars in your purse during the raid."

"None of it was mine."

I've heard that before. My disgust must show on my face because Haven continues her defense with a fervor her attorney would probably admire.

"Benny set me up and stowed stuff in my purse. He hid money and drugs and who knows what else all over the house. I'm telling you, I haven't touched a drug since I was pregnant with Daisy."

"It's not uncommon for dealers to not be users."

"I don't deal. I'd like to say I was raised better than that, but we both know that's not true. Benny and I are over for good this time."

"Yeah, because he's in jail."

"But when he gets out—we're done." Eyes narrowed in teary anguish land once again on Daisy, who now plays on the floor with Charlie and Iola. "I don't want my daughter around any of that again. I want more for her."

"I hope you mean it."

"I do. I got my GED last year, and I'm enrolled in the community college. Or I was. Things were looking up. And they will again." She licks her lips and stares at her handcuffs. "It wasn't our dad who first mentioned you to me, but a cousin."

Shocker. My bio-dad probably couldn't even recall my name.

"When I found you online last year," Haven continued, "I felt some hope for the first time in ages. Here was someone who had similar DNA, someone who'd had a rough upbringing like me, and yet you were a success. Not only a success, but it looked like you were thriving. Seeing your social media posts made me feel like there was a sister out there who could be my role model, whether she ever met me or not. You made me want to try."

I'm not sure what to say to this, so I awkwardly focus on a bit of graffiti on the wall that is a slap in the face to the rules of grammar. "That's very nice, but I assure you I still have plenty of struggles." Like knowing what to do with a five-year-old or walking toward my wedding date with the normal amount of joy and confidence.

"Just please, take care of my Daisy. You can't let my mom get to her. Promise me you won't."

It's a promise I have no power to make. "I'll take care of her while I'm here."

"Then, she can go with you to New York."

"Haven, that's not going to happen. It just can't."

"At least give it some thought. And prayer. I know you're a praying person. Don't say no until God himself tells you no."

"Look, I—"

"Time's up." The police officer tosses out some more instructions before Iola helps Daisy say her last goodbyes for the day.

"I love you," Haven calls as she shuffles out the door, while Iola holds a crying Daisy from chasing after her.

My niece crumbles into a heap on the cold, dirty floor, and as Charlie scoops down to pick her up, I take a step back, wanting to throw my hands over my ears and stop the wails.

Wanting to help Daisy.

But I have no idea how I can.

CHAPTER FOURTEEN

"WHERE AM I GOING?" Daisy asks from her throne in the backseat the next day. She looks so small nestled inside a five-point harness booster with more airbags and safety technology than my car.

"This is your new daycare we talked about." I turn on Jackson Street and worry a bit about the neighborhood this place must be in. "I'm so excited for you, Daisy. You're gonna have so much fun today." *Please, God, give her at least one minute of this thing I've called fun I've promised. I don't care how she gets it—she can eat paste for all I care. AS LONG AS IT'S FUN.*

After we drop Daisy off, we'll head to breakfast, then a local menswear store. Charlie and I had decided we'd probably go with suits instead of tuxes for the wedding. At Charlie's insistence, his groomsmen only included his dad and brother, and I'd invited my friend Jeremy because I'd picked him as one of my attendants. It makes for uneven numbers, but we'd figure that out later.

Charlie twists in the passenger seat to grin at my foster daughter. "You're going to make so many new friends."

"I don't want new friends," she says with all the conviction of a surly teenager. "I want my old ones."

Her old daycare is in a neighboring town, and the jerks had already filled her spot since the last week hadn't been paid.

"When can I see my puppy? She misses me. I bet she's crying for me. She probably stays awake all night and thinks about me and my mom and cries."

Is that what Daisy does? Stays awake all night and thinks about her mom? I've gotten in the habit of checking on her periodically throughout the night, and so far, I'd mostly found her passed out, one hand wrapped around her new favorite teddy bear and another tucked beneath her head. But I also knew we girls with unstable home lives could fake a deep sleep better than a cadaver.

"James and Millie are picking her up this afternoon." Last night they bought a dog bed, fresh puppy food that looked better than anything I've ever cooked, and a yellow and gray sweater that declared this dog was a Hufflepup.

"That's nice of them," Charlie says. "Your parents are all hands on deck with the help. Meanwhile, my dad's only effort is stirring up drama."

I take my hand off the gear shift and link Charlie's fingers with mine. It was kind of nice to not be the one whose parent was a hot mess. "We'll go into the menswear store, we'll pick the first suits you like, then get out. And if your dad gets obnoxious, I'll provide a distraction."

"How?"

"I could practice the murder scene from that play I did two years ago. Loudly. And you know how much noise radioactive aliens make."

When I stop the car at Noah's Ark Daycare, I'm relieved to find it's not a total dump. The bright yellow house-converted-into-daycare sits on Irish green grass, peppered with flower beds of every color in the Crayola box.

"Those are some nice old oak trees." Charlie points to the edge of the property and, instead of appreciating their beauty, I can only wonder about the odds of one of them crashing down on the building and hurting everyone inside.

Oh, geez. What is happening to me? Three full days as a foster parent, and I somehow get Super Mommy Anxiety Powers? Can I reject this gift?

Daisy places her soft hand in mine as we walk inside, with Charlie bringing up the rear carrying her backpack and lunchbox. Yes, they provide food, but the menu was processed junk. Not for my niece, thank you very much. Okay, Millie insisted on making her breakfast, lunch, and snacks. This kid will eat like a queen.

The place smells like glue sticks and baby wipes, and somewhere in the distance, a baby wails. I know how it feels. Alphabet letters are stamped willy-nilly on the white walls, and the carpet is woven with happy faces that seem to mock my current life situation.

The owner greets us at the door, a cheery woman who could be Mrs. Claus. "Welcome to Noah's Ark! We're so glad you're here, Daisy."

Half an hour later, Charlie and I return to the car like shell-shocked warriors finally escaping the battlefield.

"Give me the keys. Driving is the least I can do after that toddler tackled you to the ground." He slides behind the wheel, looking as dazed as I feel.

"That little brat should not be allowed to watch wrestling." Wincing, I lower my head, touching my ear first to my right shoulder, then the left. "I'll just shake off the concussion."

"Easily done. The boy's either going to be a bar bouncer or a rock star." He pulls his stainless bottle from the cup holder between us and gulps down water like it's a stronger tonic. "What did you think of Noah's Ark?"

"I think they have a flood of kids."

"And?"

"And that's a boat I don't want to be on." I buckle up and wish I had a glass of tea to hammer down. "So many children."

"Yeah." Charlie's voice sounds flippantly doubtful. "I'm sure it's within code."

"What if they don't watch Daisy?"

"They will."

"What if she chokes on a grape?"

"They'll give her the Heimlich."

"What if she misses us?"

"We'll smother her with attention tonight."

"What if she doesn't stop crying?"

Charlie stops the car mid-reverse and slips his hand behind my head, his eyes holding mine. "Iola said they're highly rated."

"Yeah, among daycares that take state vouchers. That's a small pool in this town."

"We can't send her to some Ivy League daycare."

"What if she runs with scissors?"

"She'll be fine."

But will I? I did not expect to walk out of there so wrecked. "You saw the way she clung to my leg."

"The owner said it was normal."

"Nothing is normal about Daisy's life right now. Not only is she separated from her mom, living in a new home with strangers, but now she's in a totally different daycare with kids she's never met, and adults I'm not sure we can trust."

"We give it a week, okay?" He pulls onto the road, a slow-motion as if the car is powered by my strange onslaught of sorrow. "I think the place looked very cheery."

"I hope they keep their cleaning products out of reach." Another thought slams me. "What if she eats Tide pods?"

"She'll have clean breath. Katie, she'll be fine. We'll call in an hour and check, okay?" The car hits a pothole, and his body lurches in sync with mine. "Let's go find some suits." He sends me a sweet wink. "We're getting married in T-minus ten days."

"Oh, Lord. We are."

"I love how you say that in horror. Very reassuring."

I've got to learn to not speak my every thought. This Daisy thing has loosened my filter. "Let's get me some waffles, then go find you the perfect suit." I slide my hand over his on the console. "You're going to look handsome in whatever we find."

"Nice save, Parker." He quickly kisses my cheek. "Nice save."

CHAPTER FIFTEEN

SUIT Yourself boldly perches across the street from Vivi's Bridal Boutique. While that's handy for us, it's a sore spot for Lovella, whose ex-husband Reggie runs the menswear store. Not as renowned as Lovella's shop, Suit Yourself, still holds its own, though it certainly takes a different approach.

Charlie parts a curtain of beads in the lobby, stepping into the store. "Whoa."

Whoa is right. A disco ball blinks and spins above us, and Barry White plays from hidden ceiling speakers like a husky-voiced angel. Fuzzy, chartreuse wallpaper covers the walls and begs for me to touch it. We find Charlie's dad, brother, and my good friend Jeremy waiting for us, lounged in La-Z-Boys that have been recovered in velvet the shade of a rotten orange.

"I'm already scared," Charlie whispers.

"I'm here with you every step of the way." We walk by a mannequin in a three-piece plaid suit, and I shudder. "I promise to not let you buy anything that looks like it came from a John Travolta resale shop."

He puts a hand to his forehead. "I think I just contracted Saturday Night Fever."

"Hello, son." Sterling Benson pushes the handle of his recliner and self-ejects. Popcorn remnants spill from his oxford shirt to the floor. "This place has it all. Hot dogs, chocolate chip cookies, popcorn, and sodas. Those ladies shopping for dresses really miss out."

I glance about the nightclub of a store and try not to gag on the incense. "Yeah. Who needs cocktails and elegance?" Or clean air filters.

"Right?" His dad helps Joey get vertical.

"You guys have already met our friend Jeremy." Charlie shakes Jeremy's hand while I nearly tackle my old theater friend in a bear hug.

"Yep. We all arrived early to get some snacks and take a look at the tuxedo choices."

"We're leaning toward more casual suits," I add with a bright tone I don't especially feel. I just dropped Daisy off in the care of perfect strangers who could be serial killers, and this store looks like one big lava lamp.

"They've got a deal on tuxes," Sterling says. "I'm paying for the guys' rentals but get whatever you think. Charlie, did you get my text about dinner with Joey and me tomorrow night?"

"Yeah." Charlie seems to be having trouble focusing on the sights and sounds around him. "I'm helping Katie learn lines for her new play, and we're spending time with Daisy."

"Sure, sure. It was last minute anyway." My future father-in-law looks at Charlie like there's more he wants to say but won't. Two years ago, his dad was the bank president, and unbeknownst to many of us, had a long string of shady bank deals to his credit. When a plot to buy out an entire block of In Between property and businesses went south, thanks to the investigative work of Charlie, Sterling Benson found himself implicated and almost went to jail. That last fiasco strained not only Sterling's relationship with his kids, but it completely eviscerated his marriage. I would never wish all that catastrophe and pain on anyone, but sometimes it's nice not to be the only dysfunctional one.

Between the two of us, Charlie and I have an unusually high number of jail stories, which makes us really entertaining at dinner parties.

"We're glad to help out in any way we can," Mr. Benson says.

"We?" Charlie reaches for my hand like he needs to connect to my positive vibes. Wish I had remembered to bring some.

Mr. Benson's face reddens, and he clears his throat. "Yes. Lacey sends her regards."

Judging from his face, I'm pretty sure Charlie would like to return those regards to sender.

"Hey, gentlemen!" Reggie T. Jackson, the owner of Suit Yourself, joins us, his voice as loud as his outfit. He's as gaudy as his ex-wife is chic. He wears a leopard silk shirt, the top three rhinestones unbuttoned. His pants appear to be leather or some close facsimile, in a royal shade of purple. He sports a zebra hat, and the feather perched in it nearly takes out Joey's eye when Reggie turns his smiling head. "Welcome to my den of style, providing suits for men of distinction."

I lean toward Charlie and whisper. "Are you sure you want to be a man of distinction?"

"We have classic basketball games playing on the TVs all around you, popcorn a popping, and Root Beer in my cooler in the back at your disposal. Grab yourself a snack, and let's get to shopping. Were you thinking polka dots or gold lamé?" Reggie looks between us for a beat then doubles over as he laughs. "I'm just teasing you. Look at your faces! Lord a-mercy." The man's expression turns funeral sober. "You think I can let Lovella show me up in the fancy, classy department? No, sirs and no, ma'am. This stuff out here's just to tick her off since she thought she'd take this place from me in the divorce." He holds a hand over his grinning lips. "She thinks I don't know she sends in spies. I know. Reggie knows all. Now, y'all get on back here where the sophisticated stuff is."

We follow Reggie behind a crimson velvet curtain, and I hold my breath, ready to be accosted by the spirit of disco and polyester.

But when we step into the other dimension, what I find instead is a scene straight out of *Say Yes to the Dress*. Tuxedos of this decade, a wall of ties artistically displayed in every color and style. An entire section of suits that could easily be found in the latest bridal magazine. I walk past a mannequin that doesn't have one single laser light flashing or even a hint of a ruffled shirt.

"Uh-huh." Reggie splays his arms out wide. "Contrary to what my ex says, I know what I'm doing here. Now, Charlie, you said this was a beach wedding, correct?"

"Yes, sir."

"Would you like a grass skirt or coordinating Speedo?"

Charlie blinks, still concussed from the world in whence we left. "I…no?"

Reggie's belly laughs bounces off the tasteful white walls and rises to the chandeliers above. "I'm just kidding. Suits or tuxes, gents?"

"Whatever my son wants," Mr. Benson says. "The sky's the limit. I say we get some tuxes."

Charlie's jaw flexes before he turns to the owner. "Let's see what you've got."

AN HOUR LATER, THE BOYS HAVE TAKEN ANOTHER SNACK BREAK. I find my beloved in the faux front of the store, standing beneath a TV that plays a Laker's game.

Charlie sees me and holds out his arm to walk into. "Michael Jordan. 1986. He's about to make the game-winning shot."

"We should invite him to the wedding." I lean my head on Charlie's shoulder and rest my hand on his swiftly beating heart. "How's it going?" The guys had settled on tuxes, not on suits as originally planned, but I decided to keep my mouth shut. They were not enduring fitting sessions while *Stayin' Alive* played at max volume in the store.

Charlie removes my hand from his chest long enough to kiss the center of my palm. "It's going fine."

"Ouch. I know that 'fine.'"

He doesn't even deny it. "When Dad said 'we' he meant we."

"Charlie, I doubt he was including—"

"He meant his girlfriend. Soon-to-be wife."

My brain lurches with the effort to find adequate words. A family unraveling is still new to Charlie. "I'm sorry. On the bright side, your dad's really trying."

"He offered to take me fishing."

"That's nice."

"Then he asked Joey and me if we could get matching father-son tattoos."

"Okay, a little overreach on his part."

"Between his corrupt morality and how he's treated my mom during their divorce, I can hardly stand to be around him."

I pat his chest, loving the feel of the gym-earned muscle beneath his shirt. "It's going to take some time. Trust me on that one."

"I just want to get through this wedding without tossing him into the ocean."

"I bet Reggie could sell you a Speedo for the occasion."

The subject of city gossip and our terse conversation strolls toward us, carrying a Coca-Cola in one hand and a hot dog in the other. "You can get a suit *and* lunch." His dad grins from ear to ear. "What a deal, eh?"

"Yeah." Charlie attempts a wan smile. "I guess we've about wrapped it up here."

"Yep. I'll go up and pay." His dad hesitates, adding a weird shuffling to his feet for nervous effect. "Say, son, I mentioned this to Joey but wanted to run it by you. I'll be bringing a plus-one on this trip."

"No." Charlie pulls himself to his full height, and I'm wondering if he's about to do a run-through of the ocean toss idea. "It's family only." He jerks his head toward Jeremy, who stands two coat racks away. "And that includes Jeremy."

Jeremy shoves a giant, pillowy pretzel in his mouth. "Thanks. Glad to make the shortlist."

"Lacey is going to be part of this family," his dad says. "We're getting married next month."

Charlie plants his fists on his hips and stares unblinking at his father. Should we all stand back for the explosion? Will there be yelling and fisticuffs? "You're getting married." It's not a question, but more of a disdain-soaked statement. "To this, Lacey."

"Yes." His dad's cheeks turn a light pink. "I probably could've mentioned it at a better time."

"You think?"

"I've called you a dozen times, begging you to let me fly up to see you. Since you've been back, how many times have I asked you to meet me for lunch?" He pauses for a response his son doesn't give him. "Maybe you and Katie could join us for dinner this week?"

"I said we're busy." Charlie can hardly speak for the tight clench of his jaw. "Planning a wedding."

"See, we have something in common." Sterling's smile falls. "Son, I'm marrying Lacey, and you're going to have to accept that—like your brother has."

Standing behind his father, Joey sips on a Dr. Pepper and rolls his eyes.

"I'll accept it." Charlie shoves his hand into his pants pocket and whips out car keys. "Just not today. And no strangers at our wedding."

"She doesn't have to be a stranger. I think you'll like her a lot, Charlie. Given all I'm buying here for this wedding, the least you could do is meet my future wife."

"Dad, I appreciate that you are paying for the tuxes and the reception dinner, but if it comes with strings attached, then we say no thanks."

Wait! We don't mind strings. We can live with strings for a few days. How on earth will we pay for that stuff if Charlie's dad doesn't? We're paying for a move and a new apartment.

"I'll give you some time to think about this." His dad rests his food on a nearby table holding cuff links and candles that smell like cigars. "You don't want to be too hasty. Because if Lacey doesn't go...then, neither do I."

"I guess that's your choice," Charlie thunders. "I will not dishonor my mom by making her hang out with your latest girlfriend."

"She's not just my girlfriend. I'm going to marry her. She'll be your step—"

"Katie, let's go."

"But, you guys haven't picked ties yet."

"I'll meet you in the car." Charlie storms away, hurt fueling his every step. Still munching on a hot dog, Joey goes after him.

Sterling sighs gustily. "That didn't go well."

"I'm sorry," I say, though I'm not sure why I'm apologizing. This situation is one more fault line crack neither son needs right now. I know the stress it's putting on Charlie, and it certainly can't be helping whatever is going on with Joey and Frances.

"Can you talk to him for me?"

"I don't want to get in the middle of this. You guys really have some things you need to work out." Look at me, the authority figure on family dynamics.

He stares in the direction Charlie bolted. "All their lives, I've tried not to hurt my children, but it happened nonetheless."

"Bringing the wife-to-be might be a little much for him right now. And for their mom."

"If not now, when? I've kept Lacey away from them long enough. If Charlie can't find some compassion in the goodness of his heart and let me bring my future wife, then..." The placket of buttons on Sterling's shirt expands with his deep, decisive exhale. "Then I just won't attend your wedding either."

CHAPTER SIXTEEN

THE IN BETWEEN Community Church is where I first met Jesus. I'd like to say it was a sweet, holy event, but my first impression was one of revulsion, dismay, and no-thank-you. I didn't get the point of church. The music was shockingly lacking in drum solos, and other than some summer vacation Bible schools my mom rotated me through for the sake of free childcare, I'd never actually attended a church before going with the Scotts.

Then Frances pulled me into the youth service, and, reluctantly, that's where it all came together. Probably for the sake of free cookies and mochas, but still, I surrendered to a life of faith and the pursuit of a benevolent God who loves us all as we are. When you first arrive on the scene wearing a studded dog collar and an attitude equally pointy, acceptance is a gift that unlocks even the tightest of neckwear.

Last night Charlie and I argued over allowing his dad to bring his girlfriend. When he left, I climbed into bed with a mug of chamomile and my script, only to have Daisy wake up every hour until four in the morning, crying for her mom. This Sunday morning, I could cry myself. I'm exhausted, stressed about the wedding, and I'm failing as a substitute parent. I won't even mention the fact that Daisy's puppy

Petunia likes to chew shoes and somehow snuck into my room and ate two. Not two that matched, of course.

But I'm Pastor James and Millie Scott's child, and I don't dare miss church.

"Look, Daisy. Ms. Hill brought donuts." At ten o'clock, I escort the oddly alert and unfairly energetic girl into Venus Hill's class for four and five-year-olds. Venus was three grades above me, has four children under six, and I honestly don't know how she has time to breathe. The woman deserves that entire box of chocolate eclairs she's got hidden beneath her purse on the back table. She places a glazed donut on a napkin for each child who takes a seat next to a Dixie cup of tap water.

"Welcome, Daisy." Venus shows Daisy her chair, pulling it out with enough fanfare for a queen. "I heard you'd be here, and I've been so excited to meet you."

I lean down close to Daisy's ear. "Remember what we talked about? I'm down the hall in the sanctuary with the grown-ups. I'm not going anywhere without you, and I'll be right back here after the service to get you."

With her cheeks stuffed like a winter-prepping squirrel, Daisy waves me away. "See ya."

My weary spine cracks as I straighten and smile at Venus. "She gets pretty anxious when we're apart. Cries when I leave. Sometimes throws herself on the floor."

Venus hands a donut to a small boy with more freckles than hair, then glances back at Daisy, who's chatting it up with two new friends. "Looks like she's pushing through the pain today."

Daisy could at least squeeze out a few tears. I stayed up all night for this kid. "I'll be on my way then." I raise my voice above the clash and clang of young voices. "Goodbye, Daisy. I will return."

I watch Daisy throw her head back and laugh at something a spiky-haired boy says, then go back to her donut. A full minute later, when she still hasn't so much as glanced my way, I accept the truth. I am forgotten. Thrown over for cheap carbs and a boy wearing shoes that light up when he jumps.

My path to the sanctuary is filled with well-wishers and greetings from the many who make up what James refers to as our "church family." I'm too tired for small talk, but I manage a few polite niceties for James's flock. Many of whom will be at my shower after the service and don't want to give a Walmart gift card to a snippy hag.

"There's our bride-to-be." Maxine waits for me in her usual seat. Sam sits on one side of her, and Amy stands between them.

"How did Daisy do when you dropped her off at her class?" Amy clutches her blue Bible with her name etched in swirly letters on the cover.

"She put on a brave, brave face." I squeeze into the row, kissing Sam on his stubbled cheek, then hug my grandma.

"Did you have a bachelorette party I didn't know about last night?" Maxine's lips draw back in a grimace. "You look like the walking dead."

"Thank you for the encouraging compliments." I open my church bulletin and pretend to read the prayer list. "Daisy kept me awake." The least the girl could've done was sneak me one of Venus's donuts. "But it's all fine now."

"I'm helping the youth pastor today," Amy says. "I better get upstairs. Get some rest, Katie."

Maxine pats my cheeks a little too enthusiastically. "You really do need to catch up on some Zs."

"Stop that." I swat her hands away.

"I'm trying to get some blood flowing. You can't be pale as death at your wedding shower. The churchies will think you're contagious." Her head swivels on her neck like an antenna searching for a signal. "Where's Charlie?"

"I don't know."

"Ohhh." Maxine purses her ruby red lips. "Lover's quarrel?"

"This wedding feels doomed."

"Today, your hair is doomed, but hon, not your wedding. Perk up, now. Most brides have months of pre-ceremonial stress. Yours is superdosed and packed into mere weeks. Naturally, you two are gonna fuss, and you're gonna get moody about the wedding. Don't forget, when it was time for me to marry Sam, I tried to flee the country in the back of Carmen Ortega's Winnebago, Big Bertha. Carmen realized she had a stowaway five miles down the road, but by that time I'd already calmed down and eaten her entire stash of Oreos and chugged half her Yoo-hoos."

I think that story is about 97 percent false, but it almost makes me smile.

My grandmother holds out her hand to the next person who walks by our row. "Maxine Simmons for mayor. Be sure and get out and vote this September. Hello, welcome to church. I'm Maxine, future mayor of In Between. Hi-ho, there, Trudy. You look lovely in your black dress. Know what else is black? My campaign budget. I am a fiscally efficient candidate who will use tax-payer money wisely..." Her mouth snaps shut, and her eyes grow round as the tires on her bicycle. "There's Gus McGillicuddy. How dare he step foot in this church."

"Shouldn't we be glad he's *in* church?" Sam mumbles to his wife.

She plops back down into her seat. "Not this one. This is my turf. He's not a churchgoer, and he's darkening the door of this house of God for nefarious purposes." She taps the newcomer in the seat in front of her on the shoulder. "Hi, Maxine Dayberry. I'm running for mayor, and it looks like you need a pen. That's my face on your Bic, and when you click it, my eyeballs move. Clever, huh? *Eye* think so too." She gives him a good slap on the back. "Vote for me, and God bless you and your absolute lack of humor."

"Excuse me." A nice-looking guy in a gray v-neck tee stops at the end of our row. "Is that seat taken?" He points to the empty chair now occupied by my purse.

"Sorry," says a familiar voice. "It's mine." Charlie shows some teeth, but if that's supposed to be a smile, it looks painful.

Mr. V Neck amiably moves along, while Charlie bids my grandparents good day, then settles beside me.

Everyone stands as the worship team takes to the stage and an up-tempo song begins. I feel every note of the bass throb in my head, and when Charlie tries to take my hand, I pull away.

He leans toward my ear. "I'm sorry about last night."

"It's fine."

"No, it's not." He waits out an especially loud run from the worship pastor who occasionally forgets he's not Ariana Grande. "I was upset with my dad, and I took it out on you. I'm sorry I accused you of taking his side."

I turn to Charlie and am somewhat mollified to see he looks almost as tired as I do. "I'm on your side. Always. But that doesn't mean I will always agree with you. I still think your dad should go with us to Santisto."

"Because you want him to pay for the tuxes."

We'd gone over this three times this weekend. "I said it would help, but we can make it without his financial assistance." I frown toward the stage at two ladies trying to out-harmonize the other, wishing they wouldn't be so rude so I could use this church time to have a private conversation. "My main concern—still—is that Sterling is your one and only dad. Ten years from now, I don't want you to regret his not being at your wedding."

"So you think I should suck it up and tolerate his bringing a woman who's not my mom?"

"Your dad should be at your wedding, Charlie. No matter what he's done, he does love you. Don't cut him out of this."

"But he's putting conditions on his attendance."

Charlie's not wrong. "It's not fair to you. But maybe you take the high road, so next time your dad gets the chance, he'll know where that particular exit ramp is and take it himself."

The heat leaves Charlie's eyes, and he curls his strong arm around my waist. "Have I told you lately that I love you?"

This man. He still makes my pulse leap, and my heart swoon. Today he looks especially fetching with his brown hair swooping across his forehead and his gray shirt bringing out the silver specks in his eyes. He sits in that chair with the posture and easy confidence of a contented soul, one who draws more than his share of quick glimpses from the ladies. "I love you back." We lean toward one another, my lips about to meet his—

"No PDA in church!" Maxine leans across and gives Charlie's knee a whack.

Half an hour later, James stands at his pulpit, a worn Bible in his hand. "...God satisfies the thirsty and fills the hungry with good things..."

I'm about to nod off on Charlie's shoulder when I see my cell number flash on the screen to the left of the stage. "Shoot. That's my sign to report to Daisy's classroom." I pick up my purse just in case. "This can't be good."

CHAPTER SEVENTEEN

I SPEED-WALK OUT THE SANCTUARY, down the hall, and straight to Venus's classroom.

"Is everything okay?" I ask.

Venus guides Daisy toward the door with a gentle hand at her back. "She kicked a child."

"Oh, gosh. Daisy, please apologize."

The little girl shakes her head with a firm no.

"I'm very sorry," I tell the teacher.

"She'll need to go with you."

"For one kick?"

"Followed by a roundhouse to the chest, then a punch to the nose."

Oh, glory.

"Then, there were fifteen minutes of screaming."

"Yours or hers?" Venus does not find my attempt at levity amusing. "Daisy, we're going now."

"No!"

Pulling from every elementary class I've ever been in, I try again. "I'm going to count to three. One...two..." She crosses her arms over her ruffled dress. "Two and a half. Two and three quarters..." Three minutes later, I get to three by way of inches, feet, miles, and whatever

I could recall from the metric system. I make a grab for Daisy's hand, only to have her fall to the floor, screaming like I've pulled off an arm. "Shhhh. Please." I try the words uttered by every Southern mama. "*No, ma'am*!" I give a few more tugs, which only makes her crank up the volume.

"You broke my arm!" Daisy rubs her elbow like she wants this performance considered for the next Tony awards.

"I did not," I assure Venus, who's now surrounded by six children who stare at me as if I'm about to offer free spankings to all.

"Stop hurting me." More wails from the short actress I'm barely touching. "I don't like you. I want my mommy!"

"Y'all have a good day." Venus begins to pull the door closed. "Maybe don't feed her any more sugar."

"Oh, now you suggest that." Venus, the enabler. "Come on, Daisy."

"Noooo!" She slips from my grip and takes off down the hall, screaming like she's ablaze.

Regretting my stupid high heels, I chase after her, my feet protesting with every step. We round a corner, and in between heavy breaths, I wonder what my sister's been feeding this kid. Performance-enhancing drugs? Daisy runs like a junior Olympian. From Kenya.

"Get away from meeee!" She knocks over a plant, causing dirt and leaves to fly everywhere.

"Daisy, please stop running." I'm gaining on her. I can almost reach—

Oomph.

My heel catches on the carpet, and the Berber rises up to meet me. Desperate to stay upright, my arms flail, grabbing at air and what's left of my humility.

But it's no use.

My knees hit first, then my hands. And because gravity has it out for me, I skid a good three feet, where my face meets into a Jesus Loves You doormat. "Ow."

"Katie?"

I slowly lift my head at Maxine's voice, aware I'm in the lobby. And it's increasingly filling with people. "Did I survive?"

Maxine hoots with laughter as she helps me to my feet. "I'd give you a 6.7 on form, but a perfect 10 on the landing."

"I'm okay." I wave to the concerned crowd. "I'm fine. Nothing to see here." Where did my left shoe go? "I've got to find Daisy." And some strong iced tea.

"I have her." Charlie walks toward us, with Chariots of Fire perched on his hip and cradled in his arms. Daisy's hair splays over his shirt as she tucks her head into the crook of Charlie's neck. Tears stream down her cheeks while he pats her back and coos. "It's okay, Daisy. You're safe."

"Of course, she's safe." I spit out a piece of dirt. "Meanwhile, I probably need six months of physical therapy."

Maxine hands me my purse. "Or a lobotomy."

"What happened?" Charlie asks.

I rub my aching nose. "Besides the rug burn?"

Maxine waves to a potential voter across the room then hands me my black heel. "If it's not one rash, it's another."

"Thank you for explaining the meaning of life." I get eye to eye with Daisy the Deserter. "We will talk about this later."

Her bottom lip puckers. "Can I still have cake at your wedding shower?"

At this point, I don't even feel like allowing her oxygen. "We'll see."

"Katie." Charlie's voice carries a warning. "She was running through the church, terrified because she'd lost you."

"She lost me on purpose." But then some of the heat leaves my voice as I look at the way Daisy's tired eyes regard me so anxiously, how she chews on the thumbnail she so proudly painted yesterday. "We both had a very long night. Daisy's feeling a little homesick." I reach out and straighten the bow that's barely hanging onto the top of her head.

"Sometimes a good fit makes me feel better," Maxine says. "Not that I'm easily triggered."

I open my mouth to set my grandmother straight but get interrupted by a well-wisher. Then another. "Yes, we're getting married next week," I say to Mr. Paxton. "Yes, we had to move up the date," I tell Mrs. Orsenay. "No, we're not pregnant," I remind Maxine.

"Alrighty, a quick sandwich at James and Millie's, then back here at two for the shower." Maxine rubs her hands like she's about to roll the dice at the county casino. "I call dibs on gift duplicates, and any left-over cake can be donated to the Dayberry refrigerator."

"I promised Mom I'd join her for pizza before she heads to the shower," Charlie says, clearly grateful to miss our impending estrogen fest.

I kiss him, a quick meeting of the lips that I'd cling to if we weren't standing with a five-year-old between us in a church surrounded by a hundred people. "Call your dad and tell him he's still invited to the wedding."

"Fine." He kisses me again. "But if this turns into a disaster—"

"We'll be on our honeymoon and won't care." I take a calmer Daisy from Charlie and watch him get absorbed into the crowd.

"Oh, geez. Look what cowboy just rode into my church." Maxine plants a hand at each hip and glares at a man in a denim shirt and boots that a few snakes had to die for. "What in the name of Judas are *you* doing here, Gus McGillicuddy?"

"Who's that man?" Daisy asks my grandmother.

"That man, dear, sweet, innocent Daisy, is my competition. The other individual running for mayor of my town."

Gus tips a nonexistent hat. "Hello, Mrs. Dayberry. Or as I hear some people say, Mad Maxine."

She rolls her eyes and fills Daisy in. "You run into *one* chicken truck, and everyone wants to give you a title. But don't change the subject, McGillicuddy. I know what you've done, and I won't stand for it anymore."

"Rose significantly in the polls?" He runs a hand over his black handlebar mustache that sits over a grin. "I'm sorry that's bothering you."

"Don't give me that bull." Maxine stabs a fingernail over Gus's pearl snap pocket. "You're stealing my campaign signs, and I want it to stop."

Gus frowns, wrinkling his tan forehead. "I've done no such thing."

Maxine's gasp is the kind that usually precedes an old-fashioned slap of gloves across the face. "Lyin' in the house of God. And in front of a child, no less."

"I don't have time for petty sign stealing, so you'll have to pin that on someone else."

"Not so fast." Maxine steps in front of the man when he makes to leave. "Why exactly are you at church today?"

"Because I heard the preacher was good."

"Good at what?"

He regards Maxine like she's a chocolate shake short of a Burger Barn value meal. "Preaching?"

Maxine's nostrils flare as she sniffs. "I smell deception."

"That's my Old Spice. Will you let me pass?"

"Out with it, McGillicuddy. Why are you really here?"

"I don't have to tell you why I'm at a church whose doors are open to anyone. I enjoyed the message, the music was tolerable, and it gives me a chance to meet more of my voters."

"This is my turf. The Methodists have a potluck on the second Sunday of the month. If you hurry, you can still get some hash brown casserole and that sad excuse for a pie that Dorinda Chang always tries to pass off as cheesecake." She straightens her fitted jacket. "Not that I attend two churches on the second Sunday. I've just heard."

"Maybe I will go check out the Methodists." Gus waits long enough to see my grandmother visibly relax. "Or maybe I'll be right back here on Wednesday night. Have a lovely rest of your day, Mad Maxine."

"Why you sneaky, sign-stealing—"

"Gus?" James cuts through the lingering crowd. "Hey, how are you doing?"

"He's fine," Maxine says. "He was leaving."

"Leaving?" James shakes Gus's hand. "But we have a meeting."

"I wouldn't miss that." Gus winks at Maxine then claps James on the back. "Show me the way to your office."

"I'll get to the bottom of the sign-stealing," Maxine calls. "Just see if I don't."

CHAPTER EIGHTEEN

When you've spent most of your formative years trying to be one of the unseen, events in your honor like baptisms, graduation parties, and wedding showers provide a high level of anxiety and social panic. I can't explain it. Yes, I'm an actress and thrive on people's eyes on me while on stage. But that's when I'm in character. For today's wedding shower, I'm playing me—the stressed-out bride-to-be who's carrying a notecard of acceptable reactions to gifts should my brain spasm and go numb.

Thank you, Ms. So and So. It's a lovely toaster. Get a load of that bagel option.

This gift card is just my size. I might even share it with Charlie.

I appreciate this vacuum cleaner. It looks super sucky.

And then I added one of my own: *Maxine, I'm not sure I need a pre-paid punch-card to your plastic surgeon, but it's a very nice thought, and you might still be invited to the wedding.*

Millie pulls the car into the church parking lot and gives me a knowing smile. "You okay over there?"

"Yes. It's so thoughtful of Frances, Jemma, and Violet to throw me a shower last minute."

"But...?"

She knows me so well. "It makes it all very official."

"I'd say the proposal and ring two years ago made it official. Or at least we thought it did. Katie, if you're having reservations about marrying Charlie, you know you can talk to me, right?"

Daisy leans forward, her head sticking between our two seats. "What's a reservation?"

I smile. "Something that helps you get a good table at a restaurant. No, Millie, I don't have reservations." I point the air conditioning vent on my warm face. "Well, maybe a few. But who doesn't, right?"

"I don't have any concerns about your marrying Charlie," Millie says. "But I think you have lots of things going on in that head of yours, and you should talk about them before they make you do something crazy."

"The pace of it all is throwing me, I think. It's like Charlie and I had been riding on the engagement gondola, only to get out and catch a rocket." I watch a couple of women from the church exit a car, their arms piled with colorful packages with bows so styled they defy gravity. "It's not like I had pictured it."

Millie rests her arm on the console. "Tell me how you saw your wedding."

"I thought I'd get married at the church. With James doing the service. And there would be all this time—for showers and parties and all the hoopla." Time for a sense of peace to settle in and the encompassing feeling of drowning to leave. "Charlie and I registered for our gifts in twenty minutes. I'm not even sure what we signed up for."

"I did see a laser-light karaoke machine on your Amazon list," Millie says. "But, I'd assumed you'd been hacked by your grandma."

"I want to enjoy this, but I feel so pressured and hurried. I don't want to look back on these moments and only remember the frantic pace."

"Do you want to postpone the wedding?" Her face grows taut with concern, and I know she's secretly praying I say no.

Which I do. "We can't. This ball's in motion, and if I postpone it one more time..."

"What?"

"I think Charlie's all out of understanding on that front."

"But is that what you want?" When I don't respond, Millie digs in. "You've rescheduled this wedding a few times already, and I know there was a valid reason in every instance. I can't help but wonder if you were too comfortable with the delays. And maybe that's something you need to look at."

I attempt a smile. "In all my spare time?"

"It's important you only get married when you're truly ready. But if there is hesitation, you need to know where it's coming from."

"Can I have a snack?" Daisy interrupts. "I'm hungry."

I open my door, letting the heat and humidity invade, relieved to escape this conversation. "Yes, guaranteed cake inside. You can even help me open the gifts."

"Yay!" Daisy spills out of the car, skipping into the sunshine as her dress billows around her.

"I'm always here to listen to whatever's on your mind," Millie says.

"Thanks." I wave off the weird moment I've knit and follow Daisy.

"You're doing good with her, Katie." Millie hugs me to her as we watch my niece pick a dandelion from the green grass. "I'm very proud of you."

I'm proud. Those words still bring a mist to my eyes and feed my soul like water on parched ground. "Thank you. Except for today's meltdown, she's easy to love."

Do I love Daisy? Is it just that simple? I hardly know her. And I'll be letting her go in a matter of weeks. Last night Iola finalized the plans for Daisy's departure, and I've been rattled ever since. Basically Daisy will be moved to a new home a week after I return from my honeymoon. Between our house, the respite home while we're gone, and the future foster family, that's a lot of change for one little girl. And for me.

"It's normal for five-year-olds to have meltdowns." Without breaking stride, Millie plucks a weed from the lawn. "But a kid who's had trauma is guaranteed to act out. She doesn't know how to process all her big feelings."

"I can relate to that."

"Trauma shows up in so many ways, and most are not pleasant."

"I'm sorry for all the grief I gave you and James."

Millie stops at the church doors and wraps me in a hug. "It's what we signed up for. But Katie, the aftershocks of that trauma don't stop when the original source of the pain is removed. They can linger for years." She gestures to Daisy, who flips in a cartwheel on the sidewalk, her dress flying over her head. "What you saw today was her acting out of fear and hurt that had nothing to do with you. You might not be that sixteen-year-old still lashing out, but as we age, old wounds can fester in new, more sophisticated ways. Dress up a little fancier. Do you know what I'm saying?"

Yes. No. I don't know. "I think so. But I'm going to be fine, Millie."

"If it helps, I was nervous before I married James."

"You were?" We step behind a potted shrub, out of the way of a group of women walking into the church.

"Yeah, for months leading up to the ceremony all I could think about was past boyfriends and wonder if I was making the right choice."

"How did you know for sure James was the right one and that you were ready?"

"I knew I was in love with James, but I wanted to be sure we were meant to be together forever. So I prayed for God to give me a sign, something to confirm that he was truly the guy for me."

"Did you get that sign?"

"I did." She smiles at a faraway memory.

"What was it?"

Her grin turns a tiny bit mischievous. "I don't think I'll tell you that part now. But I will say that when it arrived, it made my heart lighter, confirmed the kind of man James was, and gave me the peace I was looking for. And it made me laugh. Basically, it confirmed all the things I still love about my husband."

I nodded as if I understood. "I can't imagine you with anyone else."

"But I had to be sure. You need to be sure, as well. Sometimes it's not about if the person is right, but if the time is right. If *you're* all right."

"I do love Charlie."

"We all do." Millie waves at Frances's mother while Daisy races back to us.

Daisy jumps up and down, her dainty shoes stomping the dirt beneath her. "I want to go inside. Let's go get that cake." She reaches for my hand, wrapping her marker-stained fingers around mine. "Are you ready, Katie?"

I see the church lobby through the glass, a room bustling with activity, people here to see me and celebrate this new life stage. Then I shift my gaze to Daisy, who tugs on my hand and watches me with such expectations. "I really hope I am."

The downstairs meeting area of the church boasts an updated kitchen and a large space that can hold portable basketball goals, an uncomfortable number of chairs, or wall-to-wall tables. Today the sports equipment and youth music equipment have been tucked away, and friendly faces smiled back at me as people fill every seat in the church.

"I cannot believe this crowd," I say as I hug Frances. "Do I even know all these people?"

"Every one of them." Frances beams as she scans the successful turnout. "Friends from church, school, college, and a good number of folks from town."

I can hardly breathe with the wonder. Everywhere I turn, I see someone I know, a special person who touched some stage of my life. There's Ms. Hall, my old drama teacher. Laura, the wife of my high school youth pastor, who helped me when Millie was diagnosed with cancer. I spot Jeremy's mom, who began attending our church after the tornado hit In Between in my tenth-grade year. Then there's Loretta, former owner of Micky's Diner, who offered me a job four years ago when I came back to In Between with heartbreak and an even emptier bank account. She's now retired and travels the country with her husband in a motorhome bigger than my Chicago apartment.

Three tables of white-haired ladies wave at me like I'm a Hollywood celebrity.

"Those are the gals from Shady Pines." Maxine reaches my side with a visible blot of icing above her lip. Clearly, she's already taste-tested the party spread. "They bussed over, but probably can't stay long." She runs her hands down the skirt of her hot pink sundress. "It's casino night at the Pines, and they gotta nap before the big event."

"Katie!" Violet Newbury rushes toward me, enfolding me in her arms. My college roommate wears a T-shirt emblazoned with the face of Barbara Walters, a black skirt, and heels. Her chestnut brown hair sits crooked atop her head, just like it did when we were sophomores sitting on the floor of the Curie Hall eating pizza and discussing the woes of the day. "I'm so excited you're finally marrying that Charlie Benson." She grabs my hands and leans close. "I knew he was the one."

The room warms a degree, and I discreetly take a deep breath. "Thank you for the shower. I know it was hard to throw it together so quickly."

"Not at all." Violet waves our other old roomie over. "I'd ask Jemma to give you some marriage tips, but I don't think sorting the sock drawer and alphabetizing the spice rack will apply as much to your life as hers."

Our neurotically detail-oriented friend joins us, looking slightly miserable and in need of an EpiPen for her people allergy. "Hi, Katie." Jemma's voice is a flat, one-note tune. "I hope you know I wouldn't do this for just anyone."

I spare her the hug I *know* she doesn't want and high-five her instead. "It means a lot to me, Jemma. You two being here is exactly what I need."

"I see you've stopped delaying the wedding." Jemma twists the simple band on her left hand. "I can tell you, aside from discovering a new constellation, it's the best decision I've ever made."

"How about you, Frances?" I turn to my best friend as she stacks and restocks some decorative napkins. "Is getting married still your best decision?"

"Cake's here," Mrs. Vega calls, rolling out a towering three-tier cake on a cart. "Let's celebrate!"

Frances watches the cake, and her eyes behind her glasses get big. "I just remembered something." She disappears in a flash, going the opposite direction of the cake.

"What's up with our little nerd queen?" Maxine asks.

"I'm not sure." I hope the wedding festivities aren't triggering Frances. "But whatever it is, I don't think it's good."

CHAPTER NINETEEN

"THANK YOU FOR EVERYTHING," I say to Violet and Jemma as they clean up the cake table. I grab another petit four and wish I could eat ten more.

Violet laughs and tosses a plate of crumbs in the trash. "You've already told us that approximately a hundred times."

"Actually, it was exactly twelve." Jemma removes a pair of latex gloves used in her cleaning duties. "Once more, and I'm taking back my Crockpot."

I hug Violet and give Jemma a high-five. "I'm just glad to see you two. I wish you could be at the wedding."

"We'll both be able to make it to the reception when you return," Violet says. "Don't forget, I want to interview you for *Good Morning Dallas*."

"It's on my calendar." Violet's dating a nice man ten years her senior and giving her mother the vapors. In college, she rebuked a family tradition and left predestined med school pursuits to become a journalist. She's written for various papers, interned at a major news network in New York, and now writes and reports full time for a popular news show in Dallas. She still has her heart set on becoming a war correspondent, and I know she'll push through until she makes it.

"Jemma, how's Alex?" I ask of her husband, a boy who dared to ask her for tutoring help in college. She brought the astronomy expertise, and he brought the charm. And somehow, he won her over. They married last year on the courthouse steps because Jemma wanted nothing to do with the pomp and circumstance of a formal ceremony. I can't say I blame her. Alex teaches at a high school in Houston, while Jemma works for a lab studying black holes and other celestial things I don't understand.

"Alex wants to get a dog." Jemma's dark eyes pierce us with her trademark intensity. "I think we all know what that means."

Frances laughs and pops a few peanuts in her mouth. "We got a puppy last Christmas."

"I don't get it," I say. "What's wrong with Alex wanting a dog?"

"It's a trial run for kids." Jemma watches Daisy skipping across the room with Maxine. "First comes the canine, then comes the offspring."

"Or," I suggest, "it could just mean he wants a dog."

"I don't want children," Jemma says. "Alex knew this."

"We all have our own timelines and plans." The plastic fork in Frances's hand snaps in two. "Then, life just blows them right up."

"Wait, what?" I stare at my friend, the one who's always been the most annoying ray of optimistic sunshine. "Plans don't *have* to change, right?"

"I'm just saying that you can plan and plan, but then one day, your husband wakes up with a different idea and wants to light your old goals on fire. Or life takes a detour you never counted on, and every single element of your life gets tossed up in the air." She catches my appalled expression and recovers, slapping on a toothy smile. "But other than that, marriage is really cool." She grabs a petit four and shoves it in her mouth. "I like it."

What if one day Charlie doesn't want me to be an actress? What if he tires of life in New York? Or what if he decides our plan to hold off on children until our thirties is no longer acceptable?

"What are you hens clucking about over here?" Maxine sweeps through, carrying an empty plate she begins to fill. Again.

Violet dips the ladle into the punch and serves my grandmother another glass. "The girls are scaring Katie with their wifely woes."

"Wifely woes? Marriage is great. Otherwise, I wouldn't have done it twice." She cups a hand over her mouth and faux whispers. "And those are just the ones I've told the family about."

"What's your secret for a happy marriage?" Frances asks.

Maxine ponders this for one millisecond. "Never let your husband come to bed mad."

"You work the problem out, right?" Violet seems quite proud of her suggestion. "Even if it takes all night."

"No, I mean, if you're in a tiff, the hubs goes to the spare bedroom." Maxine's teeth snap into a carrot stick. "Until he sees the error of his ways."

"Very helpful," I droll.

"I have a few tips." Donna Benson says as she and her daughter join us. "Make sure you're a partner in all things, but especially in finances."

Mrs. Vega wanders over and lifts her glass of punch. "Embrace your differences."

Frances grins at her mom. "Then force them on your kids until one day they finally appreciate it."

Millie's the next to chime in. "The secret for keeping James happy has always been a home-cooked meal. He's never wanted much, but what he wouldn't do for my pot roast. If he had it his way, we'd never go out to eat."

"That was Charlie growing up," Donna said. "He always wanted my homemade mac-n-cheese, fried chicken, and buttery mashed potatoes and gravy—with no lumps. Right, Katie?"

"Um, right." Did buying him roasted chicken from the deli count? I have no idea how he likes his mashed potatoes. I guess, however KFC makes them.

My future mother-in-law takes a sip of punch. "When Charlie would come home from college, he'd request his favorite meal and my coconut cream pie."

"She makes the crust herself," Sadie says, as proud of her mom as if the woman landed on the moon instead of achieving a buttery, flaky baked good.

Donna's fingers absently play with Sadie's long, blonde hair. "Twice that boy flew in unexpectedly just because his sister told him I had pie in the oven."

"It's almost a curse to cook well," Millie says. "In the early days of our marriage, James was so impressed with my kitchen skills, he'd invite over couples from the church and other pastoring families, missionaries who were passing through, city dignitaries. We entertained all the time, and it was ten years before I finally put my foot down and told James that the In Between Steak House could fix up a meal quicker than I could, and we didn't have to clean up afterward."

Donna watches her daughter as Sadie leads Daisy outside to the small playground. "Katie, Charlie's told me all about the socializing expectations involved in his new promotion. Are you gonna be okay with that?"

"I'll be gone most evenings." My future mother-in-law doesn't seem too impressed with this obvious detail.

"So was my husband. Sterling was such a workaholic. We didn't have pre-marital counseling back in my day, but I'm sure that's something you guys have thoroughly discussed. It's not so much about a person being gone all the time as it is the unrealistic expectations one might have."

Did she mean Charlie might have unrealistic expectations, or my idea of working seven shows a week was out of bounds?

Millie's quick to reassure Donna. "Katie and Charlie went through all that with our pastor friend in Chicago, didn't you?"

"Yes." My cheeks hurt from all this fake smiling. "We didn't get to finish the last few weeks due to Charlie working in Canada, but I think we got the gist of it." Donna's drink pauses on the way to her mouth. "We still did a lot of work, though. Pastor Jenkins didn't flunk us." I definitely did *not* register for guilt and condemnation for this shower. Can we just put all that back in the dollar store gift bag it came in?

"I wasn't prepared to be Joey's personal assistant," Frances says, blessedly changing the subject. "He can run his own business just fine, but unbeknownst to me, I'm now responsible for reminding him about family birthdays and social events we'd agreed to." Her cheeks flush pink. "But, I'm sure Charlie can handle all that himself."

I'd had to remind Charlie of Sadie's birthday just last month *and* buy the darn present. "I can see how too much of it could make you feel unappreciated."

"Yeah. Try four years of it. And then he has the nerve to forget *my* birthday this year."

"I'm sorry." Frances seemed so unhappy. If she and Joey were struggling, then how would I ever successfully handle a marriage? My friend has never failed at anything.

"I pay someone to cook for us," Maxine says, completely unfazed. "And then I make Sam do the dishes. You ladies need to show the boys who's boss." Never one to embrace appropriateness, she pulls Maxine for Mayor pens out of her dress pocket and passes them out. "My complaint is the snoring and cover stealing. Oh, and the thermostat. Sam would keep the house cold as a meat locker in the winter and hot as his barbecue grill in the summer. The electric bill was our first big argument, and let me tell you, I won that one."

Jemma frowns at her new pen. "I love Alex but living together has been a huge adjustment. I'm not sure I've acclimated even still."

"It is hard," France says. "Suddenly, you've got twice the laundry, twice the mess, it's a turf war for the TV remote, and don't even get me started on the problems of a night owl marrying a morning person."

"I'm telling you, Katie." Donna nudges me with a friendly elbow. "I've been trying to impress this upon Frances this for years. The way to a Benson boy's heart is through his stomach. Make him his favorite meal, and all is well. These are not high maintenance children I raised." She shoots Frances a scolding look. "And you tell Joey to do his own laundry. He certainly knows his way around a washing machine. I brought up self-sufficient kids."

"So, back to this food thing," I say, still pondering my lack of cooking skills. "What's Charlie's favorite meal?"

Donna appears a little taken aback that I even have to ask. "Pork chops."

"Right, right." I guess it was too much to hope that she'd say two bowls of Cheerios.

"Katie," Millie says, "you and Charlie will be fine. You've been together a long time, so I'm sure you've worked out all the kinks.

I'm a little worried our kinks have kinks. "I better check on Daisy." And breathe air that isn't filled with wifely advice from the Betty Crocker Brigade.

"I'll go with you." Maxine dabs a napkin to the dusting of crumbs on her top lip, then links her toned arm through mine. "What's up, buttercup?"

We walk down the hall, the scent of a concrete-floored basement of this fifty-year-old church once an offense, now a small comfort. "Everyone has all these rules and must-haves for a successful marriage."

"Yeah, but use or toss, right? Not one person mentioned the value of solo vacations and hidden stashes of squeeze cheese, so what do they know? Sweet pea, nobody gets Charlie better than you. Don't sweat this. So much of marriage is figuring it out as you go. Not one of those ladies in there knew what they were doing when they first said, 'I do.'"

We reach the door to the outside play area, and I come to a halt. There's Daisy, face lit with a smile as she zooms down a slide. Her giggles sing out like melodious birdsongs as her hands lift to the sky in wild abandonment. Her joy pushes away all the fussy, crowded thoughts of being an underqualified wife.

"Look at that." Maxine chuckles softly as she watches my niece. "My new great-granddaughter is having the time of her life."

If only Daisy could have a Maxine in her corner like me. "She's starting to act more like a five-year-old."

"Because Daisy's safe and loved." My grandmother bumps her shoulder to mine. "She resembles you."

I return my attention to Daisy who now chases two other girls in a game of tag. "Her hair's as white as a cotton ball, she has skin that tans, eyes brown as chestnuts, and she's short."

Maxine's glossy pink lips curve. "She has your feisty spirit, your resilience, your heart, and your intelligent instinct for survival. You've both come a long way, and you're both going to be okay."

"I want her to be okay." Guilt weighs on my stomach heavier than Maxine's three pieces of cake ever could. "But Charlie and I just can't be full-time foster parents."

Daisy spies us standing in the glass double doors and waves, first hesitantly, then full force, her arm beckoning me to come outside.

"She's yours for now." Maxine opens the door, and the sunlight pours in. "Let's make today one of her favorites." She slips into the fenced yard, hooting and dancing her way to Daisy. She grabs my niece's little hands and skips in mad, uneven circles. Heads thrown back, the two howl with laughter.

When I was Daisy's age, I clung to these rare moments of pure, unfiltered happiness. When I had an easy hour with no drunk mother raging, no scary people looming, no nights too dark to sleep through. I hope and pray her future somehow turns out as well as mine. But the reality is her odds aren't great.

To spend time with Daisy, to be close to her, is often too much. Too many memories of my own childhood and all the guilt that I'll soon say goodbye. But most of all, my Super-Glued soul would shatter into a thousand pieces if something happened to her.

And it's only a matter of time before it does.

CHAPTER TWENTY

I THOUGHT my last connection to prison died with my bio-mom. But as I walk upstairs Monday evening to get Daisy for her video visit with Haven, my mood plummets. How is it possible I'm once again connected to a correctional facility? Why can't my biological family stick to the right side of the law?

But maybe the most depressing thought is *I* could be the one wearing prison orange if James and Millie hadn't saved me.

Walking down the hall, I see James standing covertly near Daisy's doorway, and from the sappy smile on his face, I can tell he's about to report something precious.

He motions me over, then puts a shushing finger to his lips. "Check this out," he whispers before nodding his head toward the bedroom.

I quietly peek in and see her standing in the middle of the space, surrounded by dolls and miniature teacups in every color of the rainbow. She wears one of the princess dresses I picked up for her yesterday, her tiara perched crookedly on her blonde head. Her dog Petunia dons a purple doll cape, looking very royal despite the drool. Disney music plays from some unidentified, but loud, source.

"Remind you of anyone?" James asks.

I pull back from the door. "Makes me recall the time you got a little excessive with the visual aids during a sermon."

"Come on. Think back to your first year in our home. How many times did I catch you running lines with our dog?"

"Rocky had an emotional depth and an undeniable artistic side yearning to be recognized. And an appreciation for undiscovered talent."

James laughs. "This puppy looks like him. And Daisy reminds me of you."

Still completely unaware of being watched, Daisy bows low to her yipping dog. "Good to meet you, Prince," she says with a British accent that's not half bad. "I can dance with you tonight, but I have to leave at midnight. Do you like my glass slippers?" She shows the high heels I let her borrow.

"It was the first play of the reopening of the Valiant," I whispered. "The director had just handed me the part of Juliet. I had zero acting experience, and I was scared to death I would screw it up. I wanted to do such a good job for you and Millie."

"You did a fabulous job." He nods toward Daisy, then hugs me to his side. "And you still are."

I didn't agree, but Millie told me if I believed I was killing it at this mommying stuff, I'd be abnormal.

James kisses the top of my head. "I'll leave you ladies to your visit. I'll be in my study watching football and pretending to prepare for next week's sermon if you need to talk later."

I watch James walk away, grateful for a support system in this crazy season. And even more grateful he's stashed the good snacks in that office. "Daisy, time to talk to your mommy."

She whirls around, not the least bit chagrined to find me lurking in her doorway. "I'm a princess."

"That you are."

A few minutes later, I address thank you notes while she chats like a magpie to her mother. From where I sit, out of the line of the camera, I see Haven's relieved face on my laptop screen, hear the Millie-like questions she lobs at her daughter.

"Are you brushing your teeth?"

"Yes, Mommy."

"Morning and night?"

"Yes."

"Have you been listening to Katie and doing what she tells you?"

Daisy turns to me on that one, and I give her a reassuring nod.

"Mostly," Daisy says. She holds her wiggly puppy, Petunia, who licks her face.

Haven walks Daisy through the same process she does every call. "Give yourself a great big hug. Now squeeze." Daisy giggles, and Haven's laughter echoes in the room. "That was from me. I love you, Daisy. We'll be together soon, okay, baby?"

Daisy grabs a tissue from the box I have handy and blows her drippy nose. Tears streak down her ruddy cheeks as she begins to cry loudly. "Don't go yet, Mommy."

"I have to, sweet girl. But I'll call you again in a few days." Haven blows kisses until the screen goes black.

"I know that's hard." I approach Daisy cautiously, never knowing if she'll welcome comfort or want to strikeout. "Do you want to talk about it?" Easing down slowly, I sit on the floor beside her.

Head bowed, she shakes her hair side to side in a definitive no.

But then the strangest thing happens.

Daisy rubs her snotty nose with the tissue, tosses it on the rug, then climbs into my lap.

I couldn't be more stunned if she handed me a ticking bomb.

Her arms curl around me, and her cheek presses to my chest. One small cough turns into a choked sob, and soon she's crying all over me.

I've tried to hold Daisy at arm's length. All along, I've said I wanted to honor her space. The truth is, I haven't wanted to get close. I'm leaving in four days. Most likely, we will not cross paths after this is over.

Do not get attached, I've told myself a hundred times. Seeing Daisy go to another home will wreck me, but if I'm bonded to the child, I will most likely lose my mind. A mind that needs to focus on memorizing script lines and marrying Charlie Benson.

Yet I know it's too late. This kid has slipped her way into my life, and I'm pretty much done for. What's a little heartbreak if I can be more of what Daisy needs now?

And later, when she's gone, I can mourn what her life could've been.

My arms close around her, and I breathe in her strawberry shampoo and Bubblegum breath. I hold her tightly and rock her back and forth. "It's hard to be apart from your mommy. I've been there." *God, give me the words for this child.* "But you're loved so much. Your mommy adores you, and she'll be home as soon as she can." As I say the words, I think I might actually believe them. Haven seems to genuinely care about Daisy. In the script I'd written in my head, I cast Haven as my own mother. But the part has never quite fit her. Haven's words and actions don't align with the role of Bobbie Ann Parker, no matter how much I try to make the two characters one and the same. "In the meantime, we'll color pictures for your mom and make her cards." I sway gently and rub my hand over her hair. "We can even do more of those beaded necklaces we made with Millie last night, okay?"

Finally, her little voice speaks. "I don't understand why my mommy can't come home."

Things a five-year-old shouldn't have to ponder.

"She made a mistake. Your mama was hanging out with a friend who wasn't doing the right thing, and the judge thinks..."

"That my mommy needs a timeout?"

"Exactly."

I brush away tears from her soft face, and as she sits there, the seconds turn to minutes until I know that I'm in the midst of a moment I'll likely never forget.

"Can I have ice cream?"

And, just like that, the spell is broken, and the little charmer plays her guilt card. "With extra sprinkles?" She grins.

"The only way to eat it."

Ten minutes later, Daisy sits on the back porch trying in vain to keep her bowl away from Petunia. We've laughed over the clumsiness of the puppy, watching as she chases a butterfly and trips over her own feet. I've given Daisy seconds on the whipped cream and shown her the fireflies flitting in the yard.

"Well, what do we have here?" Maxine wheels her bicycle-built-for-two into the open gate and assesses the situation. "Did someone call the girls' club meeting to order and not invite me?"

"Let me guess." I detach the puppy from its toothy grip on my shoelace. "You smelled the ice cream and pedaled right over."

"Actually, I drove the bike over in Sam's truck." Maxine gives Petunia's head a ruffle, then does the same for Daisy.

"You drove?" I'm instantly on alert, sensing the kind of danger that could disrupt the whole universe. "Whatever you have cooked up, the answer is no."

"I like your bike, Ms. Maxine."

"No, you don't," I tell Daisy. "Trust me on this."

"What?" Maxine asks innocently.

"You don't like her bicycle?" Daisy runs her hands over one shiny, pink seat, then the other. "It's so pretty."

"She doesn't ride it for fun, Daisy." I glare at my grandma and the two-wheeled broom she flew in on. "The only place that bike can take you to is a place called trouble."

"Nonsense." Maxine pffts. "Ginger Rogers and I were out for a spin tonight and thought Millie might watch dear Daisy while you and I go for a leisurely ride."

"Nope. Nothing good happens with you, your bike, and the dark of night. And James and Millie aren't home yet from the Valiant."

"Millie pulled into the garage when I arrived." Maxine tilts her head, squints an eye, and sizes up Daisy. "I guess I could indoctrinate short stuff here. Never too young to enjoy a little adventure, right?"

"Leave her out of this." I stoop down to Daisy's level. "Why don't you and Petunia go into the kitchen and tell Millie you'd like one more scoop of Rocky Road."

"Come on, Petunia." She and the puppy toddle off, leaving me alone with Ms. Crimes and Misdemeanors.

"What are you up to today?"

"I don't know what you're talking about. I'm sixty-one years old. It takes a hardened heart to condemn and discourage my effort to get more exercise in my middle age."

Parts of her face might be sixty-one, but Maxine sure is not. "Spit it out. I have a kid to take care of, lines to learn, and bags to pack. Plus, somewhere in the middle of it all, I also need to schedule at least one more panic attack."

"I'd like to remind you that it's been two years since our last stakeout."

"It was seven months ago. You made me crawl through an alleyway rife with poison ivy to spy on the new librarian, and I still need a hit of Calamine lotion every time I think about it."

"That librarian was hogging all the Harlequins and selling them to her neighbors to turn a tidy profit. She needed to be exposed. And I needed to read another book about unexpected triplets between the fireman and amnesiac princess." Her gaze raises toward the dim skyline with dignity and purpose. "I will never stop fighting for the unsung classics."

"I'm not getting on that bike with you," I tell Maxine.

"Someone has taken down all my campaign signs on the east side of town."

"And?"

"So now the east side is essentially naked. Don't you care about city beautification?"

"What do your signs have to do with beautification?"

"Have you seen those things? It's 12x24 inches of my face in vivid color and a gorgeous amount of Photoshop." She pulls her cheeks back toward her ears. "If only some doctor would figure out how to Photoshop in real life."

She'd be first in line. "Maxine, I'm not going on a ride with you. My nose still hurts where it broke during one of our 'outings' my freshman year of college."

"How many times do I have to apologize for that?" She plants a hand on her hip. "Do I not send you a box of chocolates every year on the anniversary of that terrible accident?"

"Yeah, and a giant red clown nose, just to let me know how sincerely sorry you are."

"If I've ever had a mission that needs your help, this is it." She sees my hesitation and pushes through the lull in my resistance. "Gus McGillicuddy runs his campaign out of the three-car garage in his backyard."

"Let me guess, there's a large oak tree and a pool involved."

"And a few Dobermans, but other than that, it looks like easy snooping."

"No thank you."

"He's taking my signs, favorite granddaughter of mine."

"I heard you call Amy that just yesterday."

"My loyalties change by the day. Just like the date on my birth certificates."

"Maxine, if I break something before my wedding, I will be completely devastated. I'm not wearing a nose cast in my wedding photos."

"Oh, sweet pea, I'd hire you a body double before that happened. Come on, this task will be easy."

"Then you don't need me."

Maxine closes the distance between us, her faint, expensive French perfume scenting the desperate air around her. "Let me tell you something I've never admitted to you."

"You really did get a chin job last year?"

"Okay, let me tell you something *else*." She blinks, and her hand covers her chin. "These missions are not so much about wanting an accomplice to help me break into someone's property."

Unconvinced, I cross my arms over my chest. "No?"

"No." Something like love sparkles in her blue eyes. "It's about time with my granddaughter, one-on-one, chica y chica, your Dorothy to my Blanche. Could I do these necessary and slightly shady tasks alone? Yes. Could I hire someone from the bad side of town and pay them to carry out my nefarious quests? Also, yes, though Donnie the Mooch has banned me from a certain part of Fifth Street." She grabs my hand in hers. "But each one of these little 'outings' is a memory I get to make with my granddaughter who now lives so very far away. Who's about to start her married life and slip even further away from me, I fear."

My eyes pool, and I sniff indelicately. "I'm glad you enjoy our times of larceny and bone breakage."

"I wouldn't want to do it with anyone else."

I sigh and brush away an escaped tear. "Fine. Give me my instructions."

Victory lifts those cheeks better than any surgery ever could. "Your mission, should you choose to accept it—and you do—is to ride with me past the Blevins farm to the McGillicuddy's house."

"That's ten miles away."

"So we toss Ginger in the back of Sam's truck, which stands ready and waiting, drive most of the way, then let Ginger discreetly carry us the last leg."

I'm already regretting this. "Go on."

"We peek into McGillicuddy's garage and see if we find my stolen signs." She holds up her glittery phone. "I take some snaps, then we roll out. Easy-peasy, opponent's-campaign-freezy."

"What if Gus is home?"

"He won't be. His website says he's meeting with the In Between Motorcycle Club tonight."

"He probably has his entire property covered in a security system."

In a move that shouldn't surprise me anymore, Maxine dips her hand into her blouse and slowly extracts a folded piece of paper. "I might have a map of his place with all the pertinent information. And a Rice Krispy bar, but probably only one of these is relevant."

"Are those Xs the cameras?"

"Yes. Notice there's not one on the out-buildings."

"What's the happy face symbol in the corner of his garage?"

"His freezer where he keeps his popsicles. But we digress."

"How did you get this?"

She rolls her eyes. "Come on, easy stuff."

"You bought a drone, didn't you?"

"Not important. Please join me, Katie. This could be the mission of all missions."

"That's exactly what I'm afraid of."

CHAPTER TWENTY-ONE

NO SMALL TOWN is complete without a patchwork quilt of farmland to frame it up right. And no small-town girl with two brain cells would be caught dead prowling around on one of those farms in the black of night.

"One more road, and then we'll pull off." Maxine gestures her hand toward the road illuminated in my headlights. "There it is. Turn. Turn already! What are you waiting for?"

"The cow crossing the road?"

"Not how I would've navigated the moment, but you're the driver." She flips the visor down and reapplies her red lipstick. "Pull into that field and park behind the big tree. They'll never see this truck."

These sound like famous last words before my first arrest. But like always, I obey Maxine's every command and let the truck make use of its four-wheel-drive until we bounce down a hill and, hopefully, out of sight.

"Help me grab Ginger." She jumps out of the vehicle, landing with a thud. "Good heavens, look out. This place is a minefield for cow poopies." Maxine steps gingerly, grumbling all the way to the tailgate. "Bunch of slobs. Someone needs to clean up out here."

"Maxine." My pulse accelerates, and a cold sweat dots my brow. I point to the back of the truck, looking at something that is *definitely* not Ginger Rogers, the two-seated bike. "What..is *this*?"

"It's my new four-wheeler or, as I like to call it, the 'campaign tour bus.'"

"You said we were taking Ginger."

"Yeah, Ginger 2.0."

"There is no way we're driving that out here."

"Sweet pea, did you seriously believe I'd ride a bike out in the country?" She pats the machine that weighs a good 500 pounds. "I might hurt myself."

"How exactly did you think you were going to get Ginger 2.0 out of the truck?" There's no way we can lift that thing onto the ground, so I feel some small measure of relief at that. "I'm not helping you push it out."

"I wouldn't dream of asking you to do such a strenuous task." Before I can say 'expired driver's license,' Maxine hops into the back, and with a few indelicate grunts, tosses one aluminum ramp to the ground, then another.

"You can't be serious."

"Democracy is serious. September's election is serious." She unfolds each ramp and lines them up with military precision. "And so is my four-wheeler."

"This is a terrible idea. Do you even know how to drive that thing?"

"You bet your Spanx, I do." She tosses her head back and laughs. "I wouldn't hop on this without some experience."

"I guess that makes me feel a little better."

"I watched two hours of YouTubes. Now stand back while I get this set this little filly free."

What follows is the stuff of nightmares. Mad Maxine Dayberry, former showgirl and current mayoral candidate, flies down the ramp like Evel Knievel, one hand steering, one hand punching the air. "Yeeee-haw!"

If the cows know what's good for them, they'll run far, far away.

Maxine tears through the field, then turns an abrupt U. She slams on the brakes and idles beside me. "Need a ride?"

"No."

"The answer is yes. The answer is always yes."

Ten minutes later, Ginger 2.0 stops again, which is really convenient. Because so has my heart.

"You nearly killed us." My hair hangs limp and wet with sweat against my face. "Did you even see that pond back there?"

Maxine squeegees her shirt sleeve. "Twas a little deeper than it looked. But you swim like a champ. Onto the next phase." She gestures to a dirt road. "We gotta walk the rest of the way."

I spit out a bug that needlessly sacrificed itself in my teeth. "You are definitely not driving back."

"Ginger 2.0 doesn't care for your attitude."

"Ginger 2.0 gave me whiplash." And a world-class wedgie. "Let's get this over with."

"First of all, you need to change your attitude. I can't have your bad juju on this mission, or it'll curse the whole thing."

Pretty sure it was cursed and doomed from the start. "Lead the way."

"That's better." Maxine turns toward the east, her forehead screwed into a frown. "Let me get my bearings here." She licks her finger, then holds it in the air.

"While I'm sure the direction of the wind is vitally important to your advanced tracking skills, if we could just begin walking in the direction of McGillicuddy's farm, that would be dandy."

"My goodness, you're testy. You need one of my prune smoothies." She takes off down the dirt road. "Would you like to talk about the source of these angry feelings?"

I walk behind Maxine and stare at her wet backside. "I'm looking at her."

Fifteen minutes and a few candy bars later, we arrive at Gus McGillicuddy's farm. "This is more like a compound." The thing is lit up like my mom's old prison parking lot, with the main house and all his exterior buildings aglow. "I thought you said he wasn't home."

"He's not. I'm telling you, Gus is scheduled to attend the biker meeting. He goes there every month. The coast is clear for espionage."

I slip an elastic from my wrist and wrangle my drenched hair into a ponytail. Perspiration slips down my shirt, and I wouldn't turn down a glass of water. "Why do we always have to conduct these crime sprees in the dead of summer?"

Maxine pulls out a selfie stick and takes a pic of the two of us. "Because I conduct nefarious undertakings better with a tan. Onward!"

I slap off a persistent mosquito, only to find three more zoom in like fighter pilots to replace him. Mr. McGillicuddy's home is a large, two-story rustic abode, the kind whose interior is probably decorated with deer antlers and wagon wheel chandeliers. Land as far as the eye can see stretches all around us, and hills roll in the perimeter in the distance. If we weren't here for questionable purposes, I'd appreciate it. But I just want to leave. The place is wooded enough to hide a body that would never be found. A white wooden fence separates the fields from the large manicured yard. Giant hostas surround the house, probably fertilized by the cows that stare at us from the tall grass behind the fence.

"Follow that cobblestone path." Maxine points her flashlight to the ground, illuminating a meandering path. "This leads us to the garage. Or, as I like to call it, McGillicuddy's Den of Thievery."

"Should we knock on his door just to make sure he's truly gone?"

"No, you amateur. I've been studying his comings and goings for three months."

"That'll sound good at your parole hearing. What if Gus has a family? A wife?"

"He's single. Probably why he wants to be mayor—so he can have more dating opportunities. Use his power to lure the ladies."

We walk around the house, trying to stay in the shadows like the delinquents we are. When Maxine leads me to a locked fence as tall as a Broadway billboard, I am not the least bit surprised. "I'm not climbing that."

"Right on, sweetcheeks." She swings her backpack off her shoulders, zips it open, and hands me a rope. "You're gonna scale it."

I back away from the offering, noticing the weight dangling at the end. "Are you out of your mind?"

"Do we really need to review the possible answers to this?"

Lord above. “Maxine, I’m not climbing that fence.”

“Fine.” She grabs the rope and faces the fence like her Goliath. “I’ll do it.”

CHAPTER TWENTY-TWO

SOME GRANDMOTHERS KNIT. Others bake.

Mine's a one-woman mafioso who takes no gruff and holds her granddaughter hostage.

Maxine whips the rope in a few loopy-loops, and with a battle cry, flings it up as hard as she can.

For the tenth time, it hits mid-way up the fence, then falls to the grass with more grace then it arose. "Well." She dusts off her black pants. "I really thought that watching *Wonder Woman* ten times would've prepared me more." She hangs her blonde head, which somehow still sports buoyant, perfect hair. "I give up. I guess I'll never get the proof I need that Gus McGilli*cruddy* is a lying, cheating, sign-stealing villain. He'll win the election, and I'll lose. Never mind that he broke the law and city regulations."

"You're attempting to break into his property."

"Have you ever heard of Malala? Rosa Parks? Susan B. Anthony? We are women who will bravely expose injustice and shine a light on the truth."

I step to the gate and pull down on the padlock. The thing springs open with a *clink*! "You were saying, Susan B.?"

"Hmph. Well, I guess if you want to do it the easy way, sure."

I push my grandmother into the backyard. "Let's make this quick. I want to be back for Daisy's bedtime."

"If you're not careful, you're going to bond with that girl like glue on a falsie eyelash." Maxine steps over a water hose as her feet swish through grass. "There's certainly nothing wrong with getting attached to the little pixie. Lord knows I have."

I smack another bug that just took a stinging bite from my glistening elbow and follow Maxine toward the garage. "I'm not getting attached. What I'm doing right now apparently is trespassing onto someone's private property and potentially ruining my career."

Maxine hesitates at a hazy window, eyes full of tears. "Chip off the old block. You make me so proud." She then presses her trim nose to the glass, her pen light shining. "I knew it! Right there. See?" The white of a French manicured nail taps the window like an angry bird. "There is one of my signs. That's it. I'm going in."

"No. Maxine, we can't—"

"It's unlocked." She flings the door wide open. "Which means technically, I'm not breaking in."

There's a whole fleet of warning sirens roaring in my head, but I stupidly follow her inside. "Where's the light switch?" I feel along the wall for a convenient source of power.

"I got all the light you need right here." Maxine ignites a huge silver flashlight, then after rummaging in her backpack, hands me one almost as large. "Click once for dim, twice for bright. But whatever you do, don't click it four times."

"Why?"

"That's the disco ball setting." She sets hers to bright. "No self-respecting snooper should boogie her way through a trespass."

"Are you sure there aren't cameras in here?"

"Positive. McGillicuddy used to have a security service with Longhorn Security, but Gus got mad a few weeks ago and shut down the service."

"Do I want to ask how you know this?"

"You don't. But I will say Don at Longhorn really loves a good homemade chocolate pie, and his wife just flips for a gift certificate to Tina's Fancy Nails."

The more I ask, the more I incriminate myself. "Let's speed this up, please."

"So maybe I *should* turn on the disco ball setting?" Maxine scoots her way between a tall stack of boxes, tripping over something that clangs loud enough to alert the entire county. "Watch out for this chain saw."

Oh, gosh. The building is weaponized. "Don't get any ideas about using that thing."

"Wouldn't dare." She scoots away before I call her on the bald lie. "Let's see what we have in here. Probably more of my signs." She lifts the lid on a box while I uselessly watch the front windows as if someone's going to walk by any moment. "Nothing much in here. Some clothes, a few blankets. How's that search going over there, Katie?"

"Good."

"Could you move on from your post at the door, so your answer is more convincing?"

"Fine." I sigh gustily. "But only because I want to get this over with." I search through another stack of boxes, finding nothing but tuna and bottled water. "What do you think he's doing with all this food?"

"No idea. Probably the leftover remains of reluctant voters he's kidnapped."

I move on to a closet, grateful when I find the door locked.

When I tell Maxine as much, she points that flashlight right at my face as she shakes her head. "Pick it, Houdini."

"I'm retired."

"Come on. Do a solid for your dear granny. For all we know, that's where Gus is keeping my signs."

"No. I'm walking the straight and narrow. Look elsewhere."

"Katie, get a load of that trunk behind you."

I turn to find a giant metal chest, one that looks like it was brought to shore by the Dread Pirate Roberts.

"Open it," Maxine commands.

"You open it."

She bumps me out of the way with her bony hip and lifts the creaky lid. "Well, well. What do we have here?" She pulls out one of her signs, shining a light on her cardboard face. "One more of my signs. That thieving jerk! That scoundrel of the stars and stripes! That villain of votes. That mongrel of—"

Voices from outside filter into the building, and the hair on the back of my neck stands on end. "Let's get out of here," I whisper. Then I rush through a quick prayer.

Dear God above, forgive me for my trespassing sins. Maxine is my downfall, and I have a feeling you understand. Had she been in the Garden of Eden, she would've grabbed apples on the first day and made everyone cobblers. With ice cream. Please get us out of this. Amen.

"Oh, Gus, I believe in your vision too."

Maxine and I swap a look at the feminine voice beyond the door.

"We need to get out," I whisper. "Now."

"Let's hide. We can't get out the door."

"Let me show you my latest work," Gus McGillicuddy loudly proclaims. "Get on in here, little darlin'."

Oh, geez. Oh, no. "There's no hiding here. The window!" I run to the back and raise the sash with a whoosh. "Maxine, now."

"I want to confront that rat scoundrel."

"Do it on your own property." Grabbing her hand, I lead her to our exit. "Jump."

She looks down. "That sure is a long way. I might hurt myself."

"Better to be hurt here than in prison."

"And down we go." She swings a leg over and leaps as I hear the door rattling. "Owwww! Oomph. Oh! Just got a rose bush in the tookus."

Climbing onto the sill, I hoist a leg over just like my grandmother.

Right as Gus and his lady friend step inside.

"Hey!" I hear him call as I flail all the way over, falling toward the ground, with no time to plan a proper landing.

Pain ricochets through my body as I crash and, for a moment, spots float before my eyes while I rush to rise.

"Who's out there?" Gus bellows.

"Run!" Maxine reaches for my hand, and away we go.

"Who is it, sweetie?" I hear the woman ask. "Should I call the police?"

Oh, crap. Oh, shoot. My legs ache as I run faster than my legs want to carry me. If my old high school P.E. teacher, Coach Nelson, could see me now, she'd hand me a medal. Then hand me over to the cops.

My feet slip in something squishy, and down I go again, barely catching my fall with my stinging hands. "Ewww."

"See?" Maxine calls behind me. "Rude, disgusting cows!"

I hear the rev of a motorcycle in the distance. Followed by one more. Then a whole collection of engines. "What in the world?"

"Oops." Maxine runs beside me, gracefully leaping over a hollowed-out log. "Sounds like the motorcycle meeting was at Gus's. Can the town trust someone who doesn't have an updated website?"

"We'll never outrun them."

"Maybe not. But we're sure gonna try."

My breath comes out in loud, violent bursts, and my chest burns with the effort. I'm out of shape and running out of time. "James and Millie are gonna kill us."

"Not if Gus gets to us first. Pick it up, Sweet Pea. I'm too young to die!"

The agonizing seconds turn into minutes. Minutes turn into...more minutes. Gus and his motorcycle gang get closer, and their lights illuminate the field not too far away.

"There's a hay bale at three o'clock." Maxine veers toward the left. "Dive for it and hide!"

I follow her instructions, though all I want to do is stop this cardio-fueled insanity and give myself up. I want a bottle of water, a chance to beg for immunity, and I seriously need to pee.

We make it to a hay bale.

Just as two fat cows do the same.

"Hey, move along." Maxine shoos the beasts. "Shouldn't you dudes be sleeping?" She peeks under one of the cows. "Oh, pardon me, miss. But please, do move on." She jerks her head toward the direction of Gus. "Look, Ms. Holstein, I'm asking you woman to woman to move away and find another bale of hay."

The cow just blinks, oblivious to any of the commotion.

"If you help us," Maxine continues, as if this cow understands one word of her rushed plea, "I'll come back here and purchase you, and you'll never have to hear the word 'hamburger' the rest of your days."

The cow takes a bite of hay, wallowing it between her big, slobbery lips. Then slowly ambles away.

"That's a smart cow," Maxine whispers.

"Maybe she should be mayor."

I take a small peek from our hiding spot and see Gus and five mean-looking motorcycle riders. Gus points to the wandering cow and holds his position. Four men and one woman all gawk about, the moonlight bouncing off their helmets.

"They're going," Maxine says near my ear, her staccato breaths matching mine. "Thank you, Lord, they're headed the other direction."

I'm afraid to move. I'm also afraid *not* to move. "Let's get out of here."

"Who was that woman with Gus?"

"I don't care."

"She could be his co-conspirator in sign-stealing. Gus's moral aptitude is pertinent to this election."

I wave my arm to encompass the field we're trespassing on. "I probably wouldn't poke the morality bear, Maxine."

"This was justified! He's stolen my signs. And God knows what he's doing with all that food."

I leave Maxine talking to herself and walk in the opposite direction of the house, further into the field. There has to be a road here somewhere.

"Wait for me!" She rushes up beside me, only to hand me a small bottle of water from her backpack. "Thank God we're safe, eh?"

We cover no more than fifty feet of ground when I hear the motorcycle rumbling again. "You just had to jinx it. This way!" A warm raindrop plops on my cheek, and I swipe it away. No, way, Mother Nature. Now is *not* the time.

But the weather has other ideas and cares not one whit for our plight. The sprinkles come in earnest. As does the roar of bikes.

"Hang a left!" I glance behind me, and my heart ceases to beat as I realize Maxine is no longer with me. "Maxine? Maxine!" I scan the dark field for a sign of her. "Did the turkeys get you?" Maybe her conscience got a hold of her instead, and she doubled back to come clean to Mr. McGillicuddy. "Maxine!"

Nothing. Just the bright lights of five motorcycles drawing near and the wild warbly gobbles of a security team of turkeys.

The sky decides to ramp up the drama and shoots a bolt of lightning cracking in the distance. Mottled clouds sweep over the moon and empty barrels of water, as the storm begins in earnest. The rain pelts my face in stinging slaps, and soon I can hardly see.

"Maxine!" I yell one more time.

But it's no use. She's not responding.

Getting my bearings as best I can, I aim my body toward the direction I believe most likely to lead me to our vehicle and take off in a sprint. My feet struggle to keep me upright, and my rain-soaked clothes slow me down. Yet I run as if my life depends on it.

Because I think it just might.

"Over there!" I hear someone yell, and a spotlight flashes to my left.

Lightning sparks on my right.

This is the last crazy adventure I ever go on with Maxine.

Daring a look back, I try to dislodge the water clinging to my lashes, desperate to see the status of my pursuers. And my grandmother.

I can't make out either.

Yanking out my small flashlight, I stick it between my teeth and pick up my pace.

But it's no use.

The calvary is gaining on me, I'm so wet I can hardly move, and I have no idea where I am.

Lifting my hands in the air, I wave them in surrender.

Then slip and fall once again.

In mud.

So much mud.

Oh, my gosh. What is that smell? Is this...? Did I just land in a —

Oink. Oink.

A pigsty.

Legs scrambling, arms flailing, I do my best to shove myself upright, but fall right back down again. My face goes under, and mud shoots up my nose. "Gross! Oh, my gosh. This can't be how it ends. Help!"

Vroom! Vroom!

Engines rev, and I know I'm seconds away from being taken down with vigilante justice.

Suddenly light breaks through my opposite side, and I jump to get out of the way.

An engine revs again, but this time, not from a motorcycle.

It's a mud-slinging four-wheeler.

It's Maxine.

"Jump on!" I hear her yell above the rain, as she slams on the brakes.

But the brakes and centrifugal force are no match for the flash-flooded earth and the pit of mud. Pigs squeal as they scramble the opposite direction of the crazy woman. The ATV slides sideways, and even in the dark of night, I see my grandmother's eyes wide as saucers and filled with stark terror.

"Whooaaaa, Nelly!" she cries. "Whoa, I say!"

But 500-pound four-wheelers don't respond to horse commands, and the scientific law of Mad Maxine says a crazy grandma in motion will stay in motion.

I pray to the Almighty as her body flings off the runaway machine and into the giant pond of mud.

Ginger 2.0 drives itself right into a nearby tree and crashes head-first as if she'd rather die than continue life as a mad woman's getaway ride.

"Ouch." Maxine raises up, spitting mud and calling out injured body parts. "My tushie hurts."

The fight has gone out of me, and when Gus McGillicuddy drives right to our spot, lights shining on us like the criminals we are, I don't give so much as a fight.

"Well, well." Mr. McGillicuddy climbs off his bike, the rain pinging like bullets on his helmet. "What do we have here?"

CHAPTER TWENTY-THREE

"I SAID I WAS SORRY."

It's three a.m., and I'm covered in mud and disgrace. I sit in the holding cell at the In Between jail and ignore my grandmother. "Kindly don't speak to me for a while."

She releases a long-suffering exhale tinged with a note of regret. "For how long?"

I cross my arms over my indignant chest that's caked in mud, and only God knows what other animal byproducts. "A half hour."

"That's an awfully long time."

"I once rode on the back bumper of a watermelon truck for a half-hour," a scantily clad woman chimes in. She's our only other cellmate, and given the purple bedhead and Vodka perfume, she's apparently had quite a night as well.

"I'm not a fan of watermelon," Maxine says. "Now I'd ride on the bumper of a peach truck. Definitely a cantaloupe caravan. Oranges are a maybe."

"Oranges are good," the woman says. "I get snooty when it comes to anything carrying vegetables."

"Turnip trucks can just roll on by, thank you very much."

"Amen, girl," Purple Hair says. "You get me."

"Yes." Maxine studies the three grimy walls of our cell. "That probably surprises no one."

"What are y'all in here for?" Purple Hair teeters toward us on bare feet, her body swaying as if moving to a jazz rhythm only she can hear.

"Protecting democracy." Maxine picks a leaf off her blouse. "That's what we did."

The woman nods. "I once got arrested for not moving during a protest for pay equality."

"Yes, ma'am." My grandmother's head bobs like it's the closing minutes of one of James's sermons. "We principled people gotta stick together."

I lean past Maxine, disgust and fatigue making my voice sharp as a cheese grater. "My dear granny here talked me into breaking and entering someone's property to snoop around."

Purple Hair's mouth forms an O. "That sounds a little illegal. Did you have a higher moral purpose for the betterment of mankind?"

"Yes!" Maxine's hands shoot to the ceiling in testimony. "We certainly did."

Our friend moves closer, and her scent could peel off wallpaper. "When I peacefully protested last month, I got chased away by some jerks with pepper spray."

"What a coincidence." Flicking off a grass wad from my shorts, I glare at Maxine. "Our finale also included a chase scene with pigs."

"You keep fighting the good fight," she tells us. "We cannot ever let up on the battle for a greater world."

Maxine hugs the stinky woman, her own hair a bird's nest of twigs and mud, and her clothes probably smelling like she recently rose from the swamp. "Thank you for your support. I was sitting here doubting my actions, but you've confirmed I did what needed to be done."

Oh, Lord, help us.

"The right way is often the hard way," our fellow activist says.

"Amen to that." Maxine's fingers blot at the tears filling her eyes. "What did you say you were in here for? Another protest?"

"Yeah." She runs her fingers over her head and tries to right the wrongs of her hair. "I went to my boyfriend's apartment and protested the fact that he was cheating on me with another woman."

Maxine scoots closer to her sister in distress. "Did you hold up a sign and conduct a sit-in?"

"No. I held up my fists and conducted a few punches."

"Dayberry and Scott."

I leap from the bench at the gruff voice, loving the way my last name ricochets off the walls, hoping it's the Morse code that spells freedom. "Here!" Standing front and center, I watch a hefty cop approach. He looks perturbed to be upright at this unholy hour. "Mr. Gus McGillicuddy has dropped all the charges."

"He has?" I clutch the bars with my filthy fingers.

Maxine rises from her seat, leaving the woman who has temporarily replaced me as her best friend. "But why would McGillicuddy do that?"

The officer shrugs, a dismissive roll of the head and shoulders that ends with a brain-touching eye-roll. "I forgot to ask him. Would you like to stay an extra twenty-four hours while I get his response and work up a full analysis?"

"No!" I yell. "We do not. Happy to leave. Thanks for the service. We'll leave a great review on Yelp."

"I hope you've learned your lesson." His badge reads Officer Tyrone Glee, and I'm pretty sure we're making him anything but happy. "Because I get the feeling McGillicuddy won't be so forgiving if there's a next time." He takes out a keyring that clinks and clanks like a tambourine, then unlocks the door. "Out you go."

"Best of luck!" Purple Hair yells behind us. "I won't forget you."

Maxine holds up her fist in solidarity before I yank her away, dragging her with me down the hall.

Our walk of shame is short, and soon we're escorted into the lobby.

Where four people wait for us, each one looking more put out than the other.

"Hi, Sam." Maxine fluffs her hair, and a small pinecone falls to the floor. "Sugar, what are you doing up so late? We didn't call anyone." She slides me a look. "Katie here wouldn't let me."

Millie looks like she was pulled from her bed, wearing sweats and a rare expression of disgust. James bites his lip on what I'm almost certain is a laugh.

Then there's Charlie.

My Charlie, who gets mad about as often as it snows. Who never raises his voice. Who shrugs off offenses like I shrug off exercise.

That version of my Charlie apparently stayed home.

If he were a cartoon, there would be steam coming from his ears. Rockets exploding from his head. Loud, locomotive horns blasting from his lips.

Instead, he just stares. Eyes lit like a roaring campfire. "Hello, Katie."

"Where's Daisy?" I ask, panicked they might've brought her.

"Amy's watching her at home," Millie says. "You can thank her later."

What a comfortable conversation that will be.

"It was my fault," Maxine says. "Things got out of hand."

"Things always get out of hand." Sam approaches his wife and shakes his head. He looks so disappointed, even his overalls droop. "What in tarnation got into you? I told you that McGillicuddy guy wouldn't steal your cotton-pickin' signs."

"But he did!" Maxine points a grimy hand toward me. "We saw them."

"We saw two." I step away from my grandma. I'm through being her accomplice for tonight. "Can we just go home?" I look between my parents and Charlie, not sure who I'd rather ride home with. Both are bound to chew me out good. "Who called you all?"

"McGillicuddy himself." James pulls his keys out of his pocket and begins a slow walk toward the exit. "Told me to tell you to consider the dropped charges his wedding gift."

"How...nice." I chance a look at Charlie, who's walking three paces behind me.

"Yeah," Charlie says. "McGillicuddy wished us a happy marriage." He holds open the door and the sweltering night air smells like relief and liberty. "Also mentioned he'd be gifting us some bacon." He unclenches his pretty, white teeth. "Said he got the impression you might be a fan."

CHAPTER TWENTY-FOUR

THE NEXT NIGHT, I decide to play it more low key and do something that won't end with my possible incarceration.

I decide to cook dinner for Charlie.

With James and Millie at a church event and Daisy spending a few hours playing with Sadie at Charlie's mom's, we've got the house to ourselves. And boy, do we need it.

This morning after a lengthy discussion over waffles, I finally cinched James and Millie's forgiveness. Though I get the feeling they're now afraid to let Maxine and me out of their sight. Since Charlie was working from home and not in the mood to talk, I spent the rest of the day with Daisy, taking her for a mani/pedi and introducing her to Micky's Diner. She was duly impressed with both stops.

Headlights shine on the living room wall, and I suddenly feel nauseous as Charlie parks his car. What if I went too far last night? What if it made him realize I'm not the sophisticated, completely stable wife he needs?

And what if he agreed to dinner tonight because he wants to break up? Even without my rap sheet, it's almost like I've thought our demise was eventually inevitable. Like things were too good, and I knew at some point the rug would be pulled out from under me.

Painful seconds later, Charlie raps on the door.

Even his knock sounds ticked off.

Wearing my hair down in waves the way he likes it and a wrap dress that hugs all the right curves, I nervously open the door. "Hey there."

"Hi." Charlie steps inside the foyer without so much as a kiss to my cheek. His love language is touch and doughnuts, so I know he's very upset.

"Want something to drink?"

"Can I admit you make me *want* to drink?"

"Sam says you'll eventually get used to it." I swallow against the knot in my throat and try to ignore the not-so-romantic sounds of the puppy yipping from his kennel. "If you want to get used to it."

"Of course, I want to." He shoves a hand through his hair. "I mean, I don't want to ever get used to picking you up from jail or finding out you were involved in some harebrained scheme that could've killed you."

I retreat into the living room and stand there like a guest in my own house, hands in the pockets of my dress, wishing Charlie would simply laugh this off, and we could go on with our lives.

But he won't. Because I have totally screwed up. "Would you like me to explain?"

His jaw clenched, Charlie lowers himself to the couch and regards me with unbanked anger. "You've been feeling cagey and anxious, and you love your grandmother dearly. So when she asked you to go on one of her ridiculous, not-quite-legal spying campaigns, you agreed. It gave you the adrenaline-induced thrill you were looking for, and since you were helping, you didn't have to feel guilty saying no to Maxine. Do I have it about right?"

I swallow hard and study a piece of dog hair rolling across the floor like a small tumbleweed escaping the tension. "I didn't know she had a four-wheeler."

"Oh, that makes it all okay." Charlie jumps to his feet and paces the length of the room. Twice.

"I said, I'm sorry." Many times. I've called, I've said it in person. I've texted. I even tried to find a singing telegram to show up at his door, but Tommy Tunes is slowing down at eighty-six and had to work a funeral. "Please don't be mad."

"Katie, you went on some guy's property out in the sticks, and then you broke into his garage."

"It was open. We didn't break-in." If looks could melt, I'd be a puddle on the floor. "Okay. You're right. It was stupid."

"And illegal."

"That too."

"We're about to get married."

"Also true."

"But if McGillicuddy hadn't dropped the charges, we might have had to cancel the wedding—again. Because you would've been in jail."

"I think James would've agreed to still perform the ceremony."

"Just what I want—a bride in prison stripes."

Images of my mom in her prison uniform spring to mind, and I inhale deeply trying to push the vision away. *I'm not her. I don't have to be like her.* "It was inconsiderate of me and a dumb risk." Though let the record show, I didn't break any body parts this time. "Maxine was convinced McGillacuddy had stolen her signs—which is also illegal. And so we went to check it out. We were just going to peek in the window of his garage, but the door was open. And one thing led to another."

With his head back and contemplating the intricacies of the ceiling, Charlie sighs. Again. "I don't know what to say."

I walk to him and lightly link my pinkie finger with his. "Say you'll stop being angry, and we can forget this ever happened?"

"I don't want our future children to ever hear of this."

Because he doesn't want them to think their mother is jail material. "Okay."

"And promise me you won't step foot on that guy's property again."

"I promise."

"We don't even know this Gus guy. He could be the shoot first, ask later type."

"I'll keep my distance."

"We're leaving In Between on Friday, boarding a plane, flying to

Mexico, and getting married." He waits for my nod of agreement. "I don't want anything to get in the way of that—not one more delay. I've been patient, Katie."

"You have."

"If I was into conspiracy theories, I might think you had subconsciously tried to sabotage this wedding date."

"Nope. Not me."

"Have you packed yet?"

"I've been too busy breaking and entering."

Charlie does not like this answer. "Do you need help?"

"Breaking and entering?"

"Packing."

"No. I'll get to it."

"We leave in three days." He pulls me to him and scrutinizes me like a lab specimen. "Just once when I say that, it would be cool if you had some reaction besides stark fear and slight revulsion."

"I am excited. You know me and flying." A misbehaving plane was what brought Charlie and me together four years ago. You'd think I'd put more faith in those cloud-hopping vessels of terror.

But no.

"I love you, Katie, but sometimes I worry that you're going to panic at the altar and do the runaway bride thing."

"You know I try to avoid running." Especially near pigsties.

Charlie's arms slip around me, and I can all but feel some of his anger fall away. "When that wedding march begins, can you assure me you'll be there to walk down the aisle and say 'I do'?"

I raise up on tiptoe and kiss his chin. "I do."

He stares down at me, a man trying to figure out the loco woman in his arms and whether he can take me at my word. "All right then."

I smile and lean in for a real kiss. "Okay?"

His lips brush mine as he complies. "We're okay." He pulls me against him, and as his mouth takes over, some of my anxiety lessens. When I'm in his arms, everything feels so right—as it always has. I just panic when I think about the rest of it—the hard work of being his wife, the scary travails of co-managing a home, the potential of being his children's mother.

Charlie nuzzles the space behind my ear. "Is something burning?"

"My deep and abiding love for you?"

His head lifts like a retriever on point. "No." He sniffs the air. "I smell smoke."

"The pork chops!" I limp into the kitchen, the scent an acrid fog as dark as my despair. Smoke slips from the oven in light puffs as I grab two hot pads and fling open the oven door. Coughs wrack my lungs, and I blink against the burning haze pressing against my eyes.

Charlie runs in behind me and raises the window over the sink. He opens the back door, not even bothering with the screen.

With my paisley mitts, I reach inside the oven and extract the baking dish that holds the charred, shrunken skeletons of the pork chops. Or what were pork chops. Charlie will have to take my word that that's what they were because it would take a forensic scientist to identify these ashy remains.

The heat from the nuked casserole dish radiates through Millie's discount store oven mitts, and I all but throw the pan on the stove. Tucking my nose into the crook of my arm, I sputter and gasp for air. While I try to resuscitate myself, Charlie grabs a towel and runs the pork chops outside as if the dish is a game-winning football he's carrying over the goal line.

But there are only losers here—that would be me and this dinner.

And my domestic skills. All dead on arrival.

Charlie returns to the kitchen as I'm lighting the second of Millie's lavender-infused candles. "So...pizza?" He holds up his phone. "I can call."

I slowly nod, turning on the vent over the oven, grateful I didn't set anything else on fire.

"You okay?" He pulls out a chair at the breakfast nook and gestures for me to sit. "Katie?"

"I'm fine." Flopping into the chair, I let my chin fall pitifully into my propped hand. "All I do is serve you pizza. Pizza or Chinese food."

"But those are my favorites."

"Your mom says you love pork chops and homemade mac-n-cheese."

"I do. But you don't have to make them for me."

"Yes, I do."

His head tilts as he studies me a moment. "Where did you get this idea?"

"At my bridal shower. All the ladies were doling out marriage advice like parade candy. Every single one of them said cooking was important. Your mom went on and on about how you'd always sneak home for her cooking, and you'd pick her food over a restaurant any day." I sniffle indelicately, then wince at the bitter smell still holding the kitchen hostage. "I didn't know that."

Charlie scoots his chair closer until his knees bump mine. "I'm not marrying you for your cooking skills."

That is no comfort. None at all. "I was raised with a mom who thought the kitchen was where the microwave lived. Everything we had came from a box or can. I have no natural skill with cooking, as I demonstrated tonight. All this time, I didn't think you minded, but then I heard your mom, and she acted like she was imparting the code to keeping a Benson man happy."

He leans in and kisses my flushed cheek. "You make me happy. You're my code to making this Benson man content."

"You'll get tired of takeout and sandwiches."

"You probably will too. So maybe we learn to cook together."

"In all our spare time."

He takes a gusty inhale, and I wonder what thoughts travel through that well-developed brain of his. "Things are crazy right now, and there's no foreseeable slowing down in sight. But—"

"Do you ever wish you weren't marrying an actress?"

Charlie hard blinks at the topic change. "What?"

"My job—it's not conducive to a normal life."

"I guess mine isn't right now, either." His thumb brushes a slow arc across my cheek. "Is this another worry of yours?"

"One of them, yes."

Charlie clears his throat, his eyes a little red from the smoke. "How many worries would you say there are?"

"I don't know. I stopped counting."

"After what number?"

I bite my lip, wishing I could swallow my every insecurity. "Four hundred and seven."

"Oh." He straightens and bobs his head in happy-go-lucky acceptance. "Is that all?"

My laugh is small and breathy. "Don't you have any reservations?"

"Reservations? No. Concerns, sure."

"Why haven't you talked about them?"

"I think everyone getting married or in a relationship has concerns."

"How many concerns would you say there are?" I watch him smile, loving the way it lifts his face and dimples his left cheek. How it backlights his gray eyes like a photo filter that makes him even more devastatingly handsome.

Charlie takes my hand, lifting it to his mouth and pressing a kiss to my palm, his gaze steady on mine. "Like you, I worry about not being home enough. I worry that my travel in the last few years has put too much distance between us, and that's why you're hesitant to get married."

"I'm not hesitant."

"You've canceled our wedding date twice."

"Postponed."

"Is there a difference?"

"You said you understood."

"I guess I do, but that doesn't mean that I liked it. I've worried that we've grown apart, and you felt you were marrying someone you didn't know as well as you should."

"I know you, Charlie Benson."

He laces his fingers with mine and holds our hands to his heart. "If you knew me, you'd know that I don't care if you can cook or if I can cook or if we order pizza every other night."

"I'm not sure I know how to be a wife. My extensive time watching soap operas growing up hasn't prepared me like I thought it would."

"You haven't slapped me one time."

"You haven't had a love child with my long-lost twin sister who's secretly a serial killer."

"She doesn't hold a candle to you."

I glance over my shoulder at the stove, still burping pork fumes. "She can probably manage one simple dinner."

"So can we." He rises, pulling me up with him. "Let's go to the Burger Barn, and I'll buy you a cheeseburger-shake combo."

"It is half-off night."

"Babe, you're always worth full price."

CHAPTER TWENTY-FIVE

The In Between town hall is straight out of Stars Hollow.

That is if the *Gilmore Girls* town hall burned to the ground, and Mayor Taylor forced the elementary school to open the air conditioning-deprived cafeteria that smells like paste and pickles.

"I can't believe Mother's still going through with this." Millie scans the room Wednesday night for a seat. Even though we're early, the place is already packed.

I put down my digital script of *Piloting Dreams* and hand Daisy a box of raisins. "She said she has nothing to hide."

"I've shared a bathroom with her on vacation." James shivers. "I beg to differ."

"There she is!" Ms. Hall, my former drama teacher, glides toward me, a vision in an orange caftan and matching turban. "Katie, come here and give your favorite teacher a hug."

I drop Daisy's hand long enough to embrace Ms. Hall, careful not to inhale too much of the cloud of patchouli that spins around her. "Glad you could make it tonight."

Jeremy appears beside her, fanning himself with a cardboard face of Maxine. "We're both on Team Maxine. Though I'm sweating through my shirt and not going to stay long if they don't provide snacks."

“Debates are definitely better with munchies.” Ms. Hall looks down at Daisy, who’s now clutching my hand and hiding behind my legs. “Who’s this sweet girl?”

“This is Daisy. She’s staying with me a while.”

“Aren’t you adorable?” Ms. Hall digs into her purse and produces a lollipop. “There’s plenty more where this came from. After the last debate went for three hours, I came prepared.”

“Let’s go find our seats.” Jeremy waves his goodbye, then tugs his co-worker down a large aisle.

“Hey, kids.” Sam ambles toward us, wearing his nicest overalls. He looks as tired as I feel. “I’ve got you some seats saved.” He leans down and tweaks Daisy’s nose, eliciting a giggle.

“Hola, mi gente favorita.” Maxine joins us, her hands in nonstop motion passing out fans and pens. “Did you catch that? I’m learning the old Español. Amy’s helping me.”

“I think that’s a great idea,” I say.

“It keeps my mind fresh and helps me connect better with some of my voters.” The faintest line forms between Maxine’s eyebrows. “Who knew it was such an easy language to learn?”

Sam nudges me with his shoulder. “Yesterday, she greeted a woman at the diner in Spanish.”

“I’m impressed.”

“She accidentally told the woman her husband looked like a boll weevil.”

Maxine’s hand shoots in the air and gives an enthusiastic wave. “There’s Frances. Interesting that her husband is sitting a row behind her. He doesn’t look very happy.”

I find them in the crowd and see Joey reclined in the seat behind Frances, scrolling on his phone while Frances stares straight ahead. “I’m not sure what’s going on with them.”

“Nothing a landslide mayoral victory won’t cure.” Maxine straightens her stars and stripes bow tie. She wears navy slacks, red sparkly heels, and a crisp white shirt. While it’s not what I’d wear to a formal debate, the outfit will come in handy if she’s suddenly asked to join the U.S.O.

“Look alive.” Maxine claps twice. “Here comes Pearl Shipley. She’s moderating again. During last month's debate, she blatantly flirted with Gus and mispronounced my name."

Millie rolls her eyes. "Mom, I don't think saying 'bless you' when Gus sneezed was flirtatious."

"There was a wanton invitation in her eyes. No couth at all." Maxine unbuttons the top three buttons of her blouse and extracts a small container. "Breath mint?"

"No." I pull back Daisy's outstretched hand. "But thanks."

"Maxine Dooberry." Pearl Shipley pushes the GO button on her wheelchair and zips toward us. Her voluminous black dress swallows the thin woman, but matches her large, obsidian hair. Gold filigree peacocks hold foggy-lensed bifocals dangling from the chain around her webby neck. Pearl's shrewd brown eyes narrow on my grandmother. "Gus has requested to speak to you before the debate."

"My name is Maxine *Dayberry*, and you darn well know it, Pearl Shipley. We've sat five chairs apart on bridge nights at the senior center for ten years, so don't act like you hardly recognize me."

Pearl lifts her pointed nose at this. "Gus waits for you in the kitchen. You two have five minutes before I get this party started. Don't be late."

Pearl whirrs away, and Maxine grips my arm like it's the only thing holding her upright. "Go with me. I can't face him alone."

"Come on, Daisy." James smiles at the girl. "Why don't you pick a seat and show me that coloring book." He holds out a hand, and I watch as Daisy stares at it a moment, indecision on her face. Then, without looking to me for the okay, she gently places her hand in his and follows my parents and Sam into the crowd.

Maxine snaps her fingers in my face. "Earth to Katie. Did you hear me? How can I face Gus?"

"What choice do you have? Go clear the air so he won't do it in front of two hundred people."

"He's up to something. And it's absolutely no good."

If anyone would recognize 'no good,' it's Maxine.

We weave through the throng of people, and Maxine waves and speaks to as many as she can. She passes out her card and throws out campaign promises.

"Vote for me, and I'll get rid of grocery self-checkout."

"Vote for me, and I'll put an end to that speed trap by the donut shop."

"Vote for me, and I'll make sure this year's Santa has a real beard!"

The kitchen area of the cafeteria could double as a crime scene. It's dark, it smells like something's rotting, and a lone figure stands in the glow of an overhead security light.

"Is that you, Gussy McGillicuddy?" Maxine boldly walks toward the man as he steps out of the shadows. "If you asked me to do bodily harm, I brought a witness."

The man wears a leather jacket over those tatted arms and scowls like a clandestine rendezvous in the school kitchen might not be his idea of a good time either. "Well, well. If it isn't my two interlopers. How was jail? Did you stay long enough to get the lunch special?"

"You know very well we didn't." Maxine stands toe to toe with her opponent and peers right up at him. "Though I guess I do need to thank you for not pressing charges."

He doesn't even blink. "I guess I need to thank you, ladies, for not stealing my pigs."

"We wouldn't dare," Maxine says, knowing full well there's very little she *wouldn't* dare.

"No, you were there to take campaign secrets."

I peek around my grandmother's back. "I want you to know none of that was my idea. I do not break into people's property."

He gives a mirthless laugh, his large nostrils flaring like wings on a plane. "You did two days ago."

"Oh, leave Katie alone, McGillicuddy. She's innocent in all this."

"My pigs would tell another story."

"Your pigs have no sense of personal space," I mutter.

"Why didn't you press charges?" Maxine asks. "Not that I'm encouraging you to reconsider. In fact, I'd say it was a very generous thing to do. I'd have done the same myself."

"Would you?"

"Yep, would've turned the other cheek, looked the other way, kept it on the down-low. I also would've offered refreshments, but that's just the hospitable Southern lady in me."

I watch anger flash in Gus McGillicuddy's eyes and worry he's about to change his mind about those charges. "Mr. McGillicuddy," I say over the hum of an industrial refrigerator. "Thank you. We're very grateful."

"And suspicious." Maxine's left brow arches as much as her fillers will allow. "You had some interesting things in that garage of yours."

"Not that we looked," I sputter. "I definitely didn't look. You could've had cleavers and semi-automatics in there, and I wouldn't have noticed."

He slides me an annoyed glance. "Maxine Dayberry, I highly suggest you forget whatever you saw in that garage. If I hear that you've discussed my personal belongings with one single citizen, I will have you two in cuffs quicker than you can say, Oscar Meyer." He pulls himself up even taller and looms over the both of us. "Do I make myself clear?"

I can see the wheels turning in my grandmother's mind, and it's a scary sight. "Super clear," I say in a rush. "Clear as glass. Crystal clear. Windex clear. The clearest."

His shrewd eyes hone in on Maxine, not certain he can trust her. "Don't test me on this, Dayberry." He points at her with a finger big enough to circle a throat. "You won't like the results."

"Alrighty, candidates." Pearl Shipley wheels to the kitchen door, her thick bifocals magnifying her marina green eyeshadow. "Let's get to shaking." Her blue fingernails tap her sundial-sized watch. "Time to take your places."

"Are we good here?" Maxine asks Gus.

"I'd say everything else not discussed is fair game."

Maxine's smile is sheer devilry. "I was hoping you'd say that."

CHAPTER TWENTY-SIX

PEARL DRIVES her wheelchair to the freestanding microphone while I take my seat between Daisy and James. The brave mic sits in the middle of the stage, with podiums on either side labeled with the respective candidate's name. Maxine's name placard has a definite sparkle to it, and I wonder if she snuck in early to jazz it up with her extensive craft supply. That woman keeps glitter in her purse like most women store tissues.

"Good evening, folks. I'd like to welcome you to the second debate for the position of In Between mayor. In one corner, we have Gus McGillicuddy, five-year resident of In Between and formerly of California." Pearl waits for the polite claps to subside. "He spent twenty years in the Marines before retiring. His first book of poems titled *Nothing Rhymes with Afghanistan* was published by HarperCollins and came out last year."

James and I swap a look over Daisy's head. *Poetry?*

Pearl adjusts her glasses, her breathing sounding like amplified, harsh rasps. "Mrs. Maxine Simmons Dingleberry is a mother, grandmother, and last place contestant in Mrs. Silver Texas."

"I was runner up, Pearl Shipley!"

"Dingleberry's earlier career was spent as a Vegas showgirl at the renowned Circus Circus. She loves people and has lived in In Between for all of her ninety-one years."

A strangled sound slips from Maxine's lips before she grabs her mic and bellows, "I am most certainly not ninety-one, you old bat!" She seems to remember where she is, lets her gaze sweep the crowd, then smiles. "But I'm sure when I arrive at that age in thirty years, I'll still be right here in In Between—loving life and being the competent, kind leader that I am."

Our moderator doesn't bother hiding her smirk. "First question is for Mr. McGillicuddy. Gus, tell us how you would deal with the traffic congestion..."

Thirty-five minutes later, I nearly jump out of my skin when Daisy places her hands on my legs, then crawls onto my lap. Her hair bow tickles my nose as she turns into me, wraps her arms around my neck, and rests her gossamer head on my shoulder.

What do I do here?

Worried if I make a wrong move, she'll bolt like a frightened fawn, I slowly test one hand lightly placed on her back. She snuggles in closer and sweetly pats my shoulder as if telling me "good job." I take a shallow breath and smell the goodness that is this child and her cherry lollipop.

When I look over at James, I find him watching me. Smiling. Like a proud father.

In two days, I'll drop Daisy off with the respite family Iola found to care for her while we're on our trip. What if this family is weird? Or what if they make Daisy eat her peas? What if Daisy doesn't understand and thinks she's being abandoned by me?

The closer it gets to my wedding, the more amped up I feel—full of anxiety and doubts and fears that keep me awake. Maybe I need one of Maxine's prune smoothies. I'd do anything to stop these swarming dark thoughts in my head.

"...and that's why I'll upgrade all the one-ply toilet paper in city buildings." Maxine waves to the crowd as they give her riotous applause.

"You have sixty seconds remaining on this question," Pearl tells my grandmother. "Would you like to use the rest of your allotment or surrender your time to Mr. McGillicuddy?"

Maxine grabs her microphone and bends it closer to her lips. "I'd love to use the rest of my time, Pearl. But not on this topic. Instead, I have a question for Gus." Oh, save us, Jesus. I'm pretty sure she's about to take a hot poker and nudge the devil. "I'd like to know why you've been stealing my campaign signs."

Gus McGillicuddy opens his mouth on a silent syllable, only to snap his lips shut as his brows unify in a wooly frown. "I..."

"Yes?" Maxine props a hand on her hip, somehow confident that Gus won't rat her out for how she illegally came by that information.

"First of all," Gus says, finding his voice, "I appreciate your *visit* to my campaign headquarters. It's always good to cross enemy lines and *trespass* into new territories of cooperation and camaraderie."

Oh, he's good.

"But I didn't steal your signs." Gus's eyes drop to the floor briefly. "Okay, I borrowed a couple. I wanted to see who made them so I could ask them to do mine."

"Keller Printing. The quality is stunning."

Gus concurs. "Excellent craftsmanship."

Maxine points a pink nail at Gus. "Hundreds of my signs have disappeared. Why on earth would I believe two is all your grubby mitts grabbed?"

"I'm telling you, that's all I took, and I'm sorry. I was gonna put them back, even though they were staked in my own mother's yard." He looks out into the sea of people. "She's all about voting for the woman."

An old lady stands up and raises her cane. "Fight the patriarchy!"

"Then who took the others?" Maxine demands, feeding off the energy of the murmuring crowd.

"I'm telling you, I didn't do it, and I have no idea."

"I had a Maxine Dayberry sign go missing from my yard," someone calls out.

Craning my neck with a squint, I see a bald man stand. Arthur Billings, the owner of the Burger Barn, takes off his Dekalb cap and clutches it in his hand. "I didn't think nothing of it. I don't even know who I'm voting for yet, but with as much money as Miss Maxine spends on shakes at my diner, I'd let her wallpaper my whole house in her merchandise. But I did notice my sign was gone yesterday morning."

"I'll bring by ten more." Maxine blows Arthur a kiss he does not catch. "And I'll see you and the missus on Two-For-One Tuesday."

"I had one disappear too!" calls Clarence Schmieding, owner of Tucker's Grocery.

Seven more people sound off like echoes, then soon half the hall follows in agreement.

Maxine stands before her people like she's their Evita. "Thank you, dear townspeople, for letting me know of this great travesty, this thievery of democracy, this etching away of the very fabric of—"

"Get on with it!" Someone shouts. "I gotta get home for *Real Housewives*."

She clears her throat and sends a stink eye toward the back of the room. "I want you to know that no sign stealer can dissuade me from my campaign. I'm still here, and I'm still running. So, you take one sign, I'm gonna replace it with two."

"Not in my yard!"

"Except for you, Mabel Perkins. I already know how you feel about my disrupting your begonias. Thank you all for adoring me tonight. Vote for me in September!" And with that, Maxine gathers her water bottle, her placard, and her notes. In lieu of another handshake, she gives McGillicuddy a curt nod, then steps down, becoming one with her people.

Daisy stirs in my arms, her face sweating against my skin, and her body a miniature oven. I run my hand over her hair, marveling at the softness and the girl it belongs to. This girl who shares some of my DNA—sitting here in my loose, reluctant embrace. Trusting me to keep her safe and secure, oblivious to my conflicted heart and the flurry of chaotic voters around us.

"Daisy?" I rub my hand over hers and watch her slowly awaken, her sleepy eyes fluttering. "Maxine's about to break out the T-shirt bazooka, and we want to be out of here before we suffer any head trauma."

"There's Charlie!" Daisy points down the aisle as I help her stand.

Sure enough, walking toward us like Texas's hottest bachelor is Charlie. He wears the sleeves of his oxford rolled to his forearms, and his collar unbuttoned like he long gave up on the tie.

"Hey, is it over?" He dodges a flying wad of T-shirt and joins our party of two.

"Yes. You lucky thing."

"I got here as soon as I could. I've had back-to-back meetings all day." He leans in and seals his lips to mine. This isn't any quick, polite peck, but a turn-your-knees-to-jelly, make-the-onlooking-voters-jealous kind of kiss. "I missed you."

Can't say that his lonesome feelings don't have some benefit.

He smiles into my lips. "This is where you say you missed me too."

I pat the firm muscle beneath his shirt. "Always."

"Charlie?" Daisy peers up and watches Charlie with an adoration reserved for princes and pop stars.

"Hey, sweet girl." He opens his arms, and Daisy jumps into them, swooping her up. He presses a kiss to the top of her head like it's the most natural thing, an automatic gesture born of an instinct I don't seem to have. Then again, he wasn't raised by wolves like Haven and me. "I've missed you too."

"Maxine has lots of ideas," Daisy says. "They put me to sleep."

I nod. "We all know the feeling."

She runs a small hand over the stubble on Charlie's face. "Are you going to be my uncle?"

Charlie's eyes flit to me, a challenge gleaming there. "Yes. Which makes Katie—"

"Ready to leave." I adjust my sagging purse strap on my shoulder and step into the aisle. "Let's go home and see if Millie has any cookies."

Charlie holds Daisy with one arm, and his other curves around my back. We say hello to people we pass, making our way to the exit.

"We look like a family." Daisy presses her head to Charlie's shoulder.

I continue walking, the air suddenly stifling, the room too crowded.

Tonight, I need to tell Daisy about where she's staying after we leave Friday. Iola's found a respite home that she swears is perfect. A woman with a nice pool and an even lovelier daughter.

But how do I explain this to Daisy? How do I tell her she's not coming with us to the island?

And when do I break it to her that when we return, it will be mere days before she moves to a new foster home...and Charlie and I go to New York?

Without her.

CHAPTER TWENTY-SEVEN

"Daisy will be fine," Charlie says for the third time Friday morning as he navigates the car down Harris Lane for her respite drop-off.

In the back, Daisy, who plays with a toy that deceptively looks like a tablet, is oblivious to the fact that I'm seconds away from bursting into tears, and none of this feels right. Not leaving her, not the fact that I'm a mess that I'm leaving her, not the plane we'll catch in three hours, and maybe not this rushed wedding.

The British-voiced GPS sounds especially aggressive with her directions this morning, providing updates with a frequency that borders on the neurotic.

"In a fourth mile, turn on Wyatt Street. In three hundred feet, prepare to turn on Wyatt Street. In two hundred and ninety-five feet prepare to get prepared to turn on Wyatt Street.

"We don't even know these people." I shoot a look in the backseat to make sure Daisy is still fully occupied with the beeps and dings of her talking toy.

"Iola seems to know them." Charlie makes the turn that the GPS has all but harassed us to take, only for the voice to follow up with warnings of a roundabout. "Mrs. Smartley's not going to recommend a family we can't trust."

He says that like he knows the system. As if *he's* been in foster care instead of the insulated, comfortable cocoon of the nuclear family that raised him.

I look out the window and rub a hand over my face, wishing I could wipe away my anxiety and overall terrible mood. "I'm sorry."

Charlie shoots me a quick look. "For what?"

"For all the snarky thoughts I didn't just say."

"Forgiven."

The car zips through the roundabout, and I wish it could be a time-traveling portal, throwing us into an easier, better world when we round the circle. A world where all kids have loving parents and ridiculous amounts of wholeness and self-esteem. A magical place where I don't fear screwing up the biggest job of my life. A jolly spot where the knot in my stomach unravels, making more room for nachos and less room for wedding terrors. Where I don't feel rushed onto a plane so we can sprint through our I Do's.

Instead, the road empties us into a small community called Mayflower, forty minutes outside of In Between and on the way to the Houston airport. When we arrive at 9032 Sailor Circle, it's everything I can do not to tell Charlie to keep on driving. Daisy sits at attention, looking like she's considering a tantrum. Last night when I gently told her she'd have to spend five days with new friends, it involved lots of crying. And that was just Charlie. Daisy didn't take it too well, either.

"Where are we?" Daisy's tablet slips into the floorboard as she leans forward as much as her car seat will allow.

"This is Cassie Edwards' house." Opening the car door, I act like we've just arrived at Disneyworld. "She's has a pool and a daughter your age, and she said she can't wait to do some crafts."

Daisy regards the red brick house like it's the dentist's office, and her eyes fill. "Why can't I go with you guys? Please, I'll be good. I won't kick or hit or run away. Please take me with you."

Her words could've come from my mouth twenty years ago. Bobbie Ann Parker had left me alone way too often, way too young. I'd forgotten the way I'd beg her not to go out at night, pleased with her to bring me along. *I promise I won't talk. I won't bother you. I'll take my coloring books and markers. Please, Mommy...*

Just as I open my mouth to tell Daisy I'll cancel it all and stay home, Iola Smartley walks out of the house with a woman I assume is Cassie Edwards.

"Hello." Cassie wears an easy smile and Nike running shorts that show off tan, muscular legs. Her tank top says *Love Everyone* and shows off arms that skip the light weights in the gym. "We're so glad you're going to stay with us, Daisy." A red-headed girl one Crayon taller than Daisy bounds onto the sidewalk and runs at us full force. "This is my daughter, Ava."

"Want to go play in the backyard?" Ava pops a fruit snack in her mouth and offers the rest of the bag to Daisy.

But Daisy throws herself at my legs, pressing her face into my churning stomach. *She does not want your leftovers.* But what she wants, I can't give her. "Maybe let us have a few minutes?"

Cassie nods, and power walks back inside, her calf muscles popping and her daughter skipping beside her.

A hot breeze flits across my skin as I sweep a hand over Daisy's hair. "We'll be back as soon as we can."

"That's what you said about my mommy."

Charlie squats down, his khaki shorts rising above his knees. "See this calendar on my phone?" He points to a date. "Here, we are today. And this is the date Millie and James will pick you up." His finger taps another date. "A few days later, Katie and I come back. We're going to FaceTime you every night. Mornings too, if you want."

"Just take me with you."

"We can't," I remind her as if we haven't already discussed this in triplicate. "Remember, Charlie and I are getting married. It was a plan already in the works, and we can't change it." A small fortune has already been invested or I probably would.

"Cassie and Ava are going to be so much fun," Iola adds.

"I don't want fun," Daisy cries. "I want Katie."

Iola bites back a smile. "You'll still have visits with your mom. And I'll stop by and see you."

Reaching into my purse, I pull out a small doll. "I brought you something."

Daisy reluctantly detaches and takes the toy. "Who's this?"

"You have Barbie, Ken, and now you have their niece, Daisy."

"That's not her name." Daisy brushes away tears with the back of her hand. "I've seen her on TV. This is her cousin Susie."

"Not this week, it isn't." I tug on the doll's miniature ponytail. "She has your blonde hair and pretty eyes. This cute girl is loved and safe—just like you."

"You promise me you'll be back?"

"We promise." I lean down next to Charlie. "And when we do, we'll all go get ice cream. Double scoop."

"With sprinkles?" Daisy's lip trembles, and it's the bravest tremble ever worn on a face.

"Definitely with sprinkles," Charlie says. "How about you and I go inside and look around?"

The two walk hand in hand up the flower-lined sidewalk into the house. When I hear that front door close, it sounds loud and final--like the sound of heartbreak.

"Cassie Edwards is a wonderful respite home." Iola regards me the same way she did over ten years ago as if she's not quite sure which combination of wires could detonate the bomb I'm holding. "She's been doing it for years. Keeps the kids busy and makes it fun."

"Oh, before I forget. I typed up a few tips and instructions."

Iola scans through my work. "This is five typed pages."

"Just a quick list."

"Single-spaced, eight font."

"The woman's never met Daisy. Don't you want Cassie to know she likes oatmeal for breakfast and will only wear her pink Minnie Mouse PJs if she has the matching socks?"

She consults the pages again. "Do cut up her grapes, but not her apples. Noise machine should play at a level seven, and ocean or rain sounds only."

"If Cassie wants Daisy to sleep, yes. The list is for everyone's benefit."

"I think you mean the manual." Iola laughs and tucks the papers under her arm. "I'll pass it on."

"What if Cassie doesn't watch Daisy around the pool?"

"She will."

"What if Daisy runs into the road."

"She won't."

"What if Daisy gets sick?"

"We'll take her to the doctor."

"What if—"

"Katie."

"What if Daisy wakes up in the middle of the night and wonders where I am and why she's alone?" My voice cracks in between each word.

"Oh, hon. We both know that one's inevitable." Iola pulls me to her drab Cowboys T-shirt and pats my back. "Do I need to show you the calendar on my phone? Want to see the day you come back?"

"No." My fingers are dotted with mascara as I wipe away the ridiculous tears. "That's me in there, you know?"

"Ah, there it is. I knew young Katie Parker would speak up at some point."

"I know what Daisy's thinking. She's wondering if her mom's ever truly coming back if I've dropped her off like trash."

"Katie." Iola clamps my shoulders in her oversized hands. "Her situation isn't like yours. Her mom *will* come back for her."

"Will she?"

"Yes. As we speak, there's an overcrowding issue, and Haven's probably going to be released in a few months. Even if that weren't the case, I know a loving parent when I see one. Not every kid in care has parents that don't want their kids or shouldn't have them back—quite the opposite. And *you'll* be back. In five days, your parents will return and pick up your niece, then if the three schedules you sent me are correct, in two more days, you'll return home to see her after that."

And by then, Iola would have a foster home located for Daisy, and she would soon leave us all. "Okay."

"You sound about as convinced as you were the day I left you at the Scotts."

I glance toward the street where a familiar terrible green van sits, the antennae snapped in two and a side mirror held together by duct tape. "I see you're still driving that same minivan."

"I don't give up on things just because they're broken and ugly." She pulls off her glasses and cleans them on her shirt. "And neither should you. Now, let's go back in that house and say goodbye to Daisy. Are you ready?"

No.

"I didn't think this would be so hard. I thought I'd spend some time with the girl, then easily relinquish her into someone else's care."

Iola claps a hand onto my shoulder. "Katie, I have some very bad news to break to you."

"Yes?"

"You care about Daisy."

"I can't get attached."

Iola laughs as she leads me toward the door. "Oh, girl. It's already too late."

CHAPTER TWENTY-EIGHT

It's not that I'm afraid to die.

It's that I'm afraid to die as a drink cart whizzes by my head while I'm stuffed in a seat that should hold no one bigger than a kindergartner.

Will I one day get over my fear of flying through lots of therapy and other treatment options such as hypnosis, hard drugs, or shock therapy? Perhaps. Is that relief coming today?

Apparently not.

My newly manicured nails dig into the armrests as my entire body shakes with the shimmies of the tiny plane. "The travel agent failed to mention we'd take a crop duster from Cancun to the island."

"We're almost there." Charlie clenches my nearest hand, his long legs shoved beneath his chin. "The flight attendant said it was a short ride."

"If I die, please don't let Joyce O'Shea do my makeup down at the funeral home." The woman has a heavy hand with the blush and has never met a teased updo she didn't like.

"Hola, kiddies!" Maxine sticks her head between our seats, looking fresh and fearless. Sam sleeps against the window beside her, oblivious to the shake, rattle, and roll of our soup can plane. "I can't wait to check out this resort. Eliza Biggles says it's divine, and we're going to have so much fun."

The sound of retching fills the pressurized space, and I turn in my gyrating seat to see Frances barf into a paper bag, while Joey holds her hair.

"So, we're sailing some choppy seas," Maxine says. "It's part of the vacation thrills."

I pull out my own bag just in case. "Their puke bags say Milton's Steak House."

"How convenient. I'll put mine in my purse." Maxine moves in so close, her breath skips across my neck. "Should I become ill or in need of a depository for my coconut shrimp, Island Hopper Airlines is prepared."

Forty minutes later, the plane angles toward a dusty excuse for a runway, and I pray a pathetic prayer to God, pleading for my life. The wheels touch down, and we bounce once, twice, three times. Charlie's parents took a different flight, and I wonder if theirs will be as drunk as ours. I clutch my bag and Charlie's arm in a sweaty grip as the aircraft fishtails. We whoosh through the runway sideways, a roller skate with no brakes.

Then. We stop.

Just like that.

Air returns to my lungs, and I burst into tears. "We made it." *ThankyouGodthankyouGodthankyouGod.*

"You bet your bippy we did." Maxine pulls a carryon out of a broken stowing compartment. "Though the whole plane appreciated your loud declarations of love."

An elderly stranger standing next to Jeremy raises his hand. "I know I did! Can I give you my number?"

"Welcome to Santisto Island. This is your pilot, Captain Pepe speaking." The man's crackling voice sounds like he's speaking into a Solo cup connected to a string. "Have a wonderful visit, and enjoy your stay. The flight attendant will now open the door, and you may safely exit."

The cockpit door slides, and Pepe slips out and takes off his hat. He scurries to the exit, pulls a lever, gives the door a kick, and it falls wide open. "Thank you for flying Island Hopper Airlines. We do accept tips and positive online reviews."

Here's a tip. Hand out Depends on your next flight because I nearly peed my pants on this ten-dollar plane.

"The resort said they'd have luxury vehicles waiting to pick us up." Maxine counts all four of her suitcases minutes later as the pilot/flight attendant/bag handler sets down another round of luggage.

"Well, that's it," he says. "Have a nice stay."

"Wait." I rush to Captain Pepe. "That can't be all the bags."

"I'm sorry, miss. Minus a few candy bar wrappers, the plane's empty."

A primal scream builds in my head, and I press my lips together to keep it contained. "That's not possible. I have a garment bag and a large suitcase. Bag is black, about yay big, holds my wedding dress for the most important day of my life." My voice climbs in pitch as raindrops fall from the dark skies above. "Suitcase is red with a huge purple tag, so I'd find it easily." Except now, it's gone. Easily found for someone who's not me. "Where are my bags, Pepe?"

"We brought all the cargo the mainland airport gave us, ma'am. I'm sure there's a misunderstanding, and we'll get it straightened out."

Charlie slips his arm around my waist, tethering me to him lest I go off like a rocket. "We'll get your luggage, Katie."

"But my wedding dress. All my clothes."

"At least you're already used to going without undies." Maxine opens her umbrella with a snap. "Or maybe that's just me."

~

IF THIS RESORT'S IDEA OF A LUXURY VEHICLE IS AN OLD SCHOOL BUS, I'm afraid to see what they call a deluxe wedding package.

The bus provided no air conditioning, no seatbelts, apparently no shocks, and it's driven by...you guessed it—Pepe. It may have been a short ride, but rain poured in through every open window, and dust plumed inside like our own personal hurricane.

By the time we step off, I'm a wet, windblown mess wondering if

I'm paying for the sins of my youth. Because things are just getting worse.

I yank the travel brochure out of my messenger bag and compare it to the sight before me. There is no ten-story high rise. Only a cottage on stilts with a flashing neon sign missing letters that says, "Tis Island Sort." Instead of two Olympic sized pools, I see a large above-ground that lists to one side and contains a live duck who looks mighty perturbed at the idea of sharing.

"Are these fake palm trees?" I inspect a tree that stands as tall as my head.

"Let's see." Maxine gives it a poke with her finger, and the thing goes down. "Yep."

"This doesn't look anything like the resort on your website." James holds up his phone for a visual aid. "What's going on, Pepe?"

"We assure you we still provide award-winning accommodations," Pepe says.

"Are these like participation awards?" A pale Frances sniffs plastic flowers in a clay pot.

"Welcome to Santisto Resort." A woman who could be Pepe's twin climbs down the steps of the treehouse and throws out her hands. "We've been anticipating your arrival!"

I hold up my brochure. "What happened to this resort?"

The woman slips a floral lei around my neck like it's Hawaii. Which it definitely is not. "Eh, it blew away in last month's hurricane."

Pepe nods. "But, we rebuild."

"Like tonight?" My voice is frantic. I don't want this to be my wedding experience! I mean, where do we sleep, on the bus? Do we marry beneath the sway of plastic palms while a duck does the breaststroke in the kiddie pool?

"Santisto Resort will not let you down," the woman says. "My name is Dorinda, by the way."

"My name is stressed and horrified bride." I shake her hand in manic jerks. "My bags are lost, my wedding dress is gone, we all need showers, and I don't understand why this is my life."

"Nice to meet you." Dorinda pats my arm, her brown eyes sympathetic. "If you need someone to talk to, Pepe is a therapist."

"Is there another resort or hotel on the island?" James asks.

"All full," Pepe says cheerfully. "But lucky for you, we had opening."

"I don't want to be lucky," I tell Charlie. "Let's go home."

"We can handle this," he says.

"Fly back with me now, and I'll give you ten minutes of make-out time on the plane. I will not declare my love to one single passenger during takeoff or landing."

"Next flight doesn't leave for days." Pepe grabs a suitcase that unfortunately isn't mine. "How about we show you to your cabanas? I promise things are about to get much better."

CHAPTER TWENTY-NINE

"HUTS?" Millie looks uncharacteristically *not* zen as she surveys the row of ten mini-residences that face what Pepe swears is the direction of the shore.

"Luxury cabanas," Pepe corrects. "Aren't they cute?"

At this point, a Hemsworth brother could stroll by, and I still would not find anything cute about my present circumstances. My intuition told me I should've stayed home, and I should've trusted it. Why would I think I could have a dream wedding?

Dorinda returns to our group, pausing by Pepe to whisper something in his ear. "Allow me to show you to your reserved quarters."

"Helloooo!" Maxine's raises her hand in a big wave. "I'm the leader here. The matriarch. Grandmere. Her royal highness, Duchess of In Between, Maxine Dayberry. We'd like cookies on our pillow, complimentary cocktails, and that's a big yes to tuck-in service."

Dorinda hands each of us a key. "I think you mean turn-down service."

"I'll take that too."

The hostess consults the clipboard carried under her arm. "Let's get you to your rooms so you can spend the rest of the evening at the beach."

"There is an ocean beyond those dunes, right?" Joey asks as thunder rumbles.

"Oh, yes," Dorinda says. "Anything less would be a total misrepresentation."

Right. You wouldn't want that.

"Here's the first of your four cabanas." Dorinda opens the door to hut number one.

"Whoa, whoa, whoa." Maxine steps in front of Dorinda like she is considering an altercation. "Four? I reserved six for this party."

"That's not what your travel agent requested."

"That Eliza Biddle. Sam, remind me to take her off my Christmas card list."

"I'm sure she'll be shattered."

Dorinda flips a few pages of her clipboard. "Four cabanas, two have one queen bed, one cabana has three twin beds, and the final cabana has two twins."

"Twin beds?" Frances looks like she's going to be sick again. "Seriously?"

Charlie steps up to be the voice of reason and calm. "We can make this work." He divides us into rooms, and I'm so tired I don't even care. Just show me to the shower. Hopefully, it's not outdoors with a hose and a community washcloth.

Dorinda puts James and Millie in a cabana with a queen bed and same for Joey and Frances. Hut number three houses the odd setup of three twin beds, and Charlie, Jeremy, and Sam file in there.

That leaves Maxine and me.

We follow Dorinda into the final hut, and...it's a lot.

"Holy luaus." Maxine steps inside and twirls in a full circle. "What is this wonderment?"

Wonderment? More like nightmare. The heavy scent of wet hay assaults my olfactory senses while my eyes rapidly blink to take in the visual overload. This place is straight out of 1965. "Is that a vibrating bed?"

"Haven't seen one of these in years." Maxine does a belly flop on one twin bed, and a cloud of dust plumes into the room. "Apparently, this one hasn't been used since then either. Ah, well, as long as the sheets are clean." She lifts up the white comforter to take a peek. "Okay, strikeout there. But I brought my own just in case these were deficient a few hundred thread count."

"I will leave you to unpack," Dorinda says. "Call me if I can be of service." She pauses at the door, which sticks on her first and second pull. "I pray you have a wonderful time, a blessed wedding, and that you have open hearts and minds." With that, she finally yanks open the door, then disappears.

The interior of the hut looks to be in dire need of an HGTV makeover. But it's wired for electricity, and a portable air conditioner roars in the corner, cooling the small, cramped space.

"Get a load of that authentic artwork." Maxine stands before a framed collage of work, studying the details like she's at the Louvre. "The brochure said every painting was created by a local native."

I inspect the collection of five ocean-inspired paintings and wonder if the natives might've been from the local elementary school. "Very...artsy."

"Right?" Maxine walks to one of a skirted man, the canvas much larger than the others and poised over a mini-fridge. "That's the founder of the island, King Mephisto."

A king. Sure. "Mr. Mephisto needs to wear a shirt." I drop my messenger bag onto a worn teak dresser. "And he's creepy." I take a few steps to the left, then back to the right. "His eyes follow you wherever you go."

"I bet if you rub his belly, it'll bring you good luck." Maxine gives it a try, grimacing as she draws back her fingers. "Or it disintegrates the paint and makes you lose your security deposit."

"Katie?" Charlie enters the cabana, looking more than a little disheveled.

"Hey." I hold his hand, needing a moment of grounding. "Did you get settled?" *With your clean clothes and personal items that arrived on the plane.*

"Yeah." He does a double-take at the sight of the shirtless king. "We have a painting of Queen Wilhelmina. I see her husband had a lot less facial hair."

"Get a load of this," Maxine calls.

Charlie and I squeeze into the bathroom with my grandmother, where a giant seashell of a bathtub sits in the middle of the room. Maxine, of course, sits in it. A rusty freestanding sink that looks like it was pulled from a camper is shoved in a corner, dripping a foreboding tempo. The entire room smells like mildew and bleach, making my eyes sting and water.

"I guess this is where you'll get ready for the ceremony," Charlie says.

My stomach twists at the very idea, and I wonder how current my tetanus shot is. "I suppose so. If they find my luggage. If not, I guess I'll be wearing this same outfit."

"Nonsense." Maxine climbs out of the tub. "I have a tube top and some bootie shorts that would fit like a dream. Let me know if you want to borrow them."

"I'll do that."

"Look, kids, I know these accommodations are a little dumpy, but with all I've got planned, we'll barely be in our tiki shanties to sleep."

"You're right." I twist the knobs on the faucet, only to have one come off in my hand. Who needs hot water? "This will be fine. Thank you, Maxine. We appreciate everything."

"Absolutely," Charlie says with such adorable conviction. "It's gonna be great. The important thing is we're together, and Katie and I are getting married. Nothing else matters."

"Hey, Katie!" A voice yells from the entrance. "Charlie?"

We step out of the dingy bathroom to find Jeremy wide-eyed and wringing his hands. "You guys better get out here. Things just got even worse."

"Need my black light?" Maxine asks.

"It's not the huts." Jeremy opens the door again, and this time I hear the furious yelling. "It's Charlie's mom and dad."

CHAPTER THIRTY

WE FIND Donna Benson and Sterling Benson standing in front of a lopsided hut twenty-five palm trees away, squared off like prizefighters waiting for a bell. The woman who must be Sterling's fiancée begs for them to stop yelling as she shields a transfixed Sadie behind her.

"Sterling, this is my room. I purchased the deluxe accommodations," Donna shouts. "And Sadie, get over here. I don't want you near that woman."

"You booked the room under Mrs. Benson," Sterling snaps.

"I *am* Mrs. Benson."

"But then it completely canceled *our* room."

"That's your problem."

"You did that on purpose," Charlie's dad charges. "You probably called up the Santisto Resort and told them to cancel our cabana."

Donna huffs like a charging bull. "First of all, I don't think this place even has modern convinces like phones, and I would never have canceled accommodations that Maxine is so generously paying for. Especially since I can't pay for it any way since my cheating ex-husband continues to deny the full extent of his assets."

"I've told you that isn't true. I've atoned for my financial dealings and have nothing left to hide."

"Nothing left to hide?" Donna's tired eyes land on Lacey. "Clearly."

The two burst into another round of yelling before Charlie and Joey break it up.

"Enough." Charlie stands between his parents, his arms on his mother's shoulders, while Joey holds back his dad. "We're here for a wedding—*our* wedding. Nothing is about you while you're here, got it? Now calm down or go home."

"You're completely right," Sterling says. "I apologize,...for your mother's behavior."

Donna lunges at Sterling, and down they go into the sand.

"Stop this." Joey pulls his mom off Sterling, while Charlie helps his father up and dusts debris from his shirt.

"You guys are only here until Tuesday." Charlie's face takes on a red, angry cast. "Is it asking too much for you to keep it civil and not embarrass us?"

"No." Donna glares at her ex-husband. "If he can do it, I can."

"Civility has never been a problem for me." Sterling returns to Lacey's arms.

"Neither has telling the truth or reporting accurate financial records," Donna cracks.

"At least I don't nag a person to death or—"

"Please quit," Sadie begs. "This is embarrassing."

Joey rubs his hands over his tired face and spears his parents with the death stare. "We want your assurance you'll keep the peace, or you'll be cut from all wedding activities."

Yeeesh. That's harsh. But I like it.

"We've had a long day of travel," James says. "Let's all settle in and meet up for dinner."

"And where would dinner be?" I ask. "I don't see a restaurant."

James looks about and shrugs. "I'll ask Pepe. Maybe he can build one."

~

"At least the beach is real," Frances says two hours later as all the ladies recline on teak deck chairs soaking up the rays. "I'm starting to feel better already."

I hang up the phone and drop it onto my towel. That's the fifth time I've called both airports. I rarely stick extra clothes in my carryon, so I'm beyond grateful that I let Charlie talk me into slipping in shorts, a tee, and a clean change of underwear just in case. Currently, I'm wearing one of Maxine's extra swimsuits, but it's one size too small, and the neckline can only be described as a plunging scandal.

"Still no sign of your luggage?" Millie squeezes a dollop of sunscreen into her palm then applies it to her already tanned arm.

"They've located my bags."

Everyone whoops with joy.

"They're en route to Costa Rica."

"Oh, Katie." Millie rubs the lotion into her other arm. "I'm sorry."

"They think it should reach me Sunday night."

"That's really cutting it close," says Donna, who spent the first thirty minutes of our time apologizing for her earlier behavior.

"If the bag doesn't show up in time, I'll wear one of Millie's sundresses." And cry.

"Hey, ladies." White sand crunches as Charlie approaches. "I think we have Dad's accommodations fixed."

"I'm glad." Donna pushes her sunglasses to her head. "I thought they were out of cabanas?"

"They are." Charlie sits down on the side of my chair and reaches for my hand. "But, they found an extra tent."

Maxine is the only one who dares to chuckle.

"Let's hope the storm doesn't return," I say. "Or else they'll be sleeping on someone's floor."

"I'm going to steal Katie for a few hours." Charlie's gray eyes hold a spark of mischief.

"You are?" I slip into my flip-flops, wondering what he's up to and hoping it doesn't require energy or clothing that fits.

"Don't do anything I wouldn't do," Maxine calls as we walk back toward the cabanas.

Charlie wraps his arm around my neck and kisses my warm cheek. "So basically nothing's off the table."

CHAPTER THIRTY-ONE

"WHERE'D YOU RENT THIS VEHICLE?" I pat the dusty black dash of our Geo Tracker, a turquoise, rough-riding beast that was probably born about the same time as Charlie and me.

"Take one guess." Charlie tries again to adjust the hot air blowing from the vents.

"Pepe."

"He is a marvel."

"He's also a registered nurse who can attend to small medical issues such as sore throats, fevers, and minor amputations."

"What a calming thought." With the top down, the wind whips through my hair, and I redo my ponytail. "Where is it you're taking me?"

"It's a surprise."

"Like a real surprise or a Santisto Island surprise?"

Charlie laughs. "Trust me." Consulting his phone every now and again for directions, he eventually turns the Tracker onto a dirt road.

Trees line our path, wedged so tight even a squirrel couldn't slip through. We give up on turning off the heater, but instead, relax into our seats and surrender to the jostle and toss of the vehicle. The radio only gets three stations, none in English, so Charlie shuts it off and serenades me in show tunes, most of which he has to make up words. By the time he gets to "The Schuyler Sisters," I'm singing along, my arms raised high, the wind whipping at my skin, and the sun filling me with a Vitamin D infused hope.

I let my eyes wander to my driver. Charlie's hair, the color of melted caramel and newly trimmed, blows in the hot air. Tousled beach Charlie is so different from Corporate Charlie. He wears a day's stubble on his cheeks, and a smile tugs at his full lips. I realize I love this version of him—relaxed, sun-kissed, and eyes only for me. Of all the people he loves back at the resort, I was his pick to spend time with today.

Faint lines fan at the corner of Charlie's gray eyes, and I imagine his face older, his hair gray, his expression wiser and full of years. Will he still want to explore unknown roads and sing Broadway hits he doesn't even like? Will he still steal glances on car rides? Drive with one hand on the steering wheel and one hand holding mine? Or will those hands later be at two and ten, full of caution and distance, with his focus on what's ahead?

"What are you thinking?" Charlie slips on a pair of sunglasses as he hits a pothole.

"Too many things to mention."

"Give me one or two."

I bring his hand to my lips and kiss the rough skin over his knuckles. "That maybe I shouldn't have guilted you into inviting Sterling and Lacey."

"Are you admitting you were wrong?"

"Your parents are worse than some scripted reality show."

He shrugs it off. "Hopefully, we've seen the end to the drama. What else is in that pretty head of yours?"

"How grateful I am for you." I could've missed all this—if James and Millie hadn't said yes to a wild teenage girl in need of a temporary home.

"But?" Charlie jiggles our hands as if to jostle more words.

"There's no but."

"I definitely heard one."

Fine. "I wish nothing had to change. But it will."

His dark brows dip in a frown. "Change because we're getting married?"

When you have a hundred neurotic worries, sometimes it's hard to pull one out and explain it in logical detail. "Because of time, the natural evolution of a relationship. You'll change. I'll change. Then... *we'll* change."

He watches the road narrow and steers the Tracker around a curve. "If this is an excerpt from your vows, so far I'm not loving it."

"You called it the honeymoon phase." A bird soars overhead, making free and graceful swoops toward a tree. "We're still in it. But what about when there are kids and more jobs and years of distance from family?"

"After today, I'd be okay with a little more distance from some of our family. But you say the word, and I'll move us back to In Between."

"Is that what you want?" Part of me has assumed he'd rather be home.

"I want to be the husband of a Broadway actress." His fingers tighten over mine.

"What if you don't like New York?"

"I like anywhere you are."

"You say that now, Charlie."

He slows the car over a rut and uses the time to send me a dark look. "I'm not going to change my mind. I keep waiting for you to believe that, but you're not, are you?"

"Things change. People change. Look at your parents."

"I'll make sure I don't embezzle money and conduct shady business dealings."

"Or Frances and Joey?"

"That one I can't explain. But look at your parents. And Maxine and Sam. That's your legacy."

"I'm also Bobbie Ann Parker's daughter." A woman who couldn't make a relationship last. Just like every known generation before her.

"How about we save this for another day?" The Tracker shimmies as it drives up a hill. "Things are about to get crazy, so I want this afternoon to be about you and me, and a Caribbean island we might never see again.

"Because it's going to deflate any moment and sink overnight?"

"But you know who could fix it?"

I laugh as we shout the answer together. "Pepe."

We off-road another five minutes with Charlie assuring me the dust and sweat will be worth it. I cling to the overhead handle and hope this surprise isn't on par with a lost wedding dress and inflatable palm trees.

"I think we're here." Charlie eases the vehicle onto a small gravel path and puts it in park. "Pepe said to look for a large boulder in the shape of a heart."

"That sounds very Santisto Resort."

"He swears it's real." Charlie runs around to my side and helps me out. While I'm dusting off bug parts and road dirt, he pulls out a soft cooler and a few towels from the back.

"I take it there are snacks involved in this excursion?"

"With you?" He slips his hand in mine and pulls me along. "Always."

We walk past the boulder that does indeed look like a heart and hike up a small incline. My flip-flops make for unsteady steps, and I have to drop Charlie's hand to keep my balance and swat away bugs.

The grass grows denser and taller as we round a curve, pursuing a worn path that could stand some weeding.

"Pretty sure this is it." Charlie holds back some branches from overgrown shrubs and gestures for me to keep walking. "After you."

"You want me to step through there?"

"Yes."

"It looks snakey."

"I'll slay them with my show tunes." He gives a quick nod toward the waiting wilderness. "I'm right behind you."

I'm wearing my grandmother's shrunken bathing suit, shoes that gave up an hour ago, and in a few days, I might get married in whatever I can cobble from other people's suitcases. It literally could not get worse.

So inside the shrubs, I go. I push the branches out of my way and plunge through, praying nothing bites me that requires an antidote. Because I'm not sure Pepe can make one. I hold back another monstrous shrub, letting Charlie catch up.

Then finally, I see daylight.

Stepping out the copse of trees, my feet return to sand, and my eyes adjust.

And what they see takes my breath away. "Oh. Charlie."

"Wow." The sound of rushing water nearly blots out his voice. "Pepe did not steer us wrong."

It's like we've stepped into a piece of heaven, another world far away from bickering parents and runaway wedding attire. Lush foliage frames a large, lazy pool of water so clear I can see fish swimming. Bright flowers bloom in sporadic bursts—in the ground, on the rocks, as if they refuse to be contained. Twenty feet above us, a waterfall rages, emptying water from the mouth of mammoth rocks worn smooth by time and pressure.

"Do you want to get in?" Charlie helps me draw closer, and as we near the waterfall, a cool mist sprays us.

The roaring becomes a song in the air, a sound of nature foreign to my city girl's ears. But there's something about it that invites me to jump in, to meet the fall where it kisses the pool, to baptize my body in this holy water, and rise a new creation. "Yes," I tell Charlie. "Let's dive in."

Charlie walks me to the spot Pepe suggested and holds out his hand. "Are you sure you're ready?"

It might be cold. It might hurt to go crashing through.

But I place my hand in Charlie's, and together we run off a mossy rock, lift our feet, and catapult into the pool.

I swim to the surface, laughing. And freezing. "So cold. So very cold. Charlie?" I glance about, frantic when I don't see him. "Charlie?"

Then he shoots up behind me, his laugh echoing through the rocks. "Amazing." Treading water, he kisses me, an awkward, wet, barely-meeting-of-the lips kiss.

One I'll remember forever.

"I love you." Charlie brushes the hair back from my face.

Tears fill my eyes, and I try to blink them away. "I love you too."

The waterfall rains hard behind us, filling the pool with an endless supply. We're the only two people here, the only two people on the planet, and everything is right in the world.

Until Charlie speaks.

"Sometimes, I see a familiar look in your eyes, and I get a bad feeling, Parker." His muscled arms move in sweeping arcs to stay afloat. "The look I got the night before your mom's funeral—right before you bolted out of the Valiant."

The night I kissed him and finally told him I loved him.

Then left.

A shaft of light breaks through the trees, and it cuts across Charlie's face. "Tell me you're going to be at our wedding."

"I am."

"And you're not going to run."

I shake my wet head, drops of water dripping down my cheek. "I won't."

"And you have no reservations."

It's not a question, but a statement he wants me to agree to, to pledge my allegiance to his same kind of marital faith.

Charlie's legs kick beneath the water as he tunnels both hands of water through his hair. "A guy could die in the space of your hesitations." With that, he turns away and dives back into the current. His bent arms slice into the air then disappear back into the water, propelling his lean body toward the waterfall. I watch him swim to a rock and pull himself up. Water pours off of him, sliding down curves and muscles his desk job couldn't take away.

"Wait. Charlie." I'm not nearly the graceful swimmer Charlie is, but I flap my way through the pool until I reach him. He helps me up, and I trail him to where the waterfall hisses like an angry fury. "I'm not bailing on this wedding."

"But you think about it?"

Where did this come from? "No. Not really."

"Not really?"

"I think about rescheduling."

"Again?" Charlie says this like I've asked to be waterboarded.

"Does this island wedding feel right to you?" Before he can reply, I rush to make him understand. "I wanted to marry you in a church, with James as our pastor. In a dress I wasn't rushed into buying. And one that *showed up* like it was supposed to. I don't even have underwear for tomorrow, for crying out loud."

"You can wear mine for all I care. Or none. Does it really matter? Does any of that stuff even matter?"

"Yes!" The waterfall rages behind us, and I can barely hear myself think. All I know is words are coming out, and I can't seem to stop them. "Nothing's going according to plan."

"Screw the plan."

"But this wedding is a roller coaster going off the rails. What if all these disturbances are signs we need to wait?"

"Wait for what, Katie?" Charlie stands in front of the falls, with ivy hanging behind him and branches dipping overhead. He looks like a tribal warrior, angry and ready to do battle. "You've postponed this wedding enough. The conditions are never going to be right."

"But why is that?"

All expression leaves Charlie's face. His eyes go dead. His mouth tight and grim. "It doesn't matter to me if every single detail implodes. What matters is that we love each other and we want to spend the rest of our lives together." Charlie takes a step closer. "Right?"

I feel like I'm still in that pool, drowning beneath the surface, but fighting to break through so I can finally breathe again. "Yes." My voice sounds shaky and faint against the onslaught of water. "All that matters is us."

I want to believe that. I want to think that all we need is each other and love.

But what if it's not enough?

Somewhere the young girl who was rejected by her mother and left on a stranger's doorstep is still in there—the girl who comes from a long line of mistakes and heartbreak.

And she wonders....what if *I'm* not enough?

CHAPTER THIRTY-TWO

If I sat down and wrote out all the things wrong with the Santisto Resort, the list would be enough to create at least three papier-mâché palm trees. Which I'm pretty sure the resort has tried. But one thing they do right? Food.

Saturday morning, I walk with Maxine to the office-on-stilts while the gray sky above us sprinkles the occasional raindrop. Beneath the office are a dozen large tables set for a formal meal, where three times a day, guests can grab a plate at the buffet and eat to their hearts' content. Another man and woman in resort uniform handle the food while Dorinda visits each table and refills coffee and juice. Last night's dinner outside was baked chicken, vegetables, and a dessert bar. Charlie and Joey didn't show up for the meal. After our quiet ride back yesterday afternoon, my internal alarm refuses to snooze. Is Charlie having second thoughts? Is he realizing I'm a hot mess that requires too much work?

But, on the other hand, he has no idea what my life's been like. If our childhoods shape us like ocean water over sea glass, then he's a stone, smooth and rounded without edges, while I'm coral, cutting and sharp, with a tendency to draw blood. I've endured years of therapy, read self-help books like they were Neil Simon scripts, and prayed for a normal heart until I'm sure God has considered giving me a closed mouth instead.

And still. I remain a red-headed, twenty-seven-year-old container of internal chaos, afraid anything good in my life will soon expire and be taken away. I routinely do the math on how many years Maxine might have left, though there's not a living soul beyond her who can nail down her true date of birth. I worry James and Millie's visits will gradually become more infrequent, and as Amy has her own family one day, I'll be pushed out and regarded with all the thought given to a distant cousin. I wake up many nights in a cold sweat, dreaming that Charlie leaves me for a tall, slender model of a co-worker who can pick the right wine with fish and loves nothing more than to talk sales channels and content optimization.

Each day of my abusive childhood programmed my brain, and though I've tried to rewire it to forget, it doesn't comply but instead sends signals to my heart. *Fear! Distrust! Run away!*

How do I make Charlie understand? Charlie, who grew up with two parents, siblings, a two-story house, and never had to wonder why the pantry was empty or if his mother would wake from her drug-induced sleep.

"Stop scowling." Maxine jabs me in the ribs with an elbow. "I said I was sorry for using all the hot water."

"It's fine." I pull myself from thoughts that seem to grow bleaker and race faster by the day. My hesitation is a cyclone that began as a steady whirl, and as the wedding date draws closer, it spins at a dizzying velocity. And not one person here understands.

Except maybe Pepe. Because he can do anything.

James and Millie sit at a table with Sam, who pours steaming syrup on a pancake. Sadie's to his left, scrolling through her phone, probably looking for an app to make her parents disappear.

Donna Benson passes the butter to my adopted grandfather and makes small talk about the gloomy weather. "Dorinda says there's a storm moving in, but we should still have a few hours of quality beach time..."

Charlie's dad and his fiancée eat bacon and waffles at their own table on the opposite side. They face the direction of the ocean, and the humid wind ruffles the napkins beneath their silverware.

Joey, Charlie, and Frances are nowhere to be seen, and I try not to let that spur a thousand horrible conspiracy theories.

"The blueberry muffins are to die for." Jeremy grins at me from his table he shares with two other guests, not in our party, who, no doubt are already his friends. "Dorinda says we're welcome to take them with us."

"Already got two in my shirt." Maxine hands me a plate at the buffet.

Though everything looks good, I don't have much of an appetite. I take a spoonful of eggs, a few slices of bacon, greet every table, then join my parents.

"Stick with the juice," James says as I sit down.

"No way." Maxine takes off a sun hat that could shade the entire island. "I gotta have some caffeine."

"Don't say I didn't warn you." James lifts a bite of eggs to his lips and gives me a wink.

I watch Maxine take an exploratory drink. Her eyes cross, her lips pucker, and she swallows her first sip like it's worse than her prune smoothies. "What's in that stuff, leftover fuel from the plane?"

"I talked to Daisy this morning," I tell James and Millie. Cassie and her daughter were taking her to McDonald's for breakfast.

"Is she having fun?" Millie dips her own herbal tea bag into a cracked Santisto Resort mug.

"The woman she's staying with said she is." Pushing my eggs around on my plate seems to only make them double in size. "Daisy asked me to come get her."

"We'll be home soon." Millie pats my hand. "Daisy's fine, Katie. Let this week be about you and Charlie."

"Speaking of, has anyone seen Charlie?" I pick up a piece of bacon and break it in two.

"He ate earlier," Donna says. "I think he went for a run."

If she finds it odd, I don't know the location of the man I'm about to marry, Donna's too busy throwing mental daggers at her ex-husband to say.

Ting! Ting! Maxine taps her spoon to her water glass, gaining the attention of the breakfast crew. "Today at noon, we will begin our wedding celebration festivities. The men will be led by my old college pal Jeremy, while I shall host our ladies. No idea what the menfolk have planned, but we chicas will enjoy a day at the spa, have a surf lesson, eat a five-star dinner, then end with some late-night dancing."

I'm wearing sink-washed underwear and my second day of selections from Maxine's suitcase. The top's too tight and the shorts too short—though I did find two mini-candy bars in the pockets. I'm hungover from worrying all night and, knowing Maxine, this day will involve some straight-up shenanigans. I glug down my orange juice and pray for the sugar spike to work quickly.

Fifteen minutes later, Charlie walks in and grabs a muffin. "Good morning," he says to the second shift.

"Forty-eight hours left till wedding time and counting," Maxine calls. "Today, a whole day of fun and frivolity, tomorrow the rehearsal, then on Monday, my two sweeties tie the knot." She hums a bar of "Goin' to the Chapel," while I join Charlie at the water cooler.

"Did you have a good run?" I ask, wondering how *good* can ever be associated with running.

"I did." He holds out a muffin, and I decline.

"I called you three times this morning."

"I'm sorry." He casts a look at his mother, then guides me further away from the group. "I had a long talk with each of my parents last night, and I needed to clear my head."

"Is everything okay?"

"They've assured me they'll suck it up and play nice while they're here."

"I appreciate that. It can't be easy for your mom."

Charlie wipes crumbs from his lips and wads up his napkin. "They promised to keep their distance and not add to the stress."

Like I was. "I'm sorry about yesterday. The waterfall was beautiful, and it was...a magical date." Until I made it weird. "You have to know I do want to marry you."

His stormy eyes search mine. "I want to believe that."

I rise on tiptoes and brush my lips over Charlie's. "Don't give up on me, Charlie Benson."

He wraps his arms around me, and I close my eyes and step into the embrace, wishing I could stay there all day. I breathe in the sunscreen on Charlie's skin and try to exhale the apprehension that sits heavy on my shoulders and toxifies my thoughts.

"Okay, sweet peas." Maxine stands on a chair and claps her hands. "Meet back here at noon so we can start our bachelor and bachelorette parties. Let the fun begin!"

"Charlie." Donna Benson tugs on her son's shirt, her eyes wide with renewed anger.

"Yes, Mother?"

Her attention roams to Lacey, who loudly thanks Maxine for including her. "Why is your dad's girlfriend joining the ladies today?"

"Because she doesn't qualify for the guy's excursion."

"But...but..."

"Have a fun day, Mom." Charlie returns his attention to me and kisses my cheek. "Let's hope we all still love each other when we return."

CHAPTER THIRTY-THREE

"HELLO, ladies, and welcome aboard. I will be your chauffeur and tour guide today." Pepe speaks into a portable mic/speaker combo, wearing a tropical shirt and cargo shorts. "It's about to begin raining, but the sun always shines on the Santisto Island Party Bus." He waits for our courtesy laugh, but only Lacey provides one. Donna rolls her eyes and fans herself with a napkin.

Our ride today is another school bus, this one pink and accented with red stars. The tires are jacked up so high we had to goose Maxine to give her leverage. I would like to report that she didn't enjoy it, but...it's Maxine.

Christmas lights run the length of the interior roof above our heads, and music plays from a radio on the floor. The three back rows have been removed for the Party Bar, which looks to be a particle board box laden with alcohol bottles and an Igloo cooler. It's just our group here, so we each have a fuzzy covered seat to ourselves. There's a countdown clock in my head, and it ticks incessantly loud increasing the pressure behind my eyes and the ache to my temple. Pepe's playlist of beach music doesn't help. Jimmy Buffet shouldn't be played at the same volume as Screamo.

We start with a group surfing lesson, which lasts a whole fifteen minutes before the red flags go up due to choppy waters. We barely make it back to the rental van before the clouds turn upside down and empty buckets of rain.

Half an hour later, we descend upon the spa, which is shockingly an impressively normal place, though it's arena style. Used to accompanying vacation parties, there's a large area with multiple tables for massages, surrounding chairs for clients to receive facials and beauty treatments, plus a separate room for manicures and pedicures.

And when Sarita, of the magic hands and little conversation, kneads my shoulders with the most perfect pressure, some of the pain evaporates like the lavender essential oils steaming from a nearby diffuser.

"How did you find this place?" I ask Maxine, who lies two tables over, giving specific instructions to her massage therapist, Lars.

She adjusts the cucumbers over her eyes. "Not from that stinking travel agent, I can tell you that. And to think I tipped that woman. I mean, it was a t-shirt *and* a pen, but still. What a waste of merch."

Frances, who opted for a facial, sits in a reclining chair as a woman small enough to fit in a high school locker slathers something brown on her face and spreads it with a brush. Millie sighs on the table between my grandmother and me, enjoying her hot stone massage. Donna and Lacey are both in another room getting pedicures, and I can only hope they're sitting far enough away there won't be bloodshed after the lacquer dries.

"How are you feeling, Katie?" Millie's face-down question is muffled by a towel.

"Relaxed." My voice wobbles as the massage therapist karate chops down my back. "Can we stay here forever?"

"I mean about the wedding." Outside, thunder booms and shakes the building.

"Good."

"Oh, geez," Maxine mutters.

"Leave her alone, Mom."

"I'm getting a bad feeling," Maxine says.

"I'm sure the two-foot-tall stack of pancakes you had for breakfast has nothing to do with it." Millie smacks her mom with an oily hand.

Frances chimes in from across the room. "I flipped out before my wedding."

"We remember." Maxine giggles as the therapist massages a foot. "It's perfectly normal to take a quick ride on the crazy train before you say I do."

"Can we not talk now?" I wince at the extra pressure applied to my tense shoulders. "You girls are ruining my massage."

"I didn't have a single hesitation," Donna Benson says as she enters the room in a white, fluffy robe.

"That was a quick pedicure." Maxine raises her head and regards Charlie's mom. "What did they do, paint two toes?"

"I cannot be in there one more minute with that floozy that my husband thinks he's marrying."

"Ex-husband," Maxine corrects.

"She's trying to make small talk."

"How rude." Maxine takes a bite of cucumber, earning a frown from her attendant.

"Katie," Donna continues, using an uptight tone that shouldn't be allowed in a spa, "I've raised a good boy in Charlie. He's a sure bet, and he's going to treat you like a queen." Her voice fades off as she thinks a moment. "Then again, that's how it started with Sterling in the early days."

"I can't listen to these war stories today." I grab my sheet and flip over at the direction of my massage therapist. "Maybe y'all could use this time to pray my luggage shows up."

"You think you know someone." Donna grabs a cucumber from a nearby tray and crunches into it with an angry snap. "Sterling and I dated all through college, and he was Mr. Wonderful. He was at least Mr. Not Too Bad the first five years of our marriage. But after Sadie was born, presto change-o. Mr. Wonderful was gone, and there was Mr. Secretive. Worked all hours of the day, rarely home for the kids or me. I should've known something was up, but I refused to believe the old Sterling was gone."

"How about that weather, huh?" Frances says as her esthetician removes the goop from her face. "It's really coming down out there."

"Men cannot be counted on." Donna checks her hair in a nearby mirror. "One minute you're planning your thirtieth wedding anniversary, the next you're vacationing with your ex-husband's girlfriend."

Magic Hands Serita leans down as she massages my upper arms. "Thees eez your idea of a relaxing time?"

"No," I say, wishing I were anywhere else but here.

"You want that I put the talky one in a chokehold?"

"At least I have my children." Donna raises her volume as if we can't hear her over the rain pounding on the roof. "My kids are what got me through it all." Her eyes focus on Frances for a long moment, then land on me. "So, girls...when are you two going to make me a grandmother?"

I'm about to tell Donna where she can stick her conversation topics when my phone buzzes from the chair holding my robe.

"No phones," Serita barks.

"I'm sorry." I wrap the sheet around me and slip off the bed, grateful for the out. "I better take this. Might be New York calling." Shuffling to the dressing room with my robe clutched in my grip, I lock the door and sit. "Hello?"

"Katie? It's Cassie."

"Oh, hey." The fluffy cotton robe feels warm against my skin as I slip it back on. "Is everything okay?"

"Mostly. Hypothetical question, does Daisy ever refuse to eat?"

That doesn't sound hypothetical. "No. Never."

"Oh, dear. She's not eating."

"Are you sure? The girl eats as much as a high school boy." Which I respect. Except for that one night last week when we went out for nachos. She definitely ate some of my share.

"Daisy's had a few bowls of cereal and some grapes. It's like she's on a hunger strike until you get back."

"I don't know what I can do from here. Do you need me to come home?"

"Goodness, no. I'm not calling to worry you. In my experience, when a kid gets hungry enough, she'll eat. I thought this might be normal, and you'd have some tips?"

"On our last night before I left, she ate a full t-bone, baked potato, and two ears of corn. Plus, a piece of pie." I review a list of Daisy's favorite foods, which I shouldn't have to do because if Cassie had read page seventeen of my packet, it's right there. With footnotes.

"She'll be fine." Cassie's assurance is wimpy at best. Like the very opposite of her biceps. "We'll try more of her favorite foods and see if there's any change."

"Maybe she's sick."

"She doesn't have a fever."

I didn't say she had the bubonic plague, Cassie! "Have you checked her throat? Ears?"

"Really, no need." I might as well have asked the woman if she's administered a breathalyzer.

"Does Daisy have her favorite teddy bear?"

"With her every moment."

"Did you put the framed photo next to her bed?"

"Yes. Your engagement picture is lovely."

I'm out of ideas. It's just like me and house plants. They come to me all healthy and full of life, then no matter what I do, it's a failure to thrive situation. "Did Daisy have her video visit with her mom yesterday?"

"She did. It went well, but then she cried for two hours afterward."

"Maybe that's part of it. She usually has a tough day after the visit. And now she's without my family and me as well." This is a knife right through the heart. "I'll text Iola Smartley."

"I already have. She said she'd drop by tomorrow."

"If Daisy starts to go downhill, please take her to a walk-in clinic. I'm really concerned."

"Truly, Katie, it's going to be fine. I assure you there's no emergency here."

"Tell her I love her, and I'll talk to her tomorrow."

"Don't think a thing about this conversation. We'll be fine."

But in the background, I hear a lonely wail that undoes every bit of my Swedish massage. "Is that Daisy? Is she crying?"

"I better go," Cassie says in a rush. "I'll update you if things don't improve. But don't worry—they will. Enjoy your wedding. We'll talk soon."

I let my head fall against the wall and squeeze my eyes shut. *God, what is going on? Why is everything falling apart? Can I not have an uninterrupted happily ever after? This is so my life.*

"Is everything all right?" Millie's voice calls from the other side of the door. "Katie?"

I open the door, tears coursing down my greasy cheeks.

"Oh, sweetie." Millie pulls me into a hug. "What's wrong?"

"I think I'm cursed. I'm living a terrible Lifetime movie."

"Katie, no."

"I try to be happy, and something always comes along to mess it up. My dress is lost and probably having its own vacation in Costa Rica. We're staying at a condemned island resort, Charlie's mad at me, and now Daisy's on a hunger strike. When does it end? When do I get a day with no chaos? Maybe I'm being silly to expect happiness."

"Honey, listen to yourself. This is the stress talking."

"It's not." Why don't they stick tissues in these robe pockets? "All my life, I've wanted to be normal. I wanted a normal family and a good job and a fairy tale wedding. But what happens when I try? It storms for days, a sister I barely even knew I had throws me her kid, and I'm wearing my grandmother's underwear. What next, the island sinks?"

"Only a small possibility of that. But we do have life preservers."

"I'm serious, Millie. This trip has been a series of catastrophes." Then I voice the question that has me undone. "What if my marriage is too?"

CHAPTER THIRTY-FOUR

"I HAVE good news and bad news." Maxine sits on my twin bed the next morning, poking my nose until I open my eyes.

I roll over and yank the blanket over my head, wishing with all I have that I could turn back the clock and catch two more hours of sleep. "Last time you told me this, you announced your candidacy for mayor and showed off your new lip injections. I'm still not sure which was the good news."

"Hmph." She stretches out, her back against the wicker headboard. "Those lips could've been a float in the Macy's Thanksgiving Parade. But they deflated eventually."

"And your run for mayor?"

Maxine's sigh is almost as loud as our dripping air conditioner. "Just got updated poll numbers. I think I'm going to win."

I slowly sit up, letting the blanket fall away. "Why don't you sound victorious and smug?"

"I do so love a good smug opportunity. But I can't even dredge up a decent smirk of superiority. I never expected things to go this far, Katie. One minute our corrupt mayor keels over during the Cotton Eyed Joe at a square dance, the next I'm joking that I'm going to run. Before I knew it, I had a whole election committee of white hairs making it happen. All we wanted was our senior center to get its funding back and the town to embrace a little progress. And maybe one less chicken plant."

"Are you saying you don't actually want to be mayor?"

"Katie, I'm fifty-six years old. Why would I want to take this on in my almost-golden years? But taken it on, I have, and I'll see it through. And it's only for two years, finishing out the dead **guy's** term. I can handle anything for two years. Except maybe an incontinent bladder. Or saggy eyelids."

"Quit the race."

"No way! Maxine Simmons Dayberry does not quit. Have I given you a koozie yet?"

"At least three."

Her eyes drop to my chest. "Why don't you make use of them and perk up that bra?"

A knock sounds at the door and Maxine jumps up like a shot. "Who could it be?"

I cross my fingers and wish aloud. "Breakfast in bed for the bride-to-be?"

"Something even better. So bad news is we're due for a humdinger of a storm, and the day is shot." She whips open the door, and there stands Pepe beneath a wind-whipped umbrella. "Good news is your luggage arrived. Bring it on in, Little Peepee!"

"Ees Pepe, ma'am."

"You betcha, we're peppy. At the sight of that dress just in time for tonight's rehearsal, how could we not be? Right there on the floor by the smaller puddle of leaky water will do. Thank you!" She hands him some cash and a Maxine for Mayor pen. "If you ever drive through in In Between, Texas, give us a toot."

"Yes, ma'am. I will toot your way. Now, a bit of bad news."

"Would everyone quit saying that? No more bad news." Never mind that I'm standing in front of a total stranger in Millie's extra pajamas with hair that looks like it had a starring role in a Tim Burton movie.

"This is more than a little passing shower moving in," Pepe says.

I freeze mid-zip of my suitcase. "Are you telling me we're about to have a hurricane?"

"No!" Pepe slaps his leg and laughs. "Those things don't pop up overnight." His face sobers. "But neither do tropical storms, yet Mother Nature threw us a curveball anyway."

"A tropical storm's coming?" Maxine's voice rises an octave as she grabs Pepe. "Talk to us, man. Give us the important details, and how can we stop it?"

"I'm afraid there's nothing we can do. Tropical Storm Charro will koochie koo straight for us at approximately nine p.m. She was supposed to miss us completely but looks like she got lost."

Maxine's lips thin. "I can relate, Charro."

"So, what happens?" I clutch the garment bag with my dress, a reunion I never thought I'd experience. "Is the rehearsal canceled?"

"Only moved up a few hours earlier. The storm is a category one, so I'm not too worried. There will be no danger, but it will be impossible to be outside when she strikes."

"Are we safe here?" Maxine asks. "One of us is too young to die." She points a finger at her chest. "It's me."

"Of course," Pepe says. "Perfectly safe. These huts are weather tested. You will be fine."

"These huts are made out of toothpicks." And what about my wedding? Why is this happening? *God, a tropical storm? Is this your way of ruining my happiness? Or a sign I shouldn't shackle Charlie to me?*

Maxine voices the question I haven't dared. "Will we be able to have a wedding tomorrow?"

"Yes. Certainly." He sounds so calm and casual. "Just not on the beach and not at our venue."

"Then, where?"

"I was thinking the party bus."

"Out. Shoo." Maxine pushes Pepe out the door. "You come back when you have better answers. My granddaughter didn't come all this way to get married on your hoochie bus. You go back to your office and don't show your face until you have a better solution." She sticks her head outside where the rain is already beginning in earnest and shakes her fist to the sky. "And you pipe down out there! You can't stop this wedding."

A crack of lightning is her answer.

The door slams shut, and Maxine rests the back of her hand against her forehead as she slides down the wall. "It's exhausting being us."

"At least my dress is here." I pull it from the garment bag and whisper water-logged words. "I don't think I'm meant to get married."

"Oh, my little plastic palm tree, of course, you are." Maxine's by my side in an instant, running her hand over the wrinkles in the gown. "We can steam this baby right up in the shower and surely find an iron somewhere. You're gonna look gorgeous in this dress, sweet pea."

"Standing in a hurricane?"

"Tropical storm."

"Does it matter?"

"Depends on how much wind chaffing you're up for, but yes, I think it does."

I fall back onto my bed, the dress clutched in my arms and draped around me in all its beautiful glory. "It shouldn't be this hard to get married and be happy."

"I know, sweetcheeks." The bed sinks as Maxine sits beside me. "But think of the memories you're making. This time next year you'll be laughing so hard, you'll cry."

Hot tears drip onto my dress, and I tuck my head into the lace. "Maybe lofty things like weddings aren't meant for me."

"Now, you look here." Maxine hauls me upright and gives me a shake. "Pull yourself together. Yes, things have gone terribly off-script. But the important things are still here—you, Charlie, your family, and a chocolate fountain for the reception that can be rolled into our cabana if necessary. You *are* going to be a lovely bride, and you *are* getting married." She crushes me in a smothering hug. "How about I pray for us?"

"Can it wait till after my shower?"

Her arms lock around me. "Dear God, this is Maxine S. Dayberry coming to you live from Santisto Island. And if you're unfamiliar with this place, it's because it's made of Legos and Play-Doh and not one of your creations. Now, Lord, we think you're neato, and we know you hold us in the same regard. So please open your holy ears and hear us now. This is what we need, Big G. We need the bad weather to go away, and we need these kids to get married before Katie reports for work. And Lord, give Katie a big confirmation that things will be okay and her life is in your hands. Preferably hands you're not dunking in a big water tank. Fix it, Jesus. Amen."

"Amen." I guess.

"You're going to get your happy ending, sweet pea." Maxine kisses me loudly on the cheek. "Just you wait and see."

CHAPTER THIRTY-FIVE

I'd like to say I feel like a million bucks wearing my new strapless designer dress that was a total splurge, pink heels that accent the floral pattern of the outfit, and my *own* underwear. Plus, makeup and hair that took me two nerve-wracking hours due to the electricity fizzling out three times while the storm kicked up the volume.

I'd like to. But I can't.

I feel more like Sixteen-Year- Old-Foster-Kid Katie, who dressed up and went to her first high school dance, unsure of her every breath and feeling like the imposter in a formal. It wasn't until my senior year that I didn't feel like I was playing dress-up, trying on the clothes of normal girls who didn't have a mom in jail and weren't still dragging around the shackles of poverty.

It's been a while since those emotions flared, and I didn't expect them today. Not here. When mingling with some of Broadway's finest, yes. During an elegant dinner with a table of Charlie's bosses, definitely. But at my own wedding rehearsal?

Why am I so messed up? I should be happy, jubilant, and so high on love that it doesn't matter that my heels pinch because I'm floating above it all on a cloud of bliss and invisible insoles.

"You ready?" Maxine squirts perfume on her neck, then under an armpit for good measure. "Aw, you look like a dream." Her head tilts like she's intercepted a high-pitched signal, and she regards me with furrowed-brow scrutiny. "I had so hoped the storm wouldn't bring you down. Especially now that it's taken a break just for you."

Outside the hut, the wind blows mightily from angry clouds, and rain hovers above the ocean, waiting to release the deluge like the revived waters of the Red Sea. "I'm fine—just tired. Let's go."

She gives one of the tendrils framing my head a tweak. "I'm proud of you."

I'd been warned I'd be a mushball during these wedding moments, but I wasn't prepared for the random bursts of tears that spring up at the slightest encouragement. I'm a desert, soaking up every kind word, every bolstering bit of fortitude and inspiration like meager drops of water.

"Did you ever settle on your something blue?" Maxine sashays to her suitcase, a vision in a navy sheath that complements her tan.

My brain stumbles at the topic change and the little time remaining to walk to our rehearsal. "A garter from Charlie."

"Your something borrowed?"

My confidence? "Millie's diamond earrings."

"And something old?"

"My maid of honor."

Her head lifts from the mountain of clothes and rolls her eyes. "I'll ignore that and chalk it up to your pre-wedding jitters. Now, you are under no obligation to wear this, but I'm giving it to you anyway." She holds a pearl necklace by the gold clasp, letting the beads drip from her fingers. "These were my mother's. She wore them in her wedding to my father, both of them eighteen and starry-eyed. They married during the Depression and were poor as field mice. My mother sold her cherished pearls so she could leave her folks money for the younger kids since she wouldn't be working the family farm anymore. My father was fifteen minutes late for the ceremony because, unbeknownst to my mom, he'd just saved enough to buy the necklace back and had raced to the hock shop before it closed."

"I can't accept that."

"You can. And you will." Maxine's azure blue eyes glisten as she stands behind me and pulls the ivory pearls across my neck, letting it drape in the space above my heart. "I wore these at my wedding, and Millie borrowed the necklace for hers. Giving them away has never felt right. Until now." The clasp locks with a click. "There. They look beautiful."

"Maxine—"

"Ah-ah-ah." She wags a glossy, manicured nail. "I want you to have the pearls."

"Thank you." I rest my hand over them, feel the cold texture beneath my skin. "I don't know what to say."

"Say you'll wear them sometime and one day pass them on to someone you love."

Like my own daughter. I close my eyes against the tender ache the idea brings—that someday I could have children, branches of this Scott family tree that I've been grafted into. A tree that's flourished and thrived through the years. I'm part of that, and my children will be as well.

"You know what they say about pearls." Maxine lifts a strand of my hair from beneath the necklace. "Something irritates an oyster, and over time, as it defends itself ...a pearl is born. Do you know what I'm telling you?"

"Are you my irritant?"

"Not this time." Her shell-pink lips curve. "Sometimes, beauty can be born of hardship. Without the unwanted bad stuff, there would be no pearl. I truly believe the best results can come from the roughest beginnings." Maxine rises on tiptoe and kisses my cheek. "My guess is today your mind's revisiting a lot of those old rough places, but you, my dear, are the pearl. This day and tomorrow—they are yours. You deserve them, and you gotta walk through them with the knowledge that you're meant to be here, meant to be happy and meant to be loved."

I want to admit that I'm scared, that part of me wants to stay in the room and read *People* magazine and drink diet soda and eat ice cream. But that just sounds immature and silly. Who wouldn't want this day? "I love you, Maxine."

"Not nearly as much as I love you." She hugs me close, only to withdraw at the sound of a heavy knock on the door. "Hopefully, that's not the evacuation patrol." She opens the door, and there stand our two guys. Charlie, dressed in a pale blue suit, holds a black umbrella for me, and Sam carries a gold one for Maxine.

"We thought we'd escort you to dinner." Charlie looks at me so kindly, with such reverence in his gaze, I'm nearly undone. "Care to share an umbrella and take a walk?"

"I'd love to." When I slip my arm through his, it's so final. No turning back. When I step through that doorway, it's a portal to a new life season. It's a commitment to the ceremony that is to come. A trial run of the real thing.

"You look stunning," Charlie says as we walk toward the beach. "I'm a lucky man."

"I'm the lucky one." Thunder booms around us, and I clutch Charlie's arm tighter. Panic claws at my skin from the inside, and the humidity steals my breath. My pulse thuds in my ear, and my stomach is somewhere back on the ground ten paces away. Sweat beads on my face, beneath my arms. "Charlie, I—" My phone trills from inside my clutch. "Let me silence that." But as I pull out my phone, I see the display reads Cassie. "It's Daisy."

Charlie stops mid-stride, moving us out of the way of a passing Sam and Maxine.

"Hello?" My heart hammers against my chest while faint drops of rain pepper my arms. "Cassidy?"

"Katie, can you hear me? The reception is terrible here."

"Yes, is everything okay?" My heartbeat escalates. "Where are you?"

"We're at the hospital."

"What? What happened?"

"Daisy got very sick last night. The poor girl was still throwing up her guts even this morning, so I finally took her to the emergency room. Turns out, she wasn't being dramatic with the hunger strike."

"What's going on?" Charlie asks.

"She's going to be all right." Cassidy's voice crackles like static on an a.m. radio. "But, they just admitted her this morning to give her fluids."

I should have never left Daisy. "Tell me everything."

"I guess a twenty-four-hour bug is going around at her school, and she caught it. We were up all night, and I swear I tried to keep her hydrated, but she couldn't keep anything down. She's hooked up to an IV of fluids and resting well now."

"Oh, my gosh." I want to crawl through this phone and be by Daisy's side. "Cassie, we'll fly back tomorrow morning." Charlie's eyes go wide.

"No," Cassie says. "After she gets some fluids, Dr. Dawkins swears she'll perk right up. My mom's got my daughter tonight, and I'm gonna camp out here with Daisy. I promise she's in good hands."

"I really think we should catch the first flight—"

"Katie, don't be crazy. The doctor said he expects to release her in the morning. Iola Smartley's coming by to visit, so Daisy won't lack for company. We've got this." Voices mingle on Cassie's end. "I need to go. The nurse has more paperwork, and Daisy wants her teddy bear. You go get married, and we'll see you soon."

When the call ends, my mouth still gapes open on the fifty questions I didn't get to ask. "I...I just..." My anguished eyes lift to Charlie's. "She has a stomach bug." I quickly fill him in as the evening wind attacks my updo. "Daisy's in the hospital. Alone."

"She's not alone," Charlie says softly, a man coaxing a lion to retreat. "I have a friend who's a doctor there. I'll have him check on her and give us a report."

"A pediatrician?"

"A proctologist."

"Zero help, Charlie. We should fly back."

Charlie's expression hardens. "I care about Daisy too. You know that. But we have a wedding tomorrow. It's scheduled, it's paid for, and I'm not moving the date again." The steel in his voice is unmistakable. "We can call Daisy every hour, but if they expect to release her tomorrow, there's no point in returning home."

I slowly, vacantly nod. "Okay."

"She's going to be fine. We'll make sure of it."

I glance up at the ominous clouds above us, a canvas of angry gray and dancing black. Even the stars ran away tonight. Nothing feels right, not the impending storm, Daisy's condition, or this island.

God, help me get through this rehearsal.

And if there's any reason this wedding should be stopped, then you shut it down. I keep waiting for everything to feel right. Why does everything feel so…off?

"We have a rehearsal to get to." Charlie tugs my hand, a question on his face.

This might be the most important dress rehearsal I've ever been to. And suddenly, I can't remember my lines, and I'm uncertain of my part.

I clasp Charlie's hand, wanting his touch to ground me, to reset my whirling mind and make all the frantic thoughts go away.

Lightning cracks across the heavens. Trees bow against the wind.

I step into the elements and walk with my fiancé.

Not certain that where Charlie's leading me…is where I'm meant to be.

CHAPTER THIRTY-SIX

MAXINE HOLDS up a questionable piece of fish. "What does this look like to you?"

"Food poisoning." I pluck a piece of chicken with tongs and drop it on my plate.

The wind sounds like a turban outside as my rehearsal dinner is crammed into the office space in the treehouse. Pepe and Dorinda cleared out all the business furniture, putting it who knows where and replaced it with a collection of round tables draped in linens, flickering candles, and place settings fit for royalty. Fairy lights sway above us while music plays from a speaker. Seashells decorate each table, and sand fills the bottom of every glass candle holder.

Though it's not the dress rehearsal dinner I wanted, it's still quaint and beautiful in its own way. Except for the fact that the building-on-stilts sways to the gales of the wind howling outside.

"That storm's really picking up," I say to Pepe as he passes by with bread baskets.

"Seems it's moving faster than was expected," Pepe says. "Eating quickly is not good for the digestion, but in this case, *ees* the lesser of the two evils."

Charlie's hand hesitates over a ladle. "What would be the other evil?"

"A giant wave overtaking you during your wedding rehearsal." Pepe's smile is as fake as the wood flooring in our hut. "It will be fine, though. Just chew speedy-like, eh?"

I don't want to chew speedy-like. This is my wedding rehearsal, not a hot dog eating competition.

"It's gonna be okay," Charlie whispers beside me, serving himself a scoop of pineapple rice. "Deep breaths."

My eyes slip back to the window that Dorinda tried to block with curtains. "It looks like the end of the world out there."

"Just a storm." Charlie drops some potatoes on my plate.

"The clouds look violent, the treehouse keeps swaying, and I can hear the angry ocean waves from here." I face Charlie directly. "If this were a movie, one of those Marvel heroes would be suiting up to sacrifice his life for us to the tune of a power ballad, the storm would turn into a hurricane, and not everyone would get out alive."

Charlie leans down and kisses my forehead. "We're the bride and groom. I'll request we get first dibs on surviving."

"Look at that chocolate fountain, Katie." Maxine stands behind Charlie and points with her fork to a smaller table in the far corner. "Is that a dream come true or what?"

Even the molten, spitting chocolate doesn't appeal. My stomach lurches with every lean of the treehouse as the fierce wind shoves it back and forth. "What if this place topples to the hard earth below?" I accidentally say out loud.

"I can tell you one thing." Maxine pops a crouton in her mouth. "If we go down, I'm grabbing that fountain."

The door opens like an explosion, heralding the arrival of Sterling, Lacey, and Donna.

"After you, Donna." Sterling extends a hand toward the food.

Charlie's mom attempts to right her wind-ravaged hair. "Now, you're polite? Where was this thoughtfulness when I had to ask three times for the check for our reception back home?"

Charlie growls with annoyance. "Mom, Dad, good to see you. No fighting allowed tonight, okay?"

"Family pledge." Joey sits at a table beside Frances and lifts his drink. "No Bensons are allowed to argue on the island."

Frances stabs a green bean with her fork. "Right. Joey's all about peace."

Joey's jovial expression slips into one of confusion. "What's that supposed to mean?"

"Nothing."

Charlie and I sit beside my parents, who are the epitome of calm. Millie wears a flowing sundress that accentuates her yoga arms, while James went with the island vibe and picked a linen shirt and pants the color of the sand.

"Hi, sweeties." Millie smiles at Charlie and me, and her gentle face lowers my anxiety at least .0005 percent. "Just block out the negativity and focus on the reason you're here." She demonstrates a cleansing breath as the shutters crash against the treehouse.

"Should we move so your dad and Lacey can sit here?" I watch the couple search for seats, but the only remaining ones are next to Donna.

"No." Charlie flips his napkin into his lap with a snap of anger. "We're not mediating tonight."

"I'm sorry about Daisy." James bites into a roll. "Millie and I prayed for her."

"The same thing happened to Amy when she was three," Millie says. "It's scary. But by the next day, she was doing cartwheels and jumping off the couch."

I slather a roll in butter. "I know she'll be okay, but I feel helpless so far away."

Charlie rests his arm on my chair. "We'll check back with Cassie in a few hours."

"Ohhhh!" A shriek ruptures the calm, and all heads turn. "You spilled that on purpose." Donna brushes fruit punch from her silk dress while Sterling comes at her with handfuls of napkins. "Don't touch me. Stop that!" She swats at his hands while red juice drips from the table and onto her shoes.

"I'm trying to help." Sterling tosses the napkin down and resumes his seat. "I most definitely did not empty my drink on purpose. Do you have to cause a scene everywhere you go?"

Donna looks like she's seconds away from an apoplectic fit. "You promised me you would be civil on this trip. Our son deserves that."

"Seriously, you guys." Joey slams down his fork and rises. "Knock it off. You two fought at my wedding." Donna and Sterling share a surprised look. "Yeah, I knew about it. But at least you didn't do it right in front of everyone like you have no shame."

I see Maxine pop the top on a Diet Coke and scoot her chair closer to the action.

"Mom, Dad, can I see you guys outside?" Charlie looks toward the window as thunder claps. "Or in that inconveniently small closet over there?" He taps his foot impatiently as his parents follow him into the tiny space that holds a broom and mop bucket. "We'll be back shortly."

"Don't rush on our account," Maxine hollers before running to the closed door and pressing her ear against it.

While we pretend to return to our meals, the building groans and sways like it had too much to drink before the party. Lacey sits next to Jeremy, miserably twirling a fork into her pasta, only to let it unwind and begin again. Sadie leans against Joey, her fingers angrily texting on her phone. I can hear Charlie's muffled voice but cannot decipher his words. I'll have to wait for a transcript later from Maxine. But Donna and Sterling's barbs are clear as the pool water this resort doesn't have.

"You betrayed your family!"

"You set the bar unreasonably high. I could never keep you happy."

"Our children looked up to you."

"You were always gone to those blasted society events."

Thunder shakes the treehouse, and what follows is blessed silence from inside the closet.

Then comes Lacey's meek voice. "I just wanted to thank you all for this lovely trip." Her awkward smile looks pained. "Katie, many blessings to you on your wedding."

"Um...thank you."

Like a flower finally given water, Lacey perks at my small measure of kindness. "When we get back, I hope to spend some time with you and Frances. Get to know everyone in this interesting family."

"That would be lovely." Frances picks up her lemon water and takes a swig. "If you're sure you want to join this mess."

"We're not a mess," Joey mumbles.

"Yes, we are." Frances turns on her husband. Though she speaks low, I hear her loud and clear. "Why can't you accept reality?"

"I thought I was. Maybe I *like* our reality. You're the one who's freaking out."

"Who wouldn't be freaked out, Joey? This was not in my plans. And you act like it's no big deal?"

Donna steps from the closet, red-faced and ready to glove-up for another fight. "Who's freaking out? What is this, another woman?"

Frances crosses her arms over her chest. "A female is possibly involved."

Sterling now joins the community conversation. "Joseph Aaron Benson!"

"I'm not having an affair. For the love of palm trees, Frances is—"

"Tired of you not supporting me during this difficult time."

"How can I? You won't speak to me, and you're sleeping in the spare bedroom. You've even turned the dog against me."

"That's exactly what your mother did." Sterling sends Donna a withering glare.

"You're making me the villain here," Joey snarls, "and that's not fair."

"I think it is." Frances pauses for an angry bite of cheesecake. "And you're being completely cavalier and insensitive. Things are *not* okay."

"What is happening?" Charlie resumes his seat beside me and rubs a hand over his face. "Did we somehow unleash a portal to hell?"

Tears sting my eyes. "I need an antacid."

"You tell him, Frances," Donna shouts. "These Benson men need to know when they're wrong and ruining our lives."

Charlie's dad settles back into his seat, completely oblivious to his date. "I didn't ruin your life, Donna."

"You stole money from a bank, tried to sell off an entire street in the town, then left me for our old babysitter."

"For the record, I'm thirty-one," Lacey interjects.

Donna's eyes bulge. "Nobody asked you!"

"You made it clear we were over, Donna. You told me you could never trust me again, never love someone who'd made my mistakes."

"Yeah, well, you mourned that a whole month before filing for divorce." She looks at everyone. "Twenty-four hours after the judge declared us officially over, Sterling was back at the courthouse... applying for a marriage certificate with *her*."

"Because my wife wouldn't have me."

James stands. "This has gone too far."

But Donna's not done. "Sterling, you're a thieving despot who ruined our family and tried to wreck the lives of dear people in In Between. Do you even care who you hurt?"

"I care."

"Then you bring *her* to your son's wedding? How dare you disrespect what's left of this family."

"Get a life," Sterling yells. "I'm not gonna put on sackcloth and ashes and wail in your front yard. I did that for months, and what did it get me?"

"Hopefully, a rash."

"Stop yelling! All of you." Frances slams down her water glass. "All you two think about is yourselves, and I'm sick of it!"

Ignoring this, Donna rounds on her ex-husband. "You're so immature."

"You've poisoned the minds of our children!"

"You tried to get out of helping with this wedding."

"I'm pregnant!"

I suck in a loud breath, then turn to the source of the announcement.

Dorinda drops a plate.

Heads swivel. Eyes round in shock. Mouths fall open.

"What did you say?" Maxine barks. "I think I have seaweed lodged in my ear."

Frances covers her face with her hands. "I said I'm pregnant. There." She throws her hands toward Joey. "Are you happy now?"

Joey's tan face softens. "I've said all along I am. You're the one who's freaking out."

"You bet I am. I'm 27. This was not in the plan."

"Plans change."

"Not mine. I had an order of things, and marrying you already messed that up."

That barb is so sharp, even I feel it. Tropical Storm Charro ain't got nothing on Hurricane Frances.

"Maybe some of us should leave the room?" James quietly suggests.

But Frances is a shaken champagne bottle who's come uncorked. "Since I was a child, I knew I wanted to work for NASA. Just like I knew I didn't want children until I was thirty. But now look at us."

"So, the timeline moved up." Joey rests his elbows on the table and bravely leans toward his wife. "It's going to be okay."

"Stop telling me it's going to be okay. You don't have the hard part here." A sob escapes her lips. "I'm not ready to be a mom."

Me neither, girl.

"I want to work and make a name for myself at my job. I wanted us to travel and see the world."

"We still can."

"Are you going to climb the Eiffel Tower with a baby in tow?"

Joey scoots closer and reaches for Frances's trembling hand. "I would climb Mt. Kilimanjaro carrying you and a baby if that's what you wanted."

She crumbles into him, her face pressed to his shirt. "What are we gonna do?"

Maxine cups her hand over her mouth and bellows. "For starters, you could talk louder so I can follow along. Way too much background noise out there."

"I love you, Frances. Things might be changing fast, but that's still true and always will be."

She pulls away from Joey, dabbing a napkin to her eyes. "Lately...I don't know if that's enough."

"All righty, wedding revelers!" Pepe slips back into the room. "Who's ready to continue this party?" A funeral could not have been more heavily quiet. Pepe's brown eyes assess the situation: the stilted silence thick as island humidity, the angry energy buzzing with more electricity than lightning, and the strange hissing from the direction of

Donna Benson. "We also have a Divorce Package for $199.99. If anyone here is interested, talk to me after the storm."

I feel like I just ate bad salmon. Like I've gone three rounds, each one ending in a TKO. Frances is my sane friend, my level-headed, in-love-with-life and everything is positive, friend. How did she and Joey let things get so bad? They're having a baby...and it's tearing them apart?

I steal a look at Charlie, who cuts into a steak like the cow did him a personal injustice. What if this is us in a few years—angrily airing our dirty laundry in front of God and all creation? Fifty percent of the married couples in this room are a disaster.

"The storm has progressed faster than expected," Pepe says. "Let us now adjourn to the beach for rehearsal before it hits." He looks to Charlie and me. "Let's give this wedding a try."

As Charlie holds my hand and leads me down the stairs, fear whispers taunts in my ear and pulls up every bad memory I've ever had. Feelings long dealt with hit me harder than the wind gusts, slapping me with rejection, isolation, loneliness, despair, anger. The storm has blown away the top veneer, and the buried ugliness has been set free.

God, I need to know this marriage is the right thing to do. I don't want to hurt Charlie. If Frances can't make it, how can I? I love Charlie so much, but if this wedding isn't right, you have to let me know. Make it so painfully clear.

I don't want to succeed at a wedding—just to fail at a marriage.

CHAPTER THIRTY-SEVEN

My wedding rehearsal looks like a low budget remake of *Lost*. We're on an island, the weather's clearly demon-possessed, and some of the supporting characters want to kill each other.

Walking to the beach feels about as smart as walking into a hurricane. Though the rain's little more than an occasional sprinkle, the wind blows stronger than an industrial fan in a Beyonce video. I can see the storm in the distance, and it's clearly headed this way. Frances and Joey walk silently behind us. I want to ask Frances a hundred questions, but I can tell now is not the time. Aren't baby announcements supposed to be happy? Are we living in the Upside Down?

A few rows of chairs are already set up on the sand, currently occupied by my entire wedding party. I add my shoes to the pile they've created on the boardwalk. Tomorrow, providing a Caribbean Armageddon doesn't occur, the pathway to the altar and the chairs will be decorated with tropical flowers. Charlie and I will stand beneath an archway of lilies, orchids, and hibiscus and pledge to love one another forever. Looking at that bare wooden arch right now, I'm doubting that dainty contraption will last through the night.

James stands next to Millie on a mound of sand. "I can only think of one other bride-to-be who's ever been this pretty."

"Thanks." Maxine joins us. "I was a beaut."

"We better get the ball rolling before Sterling and Donna start another fight." Millie glances back toward Charlie's snarling mom and dad.

Jeremy, Frances, and Joey settle onto a small row that separates Sterling and Donna. Lacey pats her disgruntled fiancé's arm while Donna glares at both of them over her daughter's head.

This is already going so well. Maybe I should call up *Bride* magazine and see if they want an exclusive.

Pepe clears his throat as thunder echoes in the distant hills. "Santisto Island Resort is pleased to welcome you tonight to this lovely rehearsal. I'm proud to introduce you to my son, Marco." He grins at a pimpled young man who looks to be about sixteen. "Marco will be your officiant."

What? Does this kid even have a driver's license? "Are you sure this is legal?"

"Most definitely," Pepe says. "Everything we do here is above board. Places, everyone. Take it away, Marco. And don't forget, if lightning strikes within eight miles, go inside. We've yet to have anyone die at one of our weddings. It wouldn't look good on the brochure."

Sweat glistens on Marco's pimply forehead. "Good evening to you all." More thunder booms, as if sending us ominous messages. "Let's get started, eh?"

While Marco spouts off instructions and moves people into position, my eyes pan the scene. We have Charlie's parents arguing from a few rows away. Jeremy reclines in his seat and wears a large smile because my fellow thespian thrives on quality drama. Then there's Joey and Frances who sit tilted away from one another, and if they've shared two words, I haven't caught it. My family stands on the other side, listening attentively, but stealing looks at Charlie and me like we're an illusion that might evaporate in the wind. Maxine whispers something to Sam and passes him some cash. Probably her wager on whether I'll stick this wedding out or hop the next boat back to the mainland.

"Charlie, you will wait for your bride beneath the arch," Marco instructs as said arch gives a violent lurch, bowing against the swift breeze. "Can we have the groomsmen up here with Charlie, and the bride's party ready to walk down the aisle?" He gives more directions for the order, then after everyone is in their places, Marco pushes a few buttons on his phone, and a stringed version of the wedding march lilts from a speaker.

Sadie walks down the aisle, pretending to toss rose petals. Next comes Jeremy, who sashays toward the arch like he's walking a runway.

Wearing rolled-up khakis and a white button-down, Sterling offers Frances his arm, and the two follow the path. I wonder if Frances is thinking of her own wedding, and if it fills her with nostalgic happiness —or regret.

Maxine looks positively giddy to be escorted by Joey. Her hair tosses to and fro on her head, and her long lashes flutter against the blowing sand. Her bare feet make dainty prints in the sand, and her joyous laugh almost makes a dent in my anxiety.

Almost.

At Marco's nod, James kisses my cheek, and we begin our slow walk. The waves crash so hard against the nearby shore, I can hardly hear the music. But I take a deep breath, inhaling the salty air and the hint of James's familiar cologne. I feel the warmth of my arm wrapped around his and lean closer as we approach Charlie.

Why does this feel so...off?

Maybe if Daisy was okay, I'd be okay too. Maybe if we weren't on the verge of evacuation orders, I'd not feel this reflex to run.

Or maybe I'm not supposed to marry Charlie because I could ruin his life, and things this good don't happen to girls like me.

Marco clears his throat. "I will begin the ceremony with a few pretty words. Would you prefer a quote from Taylor Swift or Bono?"

Charlie and I exchange a befuddled glance. "Just pick one," I finally say.

"Very well. It'll be a surprise."

Hey, Marco, wanna know what no bride wants on her wedding day? A surprise.

But the "minister" smiles at the small crowd, oblivious to the elements and the brewing tempers. "The red-headed guy will speak now, no?"

Jeremy makes his way to the front. "I prefer honorary bridesmaid, thank you." He pulls a tissue from his pocket. "I said I wouldn't do this, but weddings get me every time." He blows his nose with a disturbing amount of energy. "I first met Charlie in first grade. Then I met Katie in tenth."

An unoccupied chair goes cartwheeling by. "Skip to the end," Marco says. "Before we blow away listening to these riveting details."

"My speaking skills have won countless awards." Jeremy sniffs. "Mostly, participation awards, but quality hardware nonetheless."

Marco's hair dances in the growing wind. "Who gives this bride away?"

"Her mother and I do." James's hand closes over mine with a warm squeeze.

"Cool." Marco jerks his chin toward the peanut gallery. "Father of the bride, you're no longer needed."

You're no longer needed.

Marco's words echo in my ears, and white-hot panic becomes a wild beast in my soul, trashing and baring teeth. Lighting flashes from miles away, and its charge accelerates my heartbeat to a manic rhythm.

James takes his seat beside Millie, who holds the hair from her face. I always assumed if I was lucky enough to get married, James would be the one conducting the ceremony. It seems so wrong to have this total stranger marrying Charlie and me. Especially one who looks like he just finished taking his ACT and needs to speed it along so he can report to basketball practice.

Marco raises his voice over the growing roar of the elements. "At this point, I'll say some nice things about love. Love is patient, love is kind, blah, blah, blah, yadda, yadda, yadda." James puts his head in his hands as if the "minister" drove a stake right through his Ecclesiastes-loving heart. "I think you've written your own vows, right?" His head volleys from Charlie to me. "Because if not, we sell a vow upgrade for $59.99."

"We were supposed to write vows?" Charlie asks.

"Yes." Marco nods. "Is that a problem?"

"Our wedding is tomorrow," I say like Marco hasn't checked his calendar. "This is the first we've heard of bringing our own vows."

"Just share from your heart." Marco smiles like he's solved the world's problems. "Oh, I forgot. Before vows, we'll take a moment to light the unity candle." He gives a jerky nod to Pepe, who advances on us with a Bic stick lighter. "Torch that baby up."

An instrumental song plays as Charlie takes my hand. I pause mid-stride, certain the song is a screeching rendition of "Living on a Prayer."

I stumble on a shifting layer of sand, but Charlie catches me with his strong arms and guides me to the small table bearing a lone, white candle.

Marco clears his throat, and his voice fades in and out over the howling wind. "Two separate lives becoming one. Forever. Living together. Burning together. Dying together."

Lightning cracks in the distance, and I offer up a prayer that the dying together thing doesn't happen tonight.

"Each of you will pick up a small votive."

My heart thumps in my chest so hard, I can see my dress moving. With shaking hands, I pick up a candle that looks like it's seen a few weddings. Pepe touches his propane lighter to Charlie's wick, turning it into a dancing flame.

Then it's my turn.

Pepe clicks the button of his lighter once, twice. It finally reignites, struggling against the push of the air. When he tries to light my charred votive, I feel a silly pressure for mine to instantly light as well.

But it doesn't.

On the fifth try, my candle is still cold and flameless.

Sand flies into my eyes, and I blink against the gritty assault. Swiping at my face, I draw back a hand covered in mascara. Big raindrops fall on the bare skin of my shoulders, and my frizzy hair droops with each pelting drip.

"If you could hurry, ma'am," Marco says. "The storm's moving fast." He gestures wildly to the candles. "Two will become one. Come on, get unified. Quickly."

I hold my hand over my candle, attempting to block the wind, as Pepe tries one more time to bring my candle to life. Finally...success.

"Great job, Katie!" Maxine yells.

"Now light the unity candle," Marco yells over the booming thunder.

I follow the same process Charlie did, touching wick to wick. But nothing. It's too much wind, and the spray from the ocean intensifies as if someone turned a dial. After three more attempts, my hair hangs like a soggy curtain over my eyes, I taste saltwater on my lips, and my body shivers before the unwilling unity candle.

"We must move on," Marco says. "You get the idea. Tomorrow will be a success, no?"

Will it? Because I can't even handle tonight.

Charlie watches me with concern. He holds my hand extra-tight as we return to the minister, probably afraid his fiancée is a flight risk.

As the rain begins in earnest, Pepe passes out umbrellas, then rushes toward us, holding one over our heads. Our families huddle close, forming a human wall to buffer the elements. Maxine looks like a sea witch, her eyes glistening beneath the radiant light of the moon, her skin slick with rain, and her hair somehow standing on end.

The next portion of the ceremony plays out like a Caribbean version of *The Princess Bride*. "Marriage," Marco yells. "Marriage is what brings us here today as we celebrate..." He stops to spit out a leaf. "We celebrate Katie Parker Scott and Charles Thomas Benson." His voice is barely audible over the crashing surf and growing storm. "Should we move away from the sea?"

"Just keep going," Pepe yells.

Marco takes a bolstering breath and continues. "I'll say more sappy stuff here about the happy couple, then start the vows. Katie, you would begin." He pauses and shakes his head, and I'm not sure if it's my cue to speak or if Marco just needs a moment to let the water drain from his ears.

I glance at Charlie, but he's no help. I then look at Pepe, who still holds the umbrella. He merely shrugs.

"Your vows, Katie," Marco bellows.

This is miserable, and I want to cry. This wasn't how I saw my wedding. I'm in a tropical nightmare, I can't see a thing, and my photos are going to look like we're at a wet t-shirt contest. Any moment a wave's going to leap from the ocean and collect us all. "Just pretend I said my vows. I, Katie, take thee, Charlie."

The umbrella chooses that moment to flip inside out, and it pulls Pepe away like a runaway kite.

"Your turn, Charlie," Marco calls, tucking his Bible into his shirt.

Charlie holds my fingers in his with one hand but shields his face with the other. "Insert vows here. I, Charlie, take thee, Katie, forever and always, I do."

"By the power vested in me by Santisto Island and QuickieOrdinationServices.com, I now pronounce you husband and....*run for it*!"

A wave as tall as Charlie leaps from the sea and crashes over us.

Down I go, spitting and sputtering. Charlie swims to me, gasping like a beached fish. "Are you okay?" He gets to his knees and pulls me to him. "Katie, talk to me."

"This is terrible." Looking down, I notice my dress is askew and revealing more bra than anybody needs to see. "I can't do this."

"Yes, you can. Run. We gotta get out of here. The storm's too strong."

"Get off the beach!" Millie shouts. James stands twenty feet away, waving to us with both hands like we're a lost plane he's trying to guide safety.

Marco runs right past us. "Get to your cabanas. Go, go."

Pepe races by next, dropping umbrellas in his wake. "Just a reminder, we're not responsible for damages!"

"Come with me." Charlie wraps an arm around me and tugs me in the direction of his cabana as rain pours from invisible buckets. "Katie?"

But I can't follow. My feet won't move toward him. Tears freefall down my cheeks. "I can't."

Feet buried in the sand, Charlie stands there while the rain pelts his beautiful, confused face. "Please."

One word. But I can't obey it. It's too much. This has all been a horrible mistake. "How many more signs do we need that this isn't meant to be, Charlie?"

"Don't do this now," he says. "Get inside."

I shake my head, my hair stuck to my cheeks like tentacles. "I can't marry you."

"Fine." His voice duels with thunder as the trees sway in the background. "We'll go home and do it."

"No." A choking cry breaks from my lips, and I shake my head. "This is all wrong. If your parents, my bio parents, and Joey and Frances can't keep a marriage together, how can I?" I lift my hand, and the wind tries to yank it from my body. "There are too many signs that this wedding is doomed. I'm wearing a dress I didn't want, marrying in a location I'd never choose, we're sleeping in glorified haystacks at the world's worst church camp, and now a tropical storm just materialized out of nowhere and trashed our rehearsal. None of this is coincidence —not in my life."

"None of that has anything to do with us spending the rest of our lives together."

"Everything's falling apart." The wooden arch goes sailing by. "Literally."

"It's a storm. We've weathered plenty of these."

"Not like this. I'm cursed, Charlie. My wedding day is cursed, and so are my odds of being a functional wife. I can't do this to you."

Rain hits us sideways as his grip tightens. "Don't you bail on me, Parker. Not now. We've come too far."

"I love you, Charlie." A nearby fake palm tree uproots and catapults toward the ocean. "I love you too much to hurt you."

"Katie, you're scared. I know it's been a bad week."

"Get off the beach!" Marco screams from the boardwalk. "You must get inside."

A trio of chairs rolls like tumbleweeds. "There is no wedding. The venue's ruined. It's gone."

"We can still get married. Here."

Tears mingle with rain on my cheeks. "No, Charlie."

His eyes darken, like the storm clouds above us. "Admit it—you never wanted this wedding. You didn't want to get married on this island."

"Because I've had a bad feeling about it."

"You've had a bad feeling ever since I proposed."

I can't deny it, so I don't. "I love you. I wish I could make this right."

"I'm sorry the wedding's so messed up." Charlie reaches for me, trying again, but I step away. "I'll fix it when we get back to Texas."

"There's no fixing this." I look at this face I love, and my heart disintegrates into a thousand pieces of sand as I hand him my engagement ring. "Because I don't think there's any fixing me."

"Let's work this out. Please."

A lightning bolt zings over the water, much too close. I hear family far away, pleading with us to leave the beach.

"I'm going back to my cabana," I yell. "The wedding's off."

"I won't follow you," Charlie calls as I walk away. "Not this time."

"I do love you."

They're my last words before the wind pushes the world sideways and the rain floods.

I run toward James and Millie's cabana, my dress in tatters, and my heart somewhere back on the beach. Washed away with the current and taken to the murky depths.

God, tell me this was the right thing to do. Isn't it for the best?

I'm saving Charlie from a disastrous future.

I'm saving him from me.

CHAPTER THIRTY-EIGHT

I SLEPT two hours last night, hunkered down in Millie and James's hut with my grandparents. My eyes are swollen, my face blotchy, and I'm so heartsick, I can hardly hold myself upright. The storm hit full force as soon as we left the beach, and it shook the island all evening. Pepe swore our cabanas would hold up, and miraculously he was right. It sounded like a tornado would touch down any moment, but we survived the evening safe and alive.

I can't say the same for my heart.

When I walk outside at six on Monday morning, I step into a war zone. The storm might be gone, but the carnage remains. Debris as far as the eye can see. Chairs and umbrellas tossed like confetti. Fake palm trees shredded and exposed for the frauds that they are. It smells like dead, rotten fish, and my stomach tries to rebel as I breathe through my mouth.

Slipping off my flip-flops, I carry them in my hand and walk down the **boardwalk**, the painted wood rough beneath my bare feet. The sky hovers in shades of gloomy gray, blocking out the sun as if it still won't let her play. And why would it? Why would the sun shine on the day that should've been my wedding? The day that if the weather hadn't ruined, I surely would have? And pretty much did.

I stand on the spot where I would've said 'I do' to Charlie. Tears blur my vision, and I try in vain to blink them away. Everything's gone. Nothing left. Like my energy, my joy, my hope for a different life. I kick a wooden remnant of what should've been the floral archway, like a wrecked portal to what could've been a happy married life.

"Hey, kid." James walks toward me, carrying two mugs and a face of fatherly concern. "I thought you might be down here. Any word on Daisy?"

"Released from the hospital and home." I'd called and texted Cassie to the point of annoyance. "Already asking when she can get back in the pool."

He hands me a cup of coffee. "Mark that off your list of worries."

I take a tentative sip, and my taste buds rejoice. "The coffee's not instant. How'd you get this?"

"I paid Marco twenty bucks to bring me the real stuff from his house."

"My hero." I step into James's outstretched arm and lean into his sturdy side.

"Ten years ago, you couldn't stand for me to so much as hug you," he says quietly, watching the water. "Look at us now."

It's an invitation to trade witty zingers, to lighten the dark mood. But even my sarcasm muscles are spent. "Because you're a safe place, James. You and Millie both are. You've proven that time and time again."

"And Charlie?"

Seawater reaches my feet and slides over my toes, leaving bubbles in the sand. "He is."

"Then what's going on?"

"Would you believe me if I said I didn't know?"

James looks down at his mess of an adopted daughter. "Yes. I think that's fair. Why don't you hit me with some of the things going through your head."

"I want to be Charlie's wife. I want to spend the rest of my life with him."

"But?"

"But...I can't forget that I'm Bobbie Ann Parker's daughter."

"You're *my* daughter too."

It's more than sea spray stinging my eyes. "I'm terrified of messing this up. The last thing I want to do is hurt Charlie or future children."

"Why would you?"

"You know my family history. And just when I think I can put it behind me, Haven and Daisy show up as giant reminders."

"You're not genetically predisposed to divorce and dysfunction. It's not freckles and red hair. Maybe you've been conditioned to repel relationships, but that programming ended a long time ago. I'd like to think Millie and I have been good examples of a happy, functional marriage. And how to stash cookies in various places in the house to keep the peace."

"So, that's the secret?"

"I'm sorry if you thought it was grander than that. All these psychologists are way off." James chuckles.

"Part of me is afraid marriage is closing the door on a season of my life I'm not ready to leave."

James drops his arm and frowns as he lifts his cup to his lips. "Closing the door on singlehood?"

"No, it's..." I know it sounds ridiculous. It's stupid and juvenile and silly. "Closing the door on being your daughter."

"Katie—never." I'm back in his arms in a flash. This time it's a full-body hug with back-pats and his chest moving in deep-contemplative breaths. "Things will be different, but you will always be ours. Our home will forever be your home, and we'll never stop being your parents."

"Millie's going to turn my room into a yoga studio."

His breath puffs in a small laugh. "As much as I'd like to keep your bedroom a shrine to you for the rest of our days, the reality is you're twenty-seven. This is what parents do. They turn unused bedrooms into guest rooms and man caves and media rooms. It doesn't mean it's no longer your home."

James is right, but it still offends the sixteen-year-old in me who apparently will never grow up. Frances's bedroom got taken over by her younger sister the day Frances went to college, so it's not like it's an offense particular to me. "I've worn your last name proudly for years. I will never forget my adoption day—when the judge read my new name to the whole courtroom. And now? I have to give it up."

"I guess you could keep your maiden name. Make Charlie become a Scott." James watches a seagull swoop in the sky. "But it doesn't change who you belong to, right? Just like Charlie altering his name wouldn't sever him from his family."

"I suspect he might be interested in pursuing that option right now." My hair whips in my face, and I give up on trying to harness it. "Maybe it's more than letting go of my name."

"Then what is it?"

"My moving to Chicago made things different. We don't see each other like we did."

"I call you every night. I assumed that was annoying."

"It is." A laugh slips from my dry lips. "But the few nights you don't, I miss it. I miss you. And Millie."

James turns and places his hands on my shoulders. He looks at me the same way he did my senior year when I told him I was afraid to graduate. "You didn't get the childhood you deserved. Heck, you didn't get a childhood at all. I think it's natural that you want more time and wish life would slow down." As he says the words, relief fills me—not that he's fixing it. But that he's verbalizing something I don't even understand myself. "Unfortunately, life does move on. Don't you think I wish I could have more time with you? I'd turn back the clock and do your high school years all over. I miss our driving lessons when it was just you, me, and your terrible music in the car. I miss Friday nights when we'd all go to the high school football games, and I'd sit in the stands and watch you laugh with your friends."

"And invite them for pizza and ice cream after."

James turns his head, his eyes glazed with emotion. "I miss standing at my pulpit in church and looking out at the fifteenth row where you'd sit. I *still* catch myself searching for you."

Now I'm full-on crying. I rub a hand over my face, swiping away tears and what's left of last night's mascara. "Why did we have to grow up, James?"

"Aw, babe." He hugs me tightly, and I smell the ocean on his shirt. "It hurts, doesn't it?" I nod against him. "But you have my promise I'm going to keep calling daily, and so will Millie. We'll visit New York at least twice a year. We'll FaceTime and TikkyTok, and whatever else will bring you closer to us."

Twice a year. How can I live without these people like this? "I'll fly in on holidays."

"We Scotts have to stick together."

"Even if that Scott becomes a Benson?"

"Especially then."

A seagull flies overhead, its piercing cry an echo of my soul. "Why do I panic at every turn in the road?"

"Because you care. And because every plot twist requires a new way of doing things, letting go of some of the hard-earned ways that worked. Trauma teaches you to live in flight mode."

I'm so tired of running. "Part of me dreams of quitting acting, moving back to In Between, and taking Ms. Hall's place when she retires."

"Is that what you really want?"

"No. But I'd have you."

"You'll always have us. It will just continue to look different. And now you'll have a husband. One more person to keep you safe and love you."

"I want to believe that could be true."

"Why can't you?"

I know this is going to sound pitiful, but feeling as barren as this beach, I voice it anyway. "Deep down, I've never believed happy endings were for me. I've had happiness and safety since leaving my old life, but I've always feared it would erode away." Like sand in a storm. "Girls like me do not get guys like Charlie Benson or parents like you and Millie."

"Katie—"

"Until you adopted me, I spent my whole childhood wishing and dreaming about a life like this. Then, when it actually happened, I've been waiting for God to take it all away. It's all been too good to be true."

"Why would God do that?"

The knot in my throat expands. "I don't know, James. I can't explain it. And to see everything unraveling for this wedding confirmed what I'd suspected—that marital happiness was out of my reach."

James tucks me into his side again, and we watch a yellow sailboat bounce across the water. "He stilled the storm to a whisper. The waves of the sea were hushed."

The verse doesn't sound familiar. "What?"

"Good old Psalm. What I like about it is the reminder that God can stop the storm—he can completely take it away. But often, he stills it to a whisper. The storm's still there, but the noise is lessened, the intensity's held back by his hand. Because he knows we can handle it. Katie, you can handle everything that has you panicked. I don't want God to give you smooth sailing—that's a boring, uneventful life. Stop chasing safety. That's not what we're here for. Are you going to walk away from Charlie because things might get hard, and you don't know what's up ahead?"

"I assume failure is ahead."

"Don't miss out on a wonderful thing because you're afraid of the pain of failure or loss. If Maxine had known she'd lose her first husband so early, there might never have been a Millie. If we'd known Amy would go down a spiral of substance abuse, we might never have had children or never kept trying to help our daughter. But look at her now. Life is so hard, but it's also so beautiful. And you—you might've been our greatest risk. Thank God we pushed through and committed to weathering the difficult times. I wouldn't have wanted to miss out on you, Katie."

I have to look away, studying the horizon while tears drop onto the sand. "Some days, the fear is so much bigger than the hope."

"Stop thinking of hope as a feeling then. But instead, it's something you work at, something you recommit to every day. It's showing up and doing it scared. Fear is a cult that claims too many. It lures you in with faulty promises of safety. It wants to change your very identity and keep you bound to its lies. Not one decision I made out of fear has ever served me well."

"But look at Frances and Joey or Charlie's parents. They're a mess. If they can't keep a marriage together..."

"There are no guarantees. You will have hard days, but if God is a loving God, then he's going to see you through the good and the bad. He has a plan for you to help you succeed and not hurt you. To give you a hope and a future. Sound familiar?"

Jeremiah Twenty-nine. The verse that had rocked my world when I first met Jesus as a sixteen-year-old orphan. A verse I'd packed away like an old yearbook or an outdated sweater from my high school days that no longer fit or felt relevant.

But here I am needing to hear the words again.

I have a dream job waiting for me in New York. One I landed with hard work and skill—two things I can rely on. But the things acquired by love and surrender and grace—they feel like mirages and out of my control. Like there's no amount of studying or preparation, no self-reliant proficiency that can strengthen my grip on my loved ones and make them stay.

"God is for you," James says. "Just like your mom and me. And just like Charlie."

"I doubt Charlie feels that way at the moment."

"He's hurt. Tell him what last night was really about."

"He stopped calling and texting me at three a.m. I ignored him all night."

James winces. "Are you ready to talk to him?"

"I think so." Though I still have no idea what I'm going to say.

"But, are you ready to marry him now?"

The correct answer here is yes. Why can't I say it? "I'm not sure."

"I can't tell you what to do. Only you know if marrying Charlie is right. But make your decision on hope and faith—not on fear."

The tension that pulls on my spirit lessons a fraction, and I think of the sails on that boat needing slack in order to move forward. "You always know what to say."

"I don't." James kisses my windblown hair. "But I find that if I start with the basics—I love you, I want the best for you, and I'm listening—the rest seems to fall into place."

"That's what I should offer Charlie, isn't it?"

"That's worked well for me for a long time. That and the cookie stash."

"I should go find him."

James clinks his coffee mug to mine. "Godspeed, sailor. Go get your beloved."

CHAPTER THIRTY-NINE

MY BELOVED WAS GONE.

"What do you mean, Charlie left the island?" I grip the door to Joey's cabana, my fingers itching to tear it from the hinges. I ran to Charlie's hut first, but Jeremy told me Charlie had spent most of the night with his family. "Where is he?"

Joey tosses a shirt in a suitcase and joins his mom at the door. Probably to protect her from the crazy lady screeching questions. "He left early this morning."

"Charlie got a commercial flight?"

"No, hon." Donna tilts her head in sympathy. "He chartered a plane with Marco."

"Our twelve-year-old minister is a pilot too?"

"Only for the very desperate," Joey says.

And that's what Charlie is? "Then, I'll charter a plane with Pepe."

"All flights got grounded as of half an hour ago," Donna says. "We'll have to wait until visibility clears with this incoming fog."

Oh, of course, there was debilitating fog this morning. I wouldn't be surprised if we get a monsoon followed by a swarm of locusts when the fog rolls out. "Why didn't Charlie tell me he was leaving?" Today is our freaking wedding day. Or was. Or could've been.

"I was with him all night." Joey has the under-eye bags to prove it. "He called you a hundred times. Even had a plane arranged for you to get home to Daisy."

"I was busy having a panic attack and sitting in the tub to ride out the storm." Joey and his mom exchange a look that tells me neither finds my excuse terribly convincing. "You have to tell me where Charlie went."

"Back home," Joey says.

"To Chicago? To New York?"

"To In Between, dear." Donna Benson's face softens. "He said he had some thinking to do."

"I've got to get to the airport and catch him."

"It's too late." Joey's words sound like the ominous last line of a Broadway tragedy. "His plane left before sunrise."

"Then I'll call him."

"You won't be able to reach him for hours."

I cover my eyes with my hands and try not to burst into tears right here in this drippy room. "I have royally screwed up."

"That makes two of us." Pink spots dot Donna's cheeks. "I want to apologize for the little squabble between Sterling and me."

I take a peek between my fingers. "Little squabble?"

"Medium-sized."

I blink back rogue tears and face the woman who would've been my mother-in-law. "Donna, as far as fights go, it was a supersized combo with double fries and a shake."

"I'm sorry. Sterling and I have been circling each other for the better part of this year, and I'd finally had enough. My timing was unfortunate, and I hate that it contributed to what Marco calls 'the worst wedding rehearsal this island has ever seen.'"

"I have shoes older than Marco, so it's not like he could've seen too many." Plus, this island was apparently pulled out of a box and inflated minutes before we arrived.

"And I'm sorry if Frances and I spooked you," Joey adds. "Our life's been turned upside down lately, and we let it get the best of us. We promised we'd leave our quarrels in Texas, but they seemed to have jumped in our suitcases anyway."

"Yeah, why couldn't *that* luggage have gotten lost?"

"Your rehearsal dinner wasn't the best time to finally hash it out," Joey says, "but you know Frances. She keeps everything in her head and analyzes and compartmentalizes, making mental spreadsheets. Then, when she's had all she can take...." He mimes an explosion with his hands. "She erupts like a volcano."

"Volcanos usually come with warnings."

"So do tropical storms but look how that turned out."

Terrible. With my wedding venue obliterated and possibly my relationship with Charlie irreparably tattered as well. "Everyone's splitting up, and it really scared me last night." And every day.

"Who's splitting up?" Frances steps inside the cabana, her glasses as crooked as the ponytail on her head.

"I...You...I mean...." My voice rises an octave. "Who's *not* splitting up?"

"Katie, we're not getting a divorce." Frances must see complete disbelief on my face because she walks right to me and says it again. "Joey and I love each other, and we're not breaking up. Ever."

"It's none of my business."

"It is your business," she says. "We're about to be family."

That doesn't look very likely right now, but I don't need to add one more Jenga piece to what's already a precariously leaning family stack. "You guys have been fighting ever since I got back to town, and you said you're in separate bedrooms, and this wasn't the life you wanted. In fact, you said a lot of stuff that made me think you were done with your marriage."

Frances looks toward her husband, regret hardening her features. "Turns out you're not the only drama queen. I've said a lot that I would like to take back. We just found out about the baby, and I'm still in shock. Joey had five whole minutes of surprise and then was fully acclimated and ready to be a dad. Meanwhile, I'm back here at first base, still wondering how this happened and how helpless I am to how much my life is going to change."

"That's not true about only being shocked for a matter of minutes." Joey crosses the short distance in the cabana and takes his wife's hand.

"I'm completely poleaxed and scared out of my mind. But I wanted to be strong for you and act like it was all cool."

"You're telling me the calm thing was an act?"

"I thought that's what you needed—someone to be the strong one."

"What I want is someone to talk to about how freaked out I am, somebody who gets it."

"Oh, I get it." Joey runs his hand through his hair, a frustrated habit just like his brother. "I haven't slept in a month."

"And that's why I'm in the spare bedroom," Frances says. "This guy tosses and turns like a fevered pig. But I love him, and I'm keeping him." She rises on the toes of her sandals and kisses her husband's cheek. "I'm sorry if we gave you the wrong idea, Katie. Joey and I had a long talk last night while we thought the wind was going to carry us away, and we realized the important thing was that we worked through this together."

"We're going to love this baby." Joey's smile could light up that gray, foggy sky out there. "And life is going to be great when he or she arrives."

"You're going to be an aunt of a precious baby," Frances says to me. "Again."

"And I'm going to be a grammy." Donna claps her hands in glee.

"That makes Dad a grandpa." Joey sighs. "And you'll be at family functions together for many years to come. You two better figure out a way to get along."

"I know. Your father and I have really messed up. Katie, I'm sorry we ruined your rehearsal. I can assure you kids, that will be the last time Sterling and I conduct an argument in public."

I doubt that, but no time to disagree. "I have to talk to Charlie. This is a nightmare."

"But you told him you didn't want to marry him." Joey throws my words right back at me. "The guy was torn up last night. I've never seen him that upset. Of course, we also thought the fake palm trees were going to fall on our cabana at any moment and kill us, so that did add a sense of heightened conflict."

Donna sidesteps a drip from the ceiling. "What exactly is it you'd like to say to my son?"

I...I'm not sure. "I want to beg him to give me some time. To help me plan another wedding, maybe in the winter. One that's not on an island. In a storm. And to not give up on me."

"He's waited a long time to marry you, Katie," his mother says.

"Did he say anything last night that I need to know? You've got to give me something to work with here."

Joey's mouth forms a grim line, and his sad eyes meet mine. "Keep in mind he's mad. We all say stupid stuff when we're angry."

"Spit it out, Joey." I'm dying here, people.

Joey looks like he wishes a plastic tree would fall on the hut right about now. "He said you've postponed the wedding for the final time."

Dread gives me a shove harder than any tropical storm wind could ever blow. "What else?" I can tell from all the hand-wringing there's more.

"Katie." Frances pushes up her glasses then takes my hands in hers. "Charlie says he's done."

CHAPTER FORTY

In a romantic comedy movie, Charlie's flight would've somehow been delayed, and I'd race to the airport, catching him in the nick of time. I would've explained my current psychosis, he'd have a pre-boarding epiphany, and all would be well. Reunited and newly enlightened, we'd kiss as charmed travelers would clap and video our moment to post on their socials.

But this is real life, and more specifically, it's *my* real life, so the airline couldn't rebook our flights home until late Tuesday. After Pepe's toy plane flew us to Cancun, all eleven of us grabbed any flight and any seat we could, which put me on American 2407 to Houston by myself in the emergency aisle. Would I be willing to help passengers deplane should we need to unexpectedly land? No, thank you, ma'am. I would be the first one off this bird, and I'd throw elbows and trip any breathing human in my way.

Despite my dislike for flying and my ever-present belief we'd crash into a deep body of water, the plane safely and smoothly carried me to Houston. My bags obediently spun out of the luggage conveyer belt right away, no doubt making up for their former tardiness. Inside one suitcase was a wedding dress I didn't get to wear and might not ever need. The idea pained me as I wearily flagged down a taxi and rode back home.

An hour later, when I step into my dark house, I pause in the living room, my ears perked for any sound of life. The delusional, sleep-deprived portion of my brain wondered if Charlie might jump out of the shadows and yell, "Surprise! I forgive you, and let's go back to how things were!"

But Charlie isn't here, and neither is anyone else. I'd thought the next time I walked over this threshold, I'd be married. Mrs. Katie Benson. Instead, I'm still Katie Parker Scott, an adult child profoundly messed up and toxically confused. And very much not married.

Charlie still isn't answering my calls or texts, and I don't have time to research the cost of skywriting. So, after a quick shower, I strap myself into Millie's Subaru and drive like a maniac to Cassie's.

When I ring the doorbell, Cassie's daughter greets me and ushers me through the house and to the backdoor. "Daisy's been looking for you since this morning. She'll be so excited you're finally here."

"Katie!" Daisy leaps from the well-lit pool as I approach, her face alive with sun-kissed color, and her smile full of unbridled joy. Dripping wet, she launches herself toward me and tackles my legs in a hug. "I've missed you."

My sleeping heart flutters to life, and tears fill my eyes. "I've missed you too."

"Really?" She hugs me tightly.

"Yes." My hand combs across her tangled, wet hair. "Really." This kid's love and affection are so pure. I've done nothing to deserve it, and she's endured significant trauma. Yet here she is, hugging me until I'm as wet as she is, and smiling as if I've never left. "How are you feeling?"

"Good. Are we going home?"

Home.

"Daisy's been such a wonderful guest." Cassie wraps a floral towel around her swimsuit, water raining droplets on the concrete in her wake. "We went to the zoo, had a pizza party, visited the park, and pretty much lived in the pool. She begged to do a little night swimming this evening. You've got a little fish right here."

"Cassie says I should take swimming lessons." Eyes full of hope hold mine. "Can I?"

"We'll talk to your mom about it." I take a moment to enjoy the way the breath fills in and out of my lungs with less of a labored effort. I'm so glad to lay eyes on Daisy, so relieved to see for myself that's she's all right. "Your mother wants to see you after your little trip to the hospital."

She throws her small arms around my neck and hugs me with the force of a person three times her size. "I missed you so much. I'm happy you came back for me."

I hold her tight and smile into her wet hair, my clothes now soaked through. "I promised I would come back."

"**Alice**," Cassie says, "why don't you take Daisy inside and help her get her stuff together. We'll be in shortly."

But Daisy doesn't want to let go. "It's okay." I kiss the top of her damp head. "I'll be in shortly."

"Are you taking me with you when you go?" Doubt dims Daisy's smile.

"I'm not leaving without you."

"I'll wait for you in the living room. By the door."

Cassie's daughter hands Daisy a Mickey Mouse towel, then guides her inside. Daisy turns back to watch me with every other step, a sad uncertainty marring her sun-kissed face.

"How is she really?" I ask Cassie as the door closes, leaving us alone with the lapping pool and clouded moon.

"Daisy's fine." Cassie wrings out her long hair. "You'd never know she was ever sick. I'm sorry we panicked you." Her focus dips to my hand. "Tell me you didn't come back early because of my call."

"No." Speaking of things that make a person violently ill. "There was a big storm the night of my rehearsal. It devastated the beach and tore up the venue."

"I'm so sorry. With those beach weddings, I thought you'd only need a beach and a minister." Her eyes widen as she takes in my face. "But, I understand if you didn't want to get married without all the pretty setup."

"Yeah." If only it were as simple as me needing flowers and a photo-worthy backdrop. "Anyway, aside from getting sick, how was Daisy?"

"Very quiet in the beginning, but she warmed up. The girls camped out in the living room, and we kept her busy. She had two video visits with her mom, and that perked her up." Cassidy laughs as she pulls her hair into a ponytail. "Daisy lived for your phone calls. She sure does adore you."

Cassie's words are a gift I'll hold onto until I'm old and senile. "I missed her too."

She escorts me to the back door and into the house. "You have a wonderful niece, Katie."

As we step into the living room, Daisy stands in front of a TV that's playing a Disney movie, her hand in Alice's. "I do have a wonderful niece, don't I?" All this time, I haven't thought of her as mine. But I am her aunt. We're related by blood. I've tried so hard to keep my distance, but I went and fell for Daisy anyway. And maybe that's okay. Maybe I don't have to tell her goodbye forever after this week. Somehow I can be part of her life from New York. And she'll be part of mine.

Like family.

"Come back and see us again real soon." Cassie hugs Daisy, who clutches her teddy bear and grins. "Tomorrow, I get a new foster child who won't be as easy as Daisy. A teenage girl who I've been told is mad at the world. She'll be here any minute."

I want to correct her, to tell Cassie the new foster isn't mad at the world—it's her world that's mad. "I know a little bit about what that feels like." More like a lot. "Call me if you need some help."

I gather Daisy's belongings, thank the family again, then walk down the sidewalk as Daisy chatters, her thoughts coming loud and fast.

"...and then after the doctor left, a nice woman came into the room to give me something to eat, and I was hoping it was Chick-fil-A, but it was this stuff called Jell-O. It wobbled and was green and—"

"I missed you," I say abruptly, surprising us both. "Like a lot.

"Did you bring me back a present?"

"*A* present? No." Daisy's face crumbles as we reach Millie's car. "But three presents? Yes." She giggles, a lyrical sound that provides a perfect melody to the fireflies dancing over the yard. "Let's go home."

"Did you wear a princess dress and marry Charlie?"

I punch the unlock button on the key fob extra hard. "No."

"Why not?"

"There was a really bad storm on the island."

"So?"

Nothing like a five-year-old to cut right to it. "I might've panicked a bit."

"Why?"

Maybe I should've let the little interrogator spend one more night with Cassie and Alice. "Because sometimes when we're scared, we do silly things."

"Like when I kicked that girl at church?"

"Exactly."

"Or when I dumped a whole bottle of glue in Henry's hair at daycare?"

"Didn't know about that one, but that is a prime example."

"Who did you kick, Katie?"

Her face is so earnest that I have to give her the truth. "Charlie. Pretty badly."

"Just tell him you're sorry."

"I'm trying."

"Do you want me to talk to him for you?"

Is it wrong I want to say yes here? "I'll take care of it but thank you. Maybe we can both act better, knowing we're safe and loved."

"I hoped and prayed you'd come back for me, and you did." She slips her hand in mine, her eyes looking at our connection with child-like wonder. "Maybe you need to hope and pray that Charlie will stop being mad at you."

Bright headlights shine as a red Ford sedan drives down Cassie's street, then eases into her driveway. Daisy continues to give romantic advice as I watch the vehicle come to a stop and a harried young man gets out. He grabs a duffle bag from the backseat before running to the passenger door and helping a reluctant girl out.

This must be Cassie's new foster teen and her caseworker.

The girl wears a dark stocking hat and jacket, though it's hotter than an oven. She follows the guy a few paces toward Cassie's front door, her posture slumped in surrender, her head bowed, and her steps uneven in their angry cadence.

The two disappear into the house, and the door shuts with a sickening thud.

I was once that girl—scared, alone, desperate to be anyone and anywhere else.

But look how far you've come.

The thought slides between my ears, in that space where words take shape, and my own fears and dreams still rest.

It's true. I'm not that messed up teenager anymore. It's time to stop reacting from that place, to stop giving that part of my wound such life while the healing parts suffocate. I want to operate from a place of expectation like Daisy did, to move forward with a faith that good things are for me. I've got to get back to that place of hope. God's done it before—given me my parents, the best grandmother to ever leap off the assembly line, a career on stage. All things that were so impossible when I was Daisy's age.

Perhaps a long, love-filled future with Charlie isn't so impossible either—if I hope and believe. And maybe I was never going to be complete without this new addition to my family anyway. "You're a smart girl, Daisy. Do you know that?"

"Yes." She laughs, and for the first time, I see that the shape of her mouth is just like her mother's—and mine. "My mommy tells me that all the time."

Her hand still in mine, I help her get into her car seat. "How about we go see your mommy tomorrow? I think we both have things we want to tell her."

She yawns as she settles in. "I love you, Katie."

The tears are instant, and instead of shooing them away, I let them gather and fall. "I love you too." I do. I really love this kid. "Now let's go home, Daisy. Your aunt wants to hear all about your stay and how miserable you were without me."

Her short legs quit squirming, and her fingers in her hair go still. "Are you going to be my aunt?"

"Yes." I hand her one of her teddy bears, then safely secure her harness. "Yes, I am."

CHAPTER FORTY-ONE

THE CAR IDLES in James and Millie's driveway while I listen to Charlie's outgoing message, the same one I've heard a million and one times. "Charlie, please call me back. We need to talk."

"Did you call him *again*?" Daisy's toy tablet beeps as she kicks her feet against my seat.

"Yes, I did."

"He must be really mad."

How to put this in a way a five-year-old gets? "I hurt his feelings." I don't even know where Charlie is. He has to call me at some point. We have movers taking all our stuff to New York next week. Will he still go? I feel like every second I don't hear from him, I'm emotionally bleeding out, and soon there will be nothing left of me but a flood of anxiety and regret.

"He'll forgive you," Daisy says, so naive and innocent. "My mom was mad at me once for eating dog food, but she got over it after I gave her a big kiss and said I was sorry."

If only that could fix this.

Earlier on our drive home, we cruised by Donna Benson's house, as well as Sterling's. Nobody answered at Sterling's, and Donna hadn't heard from her son. When I called Frances, she and Joey were brainstorming baby names. They'd talked to Charlie briefly when he'd called simply to tell them he was okay, but he did not disclose his location. I guess he isn't ready to see me. On the bright side, it gives me time to gather my thoughts and figure out what I want to say when I do see Charlie face to face.

As we step into the house, cool air escapes outside.

So does Amy—carrying an armful of boxes. "Hey, welcome back."

"What are you doing?" I watch Daisy skip toward the kitchen as I frown at my sister.

"Packing." She leans against a porch post. "I found an apartment near downtown."

Is everything changing around here? "Why?"

She chuckles at my ridiculous question. "Because it's time. The backyard apartment has served me well, but I'm ready for my own space."

"But James and Millie will be alone."

"I won't be far. And I think they're going to be fine." She smiles as my grandmother squeezes by us, making a grand appearance in her Vote for Maxine shirt and wedge heels. The puppy runs near her feet. "They've got plenty to keep them company."

"Hello, granddaughters." Maxine picks up Daisy's puppy and gives it a pet. "I barely survived that last plane ride, but fortunately for you, I did live another day."

"Rough flight, Mom?" Millie asks as she takes the wiggly, sniffling dog and hugs it to her.

"I'll say. The turbulence got so bad, the flight attendant had to pause the drink cart. If it's too dangerous to serve me a soda, you better land that bird. Am I right?" She pets Petunia's soft head. "Also turns out the pilot does not want unsolicited advice mid-flight. Learned that the hard way."

Millie hugs me. "How are you doing, sweetie?"

Daisy meanders back into the living room, a snack in each hand. "She made Charlie mad and probably needs a timeout."

The tea kettle whistles from the kitchen, a lonesome sound that we all follow. "Has he called?" I ask.

Maxine and James sit at the table while Millie opens a cabinet and sets out mugs.

James helps Daisy onto his lap, then pretends to take a bite of her cookie. "I'm afraid not."

The water from the kettle provides a small cloud of steam as Millie pours. "I'm sure Charlie will call."

I'm glad she's certain. Because I'm not. "I think I'll run upstairs and find those souvenirs for Daisy." And text Charlie five more times.

In my bedroom, I collapse on the bed and give myself a moment to melt into a mattress that doesn't vibrate for a quarter. I'm worn out and don't know what to do to reach Charlie. Clearly, he doesn't want me to find him.

"Hey, sweet pea." The bed bounces as Maxine plops onto the mattress. "Still no word from your sweetie pie, honey dumpling?"

"No."

She flops onto her back and tucks her hands behind her head. "Iola Smartley's downstairs."

I jolt upright. "Now?"

"Yep. Said she's found a long-term foster family for Daisy."

"Daisy can't go." I shake my head to see if the idea will dislodge, but it doesn't. "I can't send her to live with another home of strangers."

"When did you decide that?"

"Tonight."

From the satisfied smile on Maxine's face, my declaration comes as no surprise. "That's my girl."

I collapse back onto the bed. "I know nothing about taking care of a five-year-old."

"So you say, but you've done okay so far. Last time I checked, Daisy's alive. A little weird, but alive."

"It's only been two weeks. Anyone could keep a kid going that long. Plus, it totally throws a wrench in my plans." Where will I find child-care in New York? A sitter for evenings? What if Haven's not out of jail before Daisy needs to start kindergarten?

Bracelets jangle on Maxine's arm as she grabs my hand. "Life has a way of working out. God turns our chaos into order, you know? Before you, I'd been praying for years for a kindred spirit, a best friend of my heart. But nobody came. Years passed, and my daughter told me she was fostering a teenage girl. No way, I said. A teenager will just be angry and troublesome. Get you a cute baby. But Millie didn't listen to me. And thank God she didn't. That teenage girl who came to live with her *was* difficult. But in no time...I knew I'd found the best friend I'd been praying for. And, my dearest sweet pea, you were worth the wait."

I've cried more in the last week than I have in my entire life. "That is the nicest thing anyone has ever said to me."

"You're the left to my right, the queso to my chip, the king-sized candy bar to my brassiere. You've taught me so much about life, about opening my heart, about taking a chance on people I don't immediately understand. You don't have to have it all figured out to love Daisy and give her a good home. Millie and James didn't. Six months into your stay with them, and they still didn't have it together.

"It felt like they knew exactly what they were doing."

"Girl, they were completely faking it. But they had the necessary fundamentals—hearts willing to help, constant prayers to a God they believed in, and a commitment to do it despite the setbacks and hard days. They were struggling with a run-down theater and a daughter even more broken. It was not an ideal scenario to add a new family member."

"But they did it anyway."

"I can tell you when it comes to kids, you're never ready, and it's never the right time. If people waited for the perfect scenario, the planet would go extinct."

"I work over fifty hours a week. What if I can't balance it all—my big break role, a new town, being a good foster mom?"

"Balance is a big fat myth pushed by people who want to sell self-help books and shame other women. What you do is determine to try your best and take it day by day. It's good advice for parenting, marriage, and pursuing the best possible moisturizer."

"I don't want to screw this kid up, Maxine."

"You won't. Honey, if anyone could screw a kid up, it's me. And have I ever harmed a hair on your head?" Her eyes narrow as she considers her statement. "On second thought, don't answer that. The point is, I've kept every kid in my care mostly alive. And you will too.

This situation is temporary, and it'll be good practice for your future children."

"I don't even want to think that far." I can't even keep it together long enough to get married. "I do want to help Haven. She's not what I expected."

"People often aren't."

"I thought she'd be as flaky and messed up as any other person in the family. But she truly loves Daisy, and she's working hard to get her back."

"And when this is over? Will you sisters go your separate ways?"

"I've tried everything to distance myself from my biological roots—physically and emotionally. I've needed that to heal and give myself a fighting chance at life. I've wanted nothing to do with Haven, and her dad will never be my father. But...meeting Daisy changed it all."

"She needs the love and support of family. You know what that feels like—to finally have a tribe of people who love you and take care of you."

"It seems very full circle, doesn't it?"

Maxine's smile is winsome as her hand holds my cheek. "God seems to know what he's doing. As do you." Her eyes light with excitement. "And I can visit and help. I can take Daisy to the theater and the zoo and picnic in Central Park. We can go see the Rockettes who turned me down forty years ago and give them the stink eye while sitting on a double-decker bus eating ice cream."

"These sound like big plans."

"That's how my granddaughter Katie and I roll." She kisses me with a glorious smack. "I love you. Always and forever." She leans in close and lowers her alto voice. "You really are my favorite."

"And you're mine. I love you, Maxine."

"Best friends forever and all that sappy jazz. Now. How about you go downstairs and tell that Iola Smartley lady you're taking Daisy to New York, and I'll find our girl and get her ready for S'mores at the fire pit." She jumps off the bed with all the agility of a twenty-year-old. "Oh, and Katie?" Her hand grips the doorframe.

"Yes?"

"Your fiancé's staying at his grandmother's house."

Charlie's in town? "How do you know this?"

"You forget my sister Sylvie's former CIA. She has ways of obtaining information best not confessed out loud."

"The house on Apple Blossom Street?"

"That's the one." Her bronzed eyelid drops in a saucy wink. "If you need a wingman for your stakeout, I'd be glad to volunteer. . .I know this property well."

CHAPTER FORTY-TWO

MAXINE WASN'T the only one who knew this house well. When I was sixteen, Maxine talked me into climbing on the back of Ginger Rogers 1.0. We pedaled to Trudy Marple's like front-runners in the Tour de France. Assuming they had a division for the mentally unsound and profoundly unfit.

The debacle was the first of many stakeouts with my grandmother and perhaps the most famous. After climbing onto a limb that hung over Trudy's house, I'd fallen into her pool. Then as I stood in my wet clothes and dripped in her kitchen, I met Trudy's grandson Charlie.

Now here I am on Apple Blossom Street again, eleven years later, this time using the front door like anyone with brain cells would do. I punch the doorbell with what's left of my polished nail after chipping and chewing my manicure on the flight home. Trudy recently moved to a nursing home, but at some point, she upgraded her doorbell to the camera kind. Somewhere, someone is getting a look at my anxious face.

I ring it again. It chimes a tinny tune and flashes small blue lights, letting me know it's alive and doing its job. When that gets no response, I pound on the door with my fist. "Charlie! Please let me in. I need to talk to you." My hands hurt from smacking them against the door, but I keep at it, yelling his name. "Charlie, you can't shut me out forever, I—"

The door flings open, and arms reach out to stop my fall.

But it's not Charlie.

"Joey?"

Charlie's brother releases his hold, then leans into the doorframe. "Um. Hey, Katie."

"You knew Charlie was here and didn't tell me?"

"Hello to you too."

"Is he here?"

Joey rubs a hand over his stubbled mouth, pausing one tedious beat. "He needs some time."

"Charlie!" I yell past Joey. "Please talk to me."

"Look, he's had a rough few days." Joey blocks the entrance like a bouncer to New York's most exclusive club. "Some stuff's come up at work, and our dad just sent word from Vegas that he and Lacey got married by Elvis."

"Skinny Elvis?"

"No, it was last minute, so fat Elvis."

"White jumpsuit?"

"With sequins."

Almost as bad as a marriage at a fake resort. "I know I hurt your brother, but I have to explain."

Joey looks sympathetic, but his loyalty lies with Charlie. "He thinks you made your feelings clear on Santisto Island."

"But—"

"What do you want from him?" Joey's voice takes on a therapist's quality, dulcet and curious.

"I want to explain that I'm sorry."

"You're sorry for how it all turned our or you're sorry you didn't say the right things?" His eyebrows drop in a frown. "The only thing Charlie needs to know is if you want to marry him or not. Your answer on the island was no. Has that changed?"

Yes. No.

Maybe?

"I think it could."

"You *think?*"

"It's very complicated."

"Only if you want it to be. Go home, Katie. Give Charlie his space. When he's ready to talk, he'll find you."

"Okay. You're right." I reach in for a hug. "Thank you, Joey."

"Frances and I love you." Joey's arms extend wide as he steps toward me.

"But, I gotta talk to Charlie." I duck beneath his embrace and shoot into the house. "Charlie?" I hear Joey call for me, but I keep trucking. Where is he? "Charlie?" I have a faint recollection of bedrooms being upstairs, so I hustle up the staircase like I'm running from an inferno. I yell his name when I reach the landing, wondering why this house has so many blasted doors. "Please talk to me."

Then I see him.

Charlie steps out of the bedroom at the end of the hall. He's so close, yet from his rigid posture and resigned face, there might as well be miles between us. "What do you want, Katie?"

"To talk to you."

"Why?" His face is covered in stubble, and his hair points in every direction. He wears an In Between Chihuahua T-shirt and bare feet stick out from his faded jeans. "I'm working. I have a work call with our office in Honolulu in ten minutes."

"I just need five."

His expression remains stony and impassive. "That's all, huh?"

"Yes. I wanted to say I'm sorry."

"I heard."

Then why not respond to my 400 texts and voicemails? "You have to know I still love you."

"And you have to know that I often doubt that."

That one cuts deep, a rusty edged razor across my heart. "We can work this out, can't we? I acted rash back in Mexico."

Charlie's hand grips the back of his neck as he looks longingly toward his room. "Admit it, Katie—you didn't want to get married on the island."

"Because I had a bad feeling about it."

"You've had a bad feeling ever since I proposed."

"That's not fair."

"Oh, it's quite fair. And quite accurate."

"I *do* want to marry you."

"True or false: you were relieved the tropical storm wiped out our plans."

"I..." My tongue tangles with my teeth, rendering my mouth useless to speak.

"Never mind." Charlie takes a step toward his room. "What am I doing?"

"Charlie, stop." I advance down the hall, determined to make him listen.

"Why?" He says it with such fatigue and futility, I want to sob.

"Because I love you." Why aren't these magical words? The open sesame to his heart?

"Maybe it's not enough." He shoves his hands through his hair, disheveling it even more. "Katie, I've been patient. I've waited for you for two years since our engagement."

"I haven't made up things just to cancel our wedding. We both agreed we were going to give our careers everything we had."

"Maybe we should've made the same promise for our relationship."

"I'm trying. It's not my fault a storm wiped out the venue. Do you want to go find someone to marry us? Right now?"

Charlie's jaw flexes, and he crosses his strong arms over his chest. "Sure."

"Okay, well, maybe not right now. I'm sweaty and a mess and—"

"Here's the difference between you and me. I'd marry you anytime, anywhere. You could smell like five-day-old stank and wear a paper bag, and I'd still happily say I do. You keep waiting for all these perfect conditions, and there aren't any."

"You've got to admit the island was next level cataclysmic, though."

Three steps separate us, and he closes the distance, his legs scissoring in angry strides. "I think you've been reading tea leaves and scanning roadsides for signs that tell you this wedding wasn't right—this *marriage* isn't right."

My voice cracks like fragile china. "I'm not afraid of a wedding." Lest we forget, productions are kind of my thing. "What I'm scared to death of is messing this up and ruining your life. Of you waking up two years from now and realizing you've had enough, that you've married a girl who can't overcome her past, can't disentangle from the ropes of dysfunction, a girl who has no idea how to be a wife."

Charlie looks battle-weary, as if he's been on the frontlines one too many times. "Have I ever made you feel inferior? Have I ever once made you feel like I had these giant expectations for you as my wife?"

"No, but—"

"But what?" His question booms and echoes in the hall.

"You've been raised in an upper middle-class world. You had two parents who loved each other and were married forever and—"

"And look how that's turned out. Katie, your past made you who you are, and that's a good thing. How many times do you have to hear that? How many times are you going to get that question on your life quiz and purposely choose the wrong answer? I love you. *You.* Every piece of you. And I would hope you'd take me as I am as well. I was about to be a husband who also had zero experience as a spouse, and maybe I had worries too." His chest rises and falls with his quick breaths. "I worry about all the plays I have to miss. I worry if I'm interesting enough for you, edgy enough, if I'll be a good dad, if you'll ever agree to a dog, and if you'll get bored and lonely when I'm gone for weeks at a time on business."

"When you're gone, all I do is watch Netflix and work and miss you." And eat unseemly amounts of ice cream, but there's no need for full Ben and Jerry transparency at this time.

"Do you know what I worry about most of all?" Pain slashes across his shadowed face. "I wonder if you will ever truly trust me with your heart."

"I do trust you."

"No, I don't think so. Or else you'd know that I can handle all your worries and fears because I've got a hundred of them myself. You can tell me anything, but you don't. You dodge and evade, and sometimes it's small and subtle, but other times it's as big as a tropical storm hitting an island."

"Give me another chance, Charlie." Sixteen-year-old me would rather die than beg, but adult me is not too proud. "Please."

"And then what? You delay that wedding date as well? Maybe we want two different things. You want me but won't commit. I can't live like that. Not anymore." His phone rings from his room, a loud chime that demands his attention. "I have a call from work I have to take."

"But we're not through talking."

"I think we are." The incessant ring continues. "For now...we are through. Goodbye, Katie." He steps through the oak-framed doorway and shuts himself inside with a click.

Leaving me standing in the cold hall.

Alone. Again.

CHAPTER FORTY-THREE

If it weren't for Daisy, I wouldn't get out of bed.

If it were not for this three-foot-three inch, milk-mustached, *Sesame Street*-watching sprite, I'd pull the cover over my head and bawl until my body dehydrated into a husk. But I can't.

For the past two days, I've put on a brave face and been super aunt, playing dolls, hosting tea parties, and riding bicycles in the neighborhood until I couldn't feel my legs. Then, after tucking Daisy in bed, I've crawled beneath my sheets and cried into my pillow until the sun comes up. When I report to work on August first, the makeup artists are really going to have their work cut out for them.

Right now, even the thought of Broadway doesn't thrill. It feels empty without Charlie.

Sitting at a traffic light now, I realize I've driven five miles on autopilot, unaware of how I even got this far. Did I stop at the four-way downtown? Did I yield on Gibbons Street? When will my mind do anything but obsess over Charlie and tell my heart to return to beating?

The clock on Millie's car reads 11:30 a.m., which means I have plenty of time to drive Daisy to her very important appointment.

Her visit to the county jail.

Iola Smartley got approval for Daisy and Haven to visit in person, so I picked Daisy up from daycare, fed her a quick PB&J, then hit the road. I may have failed as a fiancée to Charlie, but let the record show I'm about to walk my niece into a minefield of personal triggers. I haven't been to a jail or prison since my mom was alive. Who'd have thought I'd ever return—and to see family I barely know.

"Have you talked to Charlie?" Daisy asks from the backseat, like a tenacious talk show host who has yet to hear the response she wants.

"Not in a while," I say as casually as the Disney song playing on the radio. "He's very busy."

Busy ignoring me and planning a life without me.

"I saw him." Daisy chomps on a piece of gum I know will end up somewhere unsavory later.

"Oh, really?" I'm barely tuned in to her creative story. I have rocks in my stomach, and I'm still mad that Iola wouldn't transport Daisy for this visit. Jail is pretty much the last place I want to be. I don't need reminders of the place my mom never left.

"Yeah," continues Daisy, "he was sad."

"Uh-huh." I grip the steering wheel and turn left. "Daisy, I know you miss Charlie. Maybe James can take you to visit him this week." Because Charlie's sure not talking to me. I've continued my phone call and text campaign to no avail. Frances says he's still in town and remains tucked away in his grandma's house, working remotely. She doesn't know when he's leaving, but it's soon.

"But, I did see Charlie yesterday." Daisy's short legs kick my seat in an annoying rhythm. "He brought me lunch and ate with me and my friends."

I frown as the sun slants through my window. "At your school?"

"Yeah. He's been there twice. Twice since you got back."

"He has?" *Could I hide in your Hello Kitty backpack so I could see him?* Maybe I should volunteer in her class. "Did he... say anything about me?"

"He said he missed me."

"That's nice. I know he does, sweetie." But back to me. "Did he mention me?"

I watch in the rearview as Daisy ponders this question. My anticipation ratchets up with her every thoughtful second.

"Nope." She resumes her seat kicking. "No, he sure didn't. Can I have some fruit snacks?"

The county jail looks about as welcoming as a setting in a Stephen King novel. My heartbeat escalates as I pull into a weed-dotted parking spot, and old memories crash into me with their barbed wires and jagged edges.

After entering the building, we endure an airport level of security, then follow an escort through multiple doors. The police officer pushes buttons on keypads, says nothing to us, and leads us through a labyrinth of musty halls. I swear I can hear my own heart beating.

When we get to a windowed visiting room, the officer nods to a fellow cop standing outside who seems to be in charge.

"Name?" The woman asks.

As I stare at Haven through the window, I provide the person all the information, get a small pat down, then given the officer's smile to Daisy, assume we pass muster. "Y'all come on in here. Your momma's waiting for you."

Daisy squeals as soon as the door is opened. "Mommy!"

Free of handcuffs, Haven runs to her daughter with a hug and spins her around. I glance back at the officer who's locked in with us, but she only smiles. "Oh, I've missed you," Haven says.

I sit through a half-hour visit, taking in every detail. Haven bombards Daisy with questions, wanting to know everything she's missed since their last call. Minus the hair, mother and daughter look so much alike, from their small noses and pointed jaws to the way they can't keep their eyes off one another. Daisy updates her mom on all the happenings at her daycare. Apparently, a boy there has been stealing her carrot sticks, but yesterday she karate chopped him in the kneecap, and the problem was solved.

"Katie, thank you for bringing Daisy." Haven looks as nervous to see me as I am to be there.

"No problem." Oh, who am I kidding? Everything's a problem.

"I can't help but notice you don't have a wedding ring on."

"Yeah." I swallow against the familiar lump. "I didn't get married."

"What happened?" Haven hands her daughter a Crayon from the pack I was allowed to bring in.

I start to tell Haven some nice, tidy answer. But if anyone could possibly understand the all-consuming chaos and disordered thinking that's the real reason behind my lack of nuptials, it's her. "I couldn't go through with it." I give her the short version of the stormy night and the wreckage that followed.

"Wow." Haven leans back in her chair. "I thought you had it so together."

"I think I was under the illusion I did too."

"I've watched you on social media for the last few years and dreamed I could live your life. You have a college education, a booming career, and a handsome fiancé. You have a family who loves you. I'd see your photos with your parents and think how very lucky you were to have been given a new life. You got out. Not everyone does."

I know not every kid gets the redo I did. Not every foster kid gets a happy ending. "I am blessed with what I have. But nothing's perfect. Social media shows us someone's highlight reel. It's a cultivated gallery of finessed posts to make people think everything's perfect." My online life was so filtered. "It's not perfect."

She gestures to her orange jumpsuit. "Has to be better than my life."

"We're both so tied to our past, aren't we? Who we are as adults is because of who raised us and how we were treated. Instead of going to sleep every night, thanking God for my incredible family, career, and Charlie, I lie awake until all hours imagining all the ways it could be ripped away from me. So yeah, I know what it's like to finally have people in your corner and a good job, but I don't know what it's like to enjoy it, to trust that it will all be there tomorrow." Hot tears cascade down my cheeks. "I worry that any day Charlie will walk out and never look back. And my parents will slowly forget me in New York, stop calling, visit less and less—focus on their bio daughter now that she's back."

"You want to run...before someone else does the running."

It's instinctual, a survival of the fittest. "Love isn't stable in our world, Haven. It's not something you can count on, and when you do have it, it's used against you. My mom would basically ignore me unless—"

"Unless she wanted something."

"Exactly."

"That wasn't love, Katie. Or if it was, it was all your mom probably knew. I get that you're afraid, and maybe I'm the last person to give advice, but it seems to me your family *and* Charlie have had plenty of time to bail on you. And they haven't."

"Then there's the possibility of a giant meteor crashing, a rampant plague that takes everyone I love, and don't even get me started on the living nightmare I endure when Charlie rides in a car with all my family, and I think one wreck could take it all away."

"Don't forget zombies and alien attacks."

I'm completely bankrupt of humor. "You can't tell me you never worry about Daisy."

"Only every minute of the day. When she was taken into care, all I could imagine was her foster mom losing her or making her cry."

Wait a minute. "But you knew I was the foster mom..."

"The point is all we can do is our best to protect our loved ones, pray, and trust we can survive whatever life throws our way. You can't live your life worrying that everything will be taken away or you'll go mad."

"Some days, I worry I'm already there."

"You're not mad. Now your grandma—maybe. But there's still time for you to maintain your sanity. Katie, don't you believe with your whole heart that your family truly loves you?"

"Yes."

"Do you believe with every fiber of your being that Charlie loves you and wants to be your husband?"

I think about this for a moment. "I want to."

"No, don't give me that. Does he love you or not?"

"He does. But what if I can't keep a lid on all my dysfunction?"

"Then you go to therapy and keep fixing the broken parts. And trust Charlie to love you through the bad times as well as the good."

"What if I continue our family tradition of screwing up relationships? Nobody stays married."

"What if you don't?" Haven's tone fills with an amalgam of wonder and censure. "What if you're the first one in modern family history to make it? You've got something the rest of us didn't have—people who love you and fight for you. You have a chance, Katie. Don't let it go. You imagine all these scary scenarios, but the most likely cause of you losing out on a wonderful life is you and your fear. Aren't you sick and tired of living with all that worry? You owe it to yourself and Charlie to stop inviting it into your life. Fear is a liar and a destroyer."

James's words on the beach replay in my head. *"Stop thinking of hope as a feeling then. But instead, it's something you work at, something you recommit to every day. It's showing up and doing it scared."*

Haven reaches for my hand. "I need you to make it. For me, for all the kids who got the short end of the stick. So Daisy can know she comes from good stock and can see what's possible. But most importantly—do it for you. Look, run from those meteors, from the zombies, from the flesh-eating plague. But don't run from the people offering you a lifetime of love."

I sniffle and blink through my runny mascara. "I never said it was a *flesh*-eating plague. I hadn't considered that possibility, but...but I don't want to be my mom."

"Then be you. Because you're not your mom. Neither am I. And we're sure as heck aren't our bio dad. We have a chance to do better." Her eyes light on Daisy, playing in the corner. "And as soon as I get out of here, I'm going to take that chance. I've had a lot of time to think, and I've realized having a better life is more than wishing hard and envying other people's paths. Bad luck didn't land me in jail—bad choices did. This was my wakeup call. I want it to be the last one I need. Fear kept me with that loser ex-boyfriend, but no more. I can't waste one more moment on people who hold me back, and I certainly can't be a part of anything that separates me from Daisy."

Such bold words for someone who's as messed up as I am. How does she make it sound so simple? "Aren't you scared?"

"Completely. I say all that, but I have no idea how to make it happen. I don't even know where we'll live when I get out. If I don't find a good job, how will I feed Daisy or even that puppy she had to have? Who's gonna hire someone with a record?"

"James always says that God honors the brave first steps, the bold few. Maybe we can be the bold few together." I squeeze her hand right back. "I've done everything I could to put distance between me and my biological family these last ten years. But if you're up for it, I'd like to be your family. You said I have people who love and fight for me." I take a deep breath, calling on every brave cell to fight the resistance. "You have that too. In me. And so does Daisy." Freedom sings through my soul, and a pressure removes itself from my shoulders. In this moment, I know...a shackle has fallen.

Maybe I've been waiting for this total healing, to feel normal and whole before I truly commit to Charlie. But what if the healing comes in these small steps? In the chances I take, and the more I give of myself? It could be enough—for me and for a future with Charlie.

"Thank you." Haven wipes away some tears of her own. "I don't know what to say."

"I want you to know I'm taking Daisy back with me to New York. She won't be going to another foster family."

Visible relief washes over Haven's face. "Katie...thank you. Are you sure Charlie won't mind?"

"I don't know that he'll be with me in New York." It still seems so unreal. "But it was his wish all along. I was the one who didn't think I could handle it."

"And now?"

"Still questionable that I can manage your daughter with my life, but I want to try. And I'm here for you as well. We'll talk to Iola Smartley and see what resources she knows of. One way or another, I promise you and Daisy will have a safe place to stay."

"I'm not sure I can ever repay you."

"You don't have to. In our experience, help from family comes with strings attached." I lean forward, sharing a secret. "Turns out in the functional family model, that's not how it works."

"No?"

"No, it's so crazy. Help comes free and clear." I pluck a tissue from a nearby Kleenex box and blow my nose. "This model also comes with a slightly unhinged grandmother. If she offers to take you on a stakeout, for your own sake, you must decline. Outings with Maxine can null and void your functionality warranty."

Haven laughs, a melodic sound that reminds me of Daisy's giggles. "Thank you—for everything. I believe you're going to change some lives, just like your family changed yours."

"Right now, the life I want to change is my own."

"Same here. But you've gotta get Charlie back and marry that man."

"But what if—"

"No more ifs or buts. The same God who saw you through your childhood and carried you to the doorstep of the Scotts is the same one who can carry you through a lifetime with Charlie. You deserve love, Katie. We all do."

"What if he won't take me back?"

"You've got to try, right?"

"Charlie won't even talk to me right now."

"Get extreme. Get his attention. Surely you know someone who could help make that happen?"

One person comes to mind, and my lips curl in a smile. "I think I do."

"Daisy, come give mommy a hug and kiss." Haven embraces her daughter, holding her like she's not promised tomorrow. "I love you, sweet girl."

"I love you too, Mommy."

"Be a good girl for Aunt Katie?"

Daisy shrugs. "I guess."

Haven reluctantly releases Daisy, then pulls me into a hug. "You can do this. Now, get out of here. I hear Charlie buys my daughter toys, and I don't want her to miss out on an uncle." Her hand pats my damp cheek. "When you walk down that aisle, make sure your dad is the one escorting you to Charlie. Fear has no place in that wedding."

"Okay." Who'd have thought my younger sister would be the wise one?

"I've made a lot of terrible decisions." Haven pulls her daughter to her and holds her close. "But choosing genuine, real love has never been one of them."

CHAPTER FORTY-FOUR

"ARE you sure you don't want Ginger Rogers 2.0?" Maxine breathes like a charging rhino as we pedal into the night, the heat and humidity the worst of villains and the most oppressive of foes.

"Lean!" We hang a sharp left, narrowly avoiding a deer peacefully crossing the road.

"Move it, Bambi," Maxine yells. "My granddaughter's got a fiancé to win back." She reaches into her basket and grabs her road snacks. "Beef jerky?"

"No." I pedal harder, knowing Maxine's chewing is directly proportional to her decline in speed. "What if Charlie's not home?"

"He is." She chews loud enough for me and all the woodland creatures to hear. "My new drone captures brilliant pics that confirm his whereabouts."

"Your new what?"

"Nothing! Hang a right."

Soon, Trudy Marple's two-story brick colonial comes into view, and we slow. Why did I take the bike and not a car? Nostalgia's sake perhaps. But mostly for luck. Though every tandem bicycle escapade with Maxine has wrought immediate disaster, the end result has usually paid off. Even if it involved me wearing a nose cast or enduring my entire body covered in poison ivy. I pray it's worth it this time too—hives or not.

Also, the bike ride has given me time to form a game plan.

I hope my bravery lasts long enough to pull it off. As James said, one brave step is all that's required.

We park the bicycle in the shrubs that separate Trudy's house and the one next to it. Maxine wears her typical espionage outfit, complete with face paint and leaves sticking from her helmet. I shunned the Mission Impossible garb for something a bit more alluring. Tossing my protective headgear to the ground, I pull my hair from its ponytail and shake it out, happy to see some of the curling-iron styled waves survived. See, I'm finding hope already.

"Not that I'm one to eschew shenanigans, but are you sure you can't just ring the bell?" Maxine looks up at the tall privacy fence. "I don't recall Trudy's fence being so...imposing."

I slip on my small backpack. "I've been over here three times today, and nobody will answer the door."

"Did you peek into the windows? Try to pry them open? Attempt to come in with a FedEx delivery?"

"Am I your granddaughter?"

"That'll be a yes on all counts." She gives the padlocked gate a tug, but it doesn't budge. "Very well, up we go."

"We?"

"You're not going over alone. On this mission, I'm your ride or die." Maxine grabs my shirt and pulls me to her. "But let's not die, m'kay?"

"Got it. Let's go." We've been here before, climbing into Trudy's backyard when I was sixteen, so no instructions are needed. "I'll hoist you over, then you can help me up from the other side." Somehow.

"No problemo." Maxine steps into my **locked** hands, and after three tries and **a motivational talk**, she finally tumbles over. "*Oomph*."

"You okay?" I can't see a thing except for this fence.

"All my bits in place, but be warned, there's a new shrub. With pointy things all over it. Very aggressive for foliage."

"Are there still chairs out by the pool? Can you throw one over?"

"I've got something even better." The sound of rustling precedes a knotted rope flung to my side. "Getchu some of that."

Things never go well when my grandmother starts channeling The Rock. But I grab the rope, give it a tug to make sure it's anchored in her hands, and scale the fence with all the grace of a drunk squirrel.

Though I don't expect a response, I run to the back door and pound on it for good measure. "Charlie? Open up. Please."

Minutes pass, but Charlie does not appear. Discouragement spirals in my head, but I refuse to give in. "You know what we have to do."

"Phase two." Maxine crosses herself then mutters a prayer. "You have your supplies?"

"Check."

"Go get 'em, toots. Make that boy talk to you."

The tree bark rips into my skin as I climb the large oak tree that shades the entire backyard. It still hangs over that pool, but now it also puts me at eye level with Charlie's second-story bedroom. Outside lights illuminate most of the yard. "Ew, the pool's green."

"This house has been shut down for a year." Maxine stands beneath the tree, now peeling the wrapper on a Hershey bar. "Have I mentioned that I feel so cheated out of quality time with the chocolate fountain on the island?"

"We'll make it up to you later." Assuming there is a wedding later.

"You bet you will, sweet pea. Charlie can't resist you. Hey, watch that branch."

"Ouch!"

"How's the nose?"

"Filled with greenery."

"Keep going. No man can resist a grand gesture." Millie said she'd waited for a grand gesture, a big sign of confirmation that James was the one. I realized that Charlie's given me a hundred small grand gestures in all that he does—from opening my car door to visiting Daisy at daycare. It's my turn to provide Charlie with a confirming sign. I've waited for God to smite this relationship since it started, to rip it away from me because it was too good. But I'm the one who's ruined it, the one who's pulled the rug out from under Charlie numerous times.

Finally, with trembling legs and a queasy stomach, I reach the thick branch that hangs before Charlie's room. Where I hope he still is.

Just as rain begins to fall.

"Are you kidding me?" I yell into the night. "Why does Mother Nature hate me? For the love of umbrellas, give me ten minutes."

Maxine chuckles from below. "I guess this eliminates the fireworks in your bag."

The branch dips as I scoot onto it, straddling it like a bull. "This doesn't feel quite right."

"The tree doesn't care. Go."

Even beneath the canopy of the branches, the rain pelts my face and slickens my hands. "I might regret this. Maybe I should just send Charlie a certified letter."

"Not romantic at all." Maxine holds a hand over her eyes and looks way up to my location. "Get his attention and tell him how you feel. You're a new woman with new words. And you're now a wet, see-through blouse. Coincidence? Maybe not."

I bite back a smile and focus on the branch, scooting out further until I gain some clearance and get a clear shot of Charlie's window. Reaching into my bag, I bypass the sparklers and bottle rockets and grab some pebbles I nicked from Millie's flower beds. I fling one, then another. Then five more.

None hit his window. "Charlie!" I let three more pebbles fly. "Charlie, I'm here to tell you I love you. I love you, Charlie Benson."

"She loves you, Charles!" Maxine echoes nearby.

My arms and legs clutching the tree, I whip my head around. To find Maxine. "What are you doing? Get down."

"Nope. I'm helping."

"You're going to get hurt."

"I brought Roman Candles and a bull horn."

"But I didn't bring a liability waiver. Get down." The thick limb bows and shakes while rain falls. The sky's probably crying at our Lucy and Ethel antics. "Please, Maxine. I don't want you to get—"

Crack! Snap!

The branch breaks in two.

"Oh, no!" Maxine yelps, grabbing me as down we go.

We're a tangle of arms, legs, and words I didn't know Maxine even knew. The world tilts and spins, and I'm almost certain that scream I hear is my own. "Charlie!"

Maxine and I cannonball into the water.

Pain reverberates through my every bone, and my skin stings from the cold impact. For seconds, I'm disoriented in the dark abyss, but I begin to swim, hoping it's the right direction, praying my grandmother is okay. My arms flail against leaves and debris, and I kick my fatigued legs with a renewed shot of adrenaline. Eyes open, I can't see a thing. The water's dark, and there's too much gunk in the pool.

God, get us out of here safely. This is my last mission. I promise.

Mostly promise.

My legs hit a body, and I startle. Then stiffen as arms come around me with a firm hold. We shoot to the surface, and I gasp, pulling leaves from my face as I spit water back into the pool. "Charlie?"

Maxine does the backstroke nearby and grins, a blob of green on her hair. "Your hero."

His hold still strong as iron, Charlie swims us to the edge of the pool and grasps the ladder. "Get out."

"I—"

"Get out of the pool." Water sluices off his T-shirt and shorts as he pulls himself from the ledge and onto the concrete. He lies down on the ground, his breath ragged, and his anger hot enough to evaporate the rain.

Coughing, I climb the metal ladder, the rungs frigid and slimy beneath my now bare feet. "I have sandals here somewhere."

Charlie rolls to a seated position and stares up at the clouded moon. "You scared the life out of me. What do you think you're doing?"

"Crashing back into your life?"

The boy is not amused. "You interrupted an important work call. Get inside before you both get struck by lightning." He sees my hesitation. "Now."

Maxine and I follow Charlie into his grandma's kitchen, dripping the whole way. My teeth chatter and my limbs shake. Charlie looks like an angry pirate who walked his own plank.

"I'll get you some towels and fresh clothes." His eyes sear into me. "Don't move a muscle until I get back."

"You got it, sweetie." Maxine squeezes water from her locks as Charlie runs upstairs. "Man, that water was brutal. Someone needs to shock that pool. Throw in some chlorine. I mean, is that a pool or a moat?"

I hug myself and try to think warm thoughts. "He looks so mad, Maxine."

"But you finally got his attention, didn't you? And without pyrotechnics!" She brushes brown gunk from her shirt. "Though that part was a little bit of a letdown. Explosives improve every situation."

Charlie marches back down the steps, his footfalls heavy and loud. "Here are some sweats and shirts." He returns to us with hair still dripping but wearing a fresh shirt and athletic shorts. He gently hands Maxine some clothes that I know will swallow her, then thrusts mine into my arms. "Katie, are you out of your ever-loving mind?"

Maxine's hand shoots toward the ceiling. "Pick me! I know the answer to this one." Occasionally my grandmother can actually read a room, and she quickly sobers. "I'm gonna go find a bathroom to snoop through, then change. You two kiddies have a nice chat. And Charlie." Maxine pauses and pats his damp arm. "Just remember we wouldn't plummet into a nasty pool and risk bacterial brain rot for anyone."

His partial smile is lethal. "I'll keep that in mind."

Maxine slip-slaps out of the room, her bare feet leaving a slug's trail of water in her wake.

"You should get out of those wet clothes as well," Charlie says through gritted teeth. "You're going to catch pneumonia."

"Would you care?" It sounds like the worst line from my junior high fan fiction.

He draws a deep breath, his chest rising with the effort. "I would."

"Will you be here when I come back?"

Charlie's answer is to walk away.

CHAPTER FORTY-FIVE

When I emerge from the bathroom, I find my former fiancé in the den adjacent to the dining room. He's lit a fire like it's December. And maybe it is—between the two of us—where snow and ice have settled in the short time since we left the island. What I want to do is walk up behind Charlie as he stares into the flames, wrap my arms around him, and hold on until we both come back to life.

Instead, I pad cautiously into the room, my once styled hair now a wet, stringy mess. I wear Charlie's gray sweatpants with room for two of me and a Cowboys T-shirt that's weathered by many seasons of wash and wear. They smell like Charlie, and no matter what happens tonight, I'm not giving his clothes back. This time tomorrow, it might be all I have left of him.

"Hi." I join him at the hearth, letting the warmth press against my skin.

"Hey," he says with no inflection, no feeling. "Your grandma took a call on the porch."

That buys us at least five minutes of privacy. "I'm sorry I ruined your meeting." Charlie does not look at me or give me so much as a blink to let me know he heard. "I'm also sorry about your dad's marriage. I know that's not easy on you guys."

Charlie pushes away from the mantle and stands to his full, imposing height. His eyes flicker with shadows of hurt and a few feelings I'm afraid to count on. "Is this what you came to tell me? You could've texted."

"You'd just ignore it." He needs a shave, and it's all I can do not to reach out and run my hand against his cheek.

"What are you doing here, Katie?" Fatigue slips into every syllable.

"I want another chance."

"Not tonight. I have a call with Tokyo at eleven, and a video meeting with New York first thing in the morning."

"Charlie, I was wrong."

One brow arches, with a rare nod to sarcasm. "Were you?"

"Yes, I panicked. Again."

Full lips briefly press together, as if trying to hold back words. "This was more than your usual neurotic meltdown. You stood on that island and told me you couldn't marry me."

"I got overwhelmed, and everything was going wrong."

"We had Marco, the child prodigy of ministers, a marriage certificate, and our loved ones. What else did you need?"

"Apparently a few more days. And as much distance from Santisto island as possible."

"The place shouldn't matter."

"It smelled like canned tuna. Which, admittedly, did have a slight influence."

The couch groans as he sits and rests his head in his hands. "I can't keep going like this. I have to know there's a future for us."

"There is."

"One that doesn't involve you running the opposite way of the altar?"

"Yes."

"One that doesn't involve you losing your mind every time things get real?"

"Probably not." I move in front of Charlie blocking an escape. "But a future where I show up every day and pledge to be your wife and vow to love you forever."

He does not look convinced. "And what exactly brought on this radical shift?"

"A little bit of James. Also, some time in jail."

He rubs the bridge of his nose. "I don't even want to know." With a glance at his watch, Charlie exhales. "I should probably tell you this morning I called my landlord in Chicago to see if my old apartment was still available."

"You don't need it."

"Why? What's changed since we left the island?"

A hundred responses crash like bumper cars in my head, each one vying for a declaration. My brain aches as I try to sort through possible answers and which one to go with first.

Charlie shakes his wet head and begins to leave. "Never mind."

"Wait!" His stride doesn't even slow as he ambles toward the doorway. It's time to pull out the big guns and let Charlie know I'm his forever. "Marry me."

That stops him. With a hand on the back of a couch covered in doilies, Charlie slowly turns. "What did you say?"

Panic clangs in my head as I mentally rewind and replay my words. *Marry me?*

But...even with the clanging and sudden nausea, it feels right this time. "Charlie, I'm ready."

"No. You're not."

"Seriously, test me. You set the date, and I'll be there. If I have to get my understudy to go on for me or quit the play entirely, I will be at that church or justice of the peace or a canned-fish-smelling island."

"Again—why would I think this time is different? How will I know you'll show up for this wedding date? Are you telling me you're not afraid to marry me anymore?"

"No. I'm ridiculously terrified." The honesty feels like a risk, but it also feels right. "I want to do it anyway. Because I love you, and I don't want to live another day without you. I've realized fear isn't a reason to run, and if I wait for that feeling to completely abate, then I might be Maxine's age before I'm ready." Whatever that indeterminate number is. "I guess what I'm asking you is... if you'll still marry me, knowing I'm afraid."

The wait is unbearable—Charlie standing there while the pendulum of an old grandfather clock sways back and forth, the call of cicadas outside, the settling creaks and cracks of the house as if our argument is affecting its joints.

But then Charlie moves.

One slow step my way, then another.

He still looks like a thundercloud, but when he holds the space two inches away from me, I nearly convulse with all the hope.

"Tenth grade." His eyes lock on mine, and I smell the chlorine in his hair. "I sat in the fourth row of the Valiant Theater on opening night and watched you step into the role of Juliet. You were visibly shaking, your voice quivered on the first line, but a few minutes in, and you stole the show. That's the woman I fell in love with. The one who was clearly riddled with uncertainties but gave it her all anyway and didn't run away."

"But I—"

"I love you for who you are. All of it—the worries, the baggage, the obsessive need for three different kinds of ice cream in your freezer. I wanted to hear you say you could push through the fear—for me. I've needed to hear that assurance. But I've also needed time. Time and space to wrap my mind around the idea of us and whether I could imagine a life without you. I just needed some quiet time alone to really evaluate how much security I was willing to give up— as long as I had you." Charlie pauses, and the chaotic world in my head stops its angry spin, suspended in wild hope. "I also realized today that I've only given you enough room to handle this how I wanted you to."

"You came to this conclusion today? By yourself?"

"I might've had some strongly worded help. Iola Smartley stopped by this afternoon for a visit."

"She was here? Why?"

"She thought I needed a refresher course on your childhood. In detail. She was right."

If I didn't have every line and curve of Charlie's face memorized, I'd have missed the way it softened so slightly the eye could barely catch it. But I did catch it, and effervescent giddiness bubbles within me. "What did she say?"

"Iola heard about our botched wedding plans from Haven. She wanted me to understand where you were coming from—how what you went through as a kid still had ripple effects."

"It does. It makes me do crazy things and make reactive decisions. Bad ones."

"I'm trying to understand. I've grown so accustomed to this polished, evolved version of you that I've forgotten the girl you were when we first met and all the terrible things you went through. I realized this morning I have to love you both. And well."

My eyes can't keep up with the tears because I have never felt so seen. The *before* version of me will always be a part of me, and I need that to be okay. I need her to be safe and enough. "Thank you," I whisper. "I think I've waited my whole life to hear that."

"I'm trying to understand all this, but I'm not superhuman. When you keep running away from wedding dates, it feels like rejection."

"I get rejection." The catacombs of my heart were filled with its remains. "Ever since we got together, I've been expecting something bad to happen—something that would take you away from me. I'm in a constant struggle to accept the idea that full and complete happiness could be mine. That I can have it all—a miracle of a job, a loving family, and you—without a trap door waiting to open any moment to take it away."

"I'm not going anywhere." Charlie kisses the hand holding his, and a thousand burdens lift from my soul. "I haven't been the person you needed, the man who could handle the weight of your past when all of it crashed down on you all at once."

I think back to that wave at Santisto that took Charlie and me both down. The crashing water didn't pull me under. It could have, but I got up and stood on my own two feet. "People who were supposed to love me cast me aside and stopped caring. It's old stuff, but it's a trigger fear that never really goes away."

"I would never do that."

"In my head, I know that, but..." I tap the spot where there's a steady gallop beneath my sweatshirt. "My heart has been so reluctant to believe. James and Haven both told me love was worth the risk, and they're right. My family tree has a ridiculous amount of failure hanging from it. But it's time to stop letting those deep roots wrap around me and hold me back. I don't want to be tied to the failure of everyone who came before me." My breath hitches as tears come. "And there's a *lot* of failure before me. Have I mentioned that?"

"At least once or twice." His lips quirk. "But when you told me it mattered that our backgrounds were different, you were right. You come from an abusive past and will always have those battle scars. I'm sorry if I stopped being a safe place for who you were." Charlie exhales as if the words are a struggle. "If you need more time before you're ready to get married, then I'll wait—months, years. As long as I know you're in this forever, I can take it at your pace. I love you. I don't want to lose you. You're the person I want to spend the rest of my life with."

"Me and all that baggage?"

"You've been looking for the space to be anxious *and* engaged, and I didn't let you have it. But you're going to have to help me too. I need to know when your head's about to explode from worrying or when you think things are too much to bear. You can't shut me out and quit. We're too important for that. *You're* too important for that."

I feel my heart reset and resume its regular beat. "You still love me."

"I've loved you for years." Those five words rip from his throat, rough and hoarse. I want to tattoo them all over my arms, so they're never out of sight.

"Then let's do this—let's get married."

"I don't want to push you into something you're not ready for. We'll both still go to New York and— "

"But I am ready. There's never going to be a good time, and we're always going to be busy, and almost-hurricanes are gonna happen. Charlie, I want to be your wife. I want you to live with me in that shanty of an apartment in Manhattan." I grab one of his hands and hold it to my heart. "Let's get married, Charlie Benson."

He lowers his warm forehead to mine. "Is that what you want?"

"Yes. I absolutely want to be your wife. The one who can't cook, frequently flips out, and works terrible hours."

The slow curve of his mouth will light me up for years. "We'll get takeout and a Groupon for therapy."

What a strange sensation it is to laugh, to finally have relief and joy. "I love you."

"You make me crazy, but I love you too." Charlie's hands slip along the slope of my jaw and cradle my face. His eyes hold mine as he takes his time resetting, recalibrating, his thumbs sliding against my cheeks. "I've missed you." Then his mouth captures mine, warm and possessive, yet infused with a liberation I've waited to find me. I sigh into the kiss, tears dotting my skin, but I don't care. They're happy tears —finally.

My hands slide up Charlie's chest, and my palms feel contours I've memorized. The hills and valleys beneath his shirt have provided rest for my head, safety for my weary mind, and strength to lean against when mine was depleted. There's power beneath my hands, but also a gentleness that humbles me and calms my frenzied, wayward heart. My lips seize Charlie's, changing the angle of the kiss, and claiming him as mine. My nerves alight with fire, my skin tingles, and my breath rushes. Love pulses in every feathery touch of my lips, every nip of his. He is my beloved, and I am his.

Charlie rains kisses along my jaw, circling back to my cheek, then returns to my lips. When I am old, and memories elude me, I pray this one remains—a reunion of two unlikely souls, a love that began as children, and the beginning of a new story that will endure more changes and even greater storms. But we'll endure it together.

"Charlie?" I whisper.

"Yes?"

"I'm always going to be a little afraid." Balancing doubt with faith. Disbelief with hope.

"I'm here."

"There will always be voices telling me to run."

Charlie places a solitary kiss against my palm, his lips a brand, a promise, a deposit on forever. "Then run to me."

CHAPTER FORTY-SIX

Charlie and I sit on the couch in the den a half-hour later. The flames are doused in the fireplace, but there's plenty of warmth between us. My head rests beneath his chin as his arm holds me like his lost half. We can hear Maxine outside on the phone, her phone-speaking volume at a level appropriate for concerts and mobs.

"Maxine will be excited her role as maid of honor is back on." I smile at my fiancé and snuggle deeper. "Oh, and I kind of told Haven we'd take Daisy back to New York."

He grins and presses his lips to mine. "Atta girl."

"You're okay with that?"

"Been hoping you'd change your mind. Once I bought my first Barbie, I couldn't stop. I've got five in the upstairs closet. If I didn't see Daisy again, things were gonna get weird."

"I don't know how we're going to manage it."

"Day by day, Parker. We'll figure it out."

"Hey, kiddies." Maxine's bursts into the room, her hair wilted and clinging for life on her face. "The Orchards Neighborhood reports my signs went missing this morning." She scoots herself between us and whips out her phone. "This is a map I've created that shows the sign-stealing in chronological order. According to the pattern I'm seeing,

Avalon Heights will be hit next. My guess is tonight. The thief hits after ten p.m. and before sunrise." She points to the time on the screen. "We gotta move if we wanna catch that stealer of democracy, that rogue of revolution, that—"

"We get it." I stretch, my arm still a little battered from the fall.

Maxine's makeup-streaked face turns to me, then Charlie. "Wait a minute. Did I interrupt something?"

She knows full well she did. "The wedding's back on. Again. But like for real."

She whoops with delight. "So when's this next wedding date? Six months? Next year?"

"Next week," I say.

Charlie's smile freezes. "What?"

"You heard me right." I sound a lot braver than I feel.

"Wow," he says. "When you go for it, you go all in."

"I'm giving this *I Do* stuff 110 percent."

"How are we going to pull this off?" His forehead furrows. "I'm due in the New York office next Friday."

"Then I guess we're getting married Thursday night." Oh, Lord. That gives us six full days to scramble.

His hand reaches across Maxine and clasps mine. "Do you promise me you'll show up—no matter what?"

"Even if I have to dodge a palm tree, a cabana, and order Captain Pepe to fly me to your side.

"Are you sure about this?"

"I'm sure about you."

"Ohhh." Maxine smacks her lips against my cheek, then Charlie's. "Sweet peas, this is an answered prayer. Now, if I can just get the good Lord to answer the one about the Powerball and my own monarchy, I'll be set." She stands and does a shimmy-filled happy dance. "The wedding is on! Full steam ahead. Throw your rice. Blow your bubbles. Release the doves!"

A phone rings upstairs. "That would be Vancouver calling back." Charlie bounces up. "I gotta take it."

"We'll see ourselves out." I move in and give him a quick peck on the lips. "Call me later and tell me how it went."

He catches my hand and smiles. "You sure about this warp-speed wedding?"

"She's totally, positively certain." Maxine pushes me toward the front door. "Now you two quit canoodling. We need every precious second."

"I love you," I call to Charlie as he runs to his phone, and I'm shoved outside.

The door shuts behind us, and Maxine and I both stand on the porch.

Two realizations hit me like an ice bath over the head. "We don't have a car." I hold out a hand and am grateful to find it's barely raining now. "Also...how do I plan a wedding in six days?"

"We don't consult my travel agent, I can tell you that. You and I can do this." Maxine walks through the wet grass, her feet swishing against the trimmed blades of sod. "Don't bother Charlie again with our lack of transportation. Ginger Rogers was good enough to get us here—she can see us home."

I'd prefer an air-conditioned car, but one more ride for old time's sake will suffice. I can work off the last few nights of holding my new boyfriends, Ben and Jerry, in my arms.

Two blocks later, we both pedal with a little less energy than our initial voyage. Also, the scenery does not look like the pathway home. "You're taking us to Avalon Heights, aren't you?"

Maxine gives me a thumbs up and turns left. "Maybe we can catch our crook."

"What will you do with this person if you find him or her?"

"For the sake of possible returns to the In Between PD, it's best you don't know."

Five minutes later, Ginger Rogers rolls into the neighborhood. The collection of single-story brick homes sit on full acre lots with magazine-worthy landscaping. Rustic street lights illuminate our trail as we circle the outside perimeter, then begin pedaling down each individual street.

"This could take hours," I whine.

Maxine bikes faster, but my aching legs barely comply. I'd like to say that I'm so high on happiness from my reconciliation with Charlie that I effortlessly pick up the pace, but the truth is love won't do your cardio.

We ride the length of Haxton Street, even swooping through the cul de sac. Next, we traverse down Nickel Lane, followed by Ridley Road.

"Look! There." Maxine points to her left and slows. "I know I had signs there. Now—gone. And check out house 504. That's Laverne and Eddie's house. They *asked* me for two signs. Now they've vanished." The entire street is devoid of any Maxine for Mayor signage, so we doggedly continue to Plimpton Place. "No sign, no sign, no sign." My grandmother's voice becomes a repetitive lyric as we crawl along.

Until a shadowy figure darts across the road.

"What was that?" Maxine yells. "You there. Stop!"

The person-on-the-run dives behind a wisteria-covered mailbox and disappears.

"Stop in the name of Maxine Simmons. Citizen's Arrest!" Maxine slams on the bike brakes. "You're a true-crime podcast waiting to happen. Don't make me call *Dateline*!" Before we come to a full stop, Maxine leaps off. I watch her body wobble left then lurch right as she struggles to gain her balance. "Quit running, you little turkey." Fully upright, she shoots through a yard, following the suspicious individual.

"Be careful," I call to her, parking our bicycle in a yard and reluctantly giving chase. I can't let anything happen to my maid-of-honor. "Maxine, wait for me!"

My sandals are not made for running, and I nearly trip over a lawn chair, but still gain on Maxine, only to see her sprint into the neighboring empty lot.

"Halt there, thief," she cries. "Stoppppp!" She leaps over a row of boxwoods, mere feet from her target.

I can only watch in horror as Maxine goes airborne, her body sailing in an arc that would make the NFL proud. She tackles the person to the ground, wrapping arms and legs, then rolling down a small grassy incline. "Owwww!"

Panting like someone who hasn't worked out in a while (because I haven't), I close in on the fighting duo, wincing at the shrieks of pain and dismay.

"How dare you steal my signs." Maxine hauls the person up by the collar.

We both gasp.

"Samuel Dayberry?" Maxine cries.

Dressed in black, with tufts of hair clearly yanked by a feminine hand, Sam jerks from Maxine's hold and defiantly faces her. "Yeah, me!" He jabs his hand to his chest. "Have you been training with the Dallas Cowboys? You almost *killed* me."

My grandmother's mouth hangs agape in an unusual display of muted shock. "I...I..."

"Sam, what's going on?" I step between them, just in case Maxine's carrying one of her tasers. "You're the one who's been taking her signs?"

He retrieves his cap from the ground, dashes it against his pant leg to brush off the grass, then crushes it on his nearly-bald head. "Of course it was me."

Maxine looks at her husband as if she doesn't recognize him. "But...why?"

"Because I don't want you to become mayor."

"That's a terrible thing to say," Maxine snaps. "I support you in all your endeavors."

"You didn't support me this year when I announced my retirement. Maxine, you know I think you can do anything you set your mind too —and plenty of those you probably shouldn't. But you didn't even ask how I felt before you went off halfcocked and put your name on the ballot."

"Don't you want me to be a strong woman of leadership with a twenty percent discount at Burger Barn?"

"I want you to have everything your crazy heart desires, but Maxine, we're not getting any younger."

Her head bobbles as if Sam's slapped her. "How dare you!"

"You can pull out any one of your twenty fake birth certificates all you want, but the reality is we're both at an age where our days are limited. What if we have mere years left together?"

She sniffs in disdain. "What a terrible thing to say."

"I want us to enjoy the time we have." Sam's eyes implore Maxine to understand. "I want to buy an RV and road trip across the country. I want to hop on a plane and see Paris and Rome. Or board a cruise and sail the seas. I want to do all that—with you. In the years we've been married, we've taken three vacations, and two of those were to your sister's."

Maxine brushes dirt from Sam's black shirt. "I had no idea that's what you wanted."

"What I want is time with you—while we're able to go. While our minds are still functional." He cuts her a look. "Well, mostly."

Maxine picks up a discarded, bent sign. "If you wanted me to quit the campaign, why didn't you just say so? All you had to do was ask."

"I tried."

"Really? What did I say?"

"You offered me a bumper sticker and a koozie."

"They are of exceptional quality." A slow smile spreads on Maxine's face. "I'm sorry I didn't listen, my little lamb chop. If you want me to quit, I will."

Sam frowns. "Just like that?"

"Just like that. The reality is, I don't really want the job. It was an idea that kind of spun out of control. And, I'll admit, though it's so unlike me, I enjoyed the attention."

I'm sure Sam is shocked.

"I'll need to have a talk with McGillicruddy to make sure he's up to the task and truly understands the people of In Between," Maxine says. "But if I'm satisfied, I will withdraw." She hugs her husband and kisses his papery cheek. "Your vote is the only one I need, Samuel Love Muffin Dayberry."

Sam hugs his wife back, then notices my presence. "Wait a minute. What are you two doing out tonight? Tell me you didn't schedule another shenanigan."

"We did." I join the huddle. "But this one ended successfully."

"You both look like doused cats."

I hold up my hand, where my engagement ring sits once more. "I'm engaged."

"Does this mean I have to buy another gift?"

"No, but it's for reals this time," Maxine says to Sam. "And as soon as we get this wedding put together and these kids married, we'll go shop for that RV."

"Really?" Sam grins like a lovesick teenager.

"Yes." Maxine threads her arm in his, as the two reroute and limp toward the bicycle. "As long as you let me drive."

"Not a chance." Sam leans over and kisses his wife. "I said I want to enjoy our final years. Not go out in flames."

CHAPTER FORTY-SEVEN

"LET'S play a little game called panic attack or ulcer." Four days later, I roll down the window in my rental car and drag in the hot air like it's my only source of oxygen. "Why did I think a rushed wedding was a good idea?"

"Because you love your Charlie sweetcheeks." Maxine closes her compact, then dabs her lipstick on a tissue. "It's coming together like a dream."

"Yeah, a fevered one."

"It's going to be so worth it. This wedding preparation might be more rushed than me at a Neiman Marcus sale, but look how customized it is."

It's true. Catering would be handled by none other than Burger Barn. Jeremy got the In Between High School orchestra to play our wedding march, as well as the select choir to sing. James would, of course, perform the service. "The important thing is the groom is Charlie."

"Who else who it be?" Maxine turns her air vents toward her armpits.

I laugh as I aim the car onto a familiar dirt road. "I mean, I'm finally at the point where that's all that matters."

"The scary voices are gone?"

"Only scary voice this week is yours."

She pops a piece of gum in her mouth and grins. "Your venue is sublime."

James's church was already booked, so we had to improvise. But the alternative turned out better than I could've imagined. "It all feels right this time."

"Good. I don't want to do this again. Turn at that cattle guard. Yep, right there's our next stop."

We've spent every waking hour, and some sleeping ones as well, making preparations for my wedding. It was all hands on deck from every family member. Despite moving into her new apartment, even Amy pitched in. With two days left, I've slept very little, my mind racing nonstop with my monster to-do list and details that sprint through my head.

"Nice of you to go with me on my errand." Maxine checks her manicure, a telling sign she's nervous. "Let me handle the talking, okay? I have a strategy."

"Those words always bode well for us."

"I think things will be a-okay." She pats my hand on the gear shift. "*Or* we're never seen from again. Kind of a toss-up."

Glory.

The car bounces over a red dirt road, and dust plumes behind us. I'm a little uneasy about this one myself, but that's probably just some farmland PTSD.

Because we have arrived at Gus McGillicuddy's.

The Ford sedan ambles down the driveway, and I ease it to a stop. "Are you sure about this?"

"Yes." Maxine pops a small bubble. "It's what my Sammy wants me to do. And he's right. Feel free to stay in the car. I only needed you for the ride and the moral support."

"No way. It's my turn to play wingman." I give her a bolstering smile. "This is such a responsible thing to do." I sniff loudly. "I do believe you're growing up on me. "

"Oh, shucks. I can't help all this maturity. It's seeping out of my salon-steamed pores."

Together we walk up the sidewalk as birds chirp in nearby trees and cows moo in the distance. They all probably see us and are sending out distress signals.

Standing on a faded welcome mat, we don't even get the chance to ring the bell.

The door flies open, and in that gaping space stands Gus McGillicuddy. "Trespassing in broad daylight now?"

Maxine doesn't so much as flinch. "I come in peace, Gus McFuddyDuddy."

The man's left eye twitches, and I know that reflex well. It's the look of restraint one employs when trying not to roll your eyes at Maxine. "Come on in. But I only have a few minutes before I need to leave."

"Oh, going to your next anger management session?" Maxine steps inside, and I follow.

At Gus's bidding, we walk through a tiled foyer that empties us into a massive living room. A two-story ceiling steeples above, and the afternoon light shines right through the wrap-around windows. There is wood everywhere—trim, flooring, picture frames that show Gus apparently has some configuration of family and was not raised by wolves.

"You can take a seat as long as you don't get too comfortable and get an inclination to stay." In a surprisingly polite move that reminds me of Charlie, Gus waits for us to settle onto the leather couch before taking a seat in an adjacent chair himself.

Maxine leans forward, elbows on her knees, and steeples her fingers. "Gussy, it's time we faced facts. Sweet thing, you're not going to win this race."

He looks neither offended nor taken aback. Just...resigned. "My numbers could be better."

"Hon, if your numbers get any worse, you'll be in the negatives."

"That's not actually possible."

"I'm not here to quibble over mathematicals. I thought you might want to..." Maxine taps a finger to her chin as if trying to find her thought. Which I know she has not misplaced. "I thought you might want to concede. Save some face. Gallantly bow out. Ride into your cowboy sunset. Resume your life of cows and manure."

Now it's Gus who hinges forward, his dark eyes intense and focused on his rival. "Mrs. Dayberry, do you really want to be mayor?"

"Do birds fly? Does the sun rise? Does my favorite plastic surgeon give me big discounts on his 'spa weekends' in Florida? Yesses all around."

"You want to run a town, field complaints all day long about potholes and traffic lights and property taxes?"

Maxine chomps her gum a little harder. "Sounds...a little bit of a downer, but I can hang."

"You want to get those calls at two a.m.?"

"I can't say that I like my beauty sleep interrupted." She pats her cheeks. "It makes me puffy."

"You have to be at every civic event and often show up at school functions."

"I'm usually there already."

"You have to balance the budget and find new ways to fund projects. You deal with phone calls and spreadsheets all day."

My grandmother shrugs a shoulder. "I'll hire a good assistant."

"You're ready to go back to work full time? Your freedom to come and go, visit family, and all your social obligations will be over."

"I wouldn't be able to fly to New York whenever I wanted?"

"You'd be on call twenty-four-seven. So even if you did fly out to see your granddaughter here, if an emergency came up in town, you'd have to jet right on back home. And why? Because you're the one in charge."

"The job of mayor was a lot sexier when Reva did it on *General Hospital*."

"Why are you really doing this, Maxine?"

"Because." Her angry expression softens. "In Between has all these new things—a fancy coffee house, hiking paths, mountain bike trails, the new amphitheater for those noisy concerts put on by pink-haired teenagers who make more in a show than I did in my entire working career. Meanwhile, the senior citizen population—*not* that I am one—is being left behind. The senior center has gone to ruin. The last mayor slashed the budget so much we can barely afford to pay someone to clean the loo, let alone come out and teach ballroom dancing, tae kwon do, and my favorite—flaming aerial yoga." Gus's brows disappear into his Stetson while Maxine takes a breath. "Those old people feel forgotten. And if they don't have anything to do, they feel bored. And boredom could lead to nefarious activities."

"Like breaking into my garage and four-wheeling through my livestock?"

"Your pigs told us they were lacking in fun as well. We were glad to provide them some entertainment."

"Here's the deal, Mad Maxine." If he sees my grandmother stiffen, he plows on ahead anyway. "You're popular in this town."

"Thank you for recognizing a powerful and obvious truth."

"So, maybe you win."

"I think the descriptor you're looking for is *certainly*."

"Okay, you win. But you've won on a popularity contest. Because you're an In Between staple. You bring some familiarity and razzle-dazzle." She preens at that. "Meanwhile, I'm rough and gruff and don't say all the funny, pretty things you do at these debates. If you win, it's another case of the candidate with the most money and the best face."

"My face *has* been very expensive."

"For once, wouldn't it be nice if a political candidate won based on merit? Based on the job he or she could do? Wouldn't it be nice if the person who stepped into the role had leadership experience?"

Maxine chews her lip as she considers this. "It would. But it would also be nice if that person were me."

"Mad Maxine, you don't want to run a town. You want your senior citizen issues addressed."

"My older *friends'* senior citizen issues addressed."

"I care about In Between. The last two mayors have been total jokes—one a crook and one a desperate replacement who doesn't know her left from her right. As a town, we're at a critical point. Businesses are interested in developing here, and people are chomping at the bit to build homes. But they want infrastructure and a solid economy—all without losing our small-town feel."

Maxine adjusts one hoop earring and sends me a furtive side-eye. "You've really thought about this, Gusto."

"If you drop out, I promise you I'll revamp that senior center and find the funding to keep it not only open but the best center in the county."

"The state," she counters.

"Okay, the state."

"And I want the local restaurants to start catering our lunches again."

"I'll talk to them myself."

"More daily activities that don't involve Bingo and crafts with some volunteer's recycled toilet paper parts."

"We'll hire the place a new director with ideas."

"A director?" My grandmother's eyes light at this. "With a salary?"

"That's usually how jobs work."

"Is there money in the city budget for that?"

"There is. I've seen the town's finances. They simply need to be managed better."

"You've studied the budget?"

"Yes, haven't you?"

Maxine tucks her hair behind her ear. "Every night. Right after I read a chapter in *War and Peace*."

"I've scrutinized every available account." Gus nearly lights up with the numbers talk. "I've spent over 200 hours job shadowing with the interim mayor. I've put in countless hours in the diners talking to the good folks of In Between to hear what they need."

"I learned how to use a photo filter that takes out all my wrinkles." Maxine sighs and looks at her opponent as if really seeing him. "So, maybe you are the more qualified and prepared between the two of us. To be honest, I might entertain your idea to walk away from the job of mayor if I knew our town was finally in good hands."

"I won't let you down. This city's important to me. In Between has enormous potential, and I have the vision and drive to make sure it achieves it."

Maxine's head lowers as if she's giving this considerable thought, while I continue to sit like a statue beside her, full of respect and pride. Man, I hope I'm this cunning and clever when I'm her age.

My grandmother looks toward the enormous antler chandelier above us and takes a shuddering breath. She even wipes at a faux tear. "Okay, McGillicootie. I do believe you have In Between's best interests at heart."

"Does this mean you'll withdraw?"

"It means, Mr. Mayor, when you post that director job, I'll be the first application in your Inbox."

"The job is yours. If you keep quiet about anything else, you might've found in my garage."

"The heavy arsenal of food and clothing?"

"None of anyone's business."

"Is that for your hidden cult?"

"No."

"Your secret harem?"

"Also, no."

Maxine circulates her gum a few rotations. "You know what I think? I think—"

"Hey, Gus, honey. I'm sorry I'm late. I—"

All heads turn at the sharp intake of breath and the familiar voice.

"Amy?" Maxine's on her feet quicker than flies on a cow tail. "What in the name of older men with mustaches are you doing here?"

My adopted sister's mouth opens like a hooked fish. But only broken syllables slip out.

Gus's cowboy boots click on the floor as he rounds to Amy's side. "She's here to see me."

Maxine coughs and sputters. "Just swallowed my gum."

I give her a solid pat on the back, then another for good measure. "Hey, Amy. Nice to see you."

Amy looks like she wants to cry. "I guess I owe you two an explanation."

"Are you dating Gus? My opponent?" Maxine flings a hand toward the man. "Amy Scott, are you the hanky to his panky?"

"It's not what it looks like," she says.

Maxine's head bobs with attitude. "It looks like you two are secretly a couple, and you didn't want your family to know."

"Okay, that's exactly what it looks like. But my intentions were good. I didn't want to hurt you or make you feel betrayed. Gus and I met at a donation drive in Houston for refugees. We worked together on a task force, and...I fell for his generosity and caring heart."

"Obviously, it wasn't his topiary of a mustache." Maxine pivots to face Gus. "So that's what all those clothes and food items were for."

"I won't explain myself, Mrs. Dayberry, nor will I defend my actions. I hope we can keep this between all of us."

"I'll stay mum," Maxine says, "but maybe people need to see that side of you, Goose. You're afraid of offending one political side or another but having a heart crosses all party lines." She wraps her arm around my waist and pulls me to one side, then drags Amy to her other. "We take care of our children here. Families are important, no matter how we find them. One of my favorite books says, 'for I was hungry, and you gave me something to eat. I was thirsty, and you gave me something to drink. I was a stranger, and you invited me in. I needed clothes, and you clothed me. I was sick, and you looked after me."

His forehead wrinkles in thought. "What book is that from?"

"I think it's Harry Potter." She looks to me for help. "Which character said that? Dumbledore?"

My teeth press into my lip. "Probably a Weasley."

"Oh, sure." Maxine nods once then gets back to business with McGillicuddy. "Look, soldier, how about I help you with some of your PR—showing In Between you've got a heart as big as that handlebar hairpiece above your lip, and you promise me in writing that funding will be restored to the senior center."

Gus sticks out his tattooed arm, his hand open for Maxine to shake. "Deal."

She places her dainty hand in his. "I'll post a concession speech on my social media tonight. I do hope I still have some sparklers somewhere. And a nose kazoo. Katie will, of course, mime the death scene from *Romeo and Juliet*."

I frown. "No, she won't."

"You're right. The melting scene of *Wicked* will work so much better." She bows to her new friend. "Best of luck to you, Gusto. I charge you with taking care of my town. And if you don't, I will find some way to make your life miserable."

"I'm backed up by a motorcycle gang of ex-military vets."

"My sister is retired CIA and makes people disappear on the daily."

"That doesn't really scare me."

"Her last enemy woke up in Shanghai wearing a face identical to Jerry Seinfeld's."

"So?"

"She was a woman."

"Duly noted."

"And if you hurt so much as a hair on Amy's head or one eensy teensy feeling of hers, I will hunt you down myself. You're not the only one who knows how to brush hog a field. Those big old blades could cut something right up." She scissors her fingers for visual effect. "Do you hear what I'm not saying because it would be legally incriminating?"

Gus's gaze rests on Amy, and when he smiles, his eyes twinkle. "I hear you, Mad Maxine. I'll do you right. I'll take care of you and this whole town. And I assure you I'll do everything in my power to make your granddaughter happy."

"That's a promise?" Maxine asks.

"I swear on my favorite pig." Gus sends me a pointed look. "Probably one you've met."

"Then be happy, my dears." With a hug to Amy and a fist bump to Gus, Maxine shouts her goodbyes and leads the two of us out the door.

"That was quite the setup," I say as we get back in the car. "You sly vixen, you."

Maxine chortles and turns the music up. "Everything's negotiable, sweet pea." She sighs. "Though I do hope Amy's happy. She deserves someone to treat her right. It's her turn." Reaching into her floral blouse, she pulls out a small device. "Didn't need this thing."

I jerk the steering wheel to the left, dodging a chicken. "Is that a recorder?"

"Currently transmitting to my laptop at home." She chunks it in her purse. "If Gus whacked us and tossed our bodies in the pond, I wanted evidence."

Good heavens. "Your mind is a fright."

She giggles and fluffs her hair. "But you love me. So now, let's go celebrate."

"Shakes at the Burger Barn?"

"No. Lovella's bridal shop." Maxine reapplies lipstick on her smiling lips. "I put the most gorgeous dress on hold a few weeks ago, and it's time I picked up my sweet reward." She slips on her movie star sunglasses. "I think you're going to love it."

CHAPTER FORTY-EIGHT

When you're a kid who's raised by an abusive, addict of a mom and move with the frequency of a stray cat, you don't have a lot of time to build fantasies of your future wedding day. Fairy tales were a luxury only for other girls.

But today...I'm the princess.

The bride.

In a total surprise to me, all the details have blessedly, magically, come together to be perfect. Yes, I was scared to take the leap into marriage with Charlie not quite two weeks ago, but the destination wedding hadn't ever been right. Now all is in alignment, and except for my dress being altered a little too tight, I breathe easy and can almost enjoy myself.

With twenty minutes until wedding time, my parents knock on my old bedroom door. I stand in front of the mirrored dresser, still decorated with ribbons and forensic tournament trophies, and check my appearance one last time.

"How are you feeling?" Millie asks as they step inside.

"Nervous." Her face blanches, and James loses his smile. "But not runaway bride nervous. I'm happy to be marrying Charlie."

James regards me in the mirror. "It's a big day."

"Like bigger than the butt bow on the maid of honor dress Maxine made me wear in her wedding to Sam."

"Amy took Daisy on over for photos," James says. "She looked adorable. And quite excited to be a flower girl."

My niece has captured all of our hearts. She tried to talk me into letting the puppy be part of the wedding, but I held tight to my refusal. Haven told James and Millie yesterday that she wanted them to have the puppy, as long as Daisy could visit anytime she wanted. I think they'll be seeing a lot of each other when Haven's released.

"You look beautiful, Katie." Millie straightens the paisley lace at my shoulders. "That dress was the right one all along."

I do a slow turn in my gown—the same one Frederico brought to Lovella for the trunk show. The lace bodice is a little itchy, but the full skirt and long train feel like me. My hair heated in waves and gathered at the nape of my neck makes Maxine's pearl necklace stand out even more. "I can't believe Maxine went back to the bridal shop that day and bought it."

"I can," James said. "Your grandmother's crazy about you...and just crazy in general."

Reaching for the tube of pale pink gloss that promises not to budge for five hours, I give my mouth one last coat. "Thank you for arranging the venue, Millie. I couldn't love it more."

She gives me a quick, loose hug. "I don't want to muss you, but I'm so darn proud of you. I can't stop hugging you. I've prayed for this day for years."

"It almost didn't happen," I say.

"So, you had a dress rehearsal." James adjusts his tie in the mirror, but his steady gaze rests on me. "Today's the real performance, and it's going to be a hit."

I think it might be.

Turning, I face my parents. They both look like a million bucks in their wedding finery—Millie in a full-length champagne-colored sheath with satin scoop neck and lacy three-quarter sleeves, plus a back that dips into a V. She's a knockout.

James wears a dark gray three-piece suit with a pink tie and matching pocket square. Because the guys wanted a little personality, they're all wearing bright pink socks likes James does now. If there was a Pastor GQ magazine, he'd be the cover model.

"I have something I want to tell you two," I say.

Millie sits on the bed. "Oh, no."

James frowns. "In my officiating experience, pre-wedding declarations are not advisable."

"Hopefully, this one is okay." I love these two so much. I wish I could take them with me to New York and never let them go. "I've been doing a lot of thinking, and I realized something needs to change."

Millie elbows her husband, who now sits beside her. "James's obsession with processed foods?"

"Today, my name changes for what will be the last time." God willing. "I think yours should as well." I've only waited years to say this, and I'm not certain what's ever held me back. But I cut loose from one more shackle. "What do you say...Mom and Dad?"

"Oh, my." Millie's hands fly to her mouth and tears well in her eyes. "James, our daughter finally called us Mom and Dad."

James says nothing. Just stares.

Uh-oh. Maybe this was a terrible idea. "What do you think?".

After a lengthy stretch, James finally speaks. "What do I think?" James stands and opens his arms wide. "I think it's about time. I've waited an eternity to hear those words." With zero care for my dress, he pulls me close, and soon we're a three-person hug.

I'll need to retouch my makeup, and my hair will have to be restyled. But I don't care.

This day, this moment will never come again. I recall the first time these two dared to hold me close. I was a scared, frightened kid who barely knew how to hope there could be a future for me. A future that didn't involve the same life my biological mom had lived and her mother before her. But even then, I never dreamed that life could be so good. If I could, I'd go back and tell teenage Katie that it's going to be okay. One day she'll go to bed, and when she closes her eyes in the darkness, she won't be scared. One day she'll wake up, and she won't be angry. And one day, she'll put on her adopted grandmother's antique pearls and hug her mom and dad, and drive to the most sacred of places. To marry a man she thought only existed for a girl like her in her wildest of dreams.

Life will serve up more tropical storms and shake my cabana. There will be hard days.

But I'll cling to my faith, my family, and the love of Charlie Benson, and pray that if God doesn't want to calm the storms, He'll at least quiet the noise. And quiet me. He has a plan for me, and I'm fully stepping into it today. God hasn't failed me yet, and I can't approach every challenge or life event as if He might.

"Is this a private hug?" Amy steps into the room. "Or can any sister join?"

I hold out my hand to Amy. "Only my sister."

"Did you tell Katie about the apartment?" Amy asks our parents as we huddle.

"Not yet," I hear Millie say.

Tendrils escape as I lift my head. "What about it?"

"You mentioned that Haven didn't know where she and Daisy would stay when she was released." Millie looks to her husband, who nods his encouragement. "Now that Amy's moving out of our apartment, the place will be empty. We'd talked about offering it to Mother and Sam."

James shivers. "The stuff of nightmares."

"We even said we could leave it open for when you and Charlie visit." Millie lifts a piece of my rogue hair and tries in vain to tuck it back into a pin. "But then we chatted with Iola Smartley and decided we'd offer it to Haven instead. Rent-free so she can get back on her feet."

"Iola told us Haven would like to go to college," James says. "We could be her support system. All of us. If it's okay with you, Katie."

"It's wonderful." These people. My heart is about to fly right out of my lace-covered body. "You all provided a family when I had none. You've shown me how to live with generosity and dare to care—even when it's hard. I love you all so much."

"I think we need to get you to your wedding. How about I pray for us?" James asks the question I've heard a thousand times. When I first came to live with the Scotts, the request made my eyes roll. But now I cherish his every word, and thank God I have a dad who appeals to the heavens on my behalf.

We stand there as a family of four, hands clasped, heads bowed, eyes closed. Talking to a God who'd planned this day all along.

And I'm so very grateful.

"Dear God," James begins. "We thank you for Katie, our adored daughter and today, a beautiful bride..."

Time and again, God has proven He's faithful by giving me the desires of my heart. Not the college degree or the career or the miraculous role on Broadway.

But a family.

People who will be mine forever, no matter where I reside or what my path brings.

People who love unconditionally, despite the fact that we don't share blood. A family who holds my hand through the hard days and never gives up, never lets me go.

This day is possible because James and Millie Scott volunteered to take care of a foster kid.

Their yes changed the trajectory of my life, altered future generations.

Because of them, I'll never be alone. I'll never have to question whether I'm wanted or adored.

Because of them, I can give my heart away one more time.

To a man I'm going to be brave enough to love for the rest of my days.

Amen.

CHAPTER FORTY-NINE

INSTRUMENTAL MUSIC FLOATS in the air, played by a ten-piece orchestra made of students plucked from first and second chair students at In Between High.

"Thanks for assembling the musicians." I straighten Jeremy's tie as we wait in a side room. "I owe you one."

"Theater and band nerds always come through for one another."

"You're my favorite theater nerd." I hug my friend and kiss the red scruff on his cheek. Jeremy was my rock in college, my fellow thespian. We stayed up late many a night eating cheap pizza and studying lines for college productions. He's as loyal as they come, and In Between High is lucky to have him. So am I. "Love you, Jeremy."

"Love you more."

"Ready for your bouquet?" Frances holds her hands behind her back.

Given our time constraint, I was encouraged to divvy up the wedding tasks, and among other things, momma-to-be Frances volunteered to handle the flowers.

"I'm ready."

Frances watches my face with concern as she presents my flowers.

"What do you think? I know it's different, but...a traditional bouquet didn't feel right at all."

I hold the creation in my hands, words failing me. "It's...it's beautiful. Are these paper roses?" My fingers trace the swirls of the off-white flowers dotted with small black text. Gossamer ribbon wraps the base.

"Millie let me dig through the storage rooms of the Valiant," Frances says. "I found one of the scripts used in *Romeo and Juliet*. My mom helped me turn the pages into flowers."

I'm not sure even waterproof mascara can hold up to the tears of this day. "My first play at the Valiant Theater." The one that I stumbled into as a last-minute fill in with more animosity than acting experience and my destiny was set. When I stepped into that spotlight on opening night, I found my place, my purpose. "This couldn't be more perfect, Frances. I'll keep it forever."

"Pretty neato," Maxine admits with no small amount of rancor. "But get a load of my gift." She waves me toward the back door.

"You already got us a fancy vacuum cleaner. And the island wedding."

"Yeah, I wanted to make up for the fact that I basically bought you a tropical storm. Come here." She grabs my hand and drags me outside.

Where Ginger Rogers sits, shiny with a bow.

"If you're asking me to go stake out a new nemesis, now's not really a good time."

"No, sweet pea." She pats my seat on Ginger. "The bike *is* the gift."

"No."

"I can't think of a better home for Ginger than with you and Charlie. She's ready for new adventures, and so are you. Together you can create new memories. Unlike our escapades with the bike, maybe some of yours will be legal."

"Oh, Maxine." I don't care that I'm in a formal dress with perfect hair and makeup. I throw myself into my grandma's arms and hug her with all the love in my heart, soul, and spirit. "You'll always be my favorite."

"I know, toots." She pats my back and sniffles in my ear. "You'll always be mine. My soul sister. The cornbread to my beans. The glue to my lash extensions."

"I hope I can go back to New York and make you proud."

She pulls away and holds my face in her hands, her blue eyes on mine. "You already do. And you always will. You are my granddaughter, and every breath you take makes me proud."

Millie and James step outside with us, holding hands and smiling like parents about to marry off their daughter. "What are you doing out here?" James asks. "Let's get inside and get you hitched. They're starting."

"Places everyone!" My old drama teacher Ms. Hall claps her hands as we step back into the small room. She wears the more formal version of a dress from her 1975 Stevie Nicks collection. "It's showtime, boys and girls. Look alive."

"Thank you for your direction today," I say to her as we transition into the lobby, where we stand behind large closed doors.

"Oh, honey." She flops a hand, and all ten of her bangles rattle down her arm. "I wish you so much love and happiness. Like more than my ex-husband and I had. Did I tell you that man's on his fourth wife? Moved to Tacoma and..."

The grand doors open, and Jeremy walks down the aisle with Daisy as she tosses flower petals and dances her way to the front.

Next goes Sterling, who beams with pride to escort his daughter Sadie. Charlie's mom and dad swore a truce today, and so far, it's held.

Frances gives me another hug, then joins her husband. Together, the two glide across the rose-covered path on Joey's arm. I can't wait to come back home in late winter and throw my friend a baby shower. I think she's having a boy, but Charlie's money is on a girl.

Maxine turns back to me, her eyes shining. "This is it, sweet pea."

I squeeze her hand. "Made it by the G.O.G., baby."

Her rosy lips curve. "The Grace of God. You know it."

The wedding march begins, a classic tune now jazzed up by the Chihuahua orchestra.

James stands to my left, and I place my hand in his. Then reach for Millie's on my right.

My grandmother tosses back her salon-styled head and laughs. Her belly-deep chuckle echoes through the lobby as she takes Millie's hand and joins our line.

The four of us pass through the antique doors of the Valiant Theater.

Then walk down the aisle.

A family.

Together.

Forever.

CHAPTER FIFTY

We step into the theater, and if it were not for my parents anchoring my side, I would fall to the floor.

Hundreds of people fill every seat, from the balcony to the orchestra pit. They could power a small town with their smiles as they rise while the music serenades. The theater required little decoration, but I have to pause and admire the sweet peas blooming in gold buckets tied to the end of every row. I have no doubt who's responsible for that beautiful detail. Thick velvet curtains in the color of navy hang to each side of the stage where my wedding party waits. The theater is mid-production, so fabric has been thrown over the set, and I don't even mind.

When I get close enough to see Charlie, the waterworks start anew.

There's my soulmate, the person God custom made for me, standing in his light gray suit. I see a few tears track down his face as he gets his first glimpse of his bride. I say a quick prayer and make the ridiculous request to never forget every feeling, every nuance, every second of this moment. When my days turn gray or life comes at me too hard, I will think back on this small stretch of time when Charlie beheld me as if I were all he could ever want, someone worthy and beautiful...and his.

My family manages the stairs at stage left and becomes the final piece of the wedding party on stage.

James kisses my cheek then assumes his place before us where his pulpit from church now stands. I see him hesitate, taking a moment to weather the emotion before he speaks. "On behalf of the families of Katie Parker Scott and Charlie Benson, we would like to welcome you to In Between's most anticipated event."

Cheers erupt in the crowd, and I look back, humbled by their revelry.

James clears his throat. "As a parent, you think there's no greater day than the day your biological child is born—or the day the child of your heart officially joins your family. But today, I think there's no greater joy and honor than officiating the marriage of my own daughter." His smile encompasses Charlie and me. "And to marry her to a young man I've watched grow up is a dream come true for her mother and me." His gaze drops, and I see his Adam's apple bob. A big sniff sounds from his clip-on microphone. "Katie, you came to us as a foster child, doing your best to show us you didn't need a preacher, a theater-owning yogi, and one crazy grandmother. But then...we realized we needed you. And we always will. Your mom and I are so blessed by the woman you've become—the strong, successful child of God you've worked so hard to be. You've stunned us with your talent on the stage and how much you've achieved. But more importantly, you've given us immeasurable happiness to watch you become the compassionate, kind, wonderful human being you are."

Behind me, Maxine bawls into a tissue. "Yes, Lord. She's a winner."

"Today, I'd like to think that you don't leave our family to join Charlie. But our families join each other." The very thought fills me with an easy peace. "If there were another pastor here, he or she would ask who gives this bride away. So let me tell you the answer to that question— her family does. With full hearts and fervent blessings. Charlie, please take your bride's hand."

Millie moves to a seat on the front row with Daisy, Amy, and Sam, while Maxine struts to her spot behind me as my maid of honor.

Charlie stands next to me, and as his hand closes over mine, I feel the strength and warmth of his comforting touch.

James spends the next few minutes sharing stories of Charlie and me, weaving in anecdotes that draw laughter from the crowd. But James also explains how Charlie and I found one another again years ago and how hard we've worked to get to this day. He opens his Bible and reads from I Corinthians, defining love as only God and James can. "And now these three remain: faith, hope, and love. But the greatest of these is love..."

Sometime later, after three of the high school choir's finest sings Van Morrison's "Crazy Love," we repeat the vows at my dad's prompting. In the last few days, Charlie and I had a lot of deep conversations, and we discovered neither one of us really wanted to write vows. So today, I face Charlie and promise to love, honor, and cherish him.

And because my dad's in charge of the service, of course, there would be more. "And do you, Katie, pledge to bring Charlie all your hopes, dreams, and fears? And to always honor God with your life?"

I blot my nose with the tissue from my dress's fabulous pocket and grin. "I do."

"Will you love him in sickness and in health, in fame or obscurity, in small town or big city?"

I laugh with Charlie. "I will."

"Will you visit your parents at least twice a year?"

"I'll definitely try."

My dad shuts his Bible and offers the final piece for me to recite.

I breathe in the beloved scent of the theater, today a mix of oiled wood and flowers. And I offer my full heart to Charlie. "I, Katie, take thee Charlie...to be my husband, to have and to hold from this day forward, to love and to cherish till death do us part, according to God's will and providence. Before our families and friends, this is my solemn and long-awaited vow to you."

"Then, by the power vested in me as father, pastor, and your devoted champion, I now pronounce you husband and wife. Charlie, you may kiss your bride."

With that, Charlie pulls me into his arms. The lace bodice tightens as I cling to my husband and kiss him for all to see. His lips grace mine, offering a final seal to the promise we both spoke in this hallowed room.

As the crowd claps and Maxine's whistles through her chemically whitened teeth, I take it all in. This man is my husband. These are my people. This is my home. This theater is the embodiment of love.

And none of it would've been possible if my parents hadn't taken a chance.

"I love you, Mr. Benson." I kiss him again, this time with a little more heat. After all, we are on a stage, so why not give them a show?

"I love you Mrs. Benson." Not one to disappoint, Charlie dips me low and returns his smiling mouth to mine.

As the band plays "How Sweet It Is to Be Loved By You," Charlie and I make our way back down the aisle, taking our time to greet all those who've witnessed our happiest day. To think eleven years ago, I came to In Between, an angry, scared rebel of a kid. I broke into the Valiant Theater, only to have it break me—in the best possible way.

I'll move to New York with In Between in my heart and a husband by my side.

I am a living, breathing promise. A girl who got to trade her ashes for beauty.

And what a beautiful life it will be.

Charlie spins me beneath his arm as we proceed toward the exit to the music, and I fall into his arms again.

Happy. Hopeful. And free.

Indeed, how sweet it is...to be loved.

PROLOGUE

Four months later...

I WAIT in the wing of the Schubert Theater, counting the seconds until my cue. It's opening night of *Piloting Dreams*, and I have drunk butterflies slam dancing in my stomach. I would blame it on the lead actress...but that's me.

We've rehearsed until I recite lines in my sleep, according to Charlie, and I'm as ready as I will ever be. I know there are theater critics out there who will write biting columns that will either make me want to kiss the director or make me want to cry.

Yet tonight, I'm not thinking about them.

This evening my family sits on the third row—my grandparents, who swung through town on their way to Connecticut, my parents, Amy and her boyfriend Gus (who has to get back for his first city council meeting), and Haven and Daisy. Even Charlie's parents are here, though we might've accidentally placed Sterling and Lacey in seats with an obstructed view.

I still have one full scene before I step onstage as Amelia Earhart, so I pull a Maxine, stick my hand down my blouse, and pull out a stowaway treasure. A note mailed to me last week from one newly re-retired caseworker.

As I have every day since I've gotten the missive, I read every line twice.

But tonight, my eyes are drawn to the words Iola's underlined, repeated words I'd forgotten we'd ever shared. Sentiments Iola Smartley told me over a decade ago when my world had stopped turning.

"Katie, one of these days really soon you're going to be able to say I know what it is to be wanted, what it is to be loved. I know what home is, and I'm right where I'm supposed to be."

I fold the letter back into its neat symmetrical square, then return it to my blouse, right over my heart.

She was right.

All those years ago, that fuzzy-headed, green van-driving woman was right. I couldn't see it then, but standing here in my costume about to walk onto a Broadway stage to deliver my first line, I'm flooded with gratitude that my own second act fulfilled her prophecy.

I do know what it is to be wanted, what it is to be loved.

I, Katie Parker Scott Benson, know what home is.

And thank God, I'm right where I'm supposed to be.

ACKNOWLEDGMENTS

I'd love to humbly thank a few people:

My readers- for still welcoming Katie Parker, Maxine, and the family into your world. I appreciate every email and message about characters who are so dear to me.

Kristin Avila- for your editing magic, for tolerating my deadline abuse, and for books recs. We have good taste.

Christa Allan—for being my literary therapist, for friendship, for the speedy way you find grammar offenses.

Erin Valentine—for your years of friendship, for still being my master teacher, for pancakes and long talks, for letting me annoy you with incessant grammar and style questions that you should charge for. (Yes, I ended that on a preposition.)

Lizann Tollett—for reminding me that Jeremiah 29:11 was and is kind of a big deal.

Amy Matayo, Karen Akins, and Ellen Matkowski—for looking at 234208349 book covers this year and pretending like you still don't hate me because you know I'll make you look at 500 more. Like next week.

J. Kramer and B. Fisher—for your support, encouragement, and bringing cookies to our Mensa meetings.

Kristin Billerbeck and Cheryl Hodde—for writing sessions and letting me benefit from your friendship and encouragement.

Rel Mollet—for being an author's best cheerleader, for your generous kindness, and for all the four million typos and errors you've caught in manuscripts.

Finally, I'm thankful to God. This series got me into traditional publishing, then later got me into indie publishing. Both events changed my life for the better and fulfilled a dream. I'm so grateful for the blessing of writing.

ALSO BY JENNY B. JONES

MYSTERY, SWEET ROMANCE

Wild Heart Summer

A Katie Parker Production, Acts 4-6

Enchanted Events Mystery Series

His Mistletoe Miracle

A Sugar Creek Christmas

Save the Date

Just Between You and Me

YOUNG ADULT

A Charmed Life series

In Between (Katie Parker, Book 1) (FREE!)

On the Loose (Katie Parker, Book 2)

The Big Picture (Katie Parker, Book 3)

Something to Believe In (Katie Parker, Book 4)

I'll Be Yours

There You'll Find Me

ABOUT THE AUTHOR

Get a free book from Jenny by signing up for her infrequent newsletter. www.jennybjones.com/news.

Award-winning author Jenny B. Jones writes romance, mystery, and YA with sass and Southern charm. Since she has very little free time, Jenny believes in spending her spare hours in meaningful, intellectual pursuits, such as checking celebrity gossip and pursuing her honorary PhD in queso. Jenny digs foster care, animal rescues, and her adorable son. She lives in the great state of Arkansas, where she's currently at work on her next novel and loves to hear from readers.

www.jennybjones.com
Insta: @jennybjonesauthor
Facebook: jennybjones
Twitter: JenBJones

Made in United States
North Haven, CT
08 November 2022